Praise for

Private Citizens:

One of Flavorwire's Most Anticipated Books of 2016

"Witty, unsparing, and unsettlingly precise, Tulathimutte empathizes with his subjects even as he (brilliantly) skewers them. A satirical portrait of privilege and disappointment with striking emotional depth." —*Kirkus* (starred review)

"Tulathimutte's debut is poetic and verbose as his characters sardonically and intellectually upend every contemporary topic presented to them. . . . *Private Citizens* is an impressive start for an edgy new writer." —*Booklist*

"*Private Citizens* is a freak of literature—a novel so authentic, hilarious, elegantly plotted, and heartbreaking that I'd follow it anywhere. Tony Tulathimutte is a singular intellect with an uncanny 40/20 vision on the world."

—Jennifer duBois, author of *Cartwheel*
and *A Partial History of Lost Causes*

"*Private Citizens* is a combustible combination of acrobatic language, dead-on observations, and hilarious, heartbreaking storytelling. Tulathimutte has created characters that are hard to forget—first they'll make you want to strangle them, then you'll end up falling in love with them."

—Angela Flournoy, National Book Award finalist
and author of *The Turner House*

"Tony Tulathimutte's *Private Citizens* is my favorite kind of novel: an entrancing narrative in which important ideas lurk around the corners and behind the curtains. It enchants, entertains, sometimes makes me chew my nails in dread, sometimes makes me laugh my ass off, and never, ever doubts my intelligence."

—Benjamin Hale, author of
The Evolution of Bruno Littlemore and *The Fat Artist*

PRIVATE CITIZENS

TONY TULATHIMUTTE

WM

WILLIAM MORROW
An Imprint of HarperCollinsPublishers

PRIVATE CITIZENS. Copyright © 2016 by Tony Tulathimutte. All rights reserved. Printed in the United States of America. No part of this book may be used or reproduced in any manner whatsoever without written permission except in the case of brief quotations embodied in critical articles and reviews. For information address HarperCollins Publishers, 195 Broadway, New York, NY 10007.

HarperCollins books may be purchased for educational, business, or sales promotional use. For information please e-mail the Special Markets Department at SPsales@harpercollins.com.

FIRST EDITION

Designed by Diahann Sturge

Library of Congress Cataloging-in-Publication Data has been applied for.

ISBN 978-0-06-239910-6

16 17 18 19 20   OV/RRD   10 9 8 7 6 5 4 3 2

For my parents—
back then, right this moment, and indefinitely

*In respect that it is solitary, I
like it very well; but in respect that it is
private, it is a very vile life.*

—Touchstone, *As You Like It,* act 3, scene 2

Prologue

September 2007

They were on a day trip, a nothing, the four of them in the hot car speeding north. All the passing and now-passed road looked faint through the filthy windows, which threw dull light onto their laps. It was ten A.M., any promise of an early start already squandered, and look, peach weather. In Sunday traffic it would be another fifty minutes, sitting still, rushing forward, all facing the same way. A fleck of fuzz stuck in Linda's eyelashes. The searing of leatherette in succulent air, a baguette rebaking in its paper sleeve, green grapes beginning to wrinkle, disks of lemon browning in iced tea. Nobody was getting enough sleep. They drove on to light and green water, sun, rest, afternoon. Last weekend before fall.

So then what? Why, Linda thought, of every possible experience, the beach? It was a failure of the imagination, budgeted and scheduled. They'd get there, trek miles down the shore until Cory deemed a spot quiet enough to lay their towels, even though by noon it would be as crowded as anywhere else. They would lie still among pasty bodies and feel tired. Will would bitch about the glare on his phone while everyone waited for him to sober up and drive them back home. And *nobody* had told her Henrik would be here.

Linda picked at the white fray of her cutoffs. Already she

missed New York—the city all others merely quoted, that tremendous vile heart pumping bedlam through its boroughs, whereas San Francisco was more uterine: passive, nonvital. Here the raindrops were smaller, the hustle slower, everything tolerated. And cities that tolerated everything tolerated mediocrity.

Which was why, unlike most Stanford grads, who'd followed the pollinating winds to San Francisco or Mountain View after graduating, she'd moved to New York, where she'd worked as an independent dominatrix, slapping, berating, and denying orgasm to ibankers five hours a week. Afternoons she'd spent swatting cigarette ash off books, and at night she'd gone to parties, where her Stanford Domme shtick gave her cred for a checkered past she didn't have: what was really checkered was her future. Her tattoo sleeves had vined out and joined between her shoulder blades, her hair went whitely afloat with bleaching, her voice turned permanently hoarse. Two years of bars and shows, dancing and reading. A bright catwalk of youth.

Then, without really meaning to, she'd stolen a miniature steel sculpture from a group show her roommates were hosting in their apartment, and was blamed for it, even though nobody could prove anything and she didn't even remember taking it. She was kicked out, and then for a few weeks she'd gone a little too hard; sure, she'd made some other friends, who were more cool than interesting . . . So after she'd gone to the ER for a hemorrhaged septum, her mom had tried forcing her into rehab, and she'd indignantly refused until she realized that it'd be hilarious, actually.

With begrudging pledges from each of her separated parents, she'd checked into a recovery center on some forested acreage in Santa Cruz. The idea at first was to see how many people she could alienate as quickly as possible—during the icebreaker, when she was asked to name her favorite book and describe her worst date, she'd said, *I guess my worst date was the time I was raped. Oh, and my favorite book is* Moby-Dick. But when she realized that rehab counselors saw this sort of snide pushback all the time, she decided not to resist, but to cooperate. In dryout couture (hoodie, ball cap, big sunglasses), she eased into a calm routine, reading until noon, affirmations after lunch, Bikram yoga, dishwashing, and nightly group discussion. She felt gratified to be the youngest resident by far, and embraced the gooey recovery bromides with perfected camp. When a starved-eyed oxycodone addict testified about seeing the afterlife during his overdose, Linda described her own bodily ascent to heaven on the backs of two angels. At group prayer, she seized people's shoulders and babbled in tongues. *You've come so far on your journey,* her counselor told her at the end of the month.

It was a pretty decent story, and more or less true. But when she'd told it to her friends just now, everyone was silent except for Cory, who'd only said, *Jesus, Linda.*

She wasn't trying to impress them or anything, she was just trying to make this whole trip less boring. Seeing her college friends after two years made her sad. It was clear now that they'd all avoided experiences, capitulated on their desires, afraid of disturbing their little routines. Linda had always had older friends, since she'd skipped two grades, and though she'd just turned twenty-one, really she'd been twenty-one since she was fourteen. But her friends were in such a weird hurry to turn thirty—not older, just *old.* When she'd moved here a few months ago, she'd thought Will and Cory would show her around, but she'd had to drag *them* to parties instead, where they'd form a sullen huddle and complain about how loud the music was, until either they left or Linda ditched them. It was super inconvenient, since by two A.M. she'd need a place to crash—she hadn't yet told them she was technically homeless—and she'd have to go home with some desperate creeper.

We could be doing something fun! Linda thought. *One day we'll be dead! So why this?* She wished they'd at least do drugs. That would make them interesting. Auden had his bennies, Milton his opium, Huxley acid, Baudelaire weed, Freud coke, Balzac fifty coffees a day—and Linda did *all* of those, plus Xanax. Even hangovers were good, sipping Bloody Marys alone in a dive bar, the slow crawl back to sentience feeling almost like accomplishment. Ugh, but there was her problem, *accomplishments*. She wasn't totally convinced that her current experience jihad was useful for her writing, and she *wanted* to be convinced. Of course, eventually *party* had to deflate from verb to noun, but there was no renouncing indulgences you hadn't exhausted.

She hadn't written, much less published, anything since college, and for this she partly blamed San Francisco, this little ukulele-strumming cuddle party. A They Might Be Giants song set in concrete. Its last influential artists were the god-awful Beats, and now it was nothing but a collapsed soufflé of sex kitsch and performance readings, book clubs, writing workshops. Haight-Ashbury radicalism had been flushed out in a thunderous enema of tourist cash; the Mission was annexed by Silicon Valley. City Lights was a good name for something that obscured stars. The little journals and bookstores were on a drip-feed of pledge drives, and the only thing to say about the McSweeney's tweehouse of interns was that they had nice packaging.

What was she even doing in this car? Why reaffirm dead friendships when she could be writing, or at least thinking about writing, instead of thinking of not thinking about it? She pinched two Xanax from her coin pocket and dry-swallowed them behind a fake yawn, put on her sunglasses, and rolled down the passenger's-side window to smoke as they passed through the northern terminus of Highway 1, where the street grid unraveled.

THE LOUD INRUSH of air flapped through the open window into the backseat, cutting into Cory's reverie about how to talk about the upcoming municipal elections. It was San Francisco's first instant-runoff mayoral vote, and emissions regulation and library fund renewal were on the ballot—but when she'd casually mentioned this a few minutes ago, Will said he didn't know there *was* an election this year, and Linda hadn't even registered to vote, and Henrik was asleep. They'd tuned her out, because political engagement somehow made you a boring caricature of the earnest liberal. She knew she risked coming off as a judgy proselytizing nag, but if she didn't bother them like this, they wouldn't be aware at *all*.

Usually she'd disguise her rants by talking about her job as an event promoter for a nonprofit, Socialize. They threw fundraising events for good causes, hiring local bands and drag queens to perform at their rallies, events that were totally every bit as good as Linda's stupid parties. Though, yes, throwing parties for money was somewhat cynical, and presumed that young people cared about progress only insofar as they could still have fun. Did people think it was enough to "be liberal"?

To feel bad but do nothing? That was of a piece with America's double exceptionalism: how you judged your nation as the most godblessed or goddamned on earth, but also stood apart from it. The body politic had become so fat, so lumpen, that it needed morality *incentivized*.

The wind battered Cory's hair around, and she held it out of her face, lamenting its impossible tangles, not dreadlocks exactly—more like anxietylocks, kelpy and worry-wadded. How could her friends know what it was like to stand on a corner, asking strangers to spend ten minutes and a few bucks on political issues that affected everyone, and getting *eye-rolled* for it? All the wave-asides from finance dicks and stroller moms, all the goddamn white earbuds that let people pretend they couldn't see or hear you, making her feel like equal parts panhandler, streetwalker, and soapbox preacher. Every weekend for two years she'd been schlepping around in her orange company T-shirt and fanny pack in Dolores Park, wiping her sideburns of sweat before delivering her rap to young people languishing on blankets: *Hey guys! What're you doing this Saturday? [Beat] Cool! Well after that, you should totally come out to [EVENT], [LOCAL ACT] is headlining, [LOCAL DJ] is spinning, it's going to be rad. Eighteen bucks at the door, and half goes to [CAUSE]. Hope I see you there! Peace out!*

At best they'd nod at her with closed-mouth smiles, taking a flyer without looking at it. And at worst? Well, she'd gotten spit on by a pro-lifer once, but that was actually validating; the worst was when, after she'd canvassed a birthday picnic, a drunk girl ran up and kicked Cory in the ass so hard her sandal came off, and the whole party laughed through their beer and smokes, knowing that Cory was professionally handcuffed to politeness, fucking *hipsters*.

For all the debasement, though, she never felt like the job was beneath her—activism was all about responsible cringing. But why the *hostility?* Sure, canvassing was cheesy and irritating and a far cry from revolution, but it wasn't lazy fatalism either. Her hair and clothes probably alienated people, but wasn't she basically like them? Didn't she work on cool projects, ride a bike, smoke weed like everyone else? . . . Yes, in fact, her event turnout had only appreciably improved once she'd started attaching little joints to her flyers. She couldn't afford much weed, so she cut them with Italian seasoning, and she streamlined her rap: *[Offer flyer] Party Saturday. [Leave]* For that, Cory was promoted from promoter to outreach manager, and all at once she was proud of her cleverness, relieved that the company was solvent, and furiously disappointed in humanity.

Will's swervy driving and the exhaust blowing through Linda's window were making Cory ill. She asked Linda to roll it up, and Linda complied with annoying slowness. Cory had assumed her friends would go on to redeem their privilege after graduating; instead they'd disappeared up their own asses. Will was some Internet douchebag, and Linda was back to getting shitfaced and thizzed and droed only weeks out of rehab. Undergrad Linda, her tea-drinking, Deleuze-reading, sweatpants-wearing college roommate, was now buried under a landfill of affectations: that wifebeater with the bra showing through the armholes and Day-Glo satin headband, all inked up like some community mural, high-waisted shorts like denim diapers. It was so depressing when women depoliticized themselves with hotpants.

Henrik, though, napping beside Cory? He was nice, considerate, sincere, even sexy in his big-bear way, and he'd never oppress you with narcissistic drama. Though in college, he'd decided to date Linda. He was a man; men liked Linda. Anyway, even niceness wasn't enough. *Nice*: from *nescire,* to not know. People *should* know! They *knew* they should know, and didn't! It was one thing to try to inform annoyed pedestrians about marriage equality, prison reform, the Ellis Act, minimum wage—but her *friends*? They'd all agree war sucks, Bush is evil, whatever, but try getting them to canvass their own goddamn corner on a Saturday afternoon.

Cory had nothing against leisure per se—she'd taken the job at Socialize precisely because it seemed to reconcile fun with purpose, but the company's struggles only seemed to demonstrate that the two canceled each other out. Her generation's failure was not of comprehension but of compassion, of splitting the indifference; its juvenile taste for making a mess; its indignant reluctance to clean it up; its limitless capacity for giving itself a break; its tendency to understand its privilege as vindication. And they weren't even happy.

Some people did care, though. Like her boss, Taren: compassionate, hardworking, a bit out of touch, but never alienated by conviction. Cory could do the easy thing and hang out only with people with matching political tastes, but she didn't want to give up on her friends like she had on her father—an objectively evil libertarian, who, after Cory had gone vegetarian in eighth grade, had snuck animal products into her food, not out of misplaced concern, just for brute enforcement of status quo—he'd laughed as he told her. (Cory had gone to the bathroom and made herself retch loud enough for everyone at the dinner table to hear, and then refused to eat for days until her father made vaguely credible threats about nose tubes.)

Dating was no easier. She always got dumped for precisely

her best qualities—dedication, intensity. Like when she'd skipped her own lunches to deliver surprise sandwiches to her last boyfriend's office and he said she was smothering him. She wanted to try dating women, but she didn't have time to figure out the Bay Area dyke scene, which was cool but sort of cliquey and mannered. She hated thinking that moral purpose asphyxiated relationships, but there it was.

Maybe she was wasting her effort on these particular friends, but you had to involve people even when they weren't grateful, even if you had to provoke and repeat, glib the message, glaze it with irony. It might annoy everyone, but if she tried and they couldn't be bothered to care, then they'd all have earned their damned futures and deserved to be lost.

ALL MORNING WILL had been irradiating the car with silent rage. He was unaware of how violently he was driving, and of the seat belt chime that had been dinging the whole ride because he refused to buckle up. He felt his brain turning red. Vanya should have been sitting next to him in the passenger's seat, right where Linda was sitting, but they'd spent all morning fighting. This trip was supposed to be his birthday celebration, which they'd already postponed for weeks now, and she'd promised *for days* that she'd come to the beach *even if* her boss called. Ellen, Vanya's boss, had texted Vanya literally an hour ago to be in at the office pronto, and when Vanya said yes, Will said he *knew* Ellen would pull this shit, and Vanya replied: "Baby, here's an idea: go without me! You haven't seen your friends in for*ever*! Do you want us to turn into one of those conjoined-twin couples who do everything together?"

Not much Will could say to that—because that was *exactly* what he wanted, but admitting that would look needy. What if he'd manned up and stood his ground? *Vanya, a promise is a promise, so go get your fucking towel.* No, he'd just send her rolling into the arms of one of those white techbro jags who were always leaving flirty comments on her Facebook and demoing their beta apps for her at parties while Will stood by flexing a red cup in his hand.

But he wasn't competing with other guys so much as with Vanya's entire life. She'd recently gotten the startup itch, and every hour she spent on biz dev webinars and skillsharing brown-bags was an hour stolen from Will. It was tough to say whether he resented the richness of her life or the blandness of his own: day drinking, blog reading, working from home with no ambitions to speak of except Vanya herself. She'd never scale back. After a year together, though, how much alone time was she strictly entitled to? True, Vanya gave Will an equally long leash, but that wasn't fair, because all he wanted to do with his free time was spend it with her.

So he'd said, fine, if you'd rather work than come along like you *said* you would, that's on you. And now he was on this stupid trip, which was her idea in the first place, out of sheer spite. It was easy to imagine another twenty-four years passing before he met a girl of Vanya's caliber, one who was moreover willing to date a short Asian guy. Before Vanya, it'd been a pathetic year of scurrying from bars to parties, getting stood up and shot down, girl after girl backing away in exotic fighting stances. And before that, twenty-two years of virginity. People assumed that longtime celibacy lowered your standards, but really it made you crazy to prove that you wouldn't settle for anything less than what was supposedly out of your league, which really fucked with your whole concept of the attainable.

He'd met Vanya at a house party last summer, when he saw

her sitting alone in the corner of the living room, texting while people were dancing. He'd been too drunk on Fernet to be properly intimidated, and he'd approached her and said something like, *I bet you're a better dancer than Michael Jordan.* She laughed, and he said, *Whoa, I can see all your teeth and they're all great,* and then he made the best and least deliberate move of his life, to just assault her with a kiss. And she kissed back! And then, when Will took her hand to lead her somewhere private, she didn't get up, but instead hung on and . . . rolled. He'd been so drunk he hadn't noticed she was paraplegic. *Perfect.*

But dating her had started to feel like paying the upkeep on a prize Lamborghini. Now he had to do things like clean his room or select clothes with attention to fabrics and seasonal palette. And smoke less. Or not really less but faster. What else could he offer? Money. He could fix her computer. And he could make her laugh by showing her his fat-kid pictures and imitating the way his mom said the word *regular,* even though he himself didn't find it funny—actually it was bound up in his whole complicated deal about Asianness.

So it was almost too bad that Vanya was *worth* the effort, surpassing every unrealistic standard that his friends had always insultingly urged him to lay aside. She was this outrageous cliché of sexiness, fashionable in wheelchair-tailored couture, in stilettos that added no height. With her bangs and faint overbite and humongous eyes, she was cute, and cute was more endearing than hot. And she was also hot. Vindicatingly. And—not that he ever bragged about this, not that he'd ever imply that this was her best quality—but in bed she was *incredibly disgusting,* indulging every tacky male fantasy, a blitzkrieg of clever fingers and smothering tits. She did everything that was too good to ask for.

The bridge yielded to highway. Will's head rushed with dark blood; he realized he was holding his breath. Though he sort of always felt that way.

I think an apology—, he began to text. But he knew it'd make him seem petty, even though against the general current of his insecurity ran a riptide of vanity, insisting in its mirthless way that he *totally* deserved Vanya; that if anything, everyone was unworthy of *him,* they just didn't know it. Will would always be the hungrier one in the relationship, a fact just shy of open acknowledgment ever since she'd caught him merging their photos together with face-morphing software to see what their kid would look like. Bottom line, he'd gotten a girl he couldn't have, one who, by some divine clerical error, precariously tolerated him. He was desiring beyond his means.

A shriek from the backseat pulled Will's attention back into the world. "*What,* Cory?"

"That guy on your left! You almost— Will, are you *texting while driving?* You *are!* Pull over!"

"Calm down. I'm touch-typing."

"Will, at least put away—"

"Yo, can I *drive?*"

He'd forgotten about Cory's control issues. Back when he'd helped her move to the city two years ago, she'd made him drive at fifty miles an hour the whole way to minimize fuel consumption. All that lofty lefty grandstanding, and here she was, insinuating he was a bad driver. He shouldn't have invited her, especially since she'd brought Linda without telling him— though he supposed he hadn't warned her Henrik would be here either.

If it came down to picking between friends like Cory, who bossed him around and only hung out when it was convenient for them or when he could do them a favor, or Vanya, who bossed him around but also fucked him, the choice was easy. If Vanya moved in with him, he'd ditch everyone else posthaste, and things would be fine, or at least it'd be harder for her to dump him on a whim. That was all he wanted.

THE CAR RECKONED down the narrowing road curving around the headlands, almost there. A tight turn caused the plastic binder to slide off Henrik's lap onto his feet, waking him. He'd wrenched his neck sleeping with his head drooped over his seat belt sash. The stitches in his tongue ached and pulsed. With sticky eyes, he glanced at Cory, who poked his nose. The ocean roiled glamorously to his left, making emblems of light jiggle on the car's ceiling. The heat itched on his face and his need to fart had a medical direness to it—possibly IBS, ulcerative colitis, Crohn's, polyps. Or death. Yeah: chronic death; death not otherwise specified.

He wished he hadn't agreed to come. Even if they made good time heading back, he'd still spend all night at the finite element analysis workstation, eating dinner from a vending machine, wiping himself down in the bathroom. And when he finally got to bed he'd still have to worry about a repeat of last night, when he'd bitten his tongue in his sleep. (A nerve-rich sense organ right between the sharpest, hardest bones powered by the strongest muscles: There was your antiteleological argument. Or evidence of Stupid Design.) He'd gone to the ER, but downplayed the pain to his doctor and was discharged with nothing but some stitches and a wad of medicated gauze to hold in his mouth. And when Will and Cory came to pick him up from the Caltrain station he'd downplayed it again, keeping his mouth closed without explaining why, and Cory had just laughed and said, *Oookay, Henrik's being weird again,* in that way people tended to talk about him behind his back right to his face.

At Stanford there was this smug saying that the students were like ducks: tranquil on the surface but paddling furiously to keep afloat. By reputation Henrik was all upper-duck: a round, approachable Danish face creased with smile lines, blond beard, huggable flannel, curly hair that was tidy only when wet. He was shy but could do eye contact. People seemed to like him when he drank, so he drank. Last time he'd been out with Will, he'd spent his rent money on rounds for the bar and done a tequila shot through his nose.

But lately he was all lower-duck, a pair of thrashing webbed feet. Effexor had not made things better and Celexa made things worse, so he was on washout, which felt like a permanent caffeine crash. Last month he'd had his Depakote upped again, bloating his face and torso, while the Topamax made his arms bony, which seemed impossible, though if you could be manic and depressive, you could probably also be fat and emaciated. He would get better if it killed him.

The pill fog had stalled his dissertation project, modeling how dermal tissues separated under various mechanical stresses. Instead he spent his time wondering whether his sink sponge was flannelly enough to throw out, whether that new freckle on his finger was lethal, and whether it was sadder to eat six boiled frozen potstickers off his cutting board or to spend a whole hour cooking and eating a proper meal while staring at his blank walls alone. It wasn't that he was falling through the cracks but that he *was* a crack, not crazy but *crazing* like a hunk of schist, full of faults and microvoids, tenuously intact.

All his friends had become self-sufficient adults, and he'd

bumbled back into the incubator. He couldn't blame them for not wanting to visit him on campus—happy hour, wine and cheese, trivia night, undergrad parties, no sir. Instead he ate Ruffles and returned Criterion Collection DVDs to the library unwatched, and took long walks for booze, single-handedly keeping the handles of Old Crow at the liquor store from acquiring that sticky layer of inventory dust. Sometimes when he passed by the Asian massage parlor on El Camino, he thought he might try to defibrillate his libido, but when he thought about it—entering some converted KFC and pantomiming with a baggy-eyed Filipina until she lifted his white modesty towel to give him a calloused handjob—shit, might as well just get an actual massage, his neck was *killing*. Not that he could afford either.

The seat belt had locked and was strangling him a bit. It was probably better now that he had a medical excuse to keep his mouth shut, because all he had to talk about was himself. He wanted to talk, but not as much as he didn't. His friends probably thought he was snubbing them, when really this was all he'd been looking forward to, and he kept his distance only because he didn't want to annoy them with his complaining. Why waste their time with self-pity? Especially with Linda here—he could see the flossy ruffle of her hair directly in front of him, through the gap in the headrest. She was blond now. Make a scene in front of her? No. Everyone had problems. Just put on some sunscreen and suck on that gauze, buddy. Keep living with chronic death. Soak that tongue in salt water.

By the time they pulled into the parking lot Henrik was asleep again, until Cory nudged his knee with hers. Daylight reddened through his eyelids. The sandy asphalt crackled beneath the gray Camry's tires as Will parked and cut the engine.

Doors opened and the clammy scent of seawater blew through. Linda blocked her fluttering eyes against the sun, tried putting her sunglasses on before realizing they were on. Her palms numb from the car seat's vibration. Substances unpleasantly metabolized. Exhaling, Cory took Henrik's elbow and told him to leave his homework in the car. Bones reordered in backs, legs under shorts felt the breeze freshen their sweat. They walked out between the bollards and across the spilled edge of sand, through dune grass yielding ticklishly underfoot. If Vanya had come they would be stopping here to collapse her wheelchair and carry her, because she was still weak in that way, no matter what.

The coast, the endlessly rewinding spills of the tide, green curbs of seawater breaking into flat white sizzling foam. The political vacuum of leisure spaces. Diagonals of sunlight carving off the last figments of fog over the water. Didn't she have another pill? Smoking and talking with towels over their shoulders. Behind the others he spat out his gauze and kicked a wave of sand over it, followed them to the concave shore. Towels down, snakes of sand filling the creases. A little crowded. But this weather. So nice. Days like this you have to have fun or you'll hate yourself when you're older.

CHAPTER 1

The Incorporation of Cordelia Rosen

It is necessary to remember that it is first the
potential oppressor within that we must resist—
the potential victim within that we must rescue.
—bell hooks

I. Live/Work

In October, Cory was promoted again, because her boss
died.

Arriving at work early on Monday, Cory had found Taren
Worth sleeping at his desk. He lay with his arms crossed at
the wrists as if to ward off life's final beating. After Cory said
Good morning to no reply, she assumed she'd caught him napping, and sat at her desk with minimal chair squeak. It wasn't
until after the office manager, Martina, showed up, and after
Cory made shushing gestures to keep her from waking Taren,
and after Martina mouthed, *What smells like shit?*, and after
the paramedics covered Taren's body while the police collected Martina's and Cory's trembling statements, and after
Cory biked home, wept in the shower, smoked a bowl, and
drank two glasses of chocolate almond milk, that she realized
that she had no idea what to do when your boss died. Why

didn't they teach it? You got math, you got sex ed—where was death ed?

Taren's timing was almost convenient: with three consecutive down quarters, Socialize was on the brink of default. For months they'd only been able to book bar venues with exposure-hungry local bands. The Oakland PD's cabaret permit sweeps were shuttering the East Bay venues, and San Francisco's dive bars were mutating into gastropubs and curio boutiques that thrived even as the economy withered. Taren had handled it with grim uncomplaining authority, and even though he'd been racking up overtime, nobody thought it'd *kill* him.

Her careworn boss. He was only thirty-four, but in hindsight he'd been a clear candidate for his version of death, with his asphalt complexion, dark purple nailbeds, drooping eye rims, a face creased like a palm. No matter his exhaustion, he always gave an unsmiling but sincere thumbs-up to Cory when she left the office. A light stutter made him seize up and squint like he was trying to read his own mind, and he'd say avuncular things like, *At this point the juice ain't worth the squeezing.*

Not knowing what else to do, the next day Cory returned to the office, a live/work loft in SoMa. The awareness that someone had died there made her sensitive to the exposed air ducts and furniture purchased from the liquidation sales of other offices. Taren's desk had been thrust aside by the paramedics, but its effects were intact, littered with consumerdrug: punctured blister packs, Dunhill soft packs, stagnant coffees, tombstone-shaped nasal sprays, ibuprofen bottles with no caps.

Lacking the wherewithal to clean it up, Cory spent the day calling venues to suspend the ongoing projects. She tidied up, cleared the whiteboard, stocked the printer paper, then sketched hands and dresses on her notepad until she remembered to fetch the mail, where she came across a delivery packet marked ATTN: CORDELIA ROSEN.

Inside was a copy of Taren's will, addressed to Cory by Taren's ex-wife, without comment. It stipulated the terms of his disposal (by incineration), the disposal of his possessions (to Goodwill), and finally an alarming dearth of goodwill:

> 3.1. To Deborah Higgins, who in marriage and sepa-
> ration treated me with contempt, ingratitude, and
> sexual spite, I leave the inconvenience of my corpse:
> the burden of my funeral expenses and the execu-
> tion of my will.

> 3.2 To my half brother Dick Macy (emphasis on
> HALF and DICK) I leave sincere wishes for a quick
> death pinned under your WaveRunner.

These were lifelong gales of resentment from the legal void, a petition to God for redress, current to two weeks. Taren had rarely discussed his home life; Cory'd figured he just had no time for personal bullshit. Her eye jumped from clause to clause, catching spurts of venom for his lawyer, for Socialize's landlord, for his therapist. She felt guilty for prying, but did he need the privacy anymore?

If Cory had known Taren was this lonely, she would've done . . . something. She could admit, now that it was too late and despite being a solid four on the Kinsey scale, that Taren was probably her ideal partner—noble, intelligent, Jewish. Naturally she'd love him—you couldn't get more unattainable than dead. The missed opportunities were coming to her now, all those late working nights, and the time they'd watched

Dark Days on the meeting room projector. Or the last time they'd been alone, two weeks ago. They'd been doing routine overtime, circles of lamplight on each of their desks as the skylight darkened, the turntable playing Nina Simone. Taren was reclined foreshadowingly in his chair, stiff and diagonal, fingers latched across his stomach. "What's up?" Cory had asked.

"My daughter," Taren muttered.

Cory pushed her chair back, casters rolling mutely over the vinyl scuff mat, and waited for the confession. "I shouldn't dump this on you," he continued, both protesting and capitulating. Cory encouraged him with appropriate subordinate concern.

"One sad truth," Taren said, "is that I achieved my goals— sort of. Owning a nonprofit, bending the arc of capitalism toward justice. I wanted to see the final swing of the materialist dialectic. But it swung the wrong way. Confidentially, our nonprofit is a nonrevenue. Everything's so small. In activism, you know, scale matters; I'm not some sentimental jerk who thinks everything's worth it as long as I ease some collective guilt. I came up rough. I'm realistic."

Taren had grown up on the fifth floor of a public housing development in Denver, living out the usual hardscrabble urban latchkey narrative, with crucial mentors and social awakenings; at Berkeley he did coke and studied public pedagogy and community organizing theory, graduating in journalism at the exact moment that O. J. Simpson and Monica Lewinsky cratered his faith in news. His girlfriend, a development economics grad student, was abruptly deidealized by an unplanned pregnancy, and Taren married her in the same civic building where she would pauperize him six years later. He waited tables until his daughter was in preschool, then got hired at the Ad Council, where he coordinated billboards telling black people to get checked for lupus, gay men to quit meth and get tested, Chinese people to seek mental illness assistance, Latinos to curb their kids' TV watching, everyone to exercise. "I was the white colonialist coming down from the mountaintop to hang fifty-foot commandments for minorities. I might as well've been wearing a pith helmet and jodhpurs."

So Taren made a Hail Mary; with a fateful loan and alimony payments yet to murder him, he founded Socialize. At the beginning, they threw $5,000-a-plate fundraising dinners that failed completely ("For some reason I expected big gives from the very echelon of society I was trying to eliminate"), so Taren took shifts at an oyster bar while the company relaunched at the opposite end of the price-point spectrum, trawling not the lunkers of philanthropy but the small fry of disposable income. He'd formulated the relationship between pragmatism, profit, and pride: put two in conflict and forget the third. Nonprofits, he learned, supplicated the idle rich, ate young hearts, and defrauded the middle class.

Then the divorce. He'd accidentally left one page of his prenup uninitialed—the pages had been stuck together with his daughter's apple juice—nullifying it. "Wiped out by a drop of apple juice! I went ballistic. For weeks I'd lie in bed with my face in a pillow and my ass in the air screaming, '*Apple* juice! *MOTHERFUCKING APPLE JUICE!*'"

Cory said, "You went bananas over apples."

Characteristically, Taren did not smile or laugh but instead nodded and said, "That's funny. I spent hours driving down Highway 1, not to relax, just to depreciate the car before my wife took half."

Twirling a pair of scissors around his finger, Taren recounted the quiet slow tragedy of therapeutic jurisprudence
and child-centered divorce, the arbitration center with its
separate entrances. He hated being an absentee dad, hated
forfeiting 60 percent of his income to support the willfully
unemployed woman who kept his daughter away from him,
while she indoctrinated his daughter with a narrative of coura-
geous single-motherhood. All she did was stick a spoon in the
kid's mouth! Whereas *he* was paying for the piano lessons and
body-positive dolls and computer camp; if he didn't, he risked
warping her with that ubiquitous American materialism borne
of aspirational envy, plus he'd go to jail. "Shitty little compromises. That's marriage: never-ending shitty little compromises.
Beestings and paper cuts unto death. That's business, too, if
you have the liability of a conscience." He smiled meaning-
lessly at Cory. "Family's overrated. Make a plan. Make money
and focus on work. Before you get old like me."

"You're not old!" Cory said. "You're seasoned."

"Pssh. Seasoned, right!" He pointed to the scorches of silver
in his hair. "Salt-and-pepper, there's your seasoning."

Taren got up and bid Cory good night. Obviously that was
the moment she should've offered him a shoulder rub, taken
his glasses off and—something. Rejection would've been disas-
trous, but if he was going to . . . goddamn internalized passiv-
ity. Now he was dead for want of vice.

Cory kept scanning Taren's will, slaloming across each page,
until on the sixth page she came across a highlighted passage:

> 14.1 I bequeath my nonprofit company, Socialize, and
> all the real property and business interests attached
> to it to my Outreach Manager, Cordelia Rosen, who

will assume the title, duties, and responsibilities of Executive Director, and will receive full control of the company's assets.

That was her. Her name. Was it even legal to saddle an employee with a debt-ridden company? Would the board approve? Did they even know Taren was dead? She could just refuse. But Taren had singled Cory out, with such fait-accompli wording. He saw potential in her. A cold, keen executive heart. Or maybe he just didn't have anybody else.

II. Benefit Is Complicity

Cory pedaled into a headwind with white scratches of rain wetting her face, navigating home by pigeon-instinct while her higher cognition performed triage. Work first: no snacks, no weed. Maybe go to the library to read case studies of companies whose bosses died. Or call Will and ask him to look up info online.

The SoMa commune Cory shared with four roommates was a converted cookie factory. There were rooms insofar as roofless partitions could be rooms; a fart in one room was heard as distinctly as a fuck in the next. Thrifty strangers constantly arrived and vanished, smoked and dealt. In the rare intervals when everyone was gone, like now, it was gorgeous with capacity.

Cory walked her white Bianchi into the hangar-size room, the flimsy ticking of its wheels tripled by the echo. Navigating to her bedroom in the far corner of the warehouse was like strolling down Market Street, with its miscellaneous zoning and visible class gradients: Roopa's tidy earth-toned den, Jinnie's live-in painting studio, the garbage bags piled in front of Laura's room awaiting disposal, Bailey's strip-club decor (leopard-print couch, mirror-plated dressers), then Cory's room, a lofted penalty box with a bare lamp and a tiny unopenable window, through which you could see the glassy teal Infinity Towers mounted like enormous humidifiers in the skyline.

Before entering her room, Cory heard the front door open distantly—probably Roopa, from the sounds of rustling vegetation. Roopa was big on food fads, and her current regimen was a self-invented one she called "ruminarianism": every day she rode the BART to Berkeley or Piedmont, wandered in meadows to pick mushrooms and herbs while listening to her iPod, then Dumpster-dove at Trader Joe's, all for a meal she'd spend two more hours cooking. She grew chanterelles in a Mycodome and sage and holy basil on the bathroom windowsill. Before this, she'd abjured meals in favor of chewing on little biscuits that looked like owl pellets; before that it was low-fat raw vegan and Master Cleanse.

If Roopa knew Cory was home, she'd want to talk at her; it was how she amused herself while cooking, recounting the quotedium of chores and bores. Cory avoided drinking water near her, to head off a sermon about how we were *literally* flushing water down the toilet and everyone should just embrace urotherapy like the ancient Egyptians.

Cory lifted up on her bedroom doorknob to keep the hinges from creaking as she opened the door, slumped in, and dropped her bag and bike helmet. She lay on her futon and gazed at the bookshelves at the foot of her bed, close enough that any minor earthquake would tip them over and kill her. It wouldn't be awful to be killed by them, she supposed: the Chomsky and Klein, Gramsci and hooks, Freire and Alinsky and Hall, even

Atlas Shrugged, which she'd read just to hate it better. But none of them told you what to do when your boss died.

She was too hungry to read anyway—her hands twitched as she overheard Roopa in the kitchen, the faucet gush, the knife clack and skillet sounds of greens on low simmer. The cozy yellow odors of dinner crept in over her partition walls. Cory considered lighting incense to counter the scent, but once cravings came, they never left until oversatisfied. She got up light-headed, helpless, and her legs forced her to the kitchen.

Roopa stood at the stove in a capital R, a hand bracing her tailbone and one leg stretched back, with her waxy black hair tressing down like a stripe of brushed pitch, ending in a horizontal slash at midwaist. Her face was babyish and marsupial-thin. She wasn't ravishing, but she wasn't unattractive, *but* men definitely treated her as if she *were* ravishing. She wore a blue apron over a brown dress with the sleeves ripped off. Cast-iron pans and stew pots were stationed over all four burners.

"Oh, you should've told me you were home, I would've made more," Roopa said. "It's potato hash with fennel and rosemary and Niman Ranch bacon and tempeh. And TVP."

"It's okay, thanks," Cory said.

"I found chèvre too. The Trader Joe's ones are ginormous. And they throw it out fully wrapped. Think how many landfill acres are taken up just by airtight cheese. Sure you don't want any?"

"Yeah, no, I'm good."

"Really? You sure?"

"Thanks, I'm fine."

Cory opened the refrigerator. It was a maddening presence—always on, drawing an eighth of their electricity, just to store food. It carried a permanent stench of chilled compost and was crammed with communal groceries; Cory spent an eternity rearranging items to get to her week-old bok choy stir-fry leftovers. It was greasy, *awfully* greasy. She could do radishes and hummus for fiber, soy milk for protein, liquid amino for more protein. She took out the hummus and the soy milk and put the hummus back in and borrowed a nectarine from Jinnie's shelf, and then took the hummus out again, jogging it in her hands to ponder its mass, its lipids and carbs, though she already knew all the numbers to the tenth decimal. Also she'd heard this particular hummus had done something bad to Palestine. Her hunger stabbed her; she tossed the hummus back in the fridge and took out her Tupperware of stir-fry. She just wouldn't eat the whole thing.

"That's your dinner?" Roopa said, in that sympathetic/annoyed tone you used with confused foreign tourists. "Where's the flavor? Aren't you at least going to heat it up and plate it?"

"Nah."

Roopa turned to the stove and mounded a plate with a few hundred thousand calories of glistening tempeh. The odor made Cory's saliva salty. "Try this. It's yummy and it's totally sanitary. Nom nom."

"Thanks, Roop, but I gotta eat this—"

"Before it goes bad? That's so *depressing*. It probably doesn't even have any nutrients after all that refrigeration. Try my food. I know it seems gross to eat 'garbage,' but people have to get over that."

Cory laid her things on the kitchen counter. When she had first moved to the city, the plan had been to recruit kindred progressives into the warehouse, maybe becoming one of those Bay Area cultural polestars. She first met Roopa at Socialize's garden harvest potluck three months ago, and, spotting a potential girlfriend or roommate or both, Cory had approached Roopa and smoked her out. As Cory wondered how to broach Roopa's sexual and political alignments, Roopa was already headed straight for those topics: two years at Oberlin as a sexual health advisor who practiced what she preached, a year in South America for her anthropology thesis ("Recuperating Presence: The Immediacy of Indigene Consciousness"—in lieu of Eurocentric written documents, she'd produced photographs and small beaded weavings). Then she'd dropped out for culinary school in Boston, dropping out again to couch-surf California.

In Cory's stoned brain, Roopa had seemed ideal, and they moved her in ASAP. But it turned out they weren't equally political, just equally pedantic. At first Cory had been thrilled that Roopa attended Socialize events, but Roopa would keep offering unsolicited advice ("I still think marriage equality isn't the issue. We need to *abolish marriage*"). In turn, Roopa brought Cory to her anarchist "salons"—usually potlucks or homebrewed pickle tastings at other collectives, where discussions played on conspiratorial themes: 9/11 was an inside job, canned tomatoes caused Parkinson's, etc. An urban primitive with pepperoni-size ear gauges wondered aloud if heterosexual intercourse was "inherently degrading." Cory got through it only by pretending she was conducting an anthropological study of failed radicalism. Roopa understood Cory's lack of enthusiasm as liberal wimpiness, which she liked taking potshots at, like now.

"I think," Cory said, "we can divest from industrial monoculture instead of relying on its waste. You know how they say benefit is complicity."

"The real waste would be to let food spoil for an empty gesture."

"Couldn't we put community pressure on supermarkets to reduce waste in the first place?"

"The fact is"—Roopa sucked a crumb that had fallen on her apron—"that the waste is there now, and it supports indigent communities."

"Well, you're right about that. Is it really okay for people like us to take free food we don't need?"

"There's plenty for everyone. Also, I'm not exactly well-off." Roopa laughed. "I'd starve if I didn't hit the Dumpsters. It's not like I'm exploiting food stamps. I'm part of the working poor."

Somehow Roopa got by, part-time and under the table, freelancing as a food photographer and botanical illustrator. Cory didn't want to have to explain the distinction between poor and broke. Spurning the nine-to-five was fine, but Cory suspected Roopa's work ethic was rooted in a determination to feel good about feeling good. Still, it was baffling how Roopa could afford San Francisco on freelance wages. Cory *did* take food stamps.

"I think you just get off on guilt," Roopa said, closing her eyes and making cumming noises as she forked up a mouthful of hash and worked it around in her mouth without chewing.

Cory's eyelids glitched. "I wasn't saying Dumpster-diving is immoral. I was only thinking maybe it'd be best not to create a social institution dependent on corporate excess."

"We're redeeming the waste. It's putting ideals into action on the most basic level."

"Spending half a day making dinner, that's 'action'?"

"That's the role food *should* play in people's lives. Food is culture, just like songs and paintings. I've had meals that made me cry. Some people are visual, others are tactile, and actually I'm a synesthete so I'm kinda both, but I also get so much meaning in through my mouth."

But so painfully little *out from* her mouth . . . "Well, air is important too. Should we spend hours every day working on breathing?"

"Doy. Ever heard of yoga? I'm only sort of kidding."

Cory wouldn't win. Roopa was rigid, the way free spirits often were, about the romance of naturopathy and well-being as morality. Photographing meals, food blogging, recreational fasting—all that time committed to sweeping the steps of her temple. It was at least as disordered as what Cory had. There was this spin, this indulgent *spin* to Roopa's charity: when she did relief in Chile, she returned with a copper-goddess tan; if she volunteered for a bake sale, it was because she enjoyed baking. Her diet was another slick win-win rationalization of glut. Good intentions notwithstanding, that was the lemon-meringue heart of her frankly dipshit worldview: that merely observing selective austerities—abstaining from work, from money—was activism, when really it was shallow *passivism* . . .

Roopa turned off the burners and unlaced her apron. She never looked tired. "Honestly," Roopa said, "people who shop in supermarkets should be forced to spend a day in a cage, like factory chickens. And those of us who didn't go to Stanford don't have the option to buy bougie farmer's market greens."

Like Cory was so rich! As if she lorded her diploma around! She hated that no matter what she did, her achievements redounded to a massively endowed, for-profit corporation—Stanford, Inc. But complaining about this would make her seem even *more* stuck-up. "Yeah, okay, Roopa? First of all, you went to Oberlin. Second, I'm just as broke as you, and my degree means nothing in the nonprofit world—well, I know privilege is invisible, but . . ." Cory pressed a thumb to her temple, where an éclat of migraine was about to light up a deep furrow of her brain. "Look, we both hate consumer waste. I prefer a policy approach, and you—well, you tell me."

Roopa leaned in and seized Cory's hand. Cory hated rhetorical touching. "All politics are spiritual issues first," Roopa said. Oh, *fuck* this. Roopa always fled to superstition. Sometimes she couched gemstones on her body to "smooth out her energy," and at day's end Cory would hear raw gems scattering on the floor as they dropped from the cups of Roopa's bra, a few more clicking down as she shook her hair. And men did love their bedazzled sex object. But more to the point, Roopa had this kernel of willed impracticality, like when Cory proposed a common-area cleaning schedule and she'd said, *I don't believe in linear time*. Irrationality was comprehensible; Roopa was *pre*rational.

Cory drew her breath for the steep ascent. "Okay, 'the spirit.' What is it? How do you base decisions on it?"

"Soul, qi, quantum energy, kundalini, whatever. It's the force field that's dissimulated throughout everything." It was extremely typical of Roopa to misuse a big word for emphasis. "It's about intuition. Instead of forcing things into this rigid paternalistic framework of, like, X equals Y."

"Isn't it *more* paternalist to assign a gender to logic?"

"I'm just saying, if you insist on denying a spiritual existence, why discuss it? You can believe in it or not."

"I don't."

"I'm sorry, but that's your limitation," Roopa said, wounded with empathy.

They were experiencing the same exact pissy offendedness. Cory tugged the hairs over her left temple, where her migraine strobed, depositing curly afterlights in the air above Roopa's head. Her kundalini visible. Cory withdrew her sweaty hand. "I'm gonna go eat in my room."

"I think my background gives me a different perspective. When my parents came over from India, they had nothing— they couldn't, like, lobby supermarkets. Minorities understand power structures."

"You know I'm *Jewish,* right?"

"Um, seriously? You're white. Sorry, but dreadlocks don't give you the voice of color."

Roopa was right, sure; but come *on,* like a cute skinny desi didn't have it *way* better than a chubby Jew! As if Roopa couldn't eat whatever, sleep whenever, fuck whomever, believe any and all woo-woo bullshit . . . Cory's irritation alerted her to the dangers of blithely dismissing people of color or bitchily undermining other women, red flags of internalized bias; though Roopa was clearly exaggerating to gain yardage—ugh, but *that* might be a privileged intuition too. Then again, who was *Roopa* to condemn privilege, as a cisgender bobo, equally inoffensive in conventional society and her so-called underground?

Cory stood and turned away before Roopa could get the wrong idea about her tears. "I'm going to my room," Cory said.

"Okay. Cory, please don't get upset. Enjoy your supper. I won't tell Jinnie you took her fruit."

Cory left a trail of smoldering footprints back to her room. Sitting on her futon, she opened the Tupperware and pushed her fork into her food and then her mouth. Frigid and bland. Cory hated being vegetarian. She loved meat but was also *mad* at it, having acquired the taste in childhood innocence. The lip-glazing completeness of a cheeseburger, bacon's salty crunch. She loved meat and hated kale and yoga and hated women who fetishized kale and yoga, capitulations to the male gaze marketed as fitness. The only problem with eating meat was that it was evil for every conceivable reason. Cory did more than abstain; she resisted.

Thoughtful people who wanted to extend their unmerited fortune to others, without expectation of profit or recognition, sheepishly accepting the discredit and liabilities of their privilege: they'd always be the most irrelevant minority. And then there was the self—the universal minority.

Cory consumed half of her cold gluey meal with her eyes closed. It was like what people would eat if they didn't have tongues. Her mouth was dry, but she wouldn't go back to the kitchen for water, so she tilted the rest of the stir-fry into her wastebasket and put out the light. She answered her stomach's aching ribbit with a dash of hot sauce, and pulled at her misery-locks, which felt like kudzu rooting into her skull. Weed would relieve the headache but it'd make her hungrier. Everything was wasting energy. She sat on her futon, adapting to the dark, and spoke aloud to her migraine.

III. The Patriarch

After an hour-long nap, during which she dreamed she was cutting a huge yellow toenail off Roopa's foot, Cory got back to work. She squinted at the printed financial records that she'd taken from the office's filing cabinets—TFS, OCF, EBITDA. Were these good numbers? What was the difference between earnings, revenue, and income? She hung a perplexed finger in her mouth. She didn't even know if they could afford an accountant: she'd need to hire an accountant to know.

She felt mute and illiterate in the language of power, which was money. She knew that corporate oligarchs used it to subvert democracy. But she was hazy on macro and micro; how US trade agreements affected sweatshop conditions in Indonesia; what the Fed *did*, exactly. Her efforts to research the housing market crisis ended in page-crumpling fury—credit default swaps? Mortgage-backed securities? Collateralized debt obligations? How could people be moral when morality obliged you to know *everything*? It was her fault for not studying econ in college, but she'd had so much contempt for the future ibankers that it had seemed principled not to.

Her landline phone felt enormous when she picked it up. She dialed, sort of hoping nobody would answer, but on the last trill of the sixth ring, someone did—it was Barr.

Cory momentarily forgot whether the caller or answerer was supposed to speak first. "Hello," they said at the same time.

"Hi, Dad, it's me. Just checking in."

"Well, that's astonishing. And to think your mother isn't around to witness this rarest of terrestrial phenomena. Years from now, I'll remember I was sitting at my desk, October 3, 2007, when my firstborn daughter, Cordy . . ."

She hated that name. In high school her mom had vetoed Delia and Cory, insisting they were respectively "too similar to" and "not as pretty as" Deirdre, her sister's name. She wished there were something worse to call him than *Dad*. "So yeah, how are things, Dad?"

"Fine, thank you. Okay then, how much money are we talking?"

"That is not fair, Dad."

"So then this is a social call?"

"Whatever. Fine. You want me to get real? I do need money."

"That's more like it."

"But not *your* money. I want to *make* money."

"I thought you were allergic."

"Dad, can I explain?"

She caught him up on Taren's death and her promotion. She had no trouble admitting that Barr had the business mind, self-made in the heyday of deregulation. After graduating from Stanford, he'd sensed a bonanza in lifting things for wimpy undergrads and founded his moving company, Barr None. Six days a week he'd carried beds and bookcases, filling his palms with slivers of wood and metal under a half inch of craggy brown callus. He franchised across Northern California, adding all-Latino landscaping and all-female cleaning services, bolstered by a series of locally famous ads that featured Barr manually decimating fad items (Beanie Babies, Foreman grills, Pokémon cards) behind a blinking toll-free number. She knew the shady pragmatics of small business ownership had shaped his cynical realpolitik, but he really believed you could run a business without one moral fiber or protein of empathy, just know-how and can-do. How could he be so pro–manual labor and so anti-Labor? So nationalist and so antinationalization? Passionate about Latin but indifferent to Latinos? Cory, at least, had collective moral purpose; she had protein and fiber.

With hindsight, Cory's sentence on Barr was *What a weird Jew.* Clearly he was out to prove something to the gentile establishment with his cash and triceps, his iron-rich Reaganism. He lived in a $1.8 million fortress in Palo Alto with a thirsty half-acre yard, but kept up the blue-collar pretenses, wearing undershirts to meetings, stretched over his hull of musclefat. His beard was the length and neatness of putting green, and he Brylcreemed his hair back from forehead to nape. In worldly matters he was amazingly, annoyingly capable, but his expertise was rotc. To him the brain was another muscle.

"Now your business," he said. "What's the product? What's your immediate revenue stream?"

"What does any of that mean? I just want advice."

"What do you *sell*?"

Cory sucked in a big preamble of a breath and then recited the mission statement: Socialize designed, coordinated, promoted, and hosted recreational events whose proceeds went to progressive causes.

"I see," Barr said, in his way-ahead-of-you way. "Commodifying liberal guilt. High elastic demand."

"Dad."

"Nothing to be ashamed of. Selling crap is how we support our base of crapmakers and crapmongers. Everyone profits when people crap."

It was one of Barr's great joys to see suckers getting screwed, and if you weren't contributing to the production order, you were getting screwed. He was the kind of hypocrite who dismissed novels because they were "made up," even though he still watched movies. He liked to stare into the windows of gyms and laugh, because he disdained both fat people and unpaid exertion.

Careful not to let actual flames escape her mouth, Cory said, "We promote culture, send business to local merchants and venues, and route disposable income to social causes."

"All right, let's hear the numbers. Numbers don't get defensive."

Against her background indignation, Cory was relieved that

she was prepared. She recited slowly, with Barr chuckling and whistling after certain figures. "You're in the proverbial truckload. Call a management consultant."

"Well, that's you. We can't afford consulting. We can't even afford Internet; we steal our neighbor's Wi-Fi."

Barr's basso profundo put an itch deep in Cory's ear. "Then find a moron to buy you out."

A lariat of stress tightened around Cory's ribs. "No way. I believe in my company. It's my coworkers' livelihoods." (That was pure fudge: most were interns or part-timers. Yet the principle stood.)

"Nemo liber est qui corporati servit."

Cory sputtered plosives, shoulder-gripping the phone and crossing her arms. She'd never fully understood Barr's dead-languages thing, but it probably related to his idea that all conflicts were battles over the dictionary: marriage defined as one-man-one-woman, life as conception. He'd homeschooled Cory and Deedee in Latin, translating poems and orations each morning, clinking scansion on his coffee mug with a butter knife while his daughters chanted, *"ARma viRUMque caNO."* It was his fault that Cory spontaneously generated puns and anagrams and portmanteaus and spoonerisms and mondegreens. It had started twelve years ago, at a Burmese restaurant in the Richmond; when Deedee offered Cory the rest of her platha bread, Cory said, *I couldn't plathably,* and Barr had laughed so hard that Cory kept doing it to please him—Indian food had her *naanplussed,* the plural of lox was *loxen,* the superlative of toilet was *toilest,* Jane Doe was married to John Deere. To encourage her, Barr hung butcher paper on the fridge to swap riffs:

I've never read Virgil, do you think Aeneid to?
  I used to read poetry Ovidly but now I think it's Juvenal
Read orations instead, they'll take Agrippa you
    I love speeches, I recite them till I'm Horace

So Barr had *raised* her to be corny and annoying. And with respect to the genetic estate she'd inherited: big butt, chunky neck, and back fat. Her adipose complex.

Barr raggedly cleared the slime from his throat. "Well, I applaud your initiative. I'm glad to help. As to raising money, there remains the matter of our loan."

Shit.

Back when Cory had been applying for schools, she and Barr had agreed, for opposite political reasons, that it would be best to avoid student loans, so she'd let Barr pay the $34,221-a-year tuition instead, vowing to repay him with side jobs. But her arrival at Stanford coincided with 9/11, turning everyone into an activist overnight: debating, learning Arabic, getting arrested, taking the Caltrain to SF to march in huge antiwar rallies with Jesse Jackson and Joan Baez. Over the summers she'd done Alternative Spring Break, Haiti relief, and documented the 2004 Summer of Love on a research grant. There wasn't any *time* to work at fucking Jamba Juice.

Soon she'd joined the Stanford Labor Action Coalition and organized protests, road blockages, sit-ins on President Hennessy's lawn, and finally her hunger strikes, starving out living wages for Stanford's custodial staff and divestment from Israel. It was an elegant way to achieve something by doing nothing, which was the only thing she'd felt absolutely qualified to do, and it felt nice to hide her little problem out in the open. Her red tent was a common sight in the Main Quad, and the *Stanford Daily* ran a front-page feature, CORDELIA ROSEN '05 SPEARHEADS HUNGER STRIKE PROTESTS, alongside a photo of her sloganeering into a bullhorn. The *Daily* named her one of the Cardinal Leaders of her class, along with the princess of Bhutan, Ben Savage, and a white novelty rapper with a big Internet following. Everyone was getting so interested in her, the message was getting out, and when after two weeks she collapsed and woke with an IV in her arm, she thought, good—everyone would know she meant business.

But when the campus humor mag ran an article in their annual fake *Daily* (SOPHOMORE SHOWS THIRD WORLD HOW AMERICA DOES STARVATION), she realized that she wasn't winning the prayers of a silent majority, but their stifled laughter. And worse, she needed to graduate. Convinced that activism should bridge disciplines, she'd taken PHIL 150 and withdrawn, taken CHEM 30 pass/fail and failed, taken LING 130 and emerged with a hair-chewing habit. By the time she earned her individually designed Liberal Studies in Classical Democracy degree, she'd borrowed just under $120,000 from Barr, not including prep school.

Barr had never pressed the issue before. "Dad," Cory said, making a wobbling sigh into defeat. "I don't know what to say. Someday, I'm serious, I'll pay it down. But now I'm really asking for your help, not money. I'll do whatever it takes, but it'll take some time and lots of work, all right?"

"Cordy, I'm just teasing. I'm glad to help, but you're going to have to be the boss. Hire, fire, get the sweat running. Hard work redeems mediocre intelligences, as Seneca says."

A tear ran onto her hand and she covered the receiver.

During her last breakup she'd broken her phone by crying into it for two hours. "I can sweat."

"That's gravy to my ears. I'll email you info."

"Okay." Oh, just say it. "Thanks, Dad, I appreciate the help."

"Take care, Cordy."

Cory dropped the phone in its cradle. From her shelves she fetched her *Compact Oxford English Dictionary*, Barr's high school graduation gift. It weighed sixteen pounds in its faux-leather hardcase—only Barr would prefer reading to be this strenuous. The dry glue in the spine crackled as she spread the lap-crushing volume open, flopping from B to E to C to Ca-, and she slid the magnifying planchette over *care*, from the Teutonic *caru*: trouble, grief. Derived from *karo*, to scream; from Old Norse *kqr*, sickbed. In Modern English: charge, oversight, protection, concern, anxiety. Yes, she would take care: of business.

She fell back, pinned under every English word. Barr would help her. All she had to do was look at an email. But incredibly—*unthinkably*—she didn't know how to email.

CHAPTER 2

His Own Devices

Thus he builds a trail of his interest through the maze of
materials available to him.
And his trails do not fade.
—Vannevar Bush

I. Vanya Pitches

The automatic front door to Vanya's apartment opened with a motor hum and hydraulic wheeze, and Vanya greeted Will with a cheeriness that perfected his dread. Her hair was wound in a compact auburn bun and draped with silky bangs, and her tight evening dress matched her grenadine lipstick. Will felt instantly second-rate: his gray sweater and black jeans might as well have been oven mitts and headgear. He should've worn the blazer, should've used shape cream and squeezed his pores. He stooped down, and she overrode his lackluster kiss with her livelier one. This meant amazing news. Last time the amazing news was her new job, and before that it'd been kittens. Amazing news never involved Will.

In any other apartment the accessible furnishings would've stood out, but Vanya's read as chic and minimalist. The mid-century decor, executed in autumnal browns and greens, was arrayed in teakwood eloquence against the walls, with no impediments except for the squat coffee table with its stack of tortoiseshell coasters. Everything was reachable via lazy Susans and swiveling bookshelves on motorized wall runners, the curtains remote-controlled. The handrails in the bathroom were the apartment's only conspicuous accessibility features. Everything was correct. Vanya didn't make messes.

She called him into the kitchen, where her purple chrome wheelchair zizzed in K-turns between stove and table. The apartment was humid with a foody savor that made the windows drool. A single dish was laid out, bracketed by one fork and one knife, heaped with couscous and a slab of lemon chicken with olive oil fluorescing beneath it. Vanya sat across from Will and placed her laptop where her dish should've been. "So, amazing news . . ."

Yesterday her boss, Ellen Stokes, gave a talk on automated user presegmentation at a Women on the Web coffee klatch, and in the schmoozing hour afterward, Vanya caught Ellen's ear and made a proposal. Among other duties, Vanya provided content for Wond.er, the flagship site of Ellen's positivity-themed blog network, featuring the usual drop-shadows and rounded corners and nostalgia listicles and videos of stranger-kindness and animal friendships. Vanya proposed a disability-oriented affiliate site, which she would run. Ellen said there wasn't room in Wond.er's org chart for new flavors of content at present, but if she were Vanya, she'd just start her own company. "Then she offered to set up a pitch meeting with her venture capital firm in Manhattan to score seed funding."

Will was interested in Vanya's career. But his *brain* wasn't—at least the part that needed to surpass a threshold of ego-relevance before it converted words into meaning. He caught something about a November meeting, the words *pro-spectus* and *monetization plan*, before wondering about the last time he'd washed his jeans, because his legs were itchy.

"—baby? Earth to baby?"

"Yeah, what's up?"

"You look like you're having a deep thought."

Will looked down. His meal was gone. "Sorry, yeah."

"So I'm tweaking my pitch and I want some feedback, okay? Let me set up."

Will stared at Vanya staring at her laptop. She cleared her throat, and two minutes later she began. "The problem with disability," she said, addressing the back row of some auditorium, "is that people have been trained to react to it with misplaced empathy. Whenever you see an amputee or a blind person or someone in a wheelchair, you think, 'How sad.' They're always jokes or pity puppets. Even when they're portrayed positively, you're supposed to feel inspired in this cheesy way, like 'Oh, I'm such a good person for seeing this paraplegic as human.' You'd never want to *be* them. The negativity is alienating and undignified. So our business goal—"

"Our?"

"We. The company."

"Oh."

"Our goal is to overhaul disability's mainstream image by offering a whole spectrum of premium lifestyle and entertainment content. Make disability exciting to watch. We call it Sable. Okay, hang on."

Vanya typed corrections, her face cold with diode light. She was so noble, like a statue of some heroic dog, reflecting decades of trained poise—Vanya the child star, the Little Miss. She'd grown up in a congenial Texas suburb, the daughter of a snack-food sales rep and a mother-slash-manager. Vlad and Randi Andreeva weren't personally ambitious, though Randi fully supported Vanya in succeeding at whatever she made Vanya do. She booked Vanya for local commercials and youth pageants and talent searches, which Vanya dominated with her huge eyes and major-league ringlets: Little Miss Border Belle, Little Miss American Cutie (Greater Houston), Little Miss Epilady™ Girls Make the Future. Randi designed a new talent routine for each competition: samisen, rhythmic gymnastics, mental arithmetic, cup stacking, celebrity impressions, and so on, later combining these routines into a tour de force. Vlad was less supportive, and shamed Vanya for the revealing competition attire that Randi made her wear.

The strictures of competition—road travel, queen duties, a ban on boys—rankled as Vanya hit high school. On weekend nights she shimmied down the drainpipe from her bedroom window and rode out to raves with friends, where she declined the little Buddha-stamped pills and looked on in wistful good-girl fascination, envying the fun that she'd quietly convinced herself she was better off for not having. This transition from Little Miss to Miss Teen had been the only lapse in Vanya's life of relentless improvement.

So it came as a perverse blessing when, at fourteen, she finished third for Miss Teen Dixie Doll, behind identical twins who'd split the tiara. During the onstage group photo, the flash-bulb caused one of the eliminees at the top of the bleachers to snap a kitten heel and crash forward onto the quarterfinalists, the semifinalists, then Vanya and the twin queens, all sixteen cascading down the steps in an anorexic avalanche. Under the scrum of Misses, Vanya broke her nose and fractured her pelvis and spine. A stray flake of bone had her in agony until after two days she awoke with no feeling below her navel. (She was luckier than the twins, who'd *really* split their tiaras and had to step down, not that they were in a position to care.)

After a year of determined physical therapy, she'd waded into the tiny pond of disability-oriented pageants (Miss Teen Enduring Spirit, Miss Teenspiration, Miss Teen Pray for a Cure), and her mom booked her as a parts model. Taking her homecoming crown and sash as an afterthought, she quit pageants for good, feeling lucky to have gotten out before hemorrhoid cream and duct tape became de rigueur. She'd realized she was "at the top of the wrong ladder," and if not for her "reboot," she wouldn't have studied new media at Vassar, moved to San Francisco, or met Will, who'd lost track of what she was saying.

"Look at the current offerings," Vanya said, diagramming her sentences with her hands. "Disability forums tend to devolve into group therapy. Sufferers bursting to swap sympathy and pain management tips. It's not fun. It's a conversation able-bodied people can't participate in, and the biggest threat to mainstream penetration. Sable will fight negativity with automated content filtering, crowd moderation, and aggressive brand management."

She looked up at Will, her long silver earrings counterswinging. To prove he was listening, Will said, "That's kinda harsh. You'll ban people for complaining?"

Vanya was happiest when fielding objections. "It's about driving expectations for community engagement. Sable will be a destination to share and have fun. Our target audience wants to participate, not mope and feel pitied."

She advanced her notes. "There's a tremendous built-in vertical: my market opportunity research shows that seventy-seven percent of *all* people with disabilities are frustrated with the lack of online community. There's so much room for category innovation in the disability space, and these are tech-savvy power users. The tent is as big as it gets: The hearing and vision impaired. Little people. MD, MS, CP, CF. The whole autism spectrum. Wounded veterans, paraplegics, diabetics.

"Though that's not how we're segmenting it—we're really going after Condé Nast, Viacom, Gawker. Land, sea, and air. Disability transcends markets, and it needs healthy images. Old media reinforced stereotypes; new media is redefining them. In the digital age, we can succeed *because* of our disability focus, not in spite of it. And that, aside from fun and profit, is my business."

Will golf-clapped and wore the printed smile that he'd iterated throughout their relationship. He considered giving honest feedback—like, how would she "transcend" the disability focus when it was the site's distinguishing feature? Why "redefine" stereotypes instead of eliminate them?—but it didn't matter what he thought. The substrata of Vanya's ambition had formed eons before they'd met. "Really engaging."

"While I'm in New York I'll be speed-dating for hires," Vanya said. "Also reconnecting with my Chi-O sisters. They're kayaking down the Hudson."

"When's that happening? I'll come along."

"No, I'll be totes swamped. You'd just end up watching movies on your laptop in the hotel room, like our Prague trip. And don't even pretend like you'd enjoy kayaking; you can't even swim."

Will wanted to point out that *she* couldn't swim either, but telling Vanya what she couldn't do was a fast way to get killed. "Why go to New York when all the tech VCs are here?"

"Ellen's contacts are there. Besides, my company is bridging old and new media, so I want East Coast connections—Silicon Valley's so incestuous. Baby, I'll only be gone for three weeks. Hang out with your college friends," Vanya said, though she'd never met them, because when he'd started dating Vanya he'd scaled back on everyone else.

"Cory and Linda? They're flakes. And Henrik's not picking up his phone."

"Baby, do I really need to plan your life for you?"

Careful not to snivel, wan smile wan smile wan smile: "It'll double as a vacation. Two birds with one stone."

"Baby, if I only get one stone, I'm aiming at one bird, okay? When it's time to decompress, I'll loop you in."

Will flexed the patience muscles in his jaw, and kept them flexed as he executed supportiveness over the next two weeks. He evaluated her wireframe UI, nodded along to n-teen more pitches, researched SEO and AdWords strategy. He ironed her tailored sit-down dresses, booked a hotel and a cheap flight, and blew out his wrists massaging her shoulders as she road-mapped her growth plan.

The night before Vanya left, the fucking was above average, and average was stellar. She lay with her legs stilled on the bed, slenderer than any vanity. A spire of lust skewered up into Will's chest. At close range he cultivated important-seeming analogies about her body parts—her nostril-shaped navel, her teeth with their nacre glassiness, her air-colored eyes, each breast as clean and touchable as an egg. The sense that she somehow smelled better than everyone else. Will resented the influence that this type of moisturized prettiness had over him, but it was an appetizing substitute for dignity. Though, being accustomed to sex at an electronic remove, Will found that this same beauty made it hard to focus—Vanya in the proximate flesh seemed like a mirage formed out of his desperation that would be pointless to embrace. If he shut his eyes he could usually make it happen, but tonight her imminent departure was putting him off.

He had a fantastic idea. He reached into his nightstand for his digital camera, activating it with a whir and a sprinkling chime.

"What are you doing?"

"Making a souvenir."

Vanya snatched the camera like a mongoose. "Baby, I'm not insane."

Will was disappointed that he didn't make her insane. "But you'll be gone for weeks. These are wartime measures."

"Nope. Nuh-uh."

"You don't trust me? I'll use 256-bit AES steganographic encryption, stored on—"

"Sorry, baby, no times a million."

"But I don't think you understand how *strong* this encryption is. It would take decades—"

Vanya kissed him. "Don't worry, you're not gonna forget this."

So Will relented, and Vanya gratuitously delivered. In the past she'd proposed handcuffs, watersports, breathplay, and tonight it was facefucking: grasping the sides of her head, her ears; sputtering and squelching as cheeks bulged and caved, hairband knocked askew, liquid eyeliner tears running to blacken the wagging suds of slobber dangling from chin and hair, eye contact unbroken. It wasn't that she didn't have a gag reflex; it was that she didn't care. How incredible that this was allowed! How bittersweet to let it pass unsaved! What could be more mature, more *considerate,* than objectifying yourself to meet the vile hard-charging demands of mainstream penetration?

But there was still the question of whether she enjoyed it, *could* enjoy it, or whether it was only tedious appeasement. She couldn't feel below her waist. "Sex is about giving pleasure too," she'd once insisted, "it's sexy and empowering." Well, that sounded like bullshit, but what did Will know about how sex went for paraplegic women? For *any* woman? "I get off on watching," she'd also claimed. Really? Watching *him* spasm, bleat, and hunch? Will figured he should be grateful that performance anxiety was moot, although he was also aware he was being denied the very pleasure of pleasure-giving that Vanya claimed was half the point.

Afterward she calmly licked up the mess. Her eyes were pink. Will lay his arm across her and nudged a bend into her knees with his own. He felt he should say something to affirm their couplehood, to cover everything the sex had left out. Sex, even explicit sex, wasn't very explicit. In fact it was downright vague.

He said, "Well, I enjoyed that."

"Right?"

"Sorry about earlier. I shouldn't have asked you to do anything uncomfortable."

"It's fine, I'm flattered."

"What about just a *few* still photos?"

Vanya's eyebrows crossed their arms, and Will backed down. All through the next morning, he was her unfaultable, inexchangeable boyfriend: making a French omelet, driving her to SFO, hefting her luggage onto the check-in scale, accompanying her to the security checkpoint, kissing her dryly. His anxiety overwhelmed any wistfulness he might've felt as security personnel steered Vanya into a screening room. He smoked four cigarettes on the drive home, parked in his garage, and checked his phone to see if Vanya had texted. But the battery was drained, and he only saw his scowling face in the dead gray crystal.

II. Regression

As Vanya filled her time with work and ambition, Will killed his. The saturating pall of loneliness was returning: its cold pinkie wending into the heart, its nauseating pressure at the temples and nuts, pulp of the teeth, root of the tongue, causing those shuddering hiccups that you didn't suppress because no one was around to hear them. His loneliness was ambidextrous and trilingual and weighed six hundred pounds.

Moderation would save him; the cardiovascular meal-cooking habits Vanya had taught him. The morning after she left, Will did his three miles on the treadmill and his accelerometer-paced crunches, flossed and showered, worked in styling cream, put on his vest and tie, and went to his bedroom to work. Any asshole with JavaScript, Python, PHP, and Ruby could print his own money, so his design and security consulting gigs were steady. He preferred never to meet his clients in person—ROI-obsessed, feature-bloating cretins, always chasing yesteryear fashions, these send-button sphinxes with their buzzword riddles.

pls use on-brand "eye-kicking" color palette signaling range/depth of integrated offerings to mission-specific users, req. touchbase at next availability thx

But the workflow was frictionless and the money invisible: click-tap, click-tap, invoice out, direct deposit in. Will low-balled the standard rate but still netted $5K for thirty billable hours. There was no way he was worth that much. Still, it beat real work.

After lunch he drove to Vanya's Bernal Heights apartment. He was impressed by her heavy accumulation of mail in a single day, a shoebox's worth of student loan bills and disability association circulars and hand-tooled letters from childhood friends, whereas Will received only Amazon packages. He watered her English ivy and fed her tuxedo cats, who wiped their faces on his shins and mewed. Vanya had toilet-trained them, so all he had to do was flush. Keeping animals indoors was stupid. The indoors was for humans.

On his way out he lingered at Vanya's bedroom. On her squat bookcase, amid photo albums and travel guides, were her five slender brown diaries. Vanya wasn't secretive about them; she journaled in front of him, and sometimes asked dubious questions ("Baby, what's the difference between pathetic, piti-ful, piteous, and pitiable?"), but he suspected nothing under-handed.

He selected a journal and opened it. The entries centered around work goals, to-dos, exercise, disability, things to discuss with Will, and the last was dated to four months ago, when she'd fully migrated to blogging. Will was annoyed that she hadn't mentioned the night they'd met, but found a bit later:

> *Tmrw nite date: boy from Lani's party*
> *—Will (get last name for goog diligence)*
> *—Stanford*

—*Works in tech!*
—*Asian (Thai)*
—*Smart, cute*
—*8PM (hard stop @ 11PM for AM mtg)*

Through slews of affirmation and epiphany, Will riffled into her past until hitting an entry from 2/17/05:

Surgery: Apr 16
—*St Francis Memorial*
—*No solids 12 hrs beforehand*
—*New clothes + higher salaries here I come LOL*

That Vanya had never mentioned any surgery made Will flash-fantasize an abortion. He flipped ahead to 4/17/05:

Recoop
—*Feeling good! 1 wk bedrest*
—*Wear sports bra + keep dry*
—*They're HUGE!* ☺

The thrill of forbidden knowledge was dampened by the feeling of having been excluded. Maybe she was ashamed, which was cool—but how did he miss it? They *were* huge. He felt fine about it, he supposed. Physical perfection seemed unreasonable to demand until you'd had your standards deranged by artisanal tits. He didn't like them because they looked real; he liked them because they looked *good*.

Come to think of it, he'd never seen pictures of Vanya predating 2006, but he'd assumed it was because that was when she'd joined Facebook. Retrieving his laptop from his bag and sitting on Vanya's bed, Will opened his photo library and stared at his thousands of Vanyas, lovely from all angles—moues and pouts, effortless bikini shots, suck-cheeked mirror selfies, cumulative miles of cleavage. (After seeing Vanya's pictures, Linda had said Vanya looked like Roman architecture, all grand arches and cunningly supported domes.) Most of her pics were online; hundreds of other losers probably downloaded and consumed them the same revolting way he did.

There weren't many pictures of them together, since Will usually held the camera. And now that he'd scrolled into the pre-Vanya era, he'd drifted into his own pictures. Last year he'd had his parents send him all of his hardcopy photos to digitize: vacation snapshots washing out to umber and pastel, school portraits and yearbooks that chronicled his travesties of hair gel, board shorts, black nail polish, lime-green contacts, obvious bids to distract from his chrysalis of acne, oversize webcomic T-shirts draping from chubby boytits . . .

God—if these ended up online! It was one thing to amuse Vanya with humiliating anecdotes of his past as if he'd outgrown it, but these? A visual primer of internalized racism and its hysterical overcorrection, the lifetime of imbecilic swerving across the center line because he wouldn't participate in the toxic alpha-male rat race that he was anyway excluded from but didn't want to be pigeonholed as another Asian castrato either. Anyone who saw these pictures could make a thousand racist assumptions and be dead right: he really *had* been a short repressed inarticulate lecherous unfuckable number whiz with strict parents. It hardly mattered if he was anything more. Even taking photos was stereotypical. Even being photographed was stereotypical. He couldn't even be *smart*. The only thing tangibly refuting his stereotype was Vanya. Had he grown around the trellis of stereotype or was he maliciously complying with it? At this point the chicken-or-egg questions were irrelevant. The choice was between inauthenticity and archetype. The latter he deemed acceptable, so long as nobody saw it.

With a quick select-all, Will deleted the photos and sanitized them in raw memory. His parents might be angry, but he was his to undo. He saw nothing worth saving. When he got home he set the hard copies on fire.

VANYA HAD BEEN gone two weeks and Will sat by his open bay window, drinking Fernet and smoking. A muscular blackfly made steely timpani noises against the screen. The barometry of Noe Valley made the clouds sit just above the roofs, cantaloupe-colored with perishing sunlight.

Will's split-level was a piece of Bay Area orthodoxy, with cornices and crown moldings, dramatized by the matte enormity of a seventy-two-inch flat-screen mounted on a bare wall, facing his tender blue recliner with its elbow-dented armrests. Some hidden low frequency constantly vibrated the apartment, so all standing liquids jittered. Two rooms stood unused. Food was delivered. In-unit laundry and treadmill. It was self-sufficient as a Soyuz capsule, and he owned it. After graduation, his parents (most likely believing it would help him attract a wife) had fronted his down payment, in the way that immigrant parents compensated for their former deprivations with savage pampering. He humored them by taking the gratuitous checks they mailed to him each month, and since he rented out the first-floor studio, he was basically being paid to live there.

He checked his phone again. Vanya had stopped answering hers, checking in only via text:

amazing mtg!!! :)))) so many posi vibes
baby I have 100x things to do brb
omg this hat I'm wearing!!! lol

Then she'd stopped replying to his emails, calls, and texts, which didn't deter him from sending them. All those buttons that thanked you for pressing them, the soft keys glowing to be stroked, were the root of so much daily suicide. You pressed them, heeded the calls to action, because you could.

He considered going out to distract himself, but the only one answering his phone calls was the electronic lady who told him to leave a message on Henrik's voicemail, and who said Cory's answering machine was full. He had other friends, technically: in the year after college Will had aggressively lurked at house parties, weekly dance nights and karaoke, street fairs, even Cory's fundraisers. He'd been a regular everywhere, and made lots of friends, but only the kind you ran into at other parties, who were glad to chitchat in a group setting but would never spare you individual time and would be sad for maybe five seconds if they heard you'd been tortured to death: which was to say, online friends. He had thousands. As a linking node, a degree of separation, Will succeeded.

Cumulatively his social network contacts numbered in the high hundreds, phone and email in the low thousands. He'd written a script to auto-sync all his phone, social network, and email contacts to a master spreadsheet because he distrusted the cloud. Each entry was tagged by date of meeting and relationship: **Friend, Family, Client.**

Filtering the spreadsheet, he sifted the ashes of his 239 **Friends** for someone to call. Besides Henrik, his **Friends** were virtually all women who'd rejected him, implicitly or otherwise.

It took only one glance at their names, vintages from his cellar of shame, to evoke the years of overaggressive texts, simpering emails, defensive Craigslist ads (**I don't belong here, but**), desperate dating site PMs (eighty attempts with only one reply: **Yuck**). But like a trail of blood drops ending, a mile-long string of zeroes terminating in a one, the entries ended on **10-09-2006**, Vanya's entry: **Girlfriend**. No more **Friends** after that.

The spreadsheet's completeness gratified him. Metadata were honest. His rejections, in sheer volume, were not insignificant—in fact they were *statistically* significant. He got up to refill his glass of Fernet and returned with the bottle. Everyone expected Asians to quantify the subjective, so why not go there? Beside each female **Friend**, he entered the date of his encounter, approximate date of rejection, and her height, age, race, ethnicity, and estimates of income, weight, IQ. The doorbell rang and he ignored it.

On a Likert scale he rated his subjective attraction and fondness, postrejection heartbreak and its duration. He downloaded a data visualization app and plotted the entries into dynamic line graphs and best-fit clusters, coaxing them into meaning. Some of the results intrigued him: the intensity of his remorse trended with height. And high intelligence correlated to his subjective attraction, but smart girls rejected him quickest. The data were glaringly silent on the most interesting questions—where he lacked in general, and what in particular. Was it pointless to pursue older, taller, poorer girls? Will leaned back and squinted, seeking the error in his error, dependencies between his dependencies. He reweighted the factors, diddled the confidence . . . It was garbage. All women appeared equally likely to reject him for any reason, which seemed pessimistic even by his standards.

Until he realized later, lying in his recliner with the ceiling cartwheeling above him, what the crucial factor really was: himself. Most women would exclude him for being five four, some for being Asian; lesbians took off another 10 percent, his standards another 50. His atheism, his dislike of the outdoors, the tongue-thrust that made it hard to say *thesauruses,* past, present, personality, inexperience—insignificance. Death by a thousand denominators.

These weren't startling data-driven insights; they only quantified what he knew. He let out the chesty belch of a veteran bachelor, got up from the recliner after a few attempts and walked back to his computer desk, overwrote the spreadsheet with a seven-pass erase, and deactivated his social network accounts. No more of that. No more knowing.

III. Screen Kiss

Will sat in his bathroom, wondering how he'd gotten there. An hour earlier he'd tried getting out of bed, but realized he wasn't in bed: he was under it, which was why he'd hit his forehead on the bed. He realized the quesadilla-like crust covering his face *was* his face. He realized he didn't have a hangover: he *was* a hangover.

As he crawled out and took to his knees, a pincer gripped his temples. He felt like he'd swallowed an unmeltable icicle. His first steps toward the bathroom triggered a mass displacement of fluids: salty gunge from sinus to throat, acid vomit from stomach to mouth, obligingly reswallowed. A reek of moldy collard greens emanated from behind his tongue, which felt like a strip of ass-wiped biltong. If for some insane reason he ever wanted to feel this way again, he would give himself a concussion and eat a live cat.

With a suffering shamble more inclined to kick aside stray beer bottles than step over them, he made a trembling grasp at the bathroom doorknob, a lurch for the sink, and held his face under the foamy column of low-flow faucet water, suckling the spout until he puked. This was the toll for mixing Fernet with brandy with rye with tequila. He sat on the tile floor to meditate, which is what he called sitting when he could do nothing but. Then he wondered how he'd gotten there.

His stillness was interrupted by a tingle at his hip, presumably the first of many organ failures, but instead it was a text from Vanya: **video chat nownownow!!!!!**

Taking one more minute to be sad, Will groaned back to his bedroom and logged in, his hangover making every keystroke feel deliberate. Vanya's chat request came in. Her hair was angled in a new Cleopatra bob, and her lovely oval face was blanched by the lightsaber glow of her screen, her complexion flawless with low resolution and high contrast. Her voice anticipated her lips by a quarter second. "Are you there? Hey, baby! Oh-em-gee, did you see the news?"

"What news?"

"I just posted it, you didn't see?"

Will read her status while she paraphrased it. The investors loved loved *loved* her presentation, said her pitch was *dynamite*. They'd more or less guaranteed her seed funding; then they'd said what the hell, and gave her seed funding.

"One point five *mil*," she whispered with brute excitement, enlarging dramatically as she leaned in. "That's pocket lint for them, but for us it's *serious* F-you money. Tranches of two hundred K every quarter for two years. We're backed!"

"Oh. That's awesome."

"Every time we met, they wanted more than I'd even prepared, so we just improvised all these concepts, it snowballed—
baby, it could *not* have been more productive."

"Cool, cool. So, uh, when do you—"

"Get this: they want me as a spokesperson. They saw my
pageant work and video portfolio online and said I'm this *mes-
merizing* presence—they're like, 'We think you could be the
disabled Oprah Winfrey,' and attaching my face to the project
would make it more than just another blogazine. And I'm all like,
wouldn't it be way too much work to edit and produce *and* star
in a show, but then they were like, 'No, you'd just be on camera
all the time: the life of a young disabled female tech entrepreneur, twenty-four-seven.' Lifecasting! Isn't that *genius*? Real
life from the seated perspective. Getting paid to do interesting
things. Like a reality show, but *real*. God, I'm just, like, amazed!"
Vanya knocked her laptop monitor askew, and Will stared at her
ceiling, adjusting his own monitor as if that would do anything,
before she reoriented her camera—"We even came up with a
name for the show: *WHEEL and DEAL with Vanya Andreeva.*"

"That's amazing, congrats. We'll celebrate when you're back.
Thursday?"

"Okay, so, let's discuss that."

"Discuss what?"

Vanya corrected her eyeliner, using her video inset as a
mirror. "I can't leave the East Coast yet. I have to hire and
train while I'm here."

"Why are you recruiting *there*?"

For a moment Vanya sounded echoey and processed, and
her face scrambled into uneven flesh-tone rectangles, an eye
up here and a nose way around there, some sectors moving sin-

uously, others blurry and frozen. Then her beauty was redrawn. "We're doing virtual office across both coasts. The investors are super hands-on. New York's great, though. I love the pressure."

"How long's that gonna take?"

"Two more months. I've already canceled my return ticket."

Will buffered his anger with tasks. He opened and closed his calendar app, checked his email, and turned on his TV, a news report on some wildfire. Under his desk he unscrewed the liter of scotch that had permanently migrated from the liquor cabinet to his desk. "What about your apartment?"

"I'll sublet to the Chi-O listserv."

"Cats?"

"I thought you could look after them, but if not I'll fly them over. There's this airline for pets now."

Looking down at his keyboard, he said, "Vanya. Two months is, you know, ulgh. And long distance? I don't know. I mean, come *on*." His English was turning ersatz—some cheap Asian knockoff.

"So you're saying the biggest opportunity of my entire life *can't happen*."

Will sprang a defensive sheen of sweat. He wanted to look meaningfully into her eyes but you couldn't do eye contact over video chat. "Let's get married."

"Oh, ha-ha."

"Town hall, quick and simple, no big deal."

"It *should* be a big deal! Are you seriously proposing to me as a bargaining tactic?"

Will felt sullen and furtive, like a spanked kid. Good thing she'd turned him down, though. He spammed his mental keyboard, [CMD+Z]: Undo. "All right, I was kidding. But I'm not thrilled."

"I recall you saying once that mutual independence is the key to a long-term relationship."

He'd only said that because he'd wanted to seem independent. Now he gamely struck [CMD+S]: **Save**. "Tell me you love me."

"Baby? Switch off the self-pity for one second and be *happy* for me. We'll spend winter break together."

It was idiotic to challenge Vanya's five-year plan, her hero's journey: humble beginnings, trial by fire, sages, endowments, returning covered in glory, sing hosannah. She was about to graduate from the lowly phase she called Eating Shit, a.k.a. Paying Doo-Dues: gathering favors, hustling, suffering debasements from Mount Olympus. She'd bemoaned her college summer internships as modern slavery ("Though slaves didn't have to make rent"), and gotten hired after graduation as an online community rep at the Foundation for Independent Living, quitting after two months in frustration at her lack of executive power. Her superiors were mere nine-to-fivers, everyone was older than her—so embarrassing.

Then, through Chi Omega, she was introduced to Ellen Stokes, a dot-com-bubble survivor, who set the pace for Vanya's ambitions: being a fast-tracker just made you a trained seal for the establishment, whereas if you made incremental backscratches and accepted no payday until your big break, you'd build a disruptive organization with your personality in its DNA: a Virgin, an Apple, an Amazon. She was currently in her third year of Eating Shit, a phase projected to last five years tops, and by no means into her thirties, when she should be making *bank*.

Will had structured his life to avoid eating job and family shit, though he ate plenty of Vanya's. He leaned out of frame to breathe deeply, then returned to [CMD+M], **Minimize**, and [CMD+Q], **Quit**. "Okay. I guess two months is okay. I'll find you a subletter."

"Awesome. See? Teamwork. Hey, I gotta bounce. Gimme a kiss."

Will felt a ping of irritation that she didn't ask how he'd been, though he had so little to report that it would've sounded pathetic anyway. He leaned in and pecked his laptop screen as it went dark in the enormous lewd umbra of Vanya's lips.

Quitting the chat, he used his eyeglass chamois to buff away the flecks of saliva that magnified the pixels into tiny rainbows. Her absence could play in his favor. If her lease lapsed, she might move in with him when she came back.

Will finished his scotch, took up his keys, and drove downtown, returning three hours later with a $20,000 engagement ring. He left the velvet case in his jacket pocket, which he hung on its hook before standing in the hallway between his bedroom and bathroom, deciding where to spend the rest of his day.

CHAPTER 3
No Synthesis

*For no one who wholeheartedly shares in a
given sensibility can analyze it; he can only,
whatever his intention, exhibit it.*
—Susan Sontag

I. No Job

Linda had been in San Francisco for three months, subsisting on not much more than her sense of humor. She'd worn out welcomes, crashed on floors and couches, in SROs—this twenty-one-year-old with the blond blowout and winged eyeliner. From last night she had two scraped palms and a cut lip; to her name she had six Xanax and a gram of coke, a phone, and a fake ID. She would make a tough corpse to identify.

The plan for tonight was to get an apartment. She was headed to a date at a karaoke bar with Baptist, a boy she'd met three nights ago, exactly the hopeful bewildered type she knew what to do with. When she arrived, it was packed and he was sitting in a big horseshoe booth tinkering miserably with his phone. Linda's phone number was faintly legible on his upper lip, where she'd written it in a permanent-marker Fu Manchu. He was thin as a surfboard, wore pristine Chucks and a purple deep-V, and his wavy hair trailed down the side of his face in oily dangle-bangs that he kept foofing aside with little puffs from the corner of his mouth.

Baptist's willingness to show up even after she'd flaked on him for the past two nights meant one thing: license. She found that insane cruelty was usually read as flirtation, so she began by taking her birth control in front of him and making him take it too. She chased it with Jameson and lit his sleeve on fire, which he extinguished with his beer. The KJ called his name, and he did a rendition of "Jailbreak" with choreographed stage moves, though he lacked the talent to underwrite it, and as he failed to get the bar crowd to dance, his air guitar became steadily less sincere.

While he awkwardly bobbed through the interminable bridge, Linda's attention ran out across the dim loud bar. All was so douchey, so fug: the Roman sandals and harem pants, feather hair extensions, feather earrings, guys wearing T-shirts of the tech companies they worked for, or that guy wearing . . . cat ears? Cultures of permission valorized bad taste as liberation. Ecosystems needed predators. Yet San Francisco was nothing if not vegetarian.

At last Baptist blew out his voice in a flannelly falsetto, and the KJ mercy-killed his song. "Let's get out of here," Linda said, which made Baptist so sad and grateful, and arriving at his up-market loft on Shotwell, she went to his bathroom and considered her options as she pissed. Sometimes you could just plead menses, and it depended on the boy, but managing sexual expectations was still touch-and-go—exactly when, she wondered, did BJs become first base? When did P-in-V become second base? Baseball wasn't the metaphor anymore—contemporary sex was tabulated in triple digits, had endorsement deals and a steroid problem. Sex was football, it was NASCAR.

But after two years of sexual freelancing, Linda realized all she had to do was be a terrible fuck. Lie there like a French girl, pouting and looking like she was trying to die, break his rhythms, mutter things like *Could you just* and *I can't,* then push him away and deliver the worst blowjob of his god-given life, trading off between low-friction stasis and molar scrapes and pube snags and scrotum tugs, breathing effortfully through her nose to demonstrate her good faith, while ever tightening her grip around the base and crumpling its contused tip against her palate—all wrapped in an extra-thick, a knife-stoppingly thick condom. This technique, which she called the *nojob,* visited crippling introspection upon its recipient. A few minutes of this and Baptist went limp; Linda said, *It's okay!* and fell asleep, leaving him to stare out his bedroom window for the rest of the night.

Without explicitly telling him, she moved in the next day, and found that he was a born lavisher: of back rubs and pharmaceuticals and his freezerful of weed. By day he was some Silicon Valley wanker, clearly grasping for purchased cool. It was embarrassing to date a boy who bought clothes at the same boutiques she shoplifted from, and he had an annoying hard-on for novelty accessories (flashing grills, mustache tie clip) and decorative skateboard decks. He was three years older than her, but so young. Not a quick wit, that Baptist, and not an initiative-taker, nor a deep reader.

But what a *wallet!* He covered every bill without even saying *I got it,* a fair exchange for the social capital he gained by standing near her at parties. One afternoon he handed her a flight itinerary, business class from SFO to Berlin Tegel, and two days later Baptist was gallantly unsheathing his platinum AmEx all over Mitte. They exhausted themselves at trite little Neukölln discotheques and partied at the abandoned listening station at Teufelsberg, ate döner at the Turkish market by the Maybachufer, and woke in jet-lagged afternoons at their hostel, where Baptist scraped at Linda's leftover currywurst while watching her turn laps in the pool, and where many a nojob was tendered.

Occasionally Linda could be tempted to see an easy future with Baptist. She told him she was feeling feelings for him, making it seem like it was one of those jokes that were actually true, when it was really a flat-out lie. But only idiots expected sincerity; anyone with life experience perceived things through a proper corrective filter of mistrust. Unfinessed truth had the grime of rube and cliché; lying was ultimately more honest, so long as you were metahonest. It wasn't her fault if he believed her.

Around the two-week mark he began to repulse her. How in public he'd rub the back of her neck and hang his finger in her waistband, proprietary gestures hardly less demeaning than a half nelson. That hateful snowman-shaped bunch in his briefs, the lipless smirk of his cockhole, the rumpled nutsack, his weird pink circumcision. Of what club was the penis a member? Clearly one that excluded women.

One morning she doodled a little house on his back in ballpoint pen, with a footpath leading down to his buttcrack, and when he came home from work in the evening, he showed off the tattoo he'd had traced over it, his first. "You don't look happy about it." Plus she'd been doing coke four times a day and was starting to look spooky and unfresh.

So it was time to end him. Except for Henrik, an inter-minable process that felt like donating a kidney, it had never been hard to end boys; you just had to exploit the ol' masculine amour propre. *The sex isn't working*—incontestable after so many nojobs and norgasms. Or *Our body types don't match*. Or tell them you wanted a threesome with another guy. She began giving him the slip at parties and spent nights away, usually with other friends, though she ignored his calls and texts to let him assume what he'd assume. But then she discovered that he'd been logging into her email, and he tried to flirt with other girls in front of her, and one night he came home with a bloody nose saying he'd been robbed, and made her drive around the Mission with him to track down the mugger, until she called his phone on a hunch and his pocket rang—"I lied" was all he had to say.

Thus one evening in his apartment, she told him she felt they were developing apart, which was true; and that they should take a time-out to reevaluate, also true; and so she'd be moving out, but they'd still hang out all the time, which was of course untrue.

First Baptist groaned—you just didn't hear an absolutely heartfelt groan all that often. He stood and braced himself against the wall with one hand, covered his weeping face with the other, pigeon-toed and clutching at his shirt. For a moment Linda thought he would rend his garment, but instead he yanked it off, which was greatly more disturbing. His face was pruny with grief. Linda put her hand on his hot shoulder. "I'm just being honest."

"You said you loved me. You said those words: *in love*."

"Things are just weird. I can't be in a relationship right now. It's not that I'm not attracted to you—our body types just don't match. Listen, you're so *young*. You'll find someone else. It was just bad timing."

Goosed up with rage, Baptist squeezed out his words one cubic inch of air at a time. "You *owe* me."

"Wait, what?"

"Clothes, plane ticket, food, drinks, drugs. Rent. I'm twenty-five thousand dollars in debt. And I owe my dealer two thousand."

"Well, that sucks, but—"

"I pawned my guitars. I sold my company laptop; they're reviewing the building security tapes and having a meeting on Monday. I'm getting evicted. My parents are going to find out their checks aren't going toward student loans . . ."

"Whatever, bro. It wasn't a fucking loan. You spent money to get me to like you."

"Oh, okay! So that makes you a prostitute. And a pretentious *cunt*. It's all intellectual accessorizing and quippy put-downs with you. Like how you always say 'or whatever,' like what you said just accidentally spilled out of your brimming jug of cleverness."

"Obviously you don't—"

"And all your *references*! You quote books because you think nobody else reads. You recycle your jokes. You even quote your own college papers, which is pathetic! And you know what? You have *no idea* how to give a blowjob."

This was not chill.

Linda rushed to grab her purse and jacket from his couch, which is also what she would've done if a fire had broken out. "Give me that hat back," Baptist said.

Linda was wearing her yellow cap from Berlin with HIV POSITIVE stitched in green. She wasn't sentimental about it, but she wouldn't surrender crucial symbolic leverage. "You bought this for me. It was a gift."

"Linda: take it off."

"Baptist: eat a dick."

He approached her with a phoenix of hot blood spreading across his chest. She escaped, shouting back that he had a weird dick and then bursting out the door and down the stairwell, catching her heel on the last step and hammering her knee down on the marble landing, an impact that made two tears fly from her eyes. She stepped out onto the dark sidewalk with her kneecap fizzing with pain.

As soon as she made it around the corner her phone rang in her bra and she shut it off. She dry-swallowed a pill. Her phone rang again, startling her because she thought she'd shut it off. She passed a man who said, "Can I call you sometime?" Her knee cricked with each step, and at Twenty-Fourth and Valencia she sat on the church steps and lit a cigarette. When her phone rang again she lobbed it into the street, where it skipped off the windshield of a passing Prius and hit the opposite curb with the suddenly cheap-sounding sound of breaking electronics. The Prius slowed and Linda fled from the F-sharp of its blaring horn, pretending she wasn't hurt.

She felt better after scooping into her purse and poking her snowcapped fingertip into her nose a few times. The bitter nerve-killing slush, percolating to her throat, dislodged an idea: she'd go "homeless." Why not? It'd be hilarious. The only thing she needed was herself; if Baptist wanted to toss her shit, fine. That was the worst thing about cities, the lack of storage. People complained about owning a car; how about owning a body?

Like the snail ascending Mount Fuji, she millimetered her

way to Dolores Park. It was fifty degrees but her hands were numb asteroids and she had to wait for them to open before shirring the white drawstrings on her hoodie and zipping her leather jacket, piling her blond hair under her hat. At the park she settled down on some tufty unmowed grass under the palm trees, took her last three Xanax, and closed her eyes. Each time she woke it was still dark, and dew collected on her jacket like frigid sweat. At three A.M. she scavenged for something to cover herself with, and only when she was shivering under damp scraps of yesterday's *Chronicle* did she truly appreciate how much thinner the dailies had become.

II. Incomplete

Regrouping was utmost. Save cash, rest her knee—she'd had to rip her jeans over the swelling. Her contact lenses had been in so long she'd have to boil them off. After waking in the park, she hobbled to a café on Guerrero to piss and think of some places where her persona was still grata. She decided to find Eve Chimie, a friend from Brooklyn who'd once bailed Linda out of the drunk tank after Linda had climbed into a squad car at a red light and demanded a ride home. Eve had moved to San Francisco a year ago with her modelographer boyfriend to study textile design at CCA, just before Linda's exile from Brooklyn. She liked Eve because they looked very good in photos together.

Linda hopped the BART, using the ticket she'd jury-rigged by cutting the magnetic strip of a paid card into lengthwise quarters and gluing them onto duds. At the library she got Eve's San Francisco address from an old email, then caught the N to

Duboce Triangle. On her way there a man on the train shouted, "Girrrrrrrl, I haven't seen a bellybutton that fine in ten years."

She staked out Eve's apartment from a slope in the dog park across the street. Like every day before, the weather was keen blue, dusty sunlight throwing a sfumato over everything. The abundance of San Francisco's million-dollar vistas was exhausting, like daylong nudity; the very topography nestled you in its pecs and tits, its buns and bulges, especially if you were rich. Otherwise it was the same archetype metropolis pumping out chances and threats, transients sleeping in the waste heat of office buildings full of tired people. In these respects one city was as good as another—it was what happened when people shared.

Down the sidewalk, Linda spotted someone approaching who was black like Eve and had Eve's cropped hair and fendered cheekbones, and wore Eve's Marc Jacobs bag and Topshop blazer and red sunglasses—but it couldn't be Eve, because Eve didn't, Eve *wouldn't,* have a baby.

"Eve!"

Eve, as in *ever,* was not a name given to shouting—but the girl turned to Linda's compass quadrant and waved. They squealed and made cumbersomely for one another, Linda dragging her bad leg, Eve searching for a break in the curb to push her stroller down. As they hugged, Linda looked over Eve's shoulder at the baby, a saddle-colored grub who returned Linda's stare with astonished gladness.

Eve kissed Linda on the cheek. "Oh my god, what're you doing here?"

"What's *that* doing here?"

"She's mine! I made her!"

"No shit?"

"Wave hi-hi, Mercy! Linda girl, you look so *cute*." (This was patronizing—childbirth had brought Eve no lower than an eight. Some people just *were* models.) "You busy? Come over to my place, it's right there. I'll tell you the whole deal. Shit is *fucked*."

As they walked, Eve recounted how she'd gotten preggers literally *the day* she and Jared started classes at CCA, right when they'd secured their student loans and settled into their apartment. After two months of failed classes, homicidal arguments, and depressing web searches, they dropped out and did the damn parent thing. Nix substances, add omega-threes. Eight hours of easy labor in a natural birth pool, then sixteen hours of hard labor every day after that: Eve waited tables, Jared barbacked and waited tables. They didn't have friends, art, or lives. They had a baby.

They entered Eve's pink stucco apartment. On one leg, Linda helped carry the stroller up the stairs and entered a one-bedroom with ceilings you could reach on tiptoe. A TV lit the living room aquamarine with its channel selection menu. Accordion gates blocked the doorways.

Forgetting to lie, Linda told Eve everything about moving to SF, Baptist and all. Eve moaned in sympathy. "You can stay here. I need to clear it with Jared, but he loves you." (This was true—Linda had hooked up with him right around when he and Eve started dating.) "And you know, this works. I'd love to have help with Mercy, if you're down."

"Sure. I used to babysit my niece," Linda said, lying about both the babysitting and the niece, and the sibling for that matter. She dangled her hand by Mercy's face until she remembered that that was what you did with dogs. "I'm good with kids."

"Duh. You're, like, good at everything."

"Hey, can I use your shower?"

LINDA WAITED TABLES, under the table. She attended garages. She literally catered. She ghostwrote college essays. She art-modeled at SFAI and glorified soju cocktails in North Beach. Any job that didn't require her to smile. She maxed her credit. She did coke for the energy to work to buy coke. All she didn't do was sleep. But if exhaustion was the cost of radical freedom, if her thunderhead of irritability was only occasionally pierced with sky-blue instants of rapture, so be it. She gave manicures on Eve's stoop. She coolhunted. She sewed clown pants for some lady's toddler. She worked the door, the door worked her, *work* worked her. Work was not so much the proverbial toad squatting on her life, but many torpid tadpoles nibbling at it.

She needed a new phone, and though she was grateful for the free room, she didn't want to stay long enough to become Aunt Linda. So onward she trudged through the entry level. She was a barista at a Valencia café, where she stank of roasted coffee and transactions of specie, and was fired for pouring twelve-ounce mediums for customers who ordered smalls because she deeply believed that a small was twelve ounces. She got shitcanned from her SoMa bartending gig when they caught her serving the runoff from the rubber spill mats to some shiny-shirted finance bros who referred to the Mission as "The Mish." Then she was fired from a North Beach soup café after she'd left the warmers on overnight under a vat of potato-leek cream soup, and bent three steak knives chipping at the bed of anthracite it turned into; her manager fired her on the spot, and Linda did not cry, though she was bothered by how easy it was to take things seriously just because other people did.

The sense of oppression that work gave her daily recalled to her the undergrad FemStud litany of empowerment and objectification. Though this underrated the stealth agency of objects, the *objective* power of objects; the sex object in particular was no slouch. Plus, object work *paid*. Online she sold her panties, nail parings and locks of hair, used tissues and tampons, and all manner of unspeakable excreta. Domme work was viable, but she lacked the equipment for independent work, and San Francisco's dungeons were overhired.

Her last gig had her smooshing her décolletage into a pleather dirndl while a guy named Escobar chauffeured her to dive bars, where she sold toys and candy from a tray strapped to her neck, soliciting tips from the tipsy. One night a short guy in a blue gingham shirt followed Linda into the street, snapping photos of her on an SLR camera he wore around his neck. Which wasn't unusual in itself, she got stopped for street-fashion photos all the time. Then he said he had a knife. He was sweating, and when Linda covered her face from his flash he said, *Don't do that.* She held still and the man neared, snapping her from the side, from behind. When he took a knee for the upskirt, Linda's tray hit the sidewalk and she caught a fistful of his hair and scored several FemStud points on his throat, spat on his gingham and stove in his jaw as her candies tumbled downhill. The creep, snared in his camera strap, pled pure dada through his destroyed mouth until he struggled away to the brassy strains of Linda's victory fanfare, and she picked up his dropped camera and snapped a photo of him as he ran.

Yes, let them objectify: then call down the objective force.

Minutes later she climbed into Escobar's car with an empty

tray, no money, and a bloody dirndl, and this job became the latest casualty of her sensibility. Being fired was fine as long as the job was awful, she decided. Living on tips meant soliciting the last thing she wanted: approval. Life had to come from somewhere; sometimes it came from below.

Wasn't the obscene entitlement of a Stanford degree supposed to excuse her from all this? She'd grown up in a basement apartment in Waterbury with rancid orange carpeting and asbestos insulation, so when she'd arrived at Stanford, she'd been intimidated for about a week before she was thoroughly over it. All the preshie diminutives—MemChu, HooTow, TresEx, CoHo, FroSoCo—telegraphed its abdication of seriousness. Her first-year roommate wore alma mater sweatshorts while farting while doing crunches while studying for HumBio midterms. Rooming with Cory sophomore year put an even finer point on Linda's class rage, making her resent the campus's beauty: the $40,000 palm trees and sunsets washing sandstone and watered lawns in premium amber, the color of old money and tech money and patriarchy. Everything here was appallingly what it seemed. Her fellow undergrads were all careerist dickheads, thumb-sucking vegans, smug libertarians, batshit Republicans, pompous student-visa techies, precious study-abroad fuzzies, Division I Neanderthals, faculty lapdogs, marching band weenies recouping their squandered adolescences, and the unforgivably rich. Everyone seemed so well parented; everyone's semantic web architecture or microlending nonprofit or carbon nanotube dildo was going to change the world. Meanwhile the artists failed to reach quorum. Linda did respect the political agitators who blocked streets and camped out on President Hennessy's lawn, though less for their trite campus liberalism than for their structural willingness to fuck with people. Cory was okay. Everyone else was weak shit. Plus she'd been rejected from all the Ivies, so even if Stanford was good, it'd never be good enough.

Abjuring friendship, Linda had plowed through the English major requirements in two years. For her first grad seminar in American modernism, she scored a Ritalin prescription and went vagrant in Green Library for two weeks, building a thesis from her marginalia in *As I Lay Dying* ("SUFFOCATING IN PERSPECTIVE"). Contemporary writers were so shit-scared of moralizing that they delegated to their poor characters the responsibility for conveying their philosophies through indirect discourse, the indeterminate ironies of narrative distance, constraining writers from delivering the grand true-eyed pronouncements of Tolstoy or Proust. Writers had capitulated to the camera lens. Postmodern author-surrogates and clairvoyant first-persons were just Band-Aids on a fault line. We needed a return to omniscience.

On deadline day she printed off the manuscript, "Divine Intervention," running triple the twenty-page limit. She turned it in at the English building, then checked her English department mailbox daily until her manuscript appeared; the lights dimmed all around her as she scanned the margins for checkmarks and dot-dot-U smilies. She expected one kind of feedback: praise, superlative. *Cunningly prosecuted thesis—recalls Benjamin, Auerbach. Foundational text for new field of inquiry.*

But the only comment came handwritten at the end:

> *Overall cogent effort. But you've overthought it: you question modernism as a valid category, "text" as a meaningful term, you've even psychologized my personal motives for asking the question. The point isn't to outsmart the prompt or produce*

lots of uncommon words; it's to <u>answer the question</u>. You
appear eager to fast-track yourself to high-level criticism, but
this is universalized unto grandiosity. Too much analysis, no
synthesis. Stylewise: ease up on academic pleonasms, e.g.,
"employ" vs. "use," "explicate" vs. "explain," "monophonic
discourse" vs. "voice." And while I admire the economy of your
ampersands—"a-n-d" will suffice. Writing shows promise. A+
for chutzpah. Yet I resist the marching tide of grade inflation,
and so—

86

That number—a page citation? Not the grade? Not *her*
grade?—HER grade?—for *HER???* Did he fucking write it
upside down or something? Oh, here it was, the hidebound
athenaeum, drowning originality in its tin tub of status quo!
Eighty-sixing new ideas with patronizing dismissal! They
feared her jouissance! She showed "promise"? She'd shown
promise *years* ago. This from some old white dickshaker who
thought there was such a thing as *overthinking*. She showed up
at the professor's next office hours with her Add/Drop form in
hand; once he'd signed it, she told him he was everything that
was wrong with tenure.

Instead she tried a fiction writing workshop, where, in
spite of its idiotic mission of focus-grouping literature, she
could at least set her own agenda. But she quickly wearied
of her classmates' manuscripts, about characters with *pound-*
ing hearts and *wry grins* who'd *sigh* and *shrug* and *fail to meet*
her gaze, who held dying grandmothers' hands, helmed star-
ships, attended dorm parties, came out. They were *so serious*
about it! And they got *foot rubs* of praise, the bland reading
the bland—products of a contemporary literature rife with do-

mestic angst, ethnic tourism, child prodigies, talking animals, period nostalgia, affected affectlessness, atrocity porn, genre crossovers clad in fig leaves of literary technique. No ideas, only intellectual property; no avant-garde, only controversy; no ars poetica, only personal essays; no major writers, only writing majors.

Opting out of the circlejerk, Linda silently played workshop lingo bingo in her notebook: *Expand. Compress. Problematic. Tidy. Baggy. Heavy-handed. Conflict. Emotional core. Narrative arc. Chekhov's gun. Kafka's ax. Hemingway's iceberg. Moment of grace. This should be a scene. I want to know more about the mother. What's at stake. Not here on the page. The real beginning is. Sags in the middle. Ending feels rushed. What I'm interested in here. A missed opportunity to.*

Linda had plenty of ideas for new work, but, disinclined to see them puzzled over in workshop, she decided instead to submit her polished and well-graded high school stories— "Cowboys and Indians": near-future society, threatened by a saber-rattling nuclear Apache Nation, goes to war with the Indians; "Give Them Your Heart": near-future society, fetishizing women's internal organs, designs fashions around MRI and ultrasound; "The Green Death": near-future society, devastated by a money-borne pathogen, collapses.

When her turn for critique came, Linda was not surprised to find that the workshop had reserved all its venom for her— the story's "narrative voice" was "contemptuous," "mannered," "dictionary-happy"; its characters were "easy targets," "flat little dominoes" that "the author" set up just to topple over. Worst of all, her writing lacked "empathy."

Although prohibited from speaking during her critique, Linda cleared her throat and said to please spare her the bugbear of empathy—if they didn't want to read about easy targets, people should stop *being* easy targets.

"I think what I'm hearing from these comments," said the nameless twenty-seven-year-old instructor (bitch-bun, taupe snood), "is that the didactic allegorical aspects might be pulling readers out of the story. The satire's a little on the nose."

Well, Linda said, what if the author *wanted* to pull readers out? And *break* their noses?

"I guess the concern there would be that the story becomes, like, a prank? Saying nyah-nyah, see, I'm smarter than you. No one's saying it's bad, it's just . . . a chilly, sort of valueless sensibility."

Sure, Linda said, if you didn't consider taste a value.

"Okay, Linda? Since you don't seem to respond to even-handed critique, I'm gonna put this out there: the ironic, too-cool meta satire, the sneering and mocking? Is actually just a contemporary version of the bourgeois sentimentality it's trying to mock. It is not new. Really it's almost quaint. The backlash has already outlasted it. But the real problem is that it's self-indulgent."

"The last thing I want is to *indulge you,*" Linda said. She addressed the class. "Have you guys read her stories? Ooh, I had these Mennonite neighbors and they were *so weird*! My Romanian immigrant aunt had a stroke and said such *inadvertently profound things*! Fucking please."

Linda left, forgetting her bag and notebook. Why was everyone such a sucker? Why the predictable taste for relatable characters conveyed in manageable little sentences, plot leading inevitably to redemption, books to curl up with? Where were the readers who wanted to be offended by difficulty, break forms and do violence to the tongue, books to curl up and die in? This wasn't even mentioning the cringeworthy peer feedback letters she received in her mailbox ("I think the rape scene felt a little forced"). Well. At least she hadn't given them her representative work. Just some high school shit.

She took an Incomplete and resolved never to become a professor; never to professionalize, become an adjunct or MFA or teaching fellow or resident or publishing intern or editorial assistant, or "contribute" book reviews or produce "content," or give readings or interviews or freelance or blog. How pathetic to only resemble ambition, to grab at the sun from the stepladder of institution.

It'd be nice now to have banked away some of that indignation, that same grunt belief in her talent. Yet here she was, serving unpermitted mediums to people who asked for the small.

III. The Weeks

La dolce vita it was fucking not. It was especially depressing to see a woman like Eve fall to the sanctioned Stockholm syndrome of motherhood, babbling in falsetto, obsessing over BPA-free binkies and poly-blend Björns—and constantly filming Mercy sleeping, oozing, sucking on Duplo blocks, hours of baby B-roll as the chubby enigma hazed itself into subjectivity. With scary nonchalance Eve would walk around with vomit on her shoulder or tickle her constipated baby until it ejected its rancid mudslide. And she served up all the postpartum clichés about upended priorities and falling of scales. "My whole life used to be about, 'Is this decision going to be good for me? Will this make me happy?' And now it's, like, 'If I stay up an extra hour, am I good for tomorrow? Is it Jared's turn or my turn?' The decisions are just so clear now."

But by her second glass of wine Eve would start complaining about never going out anymore, not being her own person, forget art, she had *stretch marks,* everything was *over.* "Linda, it's so good you left New York. Jared and I barely survived. And now we work all day. I mean, I love her, I just hate that I had her. Anyone can raise a kid, you don't gotta be *good* at it." For his part, Jared had cleaned up—he was no longer the guy who'd squirt you with syringes of his own blood. Instead he'd surrendered his art for Thursday pickup basketball, the crack pipe for the Crock-Pot.

Linda was angry that they could settle so easily into prescribed social roles, down to the smallest exchange—arguments over buying single-ply toilet paper or refilling the Brita pitcher, then collapsing together to watch reality TV in silence, too exhausted to even make fun of it.

They were pulling Linda down. Accidental parents constantly had a telescope trained jealously out into the social universe, were always checking on the latest from Planet Abortion, and Eve would pornographically interrogate Linda about social goings-on. But Linda hadn't even gone out in weeks. And hadn't *written* in years, though she knew it was what she had to do. Since graduating, whenever she tried to write something *hard,* some diamond unscratched by sentiment, her pen went soft. But still she was too judgmental to be anything but an excellent writer. The question was whether she could be a *world-historical genius* for the canon—the *real* canon, not the dead-end Austen/Mansfield/Brontë ladycanon of apology. The last thing she wanted was to submit another callow bildungsroman, a neglected chapbook, one more helping of crème brûlée for the General Reader. She had no form and no subject. But she did have guilt—and guilt, especially Roman Catholic guilt, even shorn of belief, could never be underestimated.

Guilt, and the lack of anything to do on a Sunday morning with Mercy sleeping and Eve and Jared at work, brought her back into poetry. She could feel her poetics arriving, strong, immanent, in words hot enough to curl the paper. Poems were short. She could probably finish one before dinner. She picked up her pen, opened her notebook, put down her pen, and browsed on Eve's laptop for music. Not classical, and nothing with lyrics. Ambient drone DJ mix? Sure—whoops, don't wake Mercy. Once it was playing, she got up to collect her piss for later retail before it slipped her mind, then returned to her notebook. Her breathing was annoyingly noticeable.

Linda pressed the searing tip of her pen to the page and wrote:

Time

and gazed at it for two minutes. The blue ink looked unserious. Her handwriting was wobbly with disuse. She looked at it longer, and then she was forty-three and shortlisted for the Pulitzer and reading the introduction to the first anthology of her works: *Time, known to wend in curious directions in Troland's verse, revealed its clock face early to the American belletrist, as we discover in this volume of unerring journal writings selected from holographs held at the Ransom Center,* Time: A Life, Vol. 1, Early Works, *a ruthless conte philosophique, polymythic, polymathic, polyphonic* . . .

Linda's jaw clicked when she yawned. Afternoons were bad for writing, with their sunshine and lunchy torpor—but evenings were booked for living, and mornings for recovery. She got up for a glass of water, intuiting that her mental cloudiness was probably dehydration. She looked again at the notebook. Where was the crisis in *Time?* Some exposure to language would prime her, so she turned off the music and caught up on the *LRB* and *Bookforum* and fucking *Jezebel.* Silence was distracting her. She went out for an iced coffee and a smoke, returned with a stomachache.

She started over: ~~Time~~. Outside, a skateboarder coasted down the asphalt sounding like a far-off jet, just as Mercy's baby monitor made a crackling exhale. In a poem, that would mean something; in life it was dumb synchronicity. In the top margin she wrote: *Time as birthed. Time as noise. Time skating by.*

After a nap, it was evening, then it was night. She regarded her notebook with groggy dread, with loathing that her bottommost yearning right now was for yogurt. It was absurd that she could articulate exactly *how* she wanted to write but couldn't write it: both dirtbag lowbrow and Olympian highbrow (that was how she faced the world: one brow low, the other arched high). Not a voice of her generation, but *the* voice of *de*generation. She could even name her antecedents— Melville, Dickinson, Nabokov, Eve-via-Edie-Sedgwick, half Mann half Woolf. It bummed her out. Kierkegaard said man, as a synthesis, suffered anxiety, which bore sin and greatness. She was slightly encouraged to recall that quote, if not verbatim. In the top margin she wrote: *Kierkegaard. Man. Anxiety.*

At least Time was the proper magnitude, a top-tier human condition, like Form, Memory, the Real. Not quite Death; but Time was big news. There were Larkin's Days and Woolf's Hours and Years. Minutes and seconds were too small. But

weeks—aha!—the only unit of time based on literature! Her
ballpoint pen made flimsy rattles as she drummed it on her
teeth.

She wrote:

Time is weak

She stared confusedly, then accusingly, at her writing hand.
She was better than this, better than . . . herself? Desolation
sat like an uncle on her chest. She swept her notebook off the
desk and googled her old bitch-bun workshop instructor; a
story collection with a starred review in *Publishers Weekly*. Ew.
Linda moved to write down something about the eros of envy
but then was like fuck it. She was twenty-one, would realisti-
cally produce her mature work at twenty-five, and win awards
at thirty—and then there'd be no point. Barthes said the bliss
of the text was a precocious bliss. Greatness was a moated metropolis you were born into or not. Linda occupied its exurbs;
she was bridge-and-tunnel to genius, faux poet, proseur. Maybe
she could translate. Edit. Copyedit. Serve superior souls. Art
was so useless that effort meant nothing without overwhelming success. Process was the booby prize.

The baby monitor picked up Mercy's precrying hiccups, and
with some relief Linda went to the crib. She picked up the
convulsing screaming body. *The child's cry / melts in the wall.*
Babies: Why? It felt absurd to even name them; they were Pla-
tonic, all hardwired rootle and suckle. Kids were ids, expecting you to translate screams and smells into need: *why here,
what this, I want*—NOW. Looking after a baby, you realized
you used to be one; then, that you still *were* one, screaming to
be fed, held, changed.

Mercy went soft again and Linda laid her in the crib, rested her cheek on its cool rail. Expectations of reproduction and child-rearing underlaid women's historical shit and shackles; in her innocent way, the baby was Linda's failure. Linda switched the light off and saw, across the room, a blue-and-white nightlight in the precise sailboat shape of her exhaustion.

CHAPTER 4
Intro to Basics

I need to think about it some more.
—Joseph-Louis Lagrange

I. Soft Lab

Henrik was at the lab all night picking at his arm, which lay severed and splayed across its sterile blue diaper on the brushed-steel exam table. The hand was still intact but the cutaneous tissue on the forearm was a gouged yellow pulp, too frayed for the retractors to hook onto. He only had one cadaver limb for analysis, and he'd mutilated it. He glanced toward the closet where they stored the extra arms and legs in red bags. Behind the metal doors in the half-lit lab, the freezer compressors gulped. He wondered how long it would take them to notice a missing arm.

He gave up, peeled off his latex gloves, and dozed off on the couch in the break room. At eight he woke and went to the bathroom, combing his unbarbered blond curls flat with their own oils. He ate a ramen cup and bagged up his arm. It smelled.

At nine his labmates arrived. Henrik was a known non-talker, so nobody said hi. Luke and Tim stood at the conference room window, observing the parabolic romp of a black squirrel on a scrap of grass thirty feet away, speculating on its average lifetime migratory range. Collectively the lab spun out these hypertechnical hypotheticals for weeks, devising metrics for the crispness of apples or back-of-the-envelope budget estimates for building robotic pop stars. Henrik was trying to fix the projector so it didn't display as a big headachy trapezoid.

The chatter died down as Volger entered, his first appearance in six weeks. He'd just returned from a "vacation"—likely prospecting for a new job. In spite of his tenure, he was notorious for private-sector defection. Ken Volger's career had been launched out of Stanford in the late seventies with his plantar-pressure gait analysis research that dovetailed lucratively with the jogging craze, and he'd made several TV appearances as a "jogging expert" without any increase in fame. He'd left his postdoc to draft sneaker schematics for Nike, discovering that his research (conducted in a lab through which visiting stockholders were guided, as a demonstration of Nike's R&D supremacy) was mainly to produce meaningless radial graphs and buzzword garbage like *total-range dorsiflexion* and *ambulatronics* for use in creative. He left after his first product design, a resistance sling joining the ankles to the waist, bombed in consumer trials.

He returned to academia only to forsake it twice more on unpaid sabbatical, each time professing disgust with the pony-racing and lapdogging of department politics, each time returning when his ventures tanked. He squeaked out of junior professorship on the strength of three publications and friends in the department faculty. After nine years in mechanical engineering, he reigned over the Soft Tissue Biomechanics Laboratory, which it now seemed he was once again ready to leave.

Volger liked hovering behind whoever was presenting and

looking directly at the laptop screen instead of the wall projection; he leaned on the back of Henrik's desk chair, uncomfortably constraining its degrees of freedom. Henrik bullshitted his progress report for twenty minutes, gaining sympathetic stares from Luke and Becca, while Dian-Han and Tim smacked at breakfast burritos. Volger was squinting at Henrik's slides with a finger-mustache of scrutiny. It didn't go too badly, Henrik thought, in spite of some fudged findings, in spite of saying *this whole part over here* when he meant *the energy dissipation zone surrounding the keratin filament debond*. The gist was clear.

But Volger emailed him later that morning: Henrik, come over for a powwow.

Henrik walked to Volger's office, down the hallway he traversed forty times a day: doors plastered with quotes from Darwin, Mendel, Euler; field-specific webcomic printouts; *Stanford Magazine* clippings about the Soft Lab's research; overhead lighting and gray-green carpet with a faint stench of toluene; tenkey access panels whose steel keypad buttons had their digits rubbed away; loud old computers with one important function; tireless new computers that did all the hard thinking.

In his office Volger sat behind an oak desk the size of an air hockey table, the only wooden furniture in the building, and he reached across to offer a handshake as limp as an earlobe. Volger's hairline was in retreat, with a defiant gray wisp in the unicorn-horn region. The pointiness of his occipital bone made his head vaguely anvil-shaped, and his breath made you hold yours. His thick celluloid glasses shrank his eyes to gel caps. A ketchup-red folder sat on the desk with Henrik's project title written on a sticker: COMPUTATIONAL MODELS OF ~~VESICANCE~~ DELAMINATION IN [NATIVE?] TISSUES AT THE ~~SUBQ~~ BASAL LAYER—

PAPILLARY DERMIS JUNCTION UNDER ~~SIMULATED~~ CONDITIONS OF
[INDUCED?] NIKOLSKY I.

"How was your trip?" Henrik said.

"Fine. Good fly-fishing."

"Did—did you get any—"

"Henrik, there's lots to discuss."

"Okay."

"I want to talk big picture."

Henrik couldn't recollect any time, except on camera and during the first and last lectures of a semester, that he'd heard a physical scientist talk big picture.

"I believe science is value neutral," Volger began, "and operates on history like an enzyme, speeding us along to our destiny. If that's good, all the better; if not, you could say we're getting what we've got coming. I'd say this obliges us to work on impactful projects." Volger snapped and finger-pistoled Henrik. "What's this project achieving?"

"Well, uh. We're developing finite element models for the deformation of dermal tissue under deteriorative conditions, studying the structure-function relationship—" Henrik was regurgitating his abstract. Really he was just making a poster—one of those foamcore placards representing years of research and tens of thousands of grant dollars, which he'd bring to a two-day conference and then hang in the lab's hallway. A dozen people might read his paper, assuming it was published. Henrik opened and closed his mouth while his synapses hung fire. "I've been thinking about how our insights into bullous pemphigoid could be used to develop methods to aid the proceduralization of . . . of contributing to novel understandings of poroelastic tissue delamination that could possibly *overturn*," Henrik said, seizing a minor updraft as he sighted the end of his sentence, "the prevailing wisdom. Of the last twenty years. I'm sorry. That was sort of unfocused."

"The funding committees thought so too," Volger said, resting two fists on his desk as if waiting for Henrik to guess which one had his future in it. "The NSF and NIH flat-out rejected the grant renewal, and Dermavar cut half their give. F&A jacked up their take. The postgrant officer has got his arm way up my ass this year." Volger said this at such an even keel that Henrik almost expected good news. "Maybe we should've played the BME angle. Tissue grafts. Funding's all about telling the right kind of story."

Henrik didn't think that was the issue. Funding was more a mix of feudal patronage, Soviet bureaucracy, and star-system capitalism. Between Henrik and his money were the interests of eleven committees, public and private, prospecting for wonder pills and killer apps. Every joule of work had to be directed toward saving or justifying money, though money needed neither. Besides, what story could you craft around the infinite shrewdness and nauseating inelegance of matter?

"Unfortunately that all's woulda-shoulda-coulda," Volger continued. "The plug is pulled. Our focus kept shifting and we've been consistently dodgy about bench-to-bedside applications. Plus we're not modeling from live tissues. It adds translational work and makes the findings less robust."

"You're saying we should've used live subjects?"

"At this juncture, that's not our concern. Here's our problem. There's no money for your living stipend until we reapply."

"So, uh"—Henrik's heart went up like a balloon released outdoors—"how do I live?"

Volger picked up a pen for no reason and said, "You have a couple options."

They could give Henrik more teaching hours for up to $300 a month. Another $150 if he could swing an ASB student grant. Outside funding? They wouldn't get any more from MORF and NIH under Bush. Same with state research grants. Soft tissue delamination didn't technically qualify as orthopedics, so OREF and OSRF were out. "We still have enough to continue the project," Volger said. "Just not to keep you on it."

Since the last budget tightening, moths were swarming out of Henrik's wallet; he'd racked up $8,000 in Sallie Maes and $2,400 more across three credit cards. And for what? His work was useless. His labmate Tim was building software that took MRI scans of shattered bones and solved for optimal reconstructions. All Henrik's research would do was earn him a degree. It seemed impossible that he could've gone this far down a career path without meaning to. He had $500.

Volger twirled his pen. "In my time I've worn lots of hats I never thought I'd wear. Corporate gigs, internships, night shifts. Bartended at a Mexican restaurant. Stole equipment from other labs. Some hats fit tighter than others."

Could Henrik get a research assistantship in another department? Any landscaping experience? Babysit? Something online? No? Really? Was he on food stamps, because if not—

"These are my options?" Henrik said.

"Henrik, I'd hate to lose you. Nobody's kicking you out, but I know you've got to eat. We all hit potholes. If you care about our research as much as I do, you'll figure something out."

It was clear that Volger had delivered this spiel so many times he could do it under general anesthesia. Henrik was here by Volger's charity alone. Junior year, Henrik had taken ME 281 and 287 with him, and some well-timed manic episodes enabled him to ace the classes and volunteer for cell segmentation grunt work for eight hours every weekend. Senior year, when things went bad with Linda, Volger encouraged Henrik to apply for the grad program; Henrik had warned him that his grades weren't perfect and he still had reqs to fulfill. Volger, with a nod of his anvil, said grades were moot and helped Henrik graduate early by liberally counting transfer credits from Yale. He'd overseen Henrik closely in his first grad year—triple-check those inputs, use these tensile grips on the Instron. But then Volger left for conference season and a two-quarter sabbatical, stonewalling with his email autoresponder, and Henrik realized Volger might have a bipolar streak himself, with his sinusoidal veerings of commitment.

"Give me your decision by let's say end of month," Volger said, smiling a gray barricade of teeth. "Remember: hats."

Henrik left Volger's office scratching his beard and walked back through the bright hallway, past rooms containing the rheometer that looked like a cappuccino machine, the Instron like an upended lathe, machines far harder to replace than he was. Suppose he transferred again. He'd have to start another project from scratch. He'd have to scratch up scratch, from scratch. He took the stairs down and went into the evening. If he had no real options, it didn't matter what he did now. And when it didn't matter what he did, he read books. At Green Library, Henrik swiped his student ID and cranked through the turnstile. As a scientist you implicitly checked your dualist beliefs at the door and accepted that free will and consciousness were side effects. But it didn't feel right, that mass was just mass.

With the rumble of elevator doors opening, closing, and opening, Henrik descended into the cold, sweet-smelling stacks, where the only evidence of sunny weather was on the skin of other students. He found his aisle, punched its light switch, arbitrarily selected a slim anthology on free will, and sat on the floor with his sandals flat on the gray carpet, skimming for cruxes. Libet's readiness potential (1985) sounded like smoke and mirrors. Pereboom's hard determinism (1995) claimed that moral responsibility was still licit because you didn't blame cornflakes for being soggy but you could still hate them. Whereas Dennett (2003) boiled it down to rational evitability, squaring it with determinism by expanding the concept of self. Bostrom (2003) said we were probably computer simulations.

But van Inwagen (1975) had it down, Henrik thought drowsily: the set of all physical laws L applied to the initial state of the universe P_0 at the beginning of time T_0 would only ever result in the same world state P. Corralled in four alphanumerics—$\{P, L, 0, T\}$—reality went through its motions, with arbitrary flux at the quantum level. The shit bargain of consciousness without autonomy. Free will was placebo. And it sure wasn't free. Henrik fell asleep, resting his head on the hard determinism.

II. Washing It Down

Fog had come on with the night, sustaining the peninsular warmth in its wetness. The streetlights hung in white globes illuminating nothing but the cottony air around them. Henrik's porch light had burned out, and now his cottage, a studio on the lawny margins of campus, was visible only by the moonlight on its roof, like a film of milk. Henrik toed his way up his steps and used his wristwatch's aquamarine LED to find the keyhole, noticing that the provider was due in an hour.

When the light came on, Henrik surveyed his house with a skeptical eye and saw the blights he'd long since normal ized. The blanched rectangles on the wall where previous ten ants had hung pictures; power cords tripwiring the floor; lank peelings of clothes; mouse droppings and gravel and shaggy gray fluff that crackled and smoked whenever he vacuumed it up. The light fixture's shine was mellowed by the dust on its frosted glass bowl containing a mass grave of insects in sil houette. A rill of mystery liquid trickled down the south wall. In the kitchen fruit flies drifted like sentient pollen around wadded shopping bags containing only receipts. The tile back splash behind the stove looked like the wall a firing squad saw after firing.

He turned and paced back through the fragments of his im provised life. Did he make this mess or did it make him? He'd never lived alone. Before this it was dorms and co-ops, which other people cleaned; before that, his father's truck, which was dirty. In the curriculum of self-care he hadn't quite figured out tidying up—or washing or eating or sleeping. Basics weren't easy. What made them basic was their unvarying necessity, to which we were adapted by eons of heredity and tradition, but he had neither. Complex things were manageable—you needed only the conscious brain. But basics were never easy.

Since there was no way he could just *clean,* he would have to redefine *clean.* Try a syllogism: cleanliness was next to godli ness and God didn't exist, so cleanliness was next to nothing, so he didn't have to do anything. Or solve the higher-order prob lem, that of perspective; that was something he could change. From a drawer in the kitchen he retrieved his orange plastic pill case. He poured a glass of milk. The palliatives went down first: ibuprofen for his wrenched neck, A/B eardrops, Visine, albuterol for asthma, oxcarbazepine for convulsions, triamcino-lone acetonide for eczema, and ChapStick for good measure. Drixine in four stinging spritzes—it was good for his sinuses, but he was trying to cut back, because it was bad for his sinuses. He wiped his eyes and began the gauntlet of dicyclo-mine for his IBS, filling his palm, paving his tongue. He tipped his head forward so the pills would float up, and swallowed; they chafed against one another in their gastric bath.

How doped up would he be in forty years? How many tinctures and ampoules, carpet tacks, tubes of caulk would he need to swallow? The worst thing about pills was that they worked. Without them, you might just adapt; medical optimism suspended you in a maintenance reality. He'd never known how sick he was until he'd gotten health insurance. The pill that really wanted inventing was the bitter one that cured you of optimism and made time go faster.

Alcohol was contraindicated with half his meds but oh well. He poured frigid cheap vodka into his milk glass, garnished it with a ragged wedge of a lemon scavenged from a campus bush, and gulped it down with eight Depakote and two Topamax for bipolar. Then propranolol for the Depakote. A burst of mania might help him get through the evening. But you never got the right pole.

His pulse thumped in the pulp of his teeth. Everything looked cleaner already. Henrik reminded himself that he was doing okay, this was high functioning, things had been worse before—though *this* was pretty bad too, sure, let's own that.

In the last twenty minutes he went around like a burglar hearing a garage door open: the toilet paper roll on the coffee table, the undershirt he'd used to wipe up chicken soup—he threw these into the garbage, along with a capless ChapStick whose waxy nub was still concave with newness and empty Miller Lite cans doubled over like fortune cookies. He threw plates flocked with microwaved tomato sauce under the sink and swept all the bean cans, spaghetti sauce jars, and gas station cups off the counter into the lumpy, ripped garbage bag, which he brought out to the backyard, intending to reclaim it later, unless he decided it was better off as garbage.

The last detritus, the thing he couldn't throw out, was himself. His nose leaked; a teaspoon of phlegm kept regenerating in his throat; he blotted flop sweat in the elbow of his sweatshirt. From end to end his tract purred with insectile gurbles and blats wheezing flabbily through its maze of sphincters. Continence was a cornerstone of civility. The social contract reaffirmed itself in small diligences like these.

He padded over to the bathroom, fighting off his gray Stanford sweatshirt and husky jeans. Sometimes he fantasized about being forced through a fine steel mesh, extruding the illness from his body; or having a powerful spray of water blast clear through him to hose out the fat-soluble toxins—but his shower wasn't even strong enough to fight the sag of gravity. He stepped into the bathtub stained with a vitiligo of scum. Having run out of soap, he'd been using spray disinfectant instead, coughing against closed lips as orange-scented ammonia billowed up. The bloat of the Depakote gave him biceps like fish bellies, and his pecs were threatening to mammarize. There was lots of surface area to wash, another case of size taxation, some unit of inconvenience per kilogram. Big guys were expected to push harder, squeeze in a bit, help get this thing unstuck. And not to hurt.

He stepped out, making his nude skin toughen with goose bumps, and feeling, as he put on the same clothes, that absolute clean was another class of filth. Henrik reentered the living room. Nothing living lived here. He might need to bring some of the garbage back in.

III. O

The provider was late. Henrik sat on his couch, checking the clock on his phone (each check informing him of how much life he'd just wasted) until headlights turning into the driveway struck the window blinds yellow. Footsteps approached; the broken doorbell was pressed with a lifeless clack. He counted to ten before opening the door to a dark-skinned girl, slender as a coupon, looking much younger than her photos, ten inches shorter with her black hair dangling under a weird leather cap—not at all the seropositive coin-toss he'd sort of expected. Her black coat's fur collar was speckled with drizzle. "Hi," she said as she entered, bright with professionalism, and Henrik closed the front door with what he hoped was an unpresumptuous click.

His immediate goal was to initiate some sort of freeze-frame and get another drink. He realized how creepy it was that his shades were *already* drawn. He took her coat and slung it across the couch, asked her how the drive was. She said it was easy, the directions were good, plus she was good with directions in general. Henrik enjoyed a welling of formless rage at the institution of small talk. She took off her heels and got even shorter.

"Thanks for coming—Lucretia?"

The name given in her online ad was Lucretia Rennes, a name that declared her Euro-goth-courtesan aspirations, and was triply mismatched—Lucretia being Latin, Rennes French, and she, by appearances, subcontinental.

"Yep, Lucretia. And your name again? Heinry? Heinrich?"

"Henrik."

"Hendrik. A pleasure."

She was honeying her voice, expecting probably that he wanted to engage in a bit of can't-lose flirting. Henrik brought out two different-size wineglasses and a nearly full bottle of screw-top merlot. Midpour, she asked him to drink first. "Oh, right, sorry," he said, and drained his glass halfway.

Henrik's hairline went shiny. He felt like he'd swallowed a knotted rope, but just holding the drink in his hand was easing things. Lucretia sat on the couch, whose gouged upholstery was patched with packing tape, and Henrik took the opposing armrest. She was unfakably pretty, even in this ambiance. She had a vaguely piranhic underbite, and her dark plucked eyebrows stood out from a face otherwise paled and standardized by foundation. Her outfit ironized her mousy features: a corset intricately cinched over a flounced sleeveless blouse, some kind of rugby helmet, as many piercings as each ear would hold, as many bracelets and bangles as it seemed she could lift. Linda would probably catclaw her into little curled shavings—*God, she's an object lesson in why piercings should never outnumber natural orifices.*

Well goddammit, now he was judging the girl *he'd* invited over in the first place. All that mattered was that she looked good: that is, she was unmistakably not Linda. "I appreciate you coming out here," Henrik said. "Um. You want a snack?"

She pointed at a bump in her cheek. She was chewing gum, which couldn't have tasted good with the wine. Silence prowled in. For all the small talk, he still couldn't ask her where she lived, who she was, what she was actually thinking. "Do you go to school around here?" Henrik asked.

"Nah. Dropped out. Only thing college taught me was that I didn't need it. Tuition is criminal. Knowledge should be free. Really *everything* should be."

"So you decided not to stay?"

"Decided *not* to? The burden of proof is on college. I mean, what do you *get* for all that money? I don't need a piece of paper to prove I'm smart. School is like hiding under a big boob. Autodidact is the way to go." She meddled around in her many-cinched bag and out fell an empty keychain, an envelope, and a tampon. She found a loose Post-it note and handed it to him. "My reading list. Holistic dietetics, panpsychism, horology, apocalypse myths. It's universal wisdom. College is what, math and computers? Or books about what people said in other books? College just gets you from one desk to another. It gentrifies your mind."

Lucretia retained her wine in one cheek for about ten seconds before swishing it into the other cheek. Maybe testing for numbing sedatives. Or maybe she was just a little disgusting. "I see," Henrik said, scrunching his hands into an inarticulate ball on his lap. "So why are these books more interesting to you?"

"Why's anything interesting? I mean, like, what do you study?"

"Biomechanical engineering."

Lucretia put her hands out as if minimizing the length of something. "Exactly. Vocational education. You know eventually some bureaucrat is going to turn your work into a torture device or war machine, right?"

Henrik realized that Lucretia was running down the clock, which annoyed him, but you know what, it also annoyed him to have that thought. He had to get it started. But only after somehow assuring her that he wasn't another creep out to pump a load of death into whatever mammal he could wrestle to the ground. He had to establish some trust, at the heart of which was honesty, at the innermost and therefore smallest heart of which was talking. "If my research *could* make torture devices," Henrik said, "I'd have better funding. It's pretty pure science. My advisor says there are 'parallelisms' between our work and BME—biomedical engineering—"

"I know that."

"—but mostly I just make computer simulations and fiddle with cadaver tissue."

"Ew, really? That's kind of cool. But still, why bother? No offense, you must be really smart, but what you do sounds *totally* pointless. Where's the meaning or beauty?"

"Well . . . how do you define meaning and beauty? Like, why is horology intrinsically meaningful?"

"Because it's interesting."

"But isn't interestingness subjective?"

Lucretia looked at her wineglass for a moment, her face as inscrutable as the glass, before laughing and scratching her bangs, then troweling them back into their accustomed diagonal. "Okay! I surrender. I love you Asperger's-y types. But you admit I've got a point, right?"

How to get across that he hadn't been trying to argue or patronize her intellect, that he'd been an autodidact himself and was just trying to figure out what she meant? Oh shit—they'd been talking for fifteen minutes! Did this count? Of course it did, numbnuts! It wouldn't be decent to ask her to get started, but it wasn't like she was here for any other reason. "School's mostly a job to me."

"Well, that's—cool. Whatever makes you happy."

"I wouldn't say happy exactly."

"Oh no, why are you unhappy?"

"I didn't say I was."

"Are you?"

"Um, let's call an audible here."

"Oh."

That utterance, O. Half short of breathable oxygen; two to make *good*. Or *blood*. The standard unit of disappointment. A hug, an orgasm, but not a kiss. More than anything it was nothing, which was what they'd come to.

"Well, I guess we've come to the end of the time you paid for," she said.

"Oh, uh, really? Already?"

"No, ha—that's just something I have to say for legal reasons. Anyway, let's get to know each other better."

"Yes."

She took out her wad of gum, creases stained purple with wine, and stuck it to the foot of her glass. Henrik took her offered hand, hoping she could not feel the pulse trampolining in his fingers, and she led him into his bedroom, inviting Henrik to sit with her on the mattress on his floor.

"One sec," she said, and more items tumbled from her bag: hand sanitizer, Starlight mint, rolling papers, condom, condom, can of Mace. "Oops," she said. "Ooh, awkward. Hee-hee. I used to pack heat but I thought that was overkill." Before returning it to her bag, she pointed the Mace at Henrik and pretended to spray. "*Pssssh.*"

"Ha-ha." Henrik commended himself for suppressing his flinch.

Lucretia occupied herself with scene preparation, closing the door behind her, scattering flip-top tubes and square

packets onto the bedsheet. She removed her headgear, unfas-
tened her corset, pulled down the diagonal zippers on her skirt,
wriggled out of her bracelets, unclasped a belly chain strung
with chiming trinkets, and dismantled a talon-like fingerpiece
that seemed to require an input code, discarding everything in
a heap by Henrik's humidifier. A slender black dagger tattoo
pointed down from between her breasts, and a tiny glyph rested
at her collarbone. Her petite, faintly neuter body reminded him
of a cartoon mouse.

Henrik stripped likewise. He had the physique of a car seat,
pink as pork, and he wished he could take that off too. Lucretia
walked over and knelt between his knees.

"Just a heads-up," Henrik said, "it's been a while. I'm just
trying to find out if I'm still, you know. Well, actually there's a
lot of things. Lately things have been weird, life-circumstances-
wise. Some health stuff. I mean, nothing contagious! I'm on
medication. And I was in this relationship that kinda messed
me up."

"Hmm. Okay." She sheared her lips as if distributing lip
balm, making her neck cables flinch. "So do you want to call
me by another name, like your ex's—"

"No, that's, that's . . . wow. No. I just wanted to get on the
same page before we, you know. Rrrr. I guess I wanted to make
sure you're comfortable. I mean comfortable in the sense that
you know this isn't some meaningless recreational thing. But
it's not a serious thing either. Mainly I feel respect; I respect
you a lot for this and I want to make that known even if there
is a valid argument to be made that this is an inherently exploitative exchange. There's that cliché scenario of the sensitive
white guy finding redemption and authenticity in a sex worker
and I don't want to use you in that way or any other way. I'm

also trying not to make it your responsibility to absolve me of any of the shame I'm concerned I might feel, that's not in your job description, so if this is exhausting I apologize for that too. I try to be aware of rape issues and sex worker issues and I know rape is pretty much whatever feels like rape, which is why I wanted to make completely sure—"

Lucretia made big window-washing gestures. "Henrik, stop, stop, stop! You're way overthinking everything. Let me guess, this your first time?"

"Oh no, I've done it tons of times."

Lucretia laughed. "Paying for it, I mean."

"Oh. Yeah, first time."

"Lie down."

He lay back. This probably wasn't rape. Just the usual servitude. With one hand she dropped her hair loose, while her lips imprinted stickily down his torso like the exploratory landings of a stethoscope. He heard the cellophane rustle of the opening condom foil, felt it solemnly applied. "It feels weird."

"It's polyurethane," Lucretia said. "I'm allergic to latex."

It had the tensile properties of a garbage bag. Polyurethane was a Third Reich innovation and was also in spandex. Linda had been superstitious about birth control and made Henrik use Trojans even when he pointed out that the Trojan horse was the singular metaphor for treacherous penetration and destruction from within. He chanced a look down to see Lucretia spryly engaged in her profession; it was hard not to think of those assembly-line robots that affixed bottle caps. Through the polyurethane he felt heat but no friction or moisture. He could imagine the oily flavorless polymers she was tasting, and the saliva she produced—smearing him with digestive fluid. Heavy sheaves of hair gathered and ungathered ticklishly on his thighs, and her jangling earrings pricked tiny points of cold when they tapped on his hipbones. The opened condom foil beside him read ELECTRONICALLY TESTED.

He was losing it—losing sex. Linda once said how odd it was that you had sex, not did sex, but you did do "it," "it" being sex, not love; you neither had nor did, you *made* love. But sex was something you had or didn't have, and thus could lose. And just like having sex, you could lose sex over and over again, if it was going to be that kind of night. Over the embarrassment and pity and a feeble carburetion of lust, he mainly felt annoyed—at the ingratitude of wanting sex right up until he was having it, and the futility of coaxing his ungrateful cantilever, since effort itself made it impossible, the not wanting to not want to want.

Lucretia stopped. "Something different?"

"Okie doke."

After a buttery squirt of silicone lube, Lucretia stretched out onto her back, and as Henrik loomed over her he noticed her foot had a deep red furrow that wrapped around to her ankle, as if chopped by a hatchet. Lucretia clasped Henrik's face in her hands to steer him in for a kiss, and since he was congested he had to hold his breath. Penetration went . . . okay, with some mistargeting, but then began the missionary's lonely ordeal in the savage jungle. He felt less like he was having sex with her than intubating her. Four, five minutes of this brought a searing perpendicularity of the neck, and all the midsection strains that lust usually masked. In his head he kept repeating the word *mucilage*.

Lucretia had turned her face aside, caterwauling way out of proportion. Henrik committed himself to a sporting finish. Then he felt her shaking his shoulder. "Henrik."

"Yeah?"

"You fell asleep."

The Depakote, probably. His surrendering member dangled between his thighs, asphyxiated in its airtight hood. He wiped drool from the corner of his lips.

"Am I doing anything wrong?" Lucretia asked, shrugging quietly with her breathing.

"No, I'm sorry, I just had a long day."

"Do you want me to try something else? Any kinks?"

"I'm not sure."

". . . Like this?"

"Ow."

"Here, I'll show you something. I turn over like this, and you straddle here and go in at an angle—"

"That's a bit fancy for me."

Lucretia scooched back and investigated his face with concern. In a voice high-pitched with generosity, she said, "Do . . . you want me to watch you jerk off? Do you like pee? I could use some guidance."

Henrik sneezed and left the room covering his nose and lips to find a tissue, returning to see Lucretia keeping a straight face, humoring him with humorlessness. "You don't have to stay," he said.

"You sure?" She kissed him. "You're really sweet. I want to make you feel good."

"You're doing a great job!"

Lucretia sat up, looking unbothered. She wiped her hands on the sheets and pushed her hair back over her shoulders. "Don't feel bad, I never get off either."

He trotted to the bathroom, feeling ridiculous for still wearing the condom, which he stretched off with a loud snap. The silicone lube wouldn't wash off. When he returned to his room, Lucretia was dressed and holding the cash envelope that he'd left on his dresser per instructions.

"No tip?" she said with perky tact.

"Oh—sorry. I'll go get, uh, wait here." He went for the petty cash envelope in his underwear drawer, releasing a brink-of-tears sigh as he counted out twenty dollars in an unstackably crinkled sheaf of singles. His nudity increased. "Uh, here. Can I write a check for the rest?"

"Sure! Leave the name blank."

He left the memo line blank too. He knew it was dumb to leave a paper trail, but there wasn't much she could do to him that wouldn't make him feel somewhat grateful for the effort. Lucretia smiled and took the check. "I had fun." She pecked his beard and hugged him, and he patted her on the back as the buckles and studs of her corset pressed into his stomach. "Maybe see you again?"

"I would, but I'm cleaned out."

"Fair enough. You've got my number."

Instead of making her wait for him to dress, he walked her to the door and was thwarted by the doorknob: his lubed hands couldn't grip it. He tried clamping it between his forearms, but now the knob was slippery too. Lucretia stood behind him, making him self-conscious about his buttcrack. Henrik grinned in frustration. "Heh." Lucretia opened the door herself, and Henrik hid behind it as she left, kissing her fingertips and twiddling them at him.

The door closed and Henrik deflated with a sigh. Not enjoying sex shouldn't keep him from enjoying sort of having had sex. He surveyed his living room for forensic evidence. From under the coffee table peeped a white ear of something—the envelope that had fallen out of Lucretia's purse, addressed from the Employment Development Department of California to Laura Bernard. Well, of course her name wasn't Lucretia. Basic decency obliged him to return it to her. But nothing basic was ever easy.

Henrik did a pratfall onto his sofa, feeling the cool press of corduroy cushions against his midsection, the cycles of breath and systole. He covered his face with his greasy hands and felt his eyes squirm under their lids. *Stop,* he thought. *I own you, I am you, and I'm telling you to stop.* But nothing stopped, not the wind thrashing outdoors, or gravity, or air pressure, creaming you under its ocean of air, never explaining itself, never cutting you a break. The forwardness of time, the downwardness of gravity, shoving everything like a plow—nature always acted personally. Nothing universal about it.

CHAPTER 5
Technical Support

Machines take me by surprise with great frequency.
—Alan Turing

I. Stroke of Genius

Vanya knew about the porn. She had to. Right? Certainly she knew *of* it; that Will dabbled, fleetingly and without remorse. A few months ago she'd asked (maybe a bit too casually): *Baby, have you watched much porn?* He'd said yeah, and that was the end of it. But thank god she hadn't asked *exactly how much* he'd watched, because the honest answer would've been *most of it.* So far as Will knew, to Vanya it was a normal guy thing. A quirk . . . though quirks were usually effects and not causes of one's personality, and by that standard, Will's porn watching was no quirk—it was pure trait.

And though he hadn't watched it since he'd met Vanya a year ago, it was still a huge part of who he was, of what he'd consumed, and it was here now, and Vanya was not. What did she expect? He'd never *delete* it—it was too important, indisputably rare and beautiful. Never mind the man-hours it'd taken to download it; to create file tags and XML-formatted scene markers; to regularize the filenames and formats; to fill gaps in photo sets and find hi-res scans of DVD cases, front and back; to complete the back catalogs of particular performers (since in porn, the juvenilia was often the masterpiece); to build his seed ratio on invite-only torrent forums; to decipher thousands of CAPTCHAs to prove that he was human; or to assemble the storage solutions to house its gigascale, then terascale, then petascale volumes—he'd only watched about a third of it, so it remained in many ways a mystery even to him.

Over the years he'd cultivated an eye for composition, an ear for rhythm, and impeccable connoisseurship. That one-and-done you wanted to ID all these years? Aline Batistel, and she did a scene as Paula Becker for Brazilian *Hustler* too. That flawless blonde, whom only the collapse of the Soviet Union could produce? Alena Hemcova—or Alissa Romei, Lenka Gaborova, Katerina Strougalova . . . but drill deeper into the file hierarchy, past the MF and FFM and MMF and MMMMMF, beyond the Zenra and Private, the Woodman and Steele and ZONE-sama, the doujinshi and lemon fic, into the farlights of eros, where there was no niche he couldn't cache: eco-friendly BBWs bukkaked while cemented into sidewalks, flexi Juggalo stepdads cuckolded by butterflies, cum tributes to horses torn in half, spray-painted soup men donkey-punching intersexed RealDolls. He'd also watched gay porn in a state-of-the-union capacity—you would think the redundancy of male equipment would limit the palette, but wow, no.

Since he'd been seeing Vanya, months of sex, years in the gathering, had just sat there like regretted kitchen appliances. What to do with our useless virtuosity? His collection belonged in the Smithsonian, though that'd never happen. But why? If the objection was that porn was tasteless, profane, distorting, or exploitative, then porn was just really honest TV. And now there were canonical sex acts—the sex tape as heroic fucklore in an era of democratized you-porn. Porn was obviously art: it just had weak criticism. People driveled about its politics, culture, commerce, morality. But who was defining it? Just because porn didn't have to be good didn't mean it shouldn't be. Will had been troubled by the rise of livestreaming, which was like replacing cinema with improv; and on the other hand, an encroachment of self-aware, camp irreverence: Bangbros, Cum Fiesta, Big Sausage Pizza. You couldn't find a convincing cheerleader anymore, there were only *porn* cheerleaders, with pigtails and lollipops, hosed down with hand lotion by yard-long prop cocks to the accompaniment of thrash metal. It catered to an audience so porn-saturated that they needed to be reassured they weren't taking it too seriously. Thus irony had finally kicked in the garden walls of the orgasm, sincerity's last refuge.

The real question was whether *masturbating to porn* was an art form: not as "erotica" or performance art, but as solitary pursuit of the sublime. Someone must have done it seriously, subtly, with literacy and flair, a masturbauteur—maybe it was Will. One time he'd discovered he could play the same clip in two windows side by side and cross his eyes to stereoscope the image into 3D, so long as he took Dramamine first. Another time he'd erotically hypnotized himself with a recording of his own voice, a little squicky but more or less effective.

Now he sat half-recumbent with his undershirt bunched under his chin and twelve videos tiled across three monitors. Revisiting porn after many months refreshed all the marvelous warps in the glaze of pornic fiction. Like how it never rained. Or the beguiling divot in Nadia Nyce's forehead, which looked like Bree Olson's, who was otherwise indistinguishable from Ashlynn Brooke. That subgenre of guys offering "real" girls money to fuck on camera, thus synchronizing the fantasy with reality. The moment at the beginning of a gonzo scene where the actress switched her focus from the camera to the other actors, and audience became voyeur.

Every hour or so he wristed the sweat from his upper lip and coughed with the sudden awareness of how dry his throat and eyes were. He used to wonder at his fondness for porn actors, since he categorically resented people for whom sex came easy, but porn *wasn't* easy; everyone knew it was a clearinghouse of coercion and addiction, which cut down on smugness. Will preferred not the smirking glamoristas, not the Tori Blacks and Delta Whites, but the Sasha Greys and Anastasia Blues, those who brought their sordid biographies before the lens, the ones you couldn't watch without thinking, *My god, this girl is going to* die *someday* . . . Occasionally they were dead already, making it especially clear that when they were on your level or lower, degradation-wise, guilt increased but shame usefully decreased. All this disqualified him as a good person and a feminist, but he wasn't antifeminist either, more of a solipsist—and if solipsism was theory, then masturbation was practice.

Maybe Will liked porn for not insulting him by pretending it had anything to do with the reality of sex, or with him. How *could* he relate, when there were no Asian men in porn? They weren't any more underrepresented in porn than anywhere else, but still it bothered him sometimes to manage his desires by watching white people fucking, or white-on-Asian, or black-on-white, or sometimes white-on-black or black-on-black. Well, there was some AMWF (god bless that Lexi Belle), but it was so depressing to see the low user ratings and comments it always got. Porn from Asia was another obvious exception, but with its ludicrous censorship, even Asians denied the Asian cock, burst it into a cloud of pixels, and Will's attempts to demosaic it only yielded ghostly approximations. But there was definitely no AM-disabled-WF—Will and Vanya were unimaginable even to porn.

On day three of his binge, Will was getting impatient with the tedious editing of a POV FFFM CFNM A2M DTD BJ scene. He launched his video-editing software, and after checking on his bid for the anodized aluminum skillet he was buying for his mother, he tried trimming the clip down—too jumpy, and the cuts disjointed the sound; he fixed it with subtle cross-fades and clip stretching. He normalized the dynamic range so it didn't get all loud when the cameraman was talking. He discovered that speeding up a blowjob was hilarious, and slowing it down produced an appealingly bestial lunar-gravity effect. This was great: he could pan, crop, and zoom exactly like he . . . huh.

A pulse of red static scorched through Will's brain. *Inspiration.*

He abandoned watching in favor of editing. He sought better tools and raw files. He found an image stabilizer for handheld POV scenes, and audio filters to muffle the sucking-through-clenched-molars sound the actors made. Render times were a bottleneck in the workflow, so he hauled his old desktops out of the garage, popped in some spare RAM, and fashioned an HPC cluster to distribute the processing. After two days he was performing macro-assisted edits practically in real time, with three fingers on his trackball and his other hand striking hotkeys, occasionally leaving no free hand to jerk with yet maintaining jet-hot arousal throughout, while his overclocked towers ran double digits over operating temp, their rushing fans overwhelming the solemn allegro patter of his percussions.

At random intervals, icy glitches of repetitive strain relayed up from his middle and ring fingers to his elbows. Both wrists, velcroed into pantyhose-colored braces, bore seamy scars from carpal tunnel surgeries. His left-handed death grip triggered fat flares of pain, masked by the crackle of his limbic system. But Will outdid himself now by managing to climax hands-free, and that was better anyhow, haunted as he was by the likelihood of developing some grave asymmetry between his hands.

Admiring the clever cutaways in a Claire Bandit scene, Will began to reassess form. He stopped stroking his cock and stroked his chin instead. The usefulness of looping, skipping, pausing, the fact that porn wasn't watched so much as intensely skimmed, was proof in itself of the shortcomings of linear sex in real time. If sex was raw data, and indeed it was, it should be semantic and context-aware. A reminder to pay the water bill popped up onscreen and Will paid it, then bought some eye drops. Maybe he could try a picture-in-picture inset. Or try lifting assets from one film into another?

Lumbago pinched in his back like a bedded nail. He pirated DAZ Studio and used Vanya's hi-res photos to skin the models, just because he had so many of them. With some filtering, some relighting, a few hours of figure rigging and keyframe, he could composite her into other films, controlling each joint and gyration. Well, there was one way to get Asian men into porn: in postproduction.

He screened his works. Porn that didn't require people. What was porn, after all? A set of expectations. The frontiers were wide open: machinima, teledildonics, sexual death-matches. Using game engines, performances could happen in real time with human agents conducting virtual surrogates in constructed environments, and it'd be trivial to mod the physics, script behaviors, add or subtract orifices and phalli, random-generate genders. One man could be ten men, ten men one woman. Will realized he'd poured the foundations for the homebrew online collaborative erotic composite performative found-footage remix. The world's first, as far as he knew, and he *would* know. Dozens of cameramen, lighting and motion techs, audio engineers could collaborate over team chat in the authentically realized fantasy, in the shadow of which ordinary copulation was merely tediously possible. Better than having sex, you could *make* sex. People would only need to watch. Love would be free at last.

All of which might be nice to daydream about, but Vanya would be coming back eventually. His stroke of genius was just a tributary obsession after all, and maybe it was for the best that whatever the aesthetic pleasures, the actual physiological release felt unsatisfyingly forced, like a pepper sneeze. He resisted the shame he was supposed to feel; a life of rejection had funneled him to this meager consolation, the one kindness he could render himself, and he was supposed to feel *bad*? Fuck that. He would allow some self-pity, however, and some primal reluctance to be seen for a while. It was good that porn didn't watch you back.

He passed the week's final climax like a drain clog, and with the barrening of lust came the crushing return of perspective: that sexual release imperfectly eclipsed dread, and the vertiginous awareness of disrobing in front of your computer to watch other people fuck along with millions of other people worldwide seemed like some decisive failure of the human experiment.

With fatigue and eyestrain and simulator sickness besetting him like a flu, all enthusiasm erased, Will looked down and saw his hand, the desk, and his undershirt streaked in blood. He panicked. He searched **blood in semen**: surprisingly, it was okay. Will cleaned up and lurched into the shower more for spiritual than hygienic purposes. When he returned, his room had a heavy smell of skin. And there was nothing to do but sit at his computer again.

He'd accidentally killed a week and didn't know what to do with its corpse. How to overwrite feelings and ideas, the necropolis of streaming teens and throbbing integers and data rubbing against data. The silent tyrannized horde of his memory.

II. Progress

Will smoked rapidly as he walked, as if to form a personal nimbus in which to travel undetected. He resented each step up the boutique length of Twenty-Fourth Street, in weather that someone else might call lovely. But nothing was lovely when you were inconvenienced.

He'd obviated most errands when he'd started ordering everything online—small-batch bourbon subscriptions, Virginia-stamped cigarettes, crates of produce each Wednesday. But he now found himself suffering the outrageous indignity of mailing a letter: an invoice to a client who hadn't adopted e-billing yet. He was trudging to a metal mailbox four blocks away to deposit a piece of paper inside another piece of paper for a metal truck to trundle to some brick building and the piece of paper to be hauled in turn from one tract of earth to another, all to do what some excited electrons could do in a thousandth of the time it took to have this thought. Understanding that this was a problem of extreme privilege only made his irritation itself irritating.

The same enraged wind that had overturned the curbside recycling bins earlier in the day was now whirling bits of dried leaf into Will's eyes. He reached the mailbox, clankingly thrust in the envelope, and spat in after it. Then realized he'd forgotten the stamp. He didn't even own stamps. Fuck the paycheck.

He killed his cigarette and dropped it under his next footfall, lighting another and wondering whether there was a service that mailed his mail to the mailbox. Reality took forever—the underwater way people walked and sent their voices wobbling through the air, how printed words lay inert like bugsplat, all manifesting the basic *duh* of the physical plane. By the time he decided to go anywhere he wondered why he wasn't there already. As soon as he sent an email he felt he should already have the reply. And learning any fact, he was annoyed not to have known it already, because whenever anything happened, the conversation around it had already trended and backlashed and been reexamined and swallowed and shat and reswallowed and reshat in a thousand places online, until all thinking felt redundant. We needed brain-to-brain; only then would we catch up to real time. Right now everything progressed so slowly that by the time we arrived at the future it was the present again. Everything would be annoying until the senses were surmounted and all media fell to the liberated message.

Will checked the time. It was now, as usual. Last week Cory had called asking for computer help, and though Will was sick of being anyone's Asian tech support, he hadn't seen Cory or the sky in a while, so he'd agreed. But Cory refused to go from her place in SoMa to Will's in Noe Valley. She liked drawing ugly contrasts: in SoMa, she'd say, men in track pants scooted backward across the street in wheelchairs; in Noe Valley, women in yoga pants spanned the sidewalk with four-axle strollers. SoMa had panhandlers, Noe had accordion buskers. In Noe people stooped to pick up dog shit off the sidewalk; in SoMa people living on sidewalks stooped to shit on stoops. In the land of Have Not, even the tallest streetlights were smashed; in the land of Have, the garage lights came on when you walked by. Et cetera.

Will arrived at the half-empty Revolution Café and was not surprised that Cory hadn't shown up yet—like most Californians, she considered punctuality anal and passive-aggressive, and had groomed him to expect tardiness since college, when they'd lived together. That was around the time Will had returned from his suspension for his stupid physical altercation to find that Linda had turned his and Henrik's room into a sexual eruv. In spite of the bedsheet curtain Linda tacked up next to the bed, Will's sleep was ruined by their cooing and humping night after night, and the floor was gritty with cigarette ash and hybrid hair bunnies. Will decided he was completely over it after they appropriated the whole box of condoms he'd bought freshman year out of tragically misguided optimism.

So he'd arranged to switch rooms indefinitely with Linda and live with Cory, even though he'd previously known her only as the girl who did hunger strikes, chanting loudly by her red tent in the Main Quad. And in fact they had nothing in common except the peevish indignation of having both been friend-orphaned—but at the time, that sufficed. Together they observed Henrik and Linda's mating ritual with disinterest, agreed that couples were inherently selfish, encouraging vicarious egotism and demoting friends to second-rate conveniences. They joked about how Henrik was like Linda's kid brother, always conforming and deferring, never contesting her, not even for laughs, no matter how much she humiliated him. "He's, like, a fearminist," Cory would say, releasing a billow of pot smoke. It went without saying that Will and Cory had no attraction to each other, and they ignored the subtle pressure to pair off; besides, they had a solidarity in solitude that Will felt was purer, more uncompromised, less manipulative than love. It was important to have a friend he could complain about his friends to. Even though she was often late.

Will bought a coffee and took an al fresco table beneath the open wall's white canopies, soiled with a smear of mustard and blobby water rings from recently cleared glasses. Lighting a cigarette and balancing it at a secant on the rim of his mug, he checked his phone until Cory coasted along on her white bike, swinging in dismount. "¿*Qué pasa?*"

Hugging with double backslaps, Will noted she'd lost some gravity in her jawline—how clearly you could see the passage of time in your friend's weight swings. Her hair Venned interestingly between morning neglect and political statement, and a pair of white sunglasses sat askew on her head. She wore jeans, even though she'd once said her thighs were the natural predator of pants crotches.

He kicked out a chair for her, and she unclipped her helmet and dropped her bag with a tired *uff,* sending out a whiff of sweat and lotion. From her bag, she produced her monstrous laptop, navy blue and scuffed, quite as large as the lap it sat on. "Should we move inside?" she asked. "I'm worried it'll get swiped."

"This thing? This bread machine? If anyone steals this, I'll buy you a new one."

Cory ran her power cord into the café; her computer booted with the roar of a turboprop. She put her sunglasses on because screens gave her a faceache.

"Click there," Will said.

She looked down at the buttons and the flat little rink of touchable plastic. A mangled alphabet, a 4 under a $, an 8 under a *. Twelve kinds of F. Cory blinked hard. Beside her, Will reached over and poked the largest button. "When you press this, it's called clicking."

"Dude, I know. I'm just trying to care."

Cory belonged to that final muddy rump generation of college grads who could squeak by techlessly. She wouldn't take any class that required computers, and her thesis advisor, a kindred tech-hater, had lauded her clean typewritten drafts ("Not like these jagoffs who rip half their citations off Wikipedia. *Fuck* computers, man! At college I had a record player, bookshelf, and bong—now there's a fuckin' video arcade on every desk . . ."). Taren had been cool with it, since Cory's work was mostly outdoors.

Will thought it was bizarre how Cory lost all faith and perceptiveness whenever confronted with buttons. She typed like she was using a Ouija board. She couldn't distinguish a 0 from an O ("They're right next to each other") or maintain any conceptual separation between the Shift, CMD, CTRL, ALT, and FN keys ("They're *right next* to each other!"). Her effort came across as both naive and senile.

"I only want to learn basics. Do email, and maybe look at websites."

"All right, what's your email account info?"

Cory retrieved a leaflet from her messenger bag. "My office manager gave me this. Are these passwords? Do I need a password? . . . Don't give me that fucking look."

"Yeah, this's fine. I'll set it up through Gmail, which is a—"

"Ew, isn't that Google?"

"Yeah," Will said. "Unfortunately for you, Google is capitalism at its finest. If they wanted to enslave the world they'd have done it by now."

"They *have* done it. I don't want them attached to my name. Ulgh, those creepy black buses. All those startup douches. The rents. It's cliché to say, but tech companies have ruined the Mission. No offense."

"Gold rushes have always been 'ruining' San Francisco. Ruining it with money and jobs. It beats earthquakes."

"The way tech companies turn services into verbs and products into nouns. Doesn't it depress you that googling is called googling? That they're privatizing language? They even took the letters I and E."

"Don't forget 'You.'"

"And this doesn't bother you?"

"No."

"Well, they're counting on your blasé fatalism."

A passing bird briefly interrupted the sun. Will produced a cigarette from nowhere and leaned back. "How can you dismiss something you don't even understand on a basic level?"

"Oh, you condescending butthole. 'You don't like it because you don't get it, sweetie.' Pat me on the fucking head while you're at it."

"You're disenfranchising yourself by being ignorant about the tools everyone uses."

"By 'everyone,' you mean young, affluent, computer-trained—"

"It'll get cheaper and more widespread. Technologies like electricity and transport and birth control don't fall under your rubric because you're looking at the finger and—"

"The middle finger pointing at poor people?"

"—and not where the— Okay, whatever. Does it bother you that your phone calls go through big telecom companies?"

"Uh, yeah! I hate it *all*. I hate that I *have* to know what an iPhone is. I hate that Steve Jobs gave our commencement address. I hate that everyone knows technology and textiles are made by *slaves* and they *still* don't care. I at least want people to stop caring whether *I* care."

Will had those glasses that darkened in the light; the sunlight was bright enough that Cory couldn't see what he was thinking. He sat with his cigarette arm relaxed over the back of his chair, blowing smoke from the edge of his mouth in a diagonal jet that widened out like a speech bubble, which he filled with these words: "You know the Luddites weren't successful, right?"

"Actually they were *executed* for breaking a law that made machine-smashing a capital offense. That moment when machines officially outranked human life."

"They achieved zilch and got fucked by history. You're the one who wants everyone engaged in community. Now it's online."

"The Internet is a vile, omnivorous privatization machine. A technological vector of capitalist domination. Heidegger."

"Yo, you don't win arguments by saying 'Heidegger.'"

Cory dug donuts into her temples. Will's argument was: If she stood for progress, why not *technological* progress? Because social benefit wasn't consumable—people wanted hover-boards and phone cases, not infrastructure, green energy, shit, not even food production. The tech ethos was to do less with more, the false empowerments of consumerism, inventing conveniences for the vanishing middle class, the Marcusian identification with property . . . plus, as technology became more complex, it got harder to regulate and appropriate, so technological progress was regress to mysticism. Ah, and it kept getting *thinner*. "I'm saying that building communities on private infrastructure is bad. The way I understand it—"

"You don't, but go on."

"—the Internet's a shopping mall. A global corporate holding pen masquerading as public commons. The public doesn't work if nobody's *in* it. You can't protest online; there's no space. The overlords who turned the world into property are now making property proprietary and virtual. Molding and standardizing human relationships to function as components in the assembly line. And don't forget, it was all developed with *taxpayer money* for the *military* and thrives on *government subsidies,* like all supposedly bootstrapped free-market horseshit."

Fuckin' Cory—she thought she could tar him as some cryptoconservative just because he wasn't an activist. Sure, technology was awful; just less awful than most things, and much less than she thought. "People want shopping malls," Will said, "and they'll make them, because convenience trumps freedom every time. Don't blame tech for that. Dismissing the Internet is like dismissing buildings."

"You can't live in a website."

"The walking counterargument begs to differ. Are we doing this email thing or what?"

Cory relented. She felt mentally arthritic as he said *window focus* and *right-click context menu* as if those were real things. Would we even have email in five years? Would we have people? "Listen," Cory interrupted, "all I want is a list of steps."

"You won't need one if you take a minute to learn basics."

"Will, why do you insist—"

A pebble fell from somewhere and bounced painlessly off Will's skull. Cory laughed.

"Okay, break time," Will said. "You want a snack? It's on me."

Cory declined and Will went inside. Accepting Will's gifts felt like enabling some pathology his money had created. Somehow his ethics of consumption were cavalier and generous and cynical all at once: he kept loose singles in his pocket for panhandlers and flashed his membership card at ACLU canvassers, but only to shut them up. Couldn't he at least feel bad? She remembered once in Palo Alto he'd made Cory wait while he ducked into an Apple store to replace a $300 gizmo he'd accidentally swallowed ("Don't ask"). He threw out the receipt and bag and the brick of packaging, scratched his initials into the casing with his car key, and slid it into his coin pocket while walking straight past a homeless guy. He was a great object lesson in how money could make even charity frigid.

Will returned with a clear glass mug of linden tea. "Drink it."

Mezzing out for a moment, Cory stared at the shadow cast on the table by the steam, undulating like a sheer curtain. She stirred the fat dollop of honey in the bottom up into a slender cyclone and it vanished. "Let's get this over with. No abstractions, or I *walk.*"

"Fine, Jesus."

Will stepped Cory through the click-here, click-there to get to her email. Reviewing her notes, she rolled her tongue and said, "I guess that's easy enough."

She had more than a thousand unread messages, with subjects like **following up (again)** and **Calling the office NOW** and **ATTN: CORDELIA ROSEN, MESSAGE FROM A HOT WIFE**. At the top was Barr's email. Cory clicked on the message as if disarming it:

From: fatterpamilias@yahoo.com
To: cory@socialize.org
Subject: Datum Daddi
October 6, 2007 1:13 AM

Dear Daughter,

PRAISE PALLAS for your primus passus on the path to (non-)profitable proprietorship! Provided in the proceeding: a pamphlet (printable PDF) of proper preparatory preliminary punctilio. Your proud pater is pals with prominent professionals who've proffered prodigious patronage: you're pardoned from paying a penny.

BAN ERRORS; don't be SCARED LOONIER -Pa

"The fuck is that?" Will asked. "Ban errors?"

Cory teed her chin on her palm. "My dad's anagram thing."

Indeed, Barr had once bragged that he'd chosen Cory's name for its vowel/consonant mix. CORDELIA ROSEN: ODOR LARCENIES, DROOL INCREASE—or with her middle name, A RELIANCE ON DRONES. He'd probably spent all evening on this email. She'd stupidly hoped he might offer *actual* help. "Can you open the pamphlet for me?"

Will crabdanced his hand across the keyboard. "Oh, Handshake," he said, reading the file. "Vanya went there. Public speaking, networking, all that biz-dev happy horseshit. Self-satisfaction guaranteed."

"Should I go? I'm clearly too stupid and young to run a company."

"Bullshit. This is the valley of preteen CEOs. Vanya's younger than you and she's starting a company now."

"Oh right, Vanya. How's she? Is she still, um, hot?"

"Continuously."

Cory lifted her sunglasses and rubbed her face. "Well, thanks, dude. For the help. Want to take a walk?"

"To where?"

"Nowhere. It's nice out."

"Ulgh. Can we at least walk toward my house?"

Cory tossed a crushed napkin at Will, which bounced off his chin and onto his plate. "You're such an agoraphobe."

"Claustrophile."

"Don't you ever want to get out into nature?"

"Only if I couldn't."

"Just appreciate it," Cory said. "We just stared at a screen for an hour, you can't do five minutes of sunset?"

They bussed their table and strolled west to Noe Valley. "You know," Cory said, "the inability to enjoy nature without dominating it is a major cause of conflict."

"*You're* a major cause of conflict."

The air was so warm and clean, Cory couldn't feel it entering or leaving her nose. The evening light seemed injected with a vitreous dye as the sun sank in a hurry. Ah, stay! Enjoy your own colors! Nature was so indifferent to its own majesty. "Look"—pointing skyward—"so orange! And those horsetail clouds. It's like a piece of salmon!"

"Or lines of coke on an old bruise."

"Will. Don't ruin the sky for me."

Will walked beside Cory. If you preferred the indoors, everyone assumed you were scared of life or emotionally stunted. That wasn't it. It was just ugly outdoors. Sidewalks with their stubble-beards of filth; scabby trees pregnant with vermin, weeping sap, stewing in dog piss. Sure, it was nice to have some fresh air while he smoked. But he was myopic, hard of hearing, congested—reality was lo-fi, slow and obstructing, too cold or too bright, filled with scrapes, sirens, hidden charges, long distances, pollen, and assholes.

"This weather! I die!" Cory said as they hiked the steep anti-runaway sidewalk on Twenty-Fifth. At the top, she leaned on her bike with her head thrown back and mouth open like she was catching rain. "My headache is *poof,* gone!"

She took off her sunglasses and shook her hair out in the quiet orange breeze. Will suspected she was hyped on low blood sugar and due for a crash. He felt sad that he had to police his tendency to ruin things, and sad again that there was so little in the world he could enjoy nonvicariously. "Call me if you have more dumb questions."

Cory hugged Will and pecked him. "Remember how you used to wipe off your cheek? Like a widdle baybay."

"Never say that again."

"Bye, dear."

Will left, and when he glanced back from a block ahead,

Cory was still on the corner facing east down the hill, where the sinking light was flushing the low properties of the Mission royal purple.

III. First Exposure

Will looked at the calendar on his phone and counted days on fingers in his head. Vanya was gone until January, and the question was how to make her less gone, how to make the distance less long. Will had killed plenty of time; now he would kill space.

He fought noon traffic to the Best Buy downtown, turned left across a double yellow line to cut into the parking lot's inlet. Among the retail shelves was some problem decomposition to bring Vanya to him; he prowled them, looking for solutions in the conjunction of dongles. He emerged with two bags of boxes and the feeling of mild letdown that followed shopping.

That afternoon he littered his apartment with burst packaging and the sprayed sweetness of freshly opened electronics. The webcam was zip-tied to a plastic mount and clamshelled, encased in Styrofoam braces under a cardboard partition and a baggie of manuals, within the support cardboard, within the taped-up product box, shrink-wrapped and bagged. Tearing through it, he realized he'd bought the wrong converter—as usual, a male-to-female compatibility problem. He went back to the store and hated everything all over again.

Before his scheduled nine P.M. video chat with Vanya, Will kicked aside the mess in range of his webcam, made sure his tie lined up with the buttons of his red cardigan, and pulled a licked comb through his hair. The call came in. Vanya's bun was impaled by a pencil, and she bobbed as she did curls with her pink six-pound dumbbells. "Hey, baby! What'd you want to show me?"

"I've figured everything out."

He demoed the webcams, one for the living room and one for the bedroom, autoswitching the feed to whichever had more movement in it. Hook them and an omnidirectional mic to one of his porn towers, then connect that to his wall-mounted flat-screen with a DVI-to-HDMI adapter and voilà: a persistent telepresence window.

Vanya set down her weights and applauded. "Baby, that's *so* cool! How much did it cost?"

"Not much." It had cost about $400: not much. "You can set one up at your place," he said.

"Here? I can't be chatting all day."

"You can disable it whenever. And soon you're going to be on camera all the time anyway, right?" A polite lobe of Will's brain questioned whether this invaded Vanya's privacy; Will's swaggering majority lobe fired back, *IT'S A RELATIONSHIP, BRO!* And a relationship was nothing *but* a profound invasion of privacy: invasion, followed by occupation. Pissing while the other flossed, farts under shared sheets. And what was less private than sex? "It's ambient," Will continued. "Easy to hook up. I'll ship all the equipment to you, preconfigured."

Vanya screen-kissed. "Okay, I'll do it. You're nice, mister." Vanya decided things quickly and without cumbersome after-thought. "Anything else to show me?"

The engagement ring still sat in his jacket pocket. He recalled those online videos of failed wedding proposals—men rejected onstage with maximum pomp on live television, stammeringly repeating their proposals as if their girlfriends' silence was a mere issue of latency. Will shook his head, and after another cool LED kiss they disconnected. He overnighted the telepresence equipment to Vanya.

For the next two months, they lived on each other's flat-screens in the evening; Vanya called hers the Baby Monitor. The setup was more passive than he'd expected—her webcam was mounted like a security camera, so she rarely faced him, and she muted his audio while she worked. But at least Will could verify that she was in her apartment and not audition-ing his replacement. Occasionally she waved to him, and on his end he cranked the volume loud enough to hear the airy roar of traffic outside her Crown Heights sublet, and he liked being able to bless her whenever a sneeze detonated from his subwoofer.

The camera was curbing his masturbation, which was probably good. Instead he fed himself on the cookie crumbs of Vanya's web presence. He got push notifications on her social networking activity, search alerts on her name, an RSS feed on her blog. It was as preoccupying as porn, but with no finish.

During the final weeks of December, while Vanya toured Europe with her parents—instead of spending time with him like she'd promised—Will evicted his downstairs tenant, vis-ited Linda in the hospital, hired a cleaning service, jogged, and smoked.

Waiting for Vanya at baggage claim in January, Will was so anxious to see her face that he almost didn't want to. She was easy to spot leaving the elevator with her large carry-on bag in her lap, wheeling a straight path through the crowd, some giving her berth, others aggressively tailgated. She looked like an ad for herself, the new 2008 model, with fresh highlights under a Maserati-red plastic headband and the parabolas of her chest agonizing a lace-collar blouse. Taking Vanya's bag from her lap, he gave her an airport-appropriate but nonetheless French kiss.

"The TSA practically disassembled my wheelchair," Vanya whispered. "They think *I'm* a terrorist? *Kind* of ridiculous."

Her face was somehow altered; some finessing of angles, its bevel or cant, ratios ineffably more golden. Her smoky eye, bangs sliced to the brow—still the same. What was different? Her ears, her teeth? No, it all looked same and good except . . . her nose? Had it been rescaled, narrowed, planed? Had she gotten work done in New York?

"Did you get work done in New York?"

Vanya yawned largely. "Work's never done."

THEIR SEXUAL REUNION made for a gory spectacle, as Will temporarily became a carrion beetle—he lapped and nibbled, slurped and squeezed in from every angle. In his precious minute of sanity following orgasm, Vanya made him an offer over the pillow. She'd been talking him up to the executive board in New York, and they were impressed by his cheap telepresence setup and portfolio; how would he like to be Sable's chief technical officer?

"Not *just* a CTO," Vanya said. "You'll be on the lifecast anyway, so you might as well cohost, right?"

Weighing the unseemliness of becoming his girlfriend's employee, Will inquired about duties. Vanya took her laptop from the bedstand and opened her notes, hair still plastered to her forehead with fuck sweat. "You'd oversee operations and throw together cheap, stable livecasting solutions. I just sent you our current setup, take a peek?"

Will opened the attachment on his phone. Too many cords

and converters, weak battery. He met Vanya with a lordly smile. "I could do this way better."

"Do it! Do it!"

"Sure. Yeah, why not. Is this interview over?"

Will started kissing her but she nudged him back. "Actually, there's more to discuss regarding your presentation."

"I have to do a presentation?"

"I mean, your image. You'll need some media orientation—camera etiquette, style reboot, that kinda thing. Reworking the optics. You gotta get back on social media, obviously. And I was thinking maybe, like, tweak your name."

"What? My name?"

"It's impossible," Vanya said. "Will N————. It's chowder."

"I'm aware."

"We'd just change it on the website." Vanya rubbed Will's shoulder. "To make it SEO friendly. It's standard showbiz practice. Look"—Vanya splattered keystrokes across her laptop—"like how Freddie Mercury was Farrokh Bulsara or Jon Stewart was Jonathan Liebowitz."

"What about Beyoncé? Or Björk?"

"Short and catchy. Yours is neither. Baby, it's just for the show, it's not even legal."

"So I'll be what? Will Williams? Will Smith?"

Vanya smacked Will on the arm, pretty hard, he thought. Her Texan accent was becoming faintly unsuppressed. "Don't pretend I'm trying to whitewash you. Didn't your family change its name when they immigrated to Thailand? Because of that law?"

She was referring to the law that required all Thai families to have unique surnames, so they got longer and longer over time, with the consequence that now Will carried around a bulging diaper of syllables. At least his first name was unremarkable and not one of those octogenarian names Asian guys got, Albert, Arthur, Bernard, Chester, Eugene, Joseph, Harold, Howard, Norman, Victor, Vincent, Walter . . . though even *those* were better than some of Will's relatives: Phuk and Klit, Bing and Thong, Ing, Eh, Aah, the Wannatits, the Kissaporns. (This cut both ways, as any tourist named Jim or Dawson learned.)

"Visitors need to instantly grok you," Vanya continued. "You need to be conspicuous and memorable. You're a young, attractive Asian man, and if people *could* say your name, then they just *might*. What about shortening it to 'Will N——'? It's catchy, and still quote-unquote Asian-sounding."

He had no reasonable response to this. But he did have an unreasonable one: "No way. I don't owe stupid white people any courtesies."

"Oh my god, this again!" Vanya said. "I'm white, so I can't have an *opinion*? Choosing your own name is empowering. Maybe you'd be less annoyed if people didn't always trip over it."

"*I'm* annoyed? Remember that cashier last week who *sighed* at my credit card? I annoy *them*. They butcher it and then giggle and say all this dumb face-saving bullshit. 'Boy, that's a mouthful!' 'What a *beautiful* name!' 'Where's *that* from?' 'What *are* you?' It's all part of—"

"Let me guess, racism."

"—well, yeah! How people are okay with racism against Asians because they're outside the black-white binary. I'm not even talking about all the slant eyes and *konichiwas*. Like, you can still say chink on TV, and when there's any outrage, people think Asians are being humorless. Trannies, midgets, fatties, geezers, chinks, all fair game. You can outlaw hate crimes, but you can't force anyone to respect or desire you. So no one thinks we're oppressed."

Vanya loosed a spray of uppercase *eff*s and *pee*s. "Because you're *not*! Get over yourself! It's pure nineties PC self-pity. You're acting like I've never experienced discrimination, when I'm a disabled woman in tech. I'm sorry, but you've got it *so easy*. You're exempt from both white guilt and racial profiling, Stanford-educated, rich, young, male—and, hello, able-bodied! And dating a totally cute white girl! Asian privilege is the *bomb*!"

"So being marginalized and ridiculed isn't oppression?"

"Sure it is. And I'm saying you're *not*. You just like pretending you're oppressed because it lets you avoid responsibility. You're ballooning this tiny first-exposure branding issue into a race war."

"Interesting choice of words! World War II, Korea, Vietnam, the tsunami, nothing unites America better than *gooks dying by the millions*! Shit, let's just fucking nuke North Korea and China right now! Everyone wants to anyway!" Will touched his stupid forehead. "Sorry, sorry. I'm just saying my name's a trivial detail."

"Um, yeah, it's *totally* trivial, which is why I'm surprised that—" Vanya closed her laptop and rested her palms on it, grimacing at the bumpy little curb their feet formed beneath the blanket. "Why do I get so *drained* whenever I tell you my plans? Maybe because you naysay every idea I have?"

"I'm—" He almost said, *I'm not a naysayer*. "I totally support your show. But I'd like some say over how I'm presented, since it'll be so popular."

"Baby, don't patronize me. This show is my life now, and if you're going to be on it, you have to accept some tiny concessions. You know, married women have had to change their names forever. Not saying it's fair, I'm saying they compromised with the culture."

Will kicked aside the sheets to air out. Vanya would never take his name; hers was too saturated with brand equity. It'd be absurd to hyphenate or even adjoin them: N——dreeva, Andr——. At least marriage was on her mind. The engagement ring, that circle of high value, was still in Will's jacket pocket.

"You're right," Will said, though really he felt he was right, and much more mature for not saying so.

"So we're settling on N——?"

"Fine."

"Perfect. I'll handle everything." Vanya tapped at her laptop; an action item had been consummated. "Baby, long names don't put people off. Long *arguments* do."

Yes they did—and what put off people put off Vanya. Vanya sided with People, Will with Will. But the less considered re: that the better.

His name must have released some kind of stimulant from its severed end, because over the following week, Will ate more shit faster than ever, hunting bargains, researching components, drawing schematics. After six days he arrived at Vanya's place with a tangle of hardware in his shaking arms. Vanya buzzed him in. "I figured it out," he said.

Here was Vanya's sousveillance rig, a six-megapixel wearable webcam with an integrated mic. The primary webcam was a black prism the size of a cigarette lighter, with a blue LED and a lapel clip; a second HD webcam jutted upward from a flexible stand on the wheelchair's armrest to capture Vanya's face. Through a zip-tied fascicle of cords, both cameras were hooked to auxiliary batteries and three 128 GB SSDs in a single enclosure, and drew high-speed wireless from redundant EV-DO connections on two cell networks. Raw footage was automatically encoded, image-stabilized, HDR-filtered, and fed out live to the site. Vanya could type and video chat with viewers on her netbook. She was delighted that everything weighed only twenty-five pounds and stowed under her wheelchair. "An able-bodied person would get sciatica hauling this stuff around! I'm sure things'll get even lighter, but for now, my wheelchair's an asset. You're a genius! And I've been busy too. Want to see the beta client?"

Vanya logged in with her fourteen-character password, which Will made a mental note to crack later. The loud stomps of her typing made Will's wrists sympathy-tingle. The blue LED on her lapel camera flickered awake. Her screen displayed the side of Will's head, dithered and stuttering. He waved; his image remained still. "Why's it all laggy?"

"There's a six-second delay for filtering content, like on live TV. In case people try to mess with us."

Will's onscreen image waved, then turned to the screen and said in a nasal recorded voice, *Why's it all laggy?* Vanya laughed and repeated her reply in sync with her onscreen image. It repeated again in chorus, and Vanya and Will joined in with it until the air glimmered with screechy feedback and Vanya muted the speakers.

"Isn't it great?" she said. "We're feeding out to our live staging site, so technically anyone could see us right now. Baby, say something to the world."

Will looked at the blue light on Vanya's chest. Vanya was facing the screen. He looked at the screen, where he was looking at himself six seconds earlier looking at Vanya, i.e., the camera. "Hello, world," he said, and waited for his reply.

CHAPTER 6
She Can't Resist

The memory of oppressed people is one thing that cannot be taken away, and for such people, with such memories, revolt is always an inch below the surface.
—Howard Zinn

I. Handshake

Cory was due at the Handshake introduction seminar fifteen minutes ago. She was unshowered, hungry, and her anxietylocks were fraying into full-on hysterialocks, a viny mass with a corona of frizz whose ends were pompommed by stress-chewing. She pedaled awkwardly up Market Street on underinflated tires and in heels. A motorist, missing her by inches with his right turn, slowed to call her a cunt. *You almost killed me,* Cory thought; then amended: *You ARE killing EVERYONE.* How quaint cars would be. CORDELIA ROSEN = NO SIREE OLD CAR. How unbelievable that the world could sustain so many armageddons: Iraq, AIDS, Vietnam, Stalin, the Holocaust, slavery, the whole chronicle of suffering, decline, renaissance, trial by atrocity, all trumped by the very gases she exhaled. Or nukes.

The seminar was in a brutalist office building near a midsize homeless encampment and had no bike parking; she'd have to bring it in. With her bike sweat and flushed cheeks, Cory followed people in professional attire to the elevator bank. They held the door for her, and after a minute of trying to fit her bike in, she gave up and shouldered it up the stairs.

Reaching the third floor, she waited on the landing for her Lamaze breathing to subside. Inside, a vinyl banner reading HANDSHAKE WORKSHOPS hung over a row of folding tables staffed with employees. A white placard on an easel next to the door said SILENCE YOUR MOBILE. PHOTOS & NOTES PROHIBITED. Cory stashed her bike in a rear corner and headed to the tables, where she filled out an intake form with lies. Volunteers ushered her into the conference hall with a brochure and a name tag, which she left blank.

It was half-past but they hadn't started yet, probably to accommodate latecomers like Cory, who were here precisely because they needed this sort of handicap. Cory took an isolated aisle seat among the rows of pebbly black folding chairs, all facing a rostrum. Two chalkboards stood incompletely erased from some previous gathering whose lingering body heat still dampened the air. A projection panel hung above the chalkboards, displaying that shade of luminous darkness that represented black. Cory's bra straps chafed and her insoles were slushy.

The insignia on the brochure's cover was an Escheresque line drawing of two clasping hands whose wrists looped down and conjoined. The back cover featured blurbs from successful people she'd never heard of, and an introduction that she mentally copyedited:

HANDSHAKE WORKSHOPS

—YOURSELF AND MORE—

DISRUPT YOUR LIFE. Handshake is not only a world-renowned, award-winning series of lectures, workshops and colloquiums, nor is it merely an invigorating journey into the Marin Headlands. Handshake is a journey that equips you with exciting new conceptualizations and help you find deeper meaning in life which will enhance your personal effectiveness manifold.

HONESTY. PASSION. VISION. 93% percent of all Handshake graduates, from top executives to small business entrepreneurs, from big-wave surfers to golfers, from parents to painters, have indicated that their lives have been substantively revolutionized by Handshake's award-winning flagship educational offering, the Perch Program.

YOU WILL CHANGE YOUR LIFE . . . AND THE WORLD!

Cory fanned herself with the brochure, errors and all. In front of her, two men—two *guys* in hoodies and cargo shorts—sat splay-crotched. "Still in stealth mode working on rollout strategy," said the guy on the left, in a Giants cap. The back of his neck sported that line of wispy hairs you usually found under a navel. "Invite only beta. Gotta roll out the front-end and monetization, do a bit of dogfood, then UX with the unwashed before we demo at South By."

"Monetization-wise definitely freemium's the model for SaaS," replied the cropped-haired Indian guy. "And gamified coin bundles and badges and shit. Gamification plus freemium equals user acquisition."

"Dank. Can I post that? You want attrib, bro?"

That way he said *bro* with an ironic dip only made Cory loathe him in a different way. She used to think the language of power was just a substitution cipher of shibboleths. But it was more like an insect language: dense pheromone clouds communicating fear and attraction, hunger and envy, have and not.

The lights flickered. Cory turned and counted about a hundred some-odd people, some odd. A wiry man in a seersucker dress shirt and gray slacks with a worryingly conservative part in his brown hair, a sort of human wingtip, took the stage with a microphone. The house lights dimmed and the projection screen behind him displayed a large white arrow pointing downward.

"That arrow's the most important part of my discussion today," Perch said, his voice issuing from the speakers, a baritone bounce that Cory associated with gay Southern men. "Anyone know why?" He walked toward the arrow, then stood under it. Laughter crescendoed unevenly as people got the joke at different speeds. Cory jogged her legs, worrying about blood clots.

"My name is Evan Perch. I founded the Handshake Workshops in 1990, and today we've got branches in Shanghai, Tel Aviv, Busan, Oslo, Buenos Aires, Bangalore, and thirty other major cities. Our staff is seventy percent volunteer, which shows you our commitment to helping people reach their potential—we're here because we're passionate.

"People say America doesn't make things anymore. Handshake makes a special kind of person—we make makers. We make thought leaders and entrepreneurs, people who represent the best of the human condition: the crazy dreamers who look around and say, 'I can make this better.' That's the attitude that discovered continents, brought equality for all Americans, and is catapulting us into the new millennium with dazzling technologies.

"Now, unlike business development seminars that only focus on the Ps and Qs of organizational theory, Handshake recognizes the deeper truth: that your business develops only when you do. Our mission is to catalyze mass change through personal transformation."

From the back of the room came a sound like a shopping cart hitting a chain link fence. Cory's bike had toppled, and its upended wheel spun, embarrassed against momentum. Unperturbed, Perch moved his hand to his pocket and clicked to the next slide, which read **Instrumentality**.

"As any Handshake graduate will tell you, it's impossible to describe how we work; you gotta try it yourself. But generally, Handshake is a program that gives you the skill set to form revolutionary insights. And I mean 'program' literally—we've iterated our ideas into 'mental apps' anyone can apply to achieve breakthroughs. Extraordinariness is innate, but it takes a special mind-set to access. Whether you call it prayer, meditation, flow, or the zone, it's all about active self-realization.

"Collectively we call our apps 'the Instrumentality.' They draw on millennia of open-source thought: Moses, Jesus, Muhammad, Siddhartha, Confucius, Seneca, Jung, Reich, SRI International, Gandhi, Csikszentmihalyi, and Gladwell, combined with bleeding-edge cognitive-behavioral methodologies and neurobiological findings. Ancient ideas, modern messaging. The Instrumentality."

The slideshow advanced: **Ideas**. Cory's stomach revved, and she slouched to muffle it while Perch cranked his rotator cuff. "But not *all* old ideas are good. We also dismantle obsolete cultural notions. Let's start with one that drives me bonkers: the myth of modesty. I tell you, modesty—it's what we call a sham, it's fear of greatness. To paraphrase Shakespeare: conscience makes cowards of us all. But these days, America frowns on the bold. People who're just too damn honest.

"So here's the first app: *You're always someone's jerk*. People will resent you for being more open than they let themselves be. But you don't need the nitpickers and the critics. Anyone who's not on the bandwagon is dragging it down."

Cory grieved for his metaphor.

"Now, I could go on about our method, but like I said, you gotta *do* it. So let's get one of you up here." Perch surveyed the room, shading his eyes unnecessarily against the fluorescent light. His pointing finger oscillated twice over the audience, passing over wiggling arms before settling unmistakably on Cory. "The young lady in the blue shift. What's your name, hon?"

Clapping her notebook shut, Cory said, "Linda Troland."

"Linda, c'mon up here."

He indicated a microphone stand onstage, in front of the left chalkboard. Cory went up, unsure whether to grasp the mic or stand in front of it. Her face needed a wipe; her thyroid pleaded for a sandwich, a glass of soy milk, a bong rip, anything to cushion this.

"How do you spend your time, Linda?"

When she spoke, her microphone sounded quieter than Perch's. "I run an organization that throws fundraising events for progressive causes."

Perch wrote *fundraising* on the chalkboard. "Gosh, a young thing like you, managing a company."

"Well, I'm partly here to learn *how* to manage it."

"Ain't you lucky then! In the last year alone, the Instrumentality has helped hundreds of entrepreneurs, including C-level executives from HP, Genentech, Nvidia, who've found lots of success with our advanced insistence-training programs."

"But my organization is, you know," Cory said, "anticorporate. We want to change the system."

"I believe we do offer a radical approach to personal change."

"Well, I mean," Cory said, reeling her hands in front of her, "you can improve and fulfill yourself forever without doing anything socially useful. That's the *problem*. Being comfortable, gathering neat objects and experiences for your little team. That myopia about suffering which's just gotten worse since the globalized—"

"Whoa, back up! What I'm sensing, Linda, is not a management problem." Perch walked to a chalkboard. "What's our most lethal modern sickness? Cancer? You can beat it, like my wife did. Heart disease? Diet, exercise, and baby aspirin. No, the answer is cynicism." He appeared to relish the time it took to write out *cynicism*. "It's terminal. Depression, boredom, anger, and apathy are all symptoms of cynicism. And I gotta say, dismissing personal change is classic cynicism." He pivoted. "I bet you're all sick of it. You're sick of doubting whether success is achievable, whether your dreams are worth the effort, sick of people nitpicking your dreams into dust. You're sick of people not caring. That sound right, Linda?"

Cory tilted her head. "I'm not sure what this has to do with my company?"

"Forget your company. I want to know your *business*. Is

it fair to say you're skeptical about us? Got a few nitpicks of your own?"

"That's valid."

"Tell me why, hon."

Cory investigated Perch's shiny face for tone cues, but only saw an anticipatory niceness. "Well, to start with, you make entrepreneurs out to be these heroic, special white knights, when it's a fact that lots of them go on to evade taxes, buy politicians and draft legislation, plunder and dismantle public resources, and trash the environment, with zero accountability, all to enrich themselves and their shareholders."

"Linda, our core belief is that people are decent, but sometimes misguided. Seeing anybody as fundamentally evil, well, that's a cynical sham. I know I'm repeating myself, but we've only covered one app out of over a hundred that we'll install on the platform of You." As if on cue, he advanced the slide to read **You Are a Platform** and interrupted Cory's reply with an anapestic throat-clear, continuing: "Though our methods aren't for everybody."

"But you said anyone would get a breakthrough."

"Anyone who's *willing*. Some people love their convenient shams a little too much. You can't learn anything if you already 'know everything,' isn't that right? You gotta see the ulterior motives behind the arguing. Linda, keep the comments coming. I love your passion."

"Right now I'm also curious why you keep repeating certain terms"—Cory made twitching bunny ears of her fingers—"'instrumentality, sham, nitpick, cynicism.' If Handshake is about individuality, why use this preset vocab? It feels ideological."

"Tools aren't ideological, Linda. You use them however you

want. Some technologies are made from steel or silicon; our apps are made from words and ideas, distilled and honed to a razor's edge. No point making a wheel less round."

"What about tire treads?"

"Classic nitpicking! More toxic cynicism."

Cory twisted the microphone from its stand. "You might be conflating cynicism with critical thought."

"Ah, 'critical thought.' Well, *that* sure sounds smart. Must be only stupid people are happy and only the greedy succeed, right? Y'all, I'm grateful, because Linda's giving us an A-number-one opportunity to test-drive the Instrumentality. What's going on in that superbrain of yours, Linda? Trying to think of another reason why you're right and I'm wrong?"

With sweaty, shaking hands, Cory wrung her microphone like a pepper mill. "There's no ulterior motive. I just can't debate someone who evades my questions."

A few sinuses in the audience crooned disapproval. Perch switched his mic to his left hand and quelled the air with his right. "Because you're asking the wrong questions. You want me to 'prove' Handshake works. If I describe a hot fudge sundae, does that 'prove' it's tasty? You gotta *try* it. But if you can't change your mind, you ain't changing nothing."

Dehydration and hunger tingled in Cory's gums, making it difficult to dismantle Perch's reductive sloganeering, which relieved pain by amputating the intellectual appendages that felt it—yet which also seemed effective in motivating people. It smelled of remedial introspection, of another straight white patriarch using half-assed pseudoscience to tell her what reality was. Right now some decimating factoid would put Perch in his place, but all she could summon forth was a bulge of author names and annoyance. To adequately parse his bullshit she'd need three weeks to write a twenty-page paper. Her head felt thin and permeable as a salamander. "All you're doing is putting me down."

"Pardon my fronsay, but sometimes we've got to fuck with you, so you can *see* yourself. You're used to breaking things apart with the hammer of your wits; we're offering you a sackful of nails. Now, show of hands. Who thinks Linda here is holding something back?" Many hands went up. "Who thinks she's terrified of being wrong?" Hands remained up. "Already everyone sees it. Why's that? Are you afraid if you stop criticizing for one second, you'll have to change? Worried people'll ask questions about *you* instead? Like: Has nitpicking ever made Linda happy? Or is she just armoring her vulnerabilities with smartypants excuses? Even that defensive way you're wrapping your arm around you. *Sham*'s just *shame* minus the E."

Cory held her arm in place, though now it yearned painfully to straighten. The stickiness of her dry mouth crackled in the speakers. "You're just deflecting my questions with ad hominem assertions."

"Linda here's a first-rate shammer, brain like a hammer, nobody gonna scam 'er! Listen, to be honest, I've got no idea what 'ad hominem' means, but it sounds awful smart."

"It means you're attacking my character instead of—"

"Couldn't *wait* to define it for me, could she, folks?" Perch said, putting up a let-me-finish. "Linda, I hear what you're saying. You make damn sure of that. But we want to hear what you're *not* saying."

"Uh . . ."

"We're offering help. But if you're going to be cynical and nitpicky and lazy and make excuses, you'll never break through. It's why your business is in the toilet. Why you're always arguing. Why your relationships fizzle out. Am I wrong about any of that?"

Cory's vision tunneled to enclose Perch's face and his hand holding his microphone at necktie level. She watched his mouth minutely for the flick of a forked tongue.

Perch continued, "If I'm wrong, and you're not holding anything back, steak dinner's on me. Now don't poke holes in this question, answer it. What are you lying about?"

"There's no way to answer that. And to be honest, this intense hectoring is starting to feel like a cult initiation."

"You just *can't* resist!" Perch said through a pummeling smile. "Always throwing out wild defenses when your back's to the wall. Because you're 'uncomfortable.' Because honesty would transform your life, and that terrifies you. Can you swear that there's *nothing* you're lying about?" Perch showed her an almost-pinch. "Are you too damn proud to give this much? *This* tiny bit?"

What a cheap debating tactic. She'd seem pigheaded if she conceded nothing, and silence would implicate her. The audience strained to make eye contact with her. "Fine, I'll bite, but only to give an example of—"

"Let's hear it."

"So, it's a long story. My name isn't really Linda. But the reason I did that is so—"

Cory was drowned out by the audience's gullish uproar. She sucked in her lower lip, which was starting to blubber. Perch slapped his chest and hooted. "Wow. *Wow.* What *is* your name, then?"

"Cory Rosen."

"Cory, your journey's just begun. Will you continue your education with us?"

"I think my dad, uh, already signed me up."

"Well, sheee-it! See, folks, all you need is one person in your life who's committed to your success. You've taken a huge step. Everyone, give it up for Cory."

As Cory left the stage, a volunteer intercepted her to take the microphone she'd forgotten to let go of. She headed back to her seat and was too dizzy to follow the rest of the lecture. The urge to chew and gobble was coming over her. She sucked on a sour section of hair.

"Now, everyone, here's the pitch. This month we've knocked down the weekend seminar to four hundred and ninety-nine dollars. That's still a chunk, I know, but this ain't no vacation. Take this opportunity. Don't let this be another sooner-or-later. Register now.

"Once you're squared away, I'd like you to head over to that next room. We've got refreshments, and some of our graduates have set up booths for their own specialized courses you can also sign up for. Okay, everybody, thanks for listening. I wish you all remarkable deeds."

Cory clapped with palms stiffened to produce movement but no sound. She returned her notebook to her messenger bag, and as people stood, someone patted her on the back. The jet stream of bodies buffeted her into the other room, circlets of sweat collecting at everyone's hairlines. The crowd slowed to a saunter between four long blue-dust-ruffled tables, whose signs she read as she headed to the refreshments across the room:

Blanche LaPintro, Nov. 9: LATE? GREAT!: *Supercharge Your Commute*

Ellen Stokes, Nov. 12: YOU CONTAIN MONOPOLIES:
How Wond.er Leveraged and Monetized a Personal Brand

Bill Lazzard and Cat Hu, Nov. 13: THE 18-HOUR
ORGASM: *Passionate Parturition*

Talim Cook and Chester Leary, Nov. 13: WEB YOU.0:
Agile Workflows and Playflows

Hattie Dement, Nov. 14: BREATHE INPUT, BREATHE
OUTPUT: *Codejamming for Yogis*

Queeny Hartillo, Nov. 15: PRACTICUM ON
BODYSTORMING: *Shuffling Your Creative Deck*

Emerging on the other side, Cory queued up at the refreshments table, flexing her jaws. Hors d'oeuvres went tray-
to-mouth: she began at the platter of deep-fried puff pastries,
chased them with a plastic flute of sparkling cider before falling upon the croquettes, each topped with a little quiff of sour
cream and crusted with smoky brown flecks; muffling a belch,
she sampled the adorable peanut-butter-fudge mini-cupcakes.
Then she re-upped on croquettes, with another flute of cider to
cool her stomach.

Unease kicked in instantly: the suspicion that everyone
who'd seen her humiliated was now watching her pig out.
And the food, through the eyes of remorse, was pretty much
solid fat and sugar. It was delicious, which was bad because
vegetarian food had to be *really* unhealthy to taste delicious. Wait—*was* it vegetarian? Fuckin' A! The brown flecks

could've been bacon—or some frightened veal calf with shattered legs trembling against its steel peg and collar, baying through snipped vocal cords. She felt pale. *I'm sorry, piggy, I'm so so sorry,* she thought, ashamed at her childishness, then appalled that she could consider her own earnest moral sentiments childish.

The savory grease clung at the back of her tongue and perfused her sinuses. She made for the bathroom and rinsed her mouth with hot water, but more grease delectated up from her throat, so she squirted a blob of pink hand soap from the dispenser and swallowed it. Now she was full of cloying petro-puke *and* cannibalized flesh. She turned to enter a stall, lowered to her knees, and made the familiar pattern of motions, hair pushed back and three fingers snaked into her mouth, repeating nothing in her head as she sang out her stomach. As it splashed and clouded out below her, she remembered how virtuous and light it felt to have done this. Though not while you did it. Then you were alone and it always hurt.

She got up and flushed, banging her elbow on the tampon box. At the mirror she struck at wet spots in her sweater with a paper towel, then rejoined the convention hall. Everything seemed derealized, like televised fireworks, all color and brightness robbed of dimension. Heading to her fallen bicycle, she felt her shoulder gripped. It was Evan Perch; he held her canvas bag, which she'd forgotten at her chair.

"Cory, I wanted to say, you blew everyone away. I think you're ready to kick the world's butt. Even your hair's like Wonder Woman. What's your background? Italian? Black Irish?"

"White Jewish."

"Go figure. Smart, hardworking."

Cory sighed and looked out at the milling throng. The thrilling mong. "You didn't seem to feel that way onstage."

"But you see what we achieved up there? We plowed through the bullshit. Listen, I know it's uncomfortable. Honesty is hard work. So I'll fess up too. I knew your real name all along."

Cory leaned back. "Excuse me?"

"Your father told me you were coming. Friend of mine, and a terrific entrepreneur. That's why I picked you. Imagine my surprise when you tried giving me the end run! I didn't mean to embarrass you, but I fooled you a little to get you to stop fooling *yourself*." Perch laughed and put his hand on her back, easing her away from the crowd. "Cory, you're smart; that's a fact. But your brain is getting between you and success. Now you need to be *willing* to succeed. No more guilt, blame, or self-sabotage. It takes some willingness up front. One weekend. Gotta be worth a try. Risk is its own reward."

They were at one of the registration tables at the back of the room, where a clipboard materialized in Cory's hands. She couldn't concentrate with Perch watching, so she skimmed the dense text, filled in her info, and scratched her zigzag on the signature line. Cory pumped Perch's extended hand, which was dry, large, and warm, like an oven mitt in recent use. Then he was striding away, and Cory walked to her bike, winding and pulling at, sucking and spitting out her ambivalencelocks.

Now she knew why Barr wanted her to attend. Perch's insistence and utilitarianism and meaty hand recalled nobody so much as Barr himself; she'd been delivered into the suffocating confidences of a proxy father. But Taren had been a father too. Cory reminded herself that the world was full of fathers.

II. The New Management

They rode a bus up to Marin, which dropped them a three-mile hike away from the Handshake "D-Bunker," an angular art deco facility. She'd barely let her backpack touch the floor of the entryway when she and the other 149 attendees were assigned colored bandannas and divided up into Focus Associations. After some light stretching, they attended a series of "lectercizes" by moderators in gold-trimmed suits, their personalities embossed with Evan Perch's chipperness. They were corralled from one wood-paneled auditorium to another to receive suppositories of insight. #3: *Flood Yourself in Failure.* #5: *Shitkick the Nitpick.* #12: *Approach, Reproach, Rapproche.* They were told to call up their parents and confront them. During her turn at the phone bank, Cory faked a twenty-minute argument with the SFMTA transit info menu.

On Soapbox Alpha, the square parquet stage at the center of the main demonstration hall, everyone took turns recounting their failures. Cory missed much of what the others said as she planned out her own story, but when she took the stage it all splurted forth: failed relationships, body hate, the daily inability to reconcile moral urgency with lifestyle. The moderator offered follow-up prompts ("Now ADMIT that the BIG LIE OF COMPROMISE is stifling NECESSARY confrontations!"), and her associates followed suit ("WHY are you SUCH a GODDAMN SLAVE TO ACCEPTANCE?!").

That evening they performed The Handshake: half the attendees plunged their hands into buckets of ice water for two minutes, then pulled them out and grasped hands with their partners, who'd been holding their hands over a fire, sustaining the grasp and silent eye contact for ten minutes, the goals of which were to:

☞ *Prosper diagonalized contegrative social strategies*

☞ *Reinforce physiocognitive correlates of trust (mirroring / muscle empathy)*

☞ *Affirm objectivity of feeling*

☞ *Desublimate, desublimate, desublimate!*

As Cory's face touched the pillow after the first night, calories splendidly cashed, she swan-dove into sleep.

The three remaining days were a jumble of unscheduled hazing and noisy introspection. She got along fine on the two daily meals, in spite of erratic serving schedules, but had more trouble with the surprise three A.M. confrontation sessions, when people were better disposed to honesty. She and her associates drank coffee to fight hoarseness as they tenderized each other with their thoughts exactly.

Grain of salt, sure, but if Cory was here, she may as well get motivated. And it was nice to have a sympathetic audience for once, cheering her rants about corporatization, mandated by the left's apathy and single-issue fractiousness and the right's hypocritical moralizing, between which all real dialogue had been replaced by a seesaw of factional demagogy and counter-demagogy, against a backdrop of financial fraud and global

racist classist imperialist cishet patriarchal domination so outrageous yet so mundanely normalized that all informed dissent
sounded paranoid, and though the only chance of resistance
required revolutionary socioeconomic and cultural integration,
even as an organizer it felt like she was on a one-woman cru-
sade, which wouldn't matter so much if just *one* person supported her, but dating took so much time and it was so *fucking
stupid* . . . Anywhere else this would've felt self-indulgent, but
her associates applauded her "passion." The more Cory let it
out, the righter she felt.

One associate asked whether Cory was eating her feelings. No, she was getting *drunk* on her feelings, and by the
end of the fourth day, the trembling cups of pride-frustration-
shame-pity she'd guzzled had made her black out with confes-
sional intimacy. When the shuttle dropped the graduates at
the Embarcadero on Monday evening, they hugged and wept
until chinstamps of tears darkened each shoulder, relishing the
stares of pedestrians navigating around them. Let them see
some human feeling for once, Christ, are we robots? If she was
going to cry in public, she would at least refuse to apologize.

SINCE TAREN'S DEATH, a postcoup atmosphere lingered in the
Socialize offices: no one knew what to do besides present a
face of game compliance to the new regime. It felt weird acting
without Taren's say-so, but since Cory's permission binge at
Handshake, everything seemed viable. Quitting weed triggered her migraines at first, but with enough coffee, she could
bounce around until five P.M. on chickpea salad and seltzer.
She canceled Taren's final event, a pro–bike lane BMX demonstration at UN Plaza called Sick Transit, and met with a CPA,
who helped defer Socialize's debt a few months longer. She

talked the office's aging Moscovian landlord into extending their lease, citing the half-truth that Cory represented competent new management. And she forced Will to force her to learn how to google, so she could search for moneymaking schemes, yielding an antiwealth of irrelevance—she read news articles about corporate sponsorships for college students, people who sold shares in themselves, even people who'd tattooed logos on their foreheads, restoring branding to its conceptual roots: showing who you belonged to.

Work was a good excuse to keep away from home. As housemates drifted away from the warehouse, Cory had regrettably delegated housemate recruiting to Roopa, who'd brought in dozens of her former housemates from a converted bordello in East Oakland called Mr. Floppy's Flophouse, lowering the drawbridge to a siege of Burners, burlesque dancers, anarchist Christian envirocore troubadours, hacktivists, skilltoy enthusiasts, and crustpunks with bandannaed pit bulls, all subcultures attracted to large, provisional, nonflammable living spaces. They moved in three to a room with names like 8-Ball and Clèf, and Cory would dodge around clusters of them huffing THC from turkey bags or practicing LED buugeng. Trapezes and silks were hooked to the ceiling gantries, and Cory was more than once startled awake by the plasticky pop of aerialists' feet striking gym mats. On weekends they held backyard community salons: Gourmet Geophagy, Barefoot Jogging, Jelqing, Biothermal Sous Vide, Asexual Theory. With Cory in absentia, they voted to name the warehouse "Iniquity" and dubbed Roopa the Dean of Iniquity.

So it was good that Cory was too busy to feel ostracized. She bought new modular shelves and cord caddies for the office; she swept and vacuumed, rearranged desks, attempted to deodorize the air pockets that smelled like hot dogs, then lashed back her hair and gave the toilet its first-ever cleaning, sloshes echoing in the unventilated bathroom. There wasn't much to do with the waterstained concrete walls and bare dangling lightbulbs and the carpet sample they used for a welcome mat, but the office was more or less tidy when Cory woke on the couch at six A.M. on her first Monday as a superior, ready to formalize the transition.

Ramping up to a key reprioritization, the Instrumentality mandated an inventorying of synergistic relational assets, i.e., employees. She made a list on the whiteboard. There was the street team of interns who flyered for free admission. Then Martina Inez, the half-time office manager Cory liked a lot. She was a Kansas City transplant, loud and funny with a James Dean pompadour, librarian glasses, and tattered sleeveless smock dresses resewn from XXL motorcycle shirts hugging a vavooming body line that Cory would only consider fat if it were her own. Cory loved having Martina around, but a few weeks ago she'd found Martina's résumé in the office printer's tray.

John Grabanger was senior by far, a stubbly, ptotic man who tended to comport himself like some vital ambassador of the sixties sent to steer society off its present crash course—and in that sense he was conservative, the way some radicals believed their battles would never obsolesce, and rather than embrace change ended up regressing to the root of *radical: radix*, root, subterranean and immovable and bitter, as they mistook unanticipated forms of progress for decline. But Cory still appreciated his free labor.

Pascal Jeffries was the new hire, a sweet childless forty-something on whose flimsy shoulders you could easily picture a shawl. Cory had met her in 2006 when they canvassed for gun control. They'd attracted a Second Amendment fanboy who gave the usual race-coded bunk about how "decent Americans" had to defend themselves against "gangs," and Pascal had told him things like, *We cannot show a cold heart to slavery's inheritors,* and said, *Sir, would you agree to participate in an encounter session with a Lake Merritt youth named Victor?,* until the guy left with his bleeding-heart mealymouthed liberal prejudices reinforced. But she was reliable, diligent, and unpaid.

To preserve momentum, Cory had put off identifying the Trouble Vector: Luis Garcia. Ever since Cory had been promoted ahead of Luis, he'd treated her with the same contempt he'd shown to Taren. He wore noise-canceling earmuff headphones at his desk, forcing Cory to walk across the entire office to tap his shoulder whenever she needed to ask him something, causing him to yank off his headphones and glare at her. At one meeting he'd bragged about doing tina and getting jerked off in a bar booth the previous night, and another time he'd unbuttoned his jeans to show off a flare-up of crabs. Everyone else thought he was funny, defending him when Cory tried to build consensus about his inappropriate behavior—*That's how Luis do, he's just a drama queen with no filter,* Martina said. But why give him a pass for performing a stereotype, hold him to a lower standard? Come on, Cory wanted to say, you're the only queer person of color here, I *really want* you to be cool.

But even though he logged barely half of Cory's hours, he was indispensable. He was their drag liaison, moonlighting as Mozzy Creampie, and Socialize relied on his contacts for a big slice of attendance, since the queens were strong draws. Cory had considered leapfrogging Luis and forming her own drag community connections, but he'd hear about it eventually.

Beside his name, Cory wrote *manage,* then wiped the board clear.

As employees began arriving at 9:15 A.M., Cory greeted them, standing at the head of the small white conference table. She shuffled the two sheets of paper in front of her until Luis arrived twenty minutes late.

"Mornin'!" Cory said. "Fun weekends?" They sat in silence until Martina said, *Pretty good.* "Cool. Today I want to talk about the future direction of the company, which is forward, I mean, toward"—Cory made a dumbshow with her arms—"forward toward a goal we'll set together. I want us all to really *own* our work. Move in, guys, sit closer! Let's circle the wagons!"

She searched the whiteboard tray for the green dry-erase marker until she realized she was holding it. She wrote *own your work,* which felt injunctive, but there it was. "Some business first. We need cash. Cuts are gonna happen. Starting with the free sodas"—the room crackled with sucked cheeks—"I know, it sucks, but we're doing it to avoid compromising on the important stuff. No more furloughs."

"Wow, hooray," said Luis, giving a sedate fist pump.

"I've got other ideas too," Cory said. "Like, what's one thing we have plenty of?"

"Debt," said Luis.

"Leftover flyers. Instead of recycling them, we can use them as stationery."

"We're going to invoice on scrap paper?" said Luis. "Well, that's professional."

"We'll make it look cool. Okay, next item. The way the Mission's changing, the venue scene is totally different. The Knockout, El Rio, and Elbo Room are out. Twelve Galaxies is closing. The Make Out Room, Pop's, Jack's, the Phone Booth, and the

Attic will give us weekdays. We'll have to tap art spaces, cafés, even backyards. Alcohol licensing will be a problem. We're not going to drop booze, but officially we'll have to promote dry. We need to show that dry can be fun and sexy."

"Fun and sexy," Luis said. "Let's inflate condoms into party balloons! Ooh, I'm getting all *dry* just thinking about it."

Cory clapped. "Now, I've blocked out some time for brainstorming events based on our passions. What are our passions?"

Nobody spoke. How had Taren managed them? With the built-in boundaries of age and maleness, probably. "Ideas, guys? Blue-sky me!"

One hand propping up his miserable face, Luis raised his other hand. "Internet."

Cory wrote *internet* on the board. "Cool. What else?"

Luis kept his hand up. "No, let's *talk* about this. We have *no* online presence. We're called *Socialize* and we're not even on a social network," he said. "Social means Internet now."

"I've been meeting with a web developer."

"We can't afford soda or paper but we're hiring a web developer?"

"He's pro bono. It's been covered."

"Oh really?" Luis tittered. "Are you covering his pro bono?"

"Okay, Luis? Inappropriate."

John raised his hand. "Long as we're on the subject, my passion is sex."

Cory added *sex* to the board in smaller letters, pulling a face while she was turned away. "Is this gonna be relevant, John?"

"SF sex culture is strong and ripe for politics. The Lusty Lady, the Citadel, OneTaste, the Power Exchange, Open Enterprises, Mission Control, the Folsom Street Fair, the Tenderloin strip clubs, the Castro bathhouses. Once prostitution gets decriminalized next year, sex work will be a huge industry. Need I go on? Kink.com just bought the Armory for $15 million. I've visited. *Kegs* of lube."

"Websites are how people make money these days," Luis said, glazed over with tired contempt.

Cory wanted to ask how and why a website would buy a building. "What's your idea, John?"

"We could team up with the CSC for the Masturbate-a-Thon. No overhead, lots of exposure."

"Ha, exposure for real," Martina said. "They start at eight A.M. Can you imagine getting up that early to jerk off all day?"

Cory gulped down a wave of reverse peristalsis. "How does that raise money?"

"We'll charge," John said.

"Um, that might be illegal."

"Who cares? Do I have the green light?"

"Let's table it for now. Pascal, you got anything?"

Pascal lifted her head by two degrees. Her stutters made her sound anticlimactic. ". . . I think. W-we could do. Pop-up shops?"

"What're those?"

"It's like. You put up a temporary store at a bar or street corner. Anywhere. And sell things there. Or offer services. It's both a store. And an event."

"Oh, neat!" Cory said. "I like it. But what would we sell?"

"Local crafts," said Pascal. "Silk-screen stand. Vintage clothes."

"Girl, you are *shredding*! Those are great ideas!"

"Photo booths," said Martina.

"Kissing booths," said John.

"Even a basic blog with a 'Donate' button on it would be better than nothing," said Luis.

Cory's arm sprinted to record the cross talk: book swaps, speed dating, karaoke, mojitos, rescue-shelter petting zoo. "Cool," Cory said. "But we need a bigger surge of cash." She stepped back to observe the board broadly, capping her dry-erase marker with her thumb. These were good, thrifty ideas. She closed her eyes, trying to picture an event hall. It'd be chaos. Only an outdoor venue could hold enough people to—

"Oh my god!" Cory slammed her marker down onto the table and the cap popped off. "Dolores Park!"

She wished she'd been calmer because now they were expecting something brilliant. She picked up the marker again and circled the entire list. "We'll do all of it. An outdoor event with DIY attractions. Sell slots to vendors, and run some booths of our own. I mean, everyone hangs out there on weekends anyway. It's right off the J. Young and participatory. Forty years ago that park was only good for getting murdered in; now it's a symbol of civic rehab."

"It also used to be a Jewish cemetery," Luis said.

Cory stooped to pick up the marker's cap, her brain spiraling. "We can put a hiatus on charity fundraising and raise cash for our event. Shit, this is hella crazy! What do you guys think?" John and Pascal were looking concerned, and Luis was angling his phone at her. "What?"

"Your teeth," Martina said, pointing indicatively to her own.

"Something stuck?" Cory rubbed her teeth. Her fingertip shone with blood. She excused herself and went to the bathroom mirror: dark red channels edged her teeth. She ran the faucet cold and swished until the water wasn't pink, then returned to the meeting. "Sorry guys, I just started flossing again.

So, I was saying: a Dolores Park event. Big-big-big. How does that sound? Thoughts?"

Luis pouted hawk-like. "Coordinating hundreds of vendors selling bougie little earrings and knickknacks. Sounds fun."

He had a varsity letter in sideline sarcasm, that fangless type of dissent you could only counter with unflappable sincerity. "No, Luis, it's lots of *work*. That's what you *do* at *work*. Let's take it to a vote, okay? Who's interested in this event, bearing in mind that we have to raise twelve thousand dollars in six months?" Everyone raised their hands except Luis, who skittered his fingernails on the table. "Great, it's on," Cory said, feeling his hate-squint spearing through her. "Luis," Cory said, "if you're not excited about the event, there's something else I'd love you to do."

"Yessir?"

"Leave."

"What?"

Cory leaned over the table, supported by her fists. "You're out of the company. Be gone by lunchtime. I'm not Taren. If you're too good for us, if you can't deal with a female authority figure, go shit in someone else's hat. I'll even lay you off so you can collect unemployment. Deal?"

Luis's tongue skated across his teeth to form a bitchy bulge in his cheek. He knocked his chair over as he stood, collected his headphones and Members Only jacket from the closet, and slammed the front door behind him, leaving his coworkers stricken. Cory let them adjust. It felt wrong to do Taren's end-of-meeting cheer, where everyone joined their left hands ("Because the Left is *right* and the Right is *crazy*!"), so she dismissed them.

"Oh and hey, good news," Cory called out as they migrated

to their desks. "Pascal and John, you're both part-time now, if you want. Martina, you get a raise. Good job, guys."

That night, alone in the office, Cory yanked her body out of her chair like it was a goat on a leash. She cut the lights, armed the security system, and as she hustled out of the beeping room with her bike, she paused at the printout Taren had taped to the front door, a quote she'd never wanted to tell him was misattributed:

> First they IGNORE you
> then they LAUGH AT you
> then they FIGHT you
> then you WIN
> —MAHATMA GANDHI

Cory was ready—fastening her bike helmet straps under her chin—to stop being ignored and laughed at. She didn't even care if she won. She just wanted the big fight.

III. Looks/Feelings

Cory was awake at four A.M., with none of the tiredness she'd been defying all day long, staring out her window at the falling moon. A rumpled panel of streetlight rested on her sheets. She was failing even to lie still and be unconscious.

She got up and went into her closet for her scale and full-length mirror. She mounted the scale, impartial but always unfair—157. So now she couldn't even round down. She stepped off and leaned the mirror against the wall, hoping its slight inflex would flatter her. She lifted her T-shirt. In the dark her belly looked like a stack of folded dishrags. She was vegetarian and biked everywhere, so she wasn't morbidly obese, though all obesity *felt* morbid. She used to be thin, with willowy arms, an uncreased stomach; could sit on people's laps without *worry;* eat any and all unenlightened calories. But after her hunger strikes in college, her metabolism had imploded under the rebound of stress eating and dining hall starch.

Now and then she could convince herself that her very body was a fuck-you to the beauty myth, but it felt cheap to politically rationalize something unintentional. Occasionally she thought she could be pretty, given enough time and money: she had large russet eyes and a straight nose. Her breasts were washably spaced. But she knew most people would call them flappy, walleyed, unfit for photographing, glum rodents creeping underfoot amid the hormone-enhanced livestock. And all of it would worsen! At twenty-four she already saw herself prematurely aging, the shrunken teeth and crinkled knuckles— middle age, which, like the Middle Ages, was a dark age. Without her youth, she'd only have her unsexy principles.

Jesus, was this really how it had to be for women, this constant dwelling upon crampy, jiggly, gassy uglinesses? Or, equally depressing, was she *worse,* an anxious caricature of the feminized vulnerability she'd educated herself against? She felt run down by the mystifying hetero economy of looks. You wanted looks from the good-looking; looks were nonscarce, but unfairly apportioned to the good-looking. It felt awful to be leered at, and awful to be invisible. A luxury commodity that, for all its exclusivity, sure did a lot of advertising.

Cory pondered this, how it all came down to packaging, to look and feel, as she lay awake, hoping her brain would assign her partial credit.

The next day, Henrik surprised her with a phone call, in typical fashion talking without identifying himself or saying hello. Did she want to get dinner? Of course she did, and she said yes, but she didn't want to risk asking if this constituted a date. She left work early and went home to repair herself. Tonight she would perform a burlesque of gender. In the shower she used Roopa's conditioner until her knotted hair felt like something that fingers could conceivably run through. She plucked her eyebrows into neat circumflexes and borrowed Roopa's kohl and foundation. Her leg razor paused over her bush—she hated the idea of shaving, so she wavered between feminism and optimism before choosing the former. She chose a short-brimmed gray cap to cast a strategic crescent of shade over her raccoon eyes, and her blue shift dress, black heels, a dark lip, prink, sniff-check. In the mirror she looked both acceptable and not at all herself.

A half hour late for dinner, she vaulted off her bike to meet Henrik, who was leaning against the restaurant's facade in a white fleece, and they hugged over her saddle. She locked her bike to a streetlamp and entered the restaurant with the serenity of a dryad, feeling herself slip into a dangerous reverie in which they were already dating, with synchronized schedules, plans to move to a bigger place with a rooftop garden, back rubs, adopted children . . . though she'd settle for an open relationship. Or just sex. Even once. Surely Linda's claim on Henrik had expired after these two years, and really, since she'd dumped him rather spectacularly, she had no claim to begin with. It'd been years since Cory had been close to Linda anyway; Cory loved her but didn't necessarily owe her anything, and by now she'd probably had a million boyfriends; it'd be selfish of her not to forgive Cory for doing something good for herself by dating Henrik, which hadn't even happened yet and probably wouldn't, so whatever.

They were seated and the waitress came. This was that vegan restaurant where you had to order in a humiliating way. "I Am Transformed," Henrik told the waitress.

"I Am Vibrant," Cory said, "without guacamole."

She added a carafe of sangria, feeling girdled with anxiety about renegotiating friendship boundaries, but Cory would not let herself be ashamed about feeling things and saying how she felt. She mustered an ice cap of poise. "Your hair's getting so long!" she said, reaching across the table to tug on the curls grazing his shirt collar.

"Just the back part I can't cut myself," Henrik said. "Hereditary mullet."

She caught Henrik up on her work at Socialize. He listened comfortably, wiping his blond brow and sipping water. The sangria made her feel like she was in a revolving restaurant, a sweet slow headswirl. Her high heel grazed Henrik's sneaker under the table and she glanced under the table to signal that it was an accident but wished she hadn't. She laid out her Dolores Park event idea.

"Sounds fun. I'd go," Henrik said. "What are you fundraising for?"

"Everything. Any worthwhile cause."

"Isn't that spreading things kind of thin?"

Did she need to defend her eclectic politics? You were expected to wave only one flag: fighting for animal rights meant you really loved animals, but fighting for animal rights *and* trans rights and green energy and the homeless and single-payer health care implied an agenda. But you couldn't care only about what directly affected you, or about "major" causes.

Individuals, after all, were minor causes. Educated middle-class white Americans had every opportunity to spin multiple plates. In a sense she *did* support a single cause: consciousness-raising, rerouting the torrents of devotion misspent in partisanship and narco-entertainment. Why start somewhere when you could start everywhere?

"No such thing as too thin," Cory said, "as they say. Can you help me brainstorm?"

For an hour they whacked around fundraising ideas and a name for the event, until Henrik suggested "Recreate."

Cory kittened at the back of his hand with her fingertips. "That's so clever! Recreate '08. It acknowledges that things are bad without being a bummer. It's an imperative, like Socialize. And it fits with the park concept. Henrik, you're amazing."

"What's amazing is how amazing I'm not."

"Hey."

You could never tell Henrik to lighten up because he was already "just kidding," and flattery only goaded him to deeper self-deprecation and made him suspect you were being disingenuous, though he'd never accuse you to your face, and if you tried to preemptively assure him you *weren't* being disingenuous, it just proved to him that you *knew* you were. *Henrik,* she wanted to say, *I like you, just be yourself, you can't screw this up.* If only he held a certain color and size of feeling for her in his chest. Of course, having dated Linda, he'd have to downgrade lookswise, and men were oh-so-loath to. Though there had to be Good Men, smart allies with sane body standards. Henrik was Good, probably. Pushing back her forlornness, she asked how he'd been.

Cory hadn't stopped grinning once during this entire meal, which made it hard for Henrik not to grin back. If he were honest he'd tell her how he'd been sliding, having to take bigger doses of medication that he didn't have the insurance to pay for anymore. Was scared. But he couldn't take it there, not in a vegan restaurant playing MC Solaar, with Cory in flattery mode. When you accepted a hollow compliment you validated a misperception. All compliments came freighted with uncertainty, along axes of sincerity, accuracy, intention, rhetoric. Trust was an arms race: facial expressions were supposed to circumvent lying, but faces could be concealed, so you went to kinesics and paralinguistics, and still voices were misconstrued, gestures mistaken, even silence misheard. At every word you were judged by what you had the least control over: everything. Most people went with gut-feel, but that was just cognitive priming. Even total honesty didn't remain true for long, nor, if he was honest, did it mean anyone would understand or care. He wanted to say he was miserable, jobless, and frightened, but the best she could do for him was to treat him as if he weren't, so there was no point in saying so.

Cory was twisting her napkin into a stiff wand, waiting for Henrik to speak. "How's grad school?"

"I left, sort of."

Judging that they were close enough to bypass the decorum of *what* and *how come,* Cory nodded and said, "It must've been tough being stuck on campus."

"Yeah. I couldn't—yeah."

Finishing sangria three, Cory asked if he was living in the city. Yeah, he was staying with a friend in SoMa. Same as Cory! Cross streets? Seventh and Brannan? Whoa, they were neighbors! Who was the friend?

"This girl I'm seeing," Henrik said.

Cory felt a surprise warp in her inner ear, as if an elevator she was dozing in had stopped. She emptied the sangria carafe into her glass, then drank it and chewed the wine-sodden fruit. "A girl? Are you two . . ."

"Yeah, I suppose."

"Tell me about her."

"Uh, well. She's Indian. Lots of piercings and bracelets. Dropped out of Oberlin."

Cory's eyeballs moved forward. "Indian?"

"Yeah."

"Long hair? Knife tattoo here?" Cory pointed at her chest.

"You know her?"

"*Roopa?*"

"Oh. Hmm." Henrik spoke through his napkin as he blotted his face with it. "I'm not sure what her real name is."

Cory sputtered a triphthong of confusion. She looked at Henrik like she'd discovered a colony of insects inhabiting his mouth. "What?"

"We, uh, just met. How do you know her?" Henrik said in pacifying tones.

"She's my roommate. Excuse me."

Cory left for the bathroom and returned ten minutes later, eyes throbbing and pink, picking a chalky pastel mint from the dish at the bar before returning to the table. A funny breath-taking sadness tickled at her solar plexus. She looked at Henrik's right cheek, smiled with most of her face, and laughed. "Um," she said, "so that's weird. We're roommates. And you're dating Roopa."

"We haven't called it dating. Cory, are you all right? You seem kind of—"

"Yeah, drunk. Sorry," Cory said.

Bitterness was slipping out in little sighs from the side of her mouth. Smart, kind, self-aware Henrik, *dating Roopa*. Probably *fucking*. Well, Cory had staked no claim, hadn't even spent any time courting him. She stopped talking. Someone would die if she spoke again. It would take someone's head off.

They paid and stepped out into the round white zones of streetlights. It had rained, and the strengthening wind made droplets shiver on the hoods of parked cars. "Want to get a drink?" Henrik asked, and Cory didn't respond. She gaped at her bike. "What's wrong?"

She turned around, eyes streaming with icemelt. "Someone stole my bike saddle."

"Shit." Henrik looked around and patted his pockets as if hoping to find a surprise gift. "This neighborhood doesn't seem like—"

Because she'd already lost, and because she couldn't feel any worse, Cory leaned and pressed in and found herself kissing against the most unwilling face her lips had ever touched—scrunched, unconverted. He didn't even push her off. She turned back to unlock her bike. She'd been wrong: she could feel worse. "Let's talk for a minute," Henrik said.

"No, I'm going home."

"We're going to the same place."

Cory mounted her seatless bike, balancing on the pedals in heels as she skimmed away in low flight. The night wind made a blue commotion inside her dress. It felt better to go helmetless.

CHAPTER 7

Transfer to Transfer

Nothing at all takes place in the universe in which some rule of maximum or minimum does not appear.
—Leonhard Euler

I. Mode of Failure

Because it was absolutely urgent to secure new project funding right away, Henrik was procrastinating by deciding whether to call Lucretia. The sex had been terrible, but that was sex's fault; she was still the only interesting thing that had happened to him in years. Plus he still had the unemployment check she'd forgotten at his house.

His phone battery had been dead for a month, and when he plugged it in, he found he'd missed a call from Will, probably accidental. He bloodily extracted an ingrown thigh hair before dialing her number. The other end answered, jump-kicking Henrik's ear with noise.

"Hey, Lucretia? This is Henrik, from a while ago? How—"

"Ben! Why aren't you here?" Her voice was monotone with shoutedness.

"It's Henrik."

"*Spencer?*"

"Henrik!"

"SPENCER!"

"I'll text you!"

Henrik hung up and was not interested in theorizing about Spencer. He hummed the *Davy Crockett* theme as he sent his text: **Hey you left an envelope at my place when you visited. I think there's money in it. Let me know how you want to handle. Free all week.**

She replied, **lol awsome ill come tomorrow at 8? can't wait.**

He dropped his phone and capsized onto his couch, which smelled like stale popcorn and cream of broccoli, and he stayed there until tomorrow evening, when Lucretia jiggled at the doorknob as if she'd assumed it would be unlocked. Henrik let her in. She was jingling with bracelets and wearing a black dress involvingly woven with gold thread. Henrik handed her the envelope.

"Oh!" she said. "This is my roommate's. I brought the mail in that day and forgot to give it to her. Gah! Flakiness abounds."

"What did you think you were coming for?"

"I thought you were speaking code. You know, an envelope with money in it? Ha!" Lucretia touched Henrik's arm. "I don't suppose?"

"Sorry," Henrik said, jazz-handsing. "Money's weird."

"Dang! You sure?"

"Sorry for making you drive down here," Henrik said, by which he meant *Please leave*.

"No, it's fine. I love the view on 280. Sweeney Ridge looks like big cellulite butts. Oh god, I'm being so random. I skipped lunch and I'm all low-blood-sugary."

Henrik never could ignore a complaint, always suspected

they were accusations. Though his worried accommodations only came across as flyover-state politeness. "Do you want to get something to eat?"

Lucretia dimpled her cheek with an index finger. "I'm weird with dietary stuff. Cheese makes my hands bleed."

He suggested Mexican, and at Lucretia's bright affirmative, they walked to a taqueria on El Camino and collaborated on a vegan burrito the size of a rolled-up newspaper. Lucretia could talk without breaking her jaw's stride; the subject of food allergies led to health, which led to death, which Lucretia argued didn't strictly exist since consciousnesses were interconnected. Henrik asked whether that meant murder was morally trivial. She asked Henrik how he was doing. "Do you graduate soon?"

"A few more years was the plan. But there's no plan anymore."

"Well, you know my thoughts on college. Dropping out was my best decision. I can't believe it took me three years. You should move to the city."

"I couldn't afford it."

"You could at my collective. Three hundred plus utilities. Huge backyard with a vegetable garden. And we just got chickens! I haven't bought groceries in nine months. Oops, I got sauce on you." She licked his hand and laughed. "Consider it."

When they parted, Lucretia kissed his shoulder and pressed her palms together.

That night, Henrik considered it. He'd never really wanted to be a career student. A quick move could throw off his creditors. It seemed like a pretty good idea. Then after jerking off he realized it was a *stupendously idiotic* idea—if he couldn't even hold down a cushy academic gig, how would he live in the most expensive city in the US, uninsured, with a girl he'd paid to not-really-fuck two months ago?

Lucretia seemed completely optimistic, and every few hours she'd send along another text about how close her place was to the train, how cheap the utilities, any potential irony nullified by lack of punctuation. **Mooooove heeeeerrre**, read Lucretia's *n*th text. He thought of the piles of dining hall dishes ridged with hummus, the fruit fly cocoons spiculed on his trash can lid, the week-old chicken remnant in his fridge flocked with white-green mold. Not even he wanted to live with him.

"Maybe I might take you up," Henrik said on the phone to Lucretia. "Are you sure you want us to live together?"

"Well, don't put it like *that*. I have lots of housemates. And, okay, if you're weirded out by how we met, let's just agree that *that* whole phase is over."

"That's what I assumed."

"Then move here! I'm all about first-thought-best-thought. Say yes! Say yes!"

"Okay, yes."

"Woo! You're gonna love the city. Does tomorrow work?"

The next morning Lucretia's black Explorer skidded into his driveway in the afternoon, playing a cannonade of drum-and-bass. Wearing sweatclothes and an eyebrow-immobilizing ponytail, she hustled into his apartment. She ignored the plunger standing in the sink and headed for the bedroom, where she upended drawers and unplugged lamps. Henrik stopped her when she picked up a composition notebook from a box in his closet. All the white space on its cover had been filled with ballpoint pen. He stepped toward Lucretia, wondering if she would play keep-away if he grabbed for it.

"Old diary, huh?"

"You guessed it."

"I won't look. Oops!" she said, pretend-opening the pages filled with dense massacres of handwriting. "Ha."

"I can finish packing myself," Henrik said, taking the notebook. "You should see the cactus garden on campus."

While she was gone, he packed everything that wasn't garbage into garbage bags. What little mattered in his life; his life's matter. If life was matter, what form, phase, state? Was it a fabric, as the saying went, a differentially deforming continuum? Or was it the other saying, a river: fluid and turbulent? No, definitely a solid, considering its modes of failure. How it held together and fell apart. Fatigue. Fracture. Shock. Stress. Cracking. Crazing. Life was no gas. Life was definitely solid. Life was *hard*.

He packed his laptop and its charger. His toothbrush and clothes. He left the front door key on the kitchen table.

Lucretia returned in the evening, pausing in the driveway to smile at the warm midwinter sky. When he approached her car with his load of belongings, the car grunted to life, remotely ignited. Deafening EDM rippled his cheeks when he opened the door. It was like she listened to music by vibrating her brain directly. The bass frequencies sent a tingling charge into Henrik's arm hairs, and his head hairs floated in an unfalling fray. "This is my roommate's car," Lucretia said. "I hate myself for driving, but it's handy, not gonna lie. I was going to plant some trees last weekend to make up for it, but my sapling has a fungus, so."

Henrik went back in for a final check. He stared at the water trickle on the wall and the blistered latex paint around it. When he turned the light off, the mess disappeared.

II. Distance Learning

When you drove far and fast enough west, exiting Nevada on I-80 through motor-weary Reno into an onset of greenly watered life, fleeing the interior to all the traffic and habitation, lawns greened on potable water, the low church density and visible interdependence of the Bay Area, the west was qualified by a coast, and California, becoming the West Coast.

States that contradicted their geography betrayed deeper conflicts, were governed by strange rules. Henrik was born in Sheridan, Wyoming—a proper western state, like you might see in a Western—but grew up in Florida, which was southerly but somehow not Southern; Ohio, mideastern but culturally Midwest; Indiana, no longer the land of Indians; then Reno, the Biggest Little City; and a final season in continental Rhode Island.

Where from? The most honest answer would be America, broadly. Henrik was a ward of the interstate, spending his childhood in a black four-speed single-cab Chevy S-10, with decals from the previous owner that his dad didn't bother scraping off (NOTRE DAME, JAP JUNK SUCKS, Calvin pissing on a USC logo). Henrik usually claimed he was from a military family, though he and his dad hardly added up to anything so coherent as a family.

Not much distinguished his childhood from a kidnapping in progress. They never resided, only parked. They avoided cities in favor of the blight and sprawl towns that looked identical. Payless. Staples. Jenny Craig. For cash they went on courier sorties, hauling cross-country for three hundred bucks plus the cost of fuel. Off the roadside they shot prairie dogs and gophers for the culling bounty: two bucks a critter, payable on receipt of severed foreleg. The parking lots of churches and outlet malls made for camping grounds, and Dad would offer the lot managers free security in exchange for overnight parking. They covered the car with a blue tarp while they slept and woke in a stinking pouch of blood-heat blue.

Each morning they retook the highways, past ecru acres of level dry terrain, the nation's breadbasket truly resembling different types of cracker in parallax motion—the biscotti cliffs, the matzah veld, the crouton steppe. The Fenns were sunburned on opposite sides of the body, driver's and passenger's. Each smoked his own Pall Malls. Henrik dozed to the chirp of the police radar detector, tensely reassuring, like how an EKG sounds to the patient it's attached to. Lingering tang of grape Bubble Yum that once melted under his seat. Dorito grit in the upholstery seams. The rhythms of mile markers and green rectangles passing overhead, cars floating in adjacent lanes, and the dizzy upstreaming of vision after staring for hours at a moving road.

At rest stops they diced and salted potatoes and carrots and nestled them in a tinfoil papoose with a pound of pork tenderloin. They laid it in the iron braids of the manifold, slammed the hood, played *Arkanoid* in the rest stop, then ate under the wavy triangular shade of the propped hood, sitting on a searing fender in shorts, keeping the hot sagging foil balanced on their laps, popping beer caps in the car door's strike plate. Gear oil imparted a distinct flavor, which you could grow to like, if that was what you called growth.

DROWSY DRIVERS PULL OVER IF NECESSARY. They passed cars with flag mounts, flag decals, yellow ribbon decals. Salt flats. Corn shocks. Earthen sound baffles. Wawa. Hy-Vee. Big Y. H-E-B. The hundreds of abandoned cars alongside I-4 outside

Orlando looking like a preview of the Rapture. Little towns employed by enormous prisons. Views of splendor through the windshield's beveled quadrilateral: the whip of wipers biting against a single driven shade of annihilating white in Midwestern winters. Exploded moose. A swarm of pamphlet-size butterflies flapping away from a hulking black storm front. Skidding out on a teeming migration of Mormon crickets on I-80 outside Sparks. Food Lion. Piggly Wiggly. Giant Eagle.

Everywhere was the country full of emptiness and strangers dealing infinities of abuse. Eugene Fenn, traveler of America and disregarder of its laws, labored to instill disdain for all forms of authority in his only son, Henrik, whether neighbors, taxes, or employers, never acknowledging the paradox this entailed in his own parental authority. Finding state after static state deficient in liberty, they moved through, evading the humble laws imposing order onto human affairs, especially those nine-tenths comprised by possession. Eugene kept a knee brace and an eyepatch in his map hutch to invalidate field sobriety tests. They flung garbage out the window onto sixty-six interstates and into the trash cans between gas pumps. All they owned was bought from flea markets or pawn shops or shoplifted.

Eugene's sedentary obesity afflicted all his negative spaces, approaching ideal cylindricality, with a bald head doming up like a third shoulder and a face that looked like it had baked in a tandoor, except where shielded by orange chrome sunglasses. Which was not to deny a resemblance—both Fenns were tall and land-colored, with unfixed teeth and jets of bunchgrass hair on the backs of their toes, ruddier stubble that covered more cheek than it didn't. By fourteen Henrik was mingling his Norelco clippings with his dad's in the bone-colored sinks of Citgo, Sinclair, QuikTrip, ARCO.

The way a car engine consumed total silence allowed other silences to continue indefinitely. In a car you never faced each other, only forward. Dad's lips would move sometimes, murmuring things like "Not too good, not too good" or "That's right," carrying on a conversation in his head that he didn't want interrupted. In more talkative moods he would tell what he called his "stretchers": Knew this guy in Eau Claire so addicted to slots that he fed dollars to Laundromat change machines just to hear the coins paying out. Knew this guy in Sparks who taught himself to walk on his hands till his ass grew a face. This chick in South Pattaya who could fire candy corn from her snatch into a shot glass across the bar.

Henrik had managed to stitch a rough biography from these stretchers: Dropped out of high school in Utah to get a GED, left home at sixteen to work in a garage in Pittsburg, Kansas. Two years as a firefighter in Milwaukee, followed by the enlistment in the air force in '65, leading to a bloody year of rescue-and-recovery in Vietnam that he enjoyed in spite of taking a slice of flak in his ribs, though Eugene's own account of his wartime service boiled down to a single stretcher, wearyingly repeated, that for all the Bangkok poontang he'd gotten they awarded him the Purple Helmet. Though this was a stretcher rooted in the reality of the Purple Heart dangling from their rearview mirror, beside the cat-butt air freshener and a few feet from the loaded Ruger in the glove compartment.

After Vietnam, Eugene went on the road, underwritten by VA disability. In '79 he picked up Maggie Erinson, a veteran runaway with a crew cut and messed-up boundaries hustling for rides at a Sinclair station in Sioux Falls, and she became his passenger for three years before producing Henrik out of carelessness, actually birthing him in the backseat, as that stretcher went. When Henrik was four, she left to use a gas station bathroom in Milwaukee and never returned, a dubiously stretcherous detail that made Henrik occasionally wonder if his mother, too, had been kidnapped.

Their longest period of fixed residence was a ten-month stretch in 1997 when they hit a light pole head-on in Goshen, Indiana, and they took up in a double-wide trailer. Goshen had been a penitentiary of niceness, where neighborly Mennonites openly worried at their balding tires, lent them Makita drills, noted the state on their license plate. While they raised cash to fix the truck, they enlisted in the Midwest's war on boredom: football games, county and state fairs, electronic darts, bowling, motocross, ubiquitous TV, large-scale grilling. Legally ordained, Eugene prowled bars to marry drunks on the cheap. On game days, Henrik scalped Hoosiers tickets for a month's wage, while Dad stood on unattended lawns near Memorial Stadium charging ten bucks for a park-'n'-piss.

While Dad was out plying his grift, he'd drop Henrik off at the library to fill up on books. From there Henrik would walk to Goshen High and stand by fences, courts, corners, scouting the emerging hard cases, unsupervised baby-faced whiteboys who coveted their fathers' guns and girlfriends, those pissed-off soap bubbles wearing the blackest T-shirts, unresponsive to all but their peers in disaffection. Henrik spotted them easily: flannels tied around their waists like half kilts, crop tops or draping bangs that both concealed and produced acne. You walked over and said *Hey* in your boredest voice. Offer a smoke, drop the question marks. *Let's hit the mall.* They accepted Henrik, maybe seeing the advantage in befriending a silent, malleable six-foot-three kid with an age-of-purchase beard.

He grew alongside convenience stores, shattering Old

Crow bottles to radio-recorded mixtapes of Helmet, Dio, Primus, smoking ditch weed they agreed was good weed. They vandalized TVs at the landfill and played the glitched *Street Fighter II* machine at the Laundromat that let you throw fireballs in midjump. Henrik accepted that this was what normal felt like, tranquil eventlessness, and he enjoyed it until one afternoon he returned to the truck with blood on his lips and shirt. He'd said something wrong. Eugene examined Henrik's face like it was a door he'd just dented, gave him a stack of White Castle napkins and a Dixie cup of gin. "Learn from it." In two months they were moving again.

So Henrik learned. Eugene taught Henrik to drive as soon as his legs were long enough, but he forbade Henrik any official ID, so Henrik took the wheel only when Eugene was drunk. Otherwise he was an autodidact. One way or another he'd learned to read (cloudy recollections of tracing *DUCK* and *COW* on green wide-ruled paper), and thereafter Eugene registered him as homeschooled, giving him the run of his own curriculum from distance learning catalogs. The correspondence lessons were forwarded through the same RV club service as Eugene's VA checks. Boredom was the only incentive. It annoyed him to get wrong answers, so he did until he didn't. His extracurricular reading consisted of stolen library books and flea-market books, with ocher-edged pages curled with heat and crinkled with water damage, a clothespin to riffle-proof them on the highway: Choose Your Own Adventure and Encyclopedia Brown, *Madame Bovary* with eighty pages missing, Emily Dickinson, Anne Rice, Lord of the Rings, the Dalai Lama's autobiography, Jack London, novelizations from the *Predator* universe. He threw his finished books out the window.

At some point, inhaling Eugene's millionth beef or watching the odometer's nines roll over into zeroes, hustling down a windy shoulder to fetch a toaster fallen from the truck bed or getting coldcocked by the roof after they vaulted off a dead elk, a thought came like an itch in Henrik's brain—what if he was *smarter* than his dad? Could Dad score in the ninety-fifth percentile of five practice SAT IIs? Give the partial derivative of a vector function? Break down the phases of cell division? The more mutinous studying he did, the more he packed up his emotional belongings and moved upstairs into his head. (It wasn't roomy but it was quiet, furnished with a library and wall-to-wall mirrors.) He scanned obsolete college guides for schools that waived application fees, tossing in Harvard, Princeton, and Yale as moonshots. He didn't know that his application essays, which felt like mundane autobiography to him, were award-winning stretchers—knew this kid who was raised in a truck, with a Purple Heart and a cat-butt air freshener as his mobiles, who taught himself to the test.

And Eugene slunk into his own cellar, slamming the blast hatch shut, with his eyes reading the road and a mutter playing mutely on his lips, emerging only in backfires of road rage to punctuate the radio. Da' Dip. Electric Slide. Achy Breaky. Macarena—Henrik thought real life was like the Macarena.

Early in 2000, when Henrik was nineteen and passing through Rhode Island, he opened an envelope. The forwarding service had been slow in keeping up with their movements, and the envelope had been concealed in a brick of rubber-banded mail that sat in the map hutch for two weeks. By the time he noticed his name on the envelope (trimmed in the shade of dark blue named for the university that accepted him), he had only two weeks to reply. The envelope was stuffed with folders, forms, and glossy welcomes; upon his sighting the phrase *We are delighted to offer,* bliss, nausea, and dread warred in his guts.

When he could bear to read on, he saw he'd been granted a half-tuition scholarship, with additional Pell Grant funding and a fellowship for prospective STEM majors. It felt like the first thing that had ever happened to him, though really things had only ever happened to him. At last the vista of possibilities felt wider than the converging lanes at a horizon.

Despite the deadline, he put off telling Eugene for a week. The acceptance packet wrinkled and softened as he reviewed its contents in bathroom stalls—financial aid forms, reply cards, a stark little pennant. Though he'd never said so, the feeling was that Eugene wanted him to run the family business of minding their own business. Reasons emerged, as usual, to justify desire. When Henrik finally told Eugene, Eugene paused long enough that Henrik thought he'd ignore it entirely. "College is a load of penguin shit."

"I think I should try it. I could make some money."

"Money what for?"

"I don't know."

"There's a big picture," Eugene said, bumping his knuckles on the steering wheel. "And that's doing what you want."

"And what if I want to go to college?"

"Only reason you're saying that is because you ain't gone yet."

"You didn't either."

Eugene took this levelly. "I been everywhere. All over the bright blue fucking Earth and above it too. You think there's any kind of asshole I don't know? Talkin' about freedom here. Work a job, you got a boss. Run a business, you got customers. That's your life if you go to college, only worse, 'cause then you get a giant stick up your ass about being smart. Smart don't make you less stupid, though. You're never gonna get the money or respect you think you deserve. You get it by keeping your ass under your elbows and making your own way."

"I'm making my own way? We only do what *you* want."

They eased to the shoulder, crossing the corrugated rumble strip that made the car moan deepeningly as it slowed. A car at rest felt so low to the ground. The breakdown lane fizzed in the noon with bottle glass and high-reflectance asphalt. "Okay, scooter. Where you wanna go? Outer space? Pick somewhere." Cars of different colors whipped past, too fast to have shapes. "I could've given you up easy, shit. Easy. I raised you up for your own good, not mine. Put my kid in some gagglefuck group home? Not me, man." Eugene spat his cigarette out the window. "But hell if I'll keep you from fucking yourself up. I'm not your boss. Suit your damn self."

A problem with decisions between past and future was you made them in the present. Henrik said he wanted to go. Eugene kept to his word, so long as Henrik agreed not to expect any cash or list him as a parent on his application. "Understand you're handling your own shit now. Ain't no making your way back to me."

It was strange. Henrik had fought to leave, but now with his frictionless release, he felt tricked into disowning himself. Henrik wanted to smash his dad's face. But that would mean showing he felt something, and he'd rather keep things equal and deny Eugene what he'd been denied, his real thoughts.

Six months later in New Haven, Eugene had dropped Henrik off at his destination with his single bag, ignoring the clapping, hooting freshman orientation volunteers in blue shirts, and left the curb to join the stalled line of roof-racked minivans and moving trucks filing off campus, with a sunburned arm hanging from the window, slapping the side of the dirt-whitened door.

AT YALE, PROMISE became indistinguishable from purpose. Henrik maxed out his credit cap and audited multivariate calc, cognitive psych, evolutionary bio, chem and intro O-chem, mechanics, optics. Whenever he doubted the utility of learning the behavior of light around massive bodies, he reminded himself it was keeping him alive. Every morning he was up at seven A.M. without an alarm, ate a waxy dining hall apple on the walk to class, took in a lecture, lunch off a tray, lecture, lecture, problem sets in the library, a take-out dinner in his room while watching a loaned movie, and then the last two hours in the computer cluster at Jonathan Edwards, copying MP3s from the dorm network and browsing Craigslist free ads—students just threw stuff away. He had no friends, though on weekends he played Texas Hold'em with the funny unambitious stoners on his dorm floor and turned in by midnight, reading or doing problem sets in a bed that he'd double-lofted because he didn't like having space between him and the ceiling.

It was comfortable. Rooms were comfortable, and so were dining halls, and the treed quads he crossed in the still winter into heated lecture halls among hundreds of students facing the same way. Parties were the only discomforts. How did one party? Why didn't anyone do the Macarena? At orientation he sweatily lurked by snack bowls with an escape-ready smile. He was intrigued to witness the binge drinking of powerful, talented, rich legacies, but conversation was an enigma, and when approached by chipper RAs or strident networkers, his strategy was to regurgitate his admissions essay. *Your life sounds so interesting,* they'd say, then excuse themselves to the bathroom and never return. At one function he briefly interacted with a rescuer of the shy, a redhead with large smiling eyes and a loose black T-shirt (IT'S NOT GONNA SUCK ITSELF YOU KNOW) who asked him if he was the scavenger guy. She invited him back to his dorm room, where he set a land speed record for virginity loss, and disappointed her again when he told her he didn't have any weed. This happened two more times before she stopped replying to his emails.

Better than nothing, he thought. He would've happily done fifty more years of college and left a well-informed corpse. But you didn't escape initial conditions. The life pendulum swung wider and wider from the pivot of its past. The summer before his sophomore year, Henrik became a textbook case, though the textbooks were divided on calling it *agitated depression, dysphoric mania, mixed episode,* or *mixed state.* A state contradicting itself, where high met low, or as Linda put it later, where unstoppable farce met immovable abject.

Mania did a job on memory. Mostly he recalled being angry at facts. Needing to explain back at them. Breaking a finger punching a newspaper dispenser. His roommate yelling for him to turn his fucking light off at three A.M. Instead of sleeping, Henrik would scare people away from the computer cluster with questions about where they were from, what they believed in, and would they stand up for it, like would they go to war and die? In lectures with his legs V6-ing under his desk, he filled his composition notebooks, ignoring the calc professor's *horseshit* while taking unpunctuated notes on theory-of-everything from the charismatic counterlecturer in his head. He wrote arguments for and against life; he began to think the slowest and most painful form of suicide was living, running the whole decathlon of suffering, no breathers or bottled water. Fear of dying was irrational. Death was utilitarian. Decrease in net resource consumption and planetary suffering. Increase in net comedy. There was no afterlife but there was a right-before-death, and medical research said it was loopy and nice, all white lights and gentle voices. With booze it wasn't even scary. Some people with terrible lives didn't kill themselves, but that didn't mean they shouldn't. Most people weren't alive and didn't mind. You couldn't regret it.

In October, a week after his roommate had moved out, three days since he'd last slept, two days after his RA had visited to ask if everything was cool, Henrik scheduled an appointment with a distracted doctor at Student Health. After he denied having suicidal thoughts (taking twenty minutes to distinguish *thinking about suicide* from *considering committing suicide*) she sent him away with a script for Depakote and Topamax and told him to call if he experienced problems. He lay in his lofted bed at four P.M. after taking his first dose, feeling like his brain was rotating a foot above his head. Henrik dented the ceiling with a kick, climbed down from his bed to get the liter of Smirnoff from his desk, and without a thought he drank it, swallowed all his pills, climbed back up, and took a serious nap.

By sheer ineptitude he survived: Depakote only damaged the liver. He awoke in a snarl of puked sheets with an ordeal in his skull, registering his confusion at the wall clock, which read noon—had he slept for negative-four hours? Did negative sleep give you unrest? He shuffled to his RA's room; in ten minutes he was being carried out by two EMTs to Yale–New Haven Hospital, on a stretcher.

As far as Yale was concerned, with suicide it was the

thought that counted. From the hospital he was shuttled to the Mental Hygiene wing at the Department of University Health. Its waiting room was a no-occupancy purgatory for the screaming and openly resisting, and after an hour's wait the DUH nurse led him through the DUH facilities to consult the DUH officer. At the officer's request, he handed over his notebooks, answered questions about his behavior and medication. The information went to the review board, who saw his record of missed classes, TAs' and RAs' reports, and testimony from his ex-roommate, and ordered ten days of spaced-out hospitalization and valproic acid monitoring, after which they offered either involuntary or voluntary medical leave from school. In hindsight, choosing the latter eased his transfer to Stanford later on, though it didn't feel like much of a choice; it was not take-it-or-leave-it. He both took it and left.

III. All Mass Shares Identity

If Henrik had had a quieter place and more time to consider his peril, he might have. The warehouse where Lucretia lived was loud and active, and being there was like touring a foreign country where he had neither language nor currency. Discovering that Cory lived there too, not only in San Francisco but in the same *building*, seemed at first a miraculous consummation of fate, though since his dinner with her he'd sensed delta waves of malice wafting off her, her looking harried and on-task even when walking to the bathroom in her underwear.

He kept to Lucretia. On that first day, with his stuff still in her car, Lucretia toured him around Iniquity, let him feed the chickens in the backyard, introduced him to housemates. The air in her bedroom was heavy with incense, covering strong base notes of fungus and bouillon. He could reach the ceilingless tops of her pressboard partition walls on flat feet. Above her futon was a poster of arms cradling a lotus captioned YOU ARE WELCOME, and a cross-stitch that read LIFE IS A GIFT. Lucretia insisted he take the futon, nested with voluptuous down pillows and purple watered-silk sheets. She'd sleep on her yoga mat. Rent? No worries; he was a guest for now.

Henrik was anxious about what Lucretia was expecting from this bargain; if she was pulling a long con, the joke was on her, because he had nothing. But she appeared to thrive on exactly that: nothing. She scavenged and grew her own food, was uninsured, and didn't mind Henrik's silence because she was always talking. She was unconditional, projecting into everyone she met her sense of basic goodness and connection. Her generosity made Henrik want to cry, but for months now the Depakote and Topamax had been making him feel like his feelings were happening to someone else.

As Henrik pretended to sleep that night, Lucretia entered in the dark, undressing audibly. "I love guests," she said, sliding under the sheets next to Henrik. She fell asleep instantly, bunched up against him as if asking to be petted. Was she ever lonely?

After a sleepless sexless night, Henrik asked Lucretia over muesli where the nearest pharmacy was. She made her worst face and asked why. He said he needed prescriptions filled—at this, she became a flurry of snorts and book recommendations, declaring that Western medical institutions profited by aggravating illness; Big Pharma was a cartel, doctors were pushers, patients were junkies. She asked to see what he was taking, and when she laid eyes on his briefcase-size pill case, she looked like he'd just told her he was born without a heart. She made him lie down, and sent up gasps researching his prescriptions on her naturopathic reference sites. He wasn't disordered, she assured him; society was. Manic conservatives, depressive liberals. Mood-swinging markets and a demented climate. Rich against poor, white against unwhite. Henrik was just American.

Under Lucretia's advisement, he tapered off Depakote, figuring it'd run out anyway. Reluctantly she let him keep his asthma inhaler, but he white-knuckled the rest. His first weeks brought on fever and dizziness. His head felt crammed with a dull hot compost that he couldn't expel. At night he writhed in bed, pondering his status: no longer a scientist but a layperson, surrounded by the infrasonic hum of dread that he would reject his life like a donor kidney.

Launching her campaign of dietary reeducation, Lucretia recited blog posts about flavonoids and c-kit, noetics and nootropics, *New Scientist* articles linking the spike in nut allergies, bipolar, and celiac to antibiotics. She plied him with congee, barley tea, and apple cider vinegar, and shooed off noisy roommates. "Keep putting those good foods in you," she said. When he swallowed, he couldn't feel anything going down, it just vanished; but it had to come out eventually, and after being bedbound for six weeks, with light hurting his stomach and his breath turning fruity, he was pissing in his water jar, and even then Roopa uncomplainingly collected his jars and replaced them with new cloudy tinctures.

By March, his phone service was cut and his university fees went unpaid; the official transactions affirming his existence expired. He realized he was dead. His suicide had just taken a few years to kick in. It was why he couldn't move, think, say, or sense; why his body felt like a random collation of limbs and holes in space. He was a corpse and Roopa was just a nice girl patronizing him by pretending he was alive, making sure his body didn't stink too bad. It was good, death forgave. If life was a gift, it was the sort (hastily wrapped, price tag attached) that only proved the giver didn't know or care about you at all.

But in early April his death proved temporary. He slithered to the bathroom, grunting at Cory as she raced from her bedroom out the front door. He crunched at a stale ear of sourdough and drank a glass of water, noting how fresh it tasted. It might've been only a contrast to Lucretia's syrupy tonics, but he couldn't stop drinking it, and drained the glass at one tilt. He realized that he hadn't felt dizzy, shaky, or nauseated all morning. When he changed his clothes he found that he'd gone down a size, like he'd lost a whole suit of skin in her sheets. Lucretia encouraged him to keep resting, but was glad his sadhana was opening.

Was he better? The thought made him smile and sweat. So his problems were psychosomatic after all. He could live without meds if he regulated his lifestyle, could be unemployed if he grew his food. Even if her cures were placebos, wasn't placebo the best medicine? It was like some paralyzing electromagnet on his brain had been removed, like the internal gyroscope that kept him suspended in death had finally toppled, like the meniscus of anxieties he'd had had burst, spilling his enthusiasm forth.

He needed to go outside. Pulling sneakers onto his bare feet, he shuffled out of the warehouse. The air felt mentholated. Millions of data points rushed bright and sweet across his skin. Through the vapor of his breath, he saw the sideways morning light crowning the upper thirds of the buildings

across the street. Buildings taller than any person alive! A dimpled brown stream crept toward him from a Latino shopkeeper
hosing down the sidewalk. Blackflies droning around trash
cans, windshield glass kibbled in the gutter. It was all great.

On jellylegs he walked south. He'd forgotten his jacket but
didn't feel cold. He strode down Mission and up Valencia in
two hours that went by like a pop song. Everything felt solvable
with just the right application of force. He laughed and stepped
into a puddle in the gutter as the white balloons and empire
waists of a quinceañera mobbed the sidewalk. Every stranger
seemed so interesting that he wanted to follow them all day; it
was stupid how you couldn't just do that.

Henrik's shirt hung with sweat. He needed to buy Lucretia
a gift. At a bodega ATM he emptied the forty dollars from
his bank account and bought two watermelons whose green-
ness and bounty excited him. Watching the bodega cashiers
wet their fingertips on a sliced cucumber to count cash faster,
his eyes watered and something soul-like rose up in him. These
strangers stocked all these huge watermelons just for him. He
went out until he passed a man sleeping in the alcove of an
apartment entrance. He left a watermelon at the man's side so
it'd be the first thing he saw when he woke up. Another victory
for society.

That night, when Lucretia came back, he surprised her with
the other watermelon and a long to-do list. They biked out to
pizza at Pauline's, dessert at Tartine, karaoke at Encore, cocktails at KoKo and Martuni's, up and down the Seward Street
slides, roaring back to the warehouse with Lucretia riding
his shoulders. After a hot shower he entered Lucretia's room,
where she'd changed into a black camisole and green panties
and had her hair up in a thing. The partition walls teetered

when Henrik closed the door behind him. "You dress different than when we met. Lucretia." For the past several months they'd dwelt in the intimacy of personal pronouns. "Okay if I call you that?"

Lucretia turned. "Yeah, let's go with that. She's just a character, but I like her." She pulled Henrik in by his chin. "Maybe I'll make you guess my real name."

"What's the prize?"

She removed her thing and gemstones fell from her unfurled hair. She smiled with her face upturned and squinted to look posh-sexy. "Something you'll like."

"Hillary Clinton. Mike Tyson."

"One more guess."

"Roopa," Henrik said.

"What about my last name?"

"Dunno."

"Lucky for you, you don't have to."

OFF HIS MEDS, certain valves and vessels were reopening, introducing a fresh directness of the senses. Liberated from the restrictions of a paid hour, sex with Lucretia became so greatly achievable that Henrik no longer wondered what she saw in him. He felt like a man. The sex and room-sharing made them a de facto couple. And couples got married.

While Lucretia was at a textile-making class in Oakland, he wanted to make her a surprise. She liked citrus. There were crates of limes and oranges around that she never finished. He squeezed dozens of them until his hands reddened with the acid and pitchers of juice lay on the countertops. Juice or margaritas later. More fruit in less time. He bought some rum and drank half. She'd also like it if he folded her laundry, though what was dirty was unclear, and when he opened her drawer he found a dull gray pistol lying in a nest of dark camisoles. Oh right, she'd mentioned that. He picked it up, practiced some quick draws, then moved the gun to the bottom compartment of her wardrobe under a shoebox. He was overdue for a haircut, but he'd barely finished trimming the sides when he remembered there was fruit to squeeze. Already the juice pitchers were swarmed by an electron cloud of fruit flies. He stood trembling over the sink to wipe the stickiness off, aware of the supercollisions in his head, the cardiac megathrusts. An oxygenated optimism was telling him that he was better than he'd ever been, but a chronically outvoted minority voice of reason was telling him that his lack of symptoms was a symptom. That sleep was not a disease he should've cured. That wellness *was* the illness.

Well, maybe he wasn't cured, but so what, this was better because: Cured of what? Nobody who knew what was going on with war and the economy, much less determinism, could be happy about it, but at least you could understand. Just because he was on his own didn't mean he couldn't be a scientist, a higher-order Poincaré or Mendel or Ramanujan intuition maker who worked backward from the answer. Brute-force research wasn't worth the effort—the scientific method was always catching up to the eureka. Inspiration was more fruitful, like squeezing fruit.

Even when you learned why, the basics were fishy, weren't they? Like why did light radiate in all directions but time in only one? Why were atoms mostly empty? Could bicycles *really* stay upright? He began writing in a nearby cookbook, fucking grooving. This was how he could repay Lucretia. He scribbled and tore out pages when they were wrong. Words weren't doing.

When night came to help him see clear of the sun's interference, his discovery, like benzene, arrived in an image:

"What's this?" Lucretia said when he handed it to her later, now that she was awake. Clearly it was an aquarium. Picture one of those big tanks at marine parks with the portholes in the sides. An orca whale or something is swimming around in there and its movement makes either large or small waves, moving quickly or slowly. Now look at the part of the wave you see in the porthole as it's passing by. Now how can you tell if it's a wide wave moving quickly or a narrow one moving slowly? You *can't*! The two different properties, size and velocity, are indistinguishable because of the flawed terms we use.

"Henrik, love, you're losing me," Lucretia said.

Yeah but it'll make sense when I tell you this right now, so keep listening: imagine that *every* measurement is performed through a "porthole" and that properties we ordinarily see as distinct aren't, like the Heisenberg position/velocity issue, well that's because position in some way that's not obvious yet *is* velocity. *Where* we are is *what* we are. All mass shares the same identity. Make sense? The math's not there yet but it will be. So does that make sense? All mass shares—

"Back up. Can you explain—"

I *am* explaining! Just *look* at the fucking drawing if you want to get it. I put a ton of effort into making this easy to get. I'm telling you something important and you're deliberately trying not to hear me which drives me fucking insane. Hell, you don't care. Honestly it feels like we're not even dating. Are you serious or am I just a bit player in your kooky fancy-free lifestyle? We're not getting married if you're not going to hear me, honestly, I mean Christ what's your problem, I drew this specifically so you would get it.

"Okay, Henrik—"

And I *hate* when you tell me I'm smart, because you think I'm an idiot. Being all sneaky and hiding a gun in your drawer. What? You thought I didn't know? But I moved it. It's *gone*, I *moved* it.

"Henrik, you're manifesting imbalance. I feel uncomfortable and as if the dialogue isn't being respected. I think you should leave."

Fuck *you*. I'm going nowhere.

"Anthony, 8-Ball! Help!"

There was a heavy crunch at the door, and the partition wall began to bend in a big conic section toward them. The wall fell to the onslaught of Lucretia's roommates clambering in, and Henrik grappled with them before he heard an aerosol sizzle and clutched his eyes. He curled up and they pulled his undershirt and frog-marched him over the fallen partition, down cold cement on bare feet and out the heavy steel door, which closed and shot its bolt behind him.

You heard all about insanity and genius—the thin line, the alleged link. You didn't hear about the equally thin line between insanity and idiocy. Drevets et al. (1997), using PET scans of the subgenual prefrontal cortex, demonstrated a 39 percent reduction of the volume of gray matter in bipolar patients, findings corroborated in later MRI studies on prefrontal gray and white matter by Lopez-Larson et al. (2002), on gray matter density in the fronto-limbic and cingulate cortices by Doris et al. (2004), and in situ by Fenn (2008), with his stinging face, mincing barefoot up Seventh Street at eleven P.M. in white boxers and an undershirt, awaiting peer review.

Long red vectors of pain jabbed at his eyes. He searched an hour for the impossible rarity of a pay phone, and found one on the wall of a payday loan office, whose neon sign Henrik couldn't read. He felt the shape but not the temperature of the phone's receiver in his hand, its square metal keys. He misdialed and redialed until Will asked Henrik to repeat what he was saying.

"Can I stay with you," Henrik said, picking out his words like glass from a foot.

"Um. Yeah, I guess. It's kind of a party here, though."

"I don't understand."

"Never mind, fuckin' just come over. Everything cool?"

"I'll explain later."

Will gave Henrik the directions. "Before you come over, you should know—eh, actually, whatever. You want a ride? I'm not too drunk."

Henrik considered the temperature and the wind. The flap on his boxers was not the kind that buttoned. "Just give me directions."

The street skewed with a dolly zoom, each step seeming to lengthen the distance. He disrupted a pair of seagulls in single combat over a Snickers wrapper. A car passed, trailed by its reflections on nearby parked cars. When Henrik bumped into people he said *sawright,* which sounded equally like *sorry* and *it's all right;* he left a trail of *sawright*s down three miles of sidewalk.

Will's doorbell was an ugly overhead buzzer. Henrik heard the nearing bumping of footsteps, the weather strip swishing open, then, with his dirty feet and butchered hair, half-nude, a rash across his eyes, Henrik saw at the threshold, leaning on a crutch, missing front teeth, holding a wooden spoon dripping spots of tomato soup onto the threshold, Linda.

She squinted at Henrik in suspicion, then widened her eyes, expressing something opposite. Had Will set this up? They stood longer until their silence acquired rules: They would stare at each other, remaining still so as not to disturb whatever feelings had been deadened by silence in the first place. The one to speak first would have to apologize.

"Need help?" Linda said at last. Entranced, doubting his stinging eyes, he gawked at Linda, who tried again: "Do I know you? Are you lost?"

CHAPTER 8
The Interior Drama

At least she was fun!
—Gustave Flaubert

I. To Be Foul

Linda needed a reason not to write and a new place to stay. To both ends, she put her hopes into tonight's party, which Eve had invited her to. The two shared the toothpaste-dotted bathroom mirror, swapping mascara and gin and tagging each other with pumps of hair spray, while Jared chatted with the babysitter. The parents hadn't gone out since Mercy was born, and Eve's trepidation was visible as she strove to deparentalize her attire. Linda had been out of the game for a while too, but she felt good in her stolen leggings, stolen nails and eyelashes, stolen Ferragamos, a stolen color-blocked Fiorucci tunic dress cinched by a white belt reclaimed from a stolen vintage rag, her Rick Owens jacket from Berlin, a huge stolen Margiela bag to abet future stealing, and no panties.

Eve was worried they'd be late even though it was only nine. They stepped into a spore-like rain that appeared only as a vague downward trend in the air, and on the J-Church clanked along to the Inner Mission. Linda busied herself doing bumps and some shrooms she'd found in her jacket's chest pocket. It was easy to spot the place by the loiterers on the stoop smoking and adoring their phones. They followed the music and gabble to the unlocked apartment, entering a low-ceilinged living room lit with a string of Christmas lights. The tableau was unpromising: there were only about ten people, bunched into tight circles. The lower halves of the beer cans were still matte with fresh condensate; chip bags stood unopened in serving bowls.

While Eve and Jared shuffled apprehensively from room to room like prospective buyers, Linda peeled off her leather jacket and stuffed it behind a couch cushion. She stood among the quidnuncs and tryhards, aware that she could be mistaken for one of them, twenty-somethings in slouching contrapposto, clustered like stands of thistle, always smiling with friends and unsmiling when alone. She recognized a few from other parties—she waved to the gay Turkish guy whose accent she liked to imitate and got some menacing cut-eye from the girl who sold crafts on the corner in Hayes Valley, whose boyfriend Linda had blown.

Linda ventured on into another living room, one of those rooms rich people had just to have them, parquet everything, black leather everything. A tattooed Asian guy was pretending to attentively laptop-DJ but was really just playing a Kitsuné Maison compilation. The drink table held spirits, a cheese board, hummus and carrots for the anorexics. All books fit neatly on invisible shelves with their own display lighting. *Pragmatic Ajax, Beautiful Form Design, The 4-Hour Workweek, 1,000 Brain Hacks.*

It was basic as fuck but it would be a good place to crash: she would find out who lived here. Linda took a pint bottle of Wild Turkey from the bar and nursed it in the hallway until two guys approached her. They looked identical, beards and knit caps and red plaid flannels. She really couldn't tell the difference between them.

She'd missed the beginning of what one of them was saying. "It's, like, strictly an aesthetic designation. It's all image. If you look it, you're it, so anyone who's all asymmetrical-hair-big-glasses-beard-hoodies-tattoos . . ."

"But that's just, like, a subset of what I'm talking about," said the other. They even sounded the same. "There used to be, like, a cultural lineage behind it, starting with the beatniks. Lenny Bruce—"

"—and, like, Norman Mailer had that article about how quests for authenticity are perforce inauthentic—"

"It used to be a subculture but now it's kinda melted into this confederation of resuscitated subcultures, like post-punk-hard-core-New-Wave-sixties-counterculture-late-eighties-emo—"

"—right-but-also-it's-an-economic-designation-right-like-these-young-people-with-something-to-prove-about-money-so-they're-either-rich-and-want-to-feel-like-they've-succeeded-without-privilege-or-poor-and-want-to-either-reject-or-surpass-economic-value-systems-and-you-know-both-stances-require-alienation-from-the-commercial-mainstream-so-they-have-to-commit-themselves-to-esoterica-or-faux-sincere-ironic-appropriation-of-pop-culture—"

"—right-yeah-so-like-right-at-the-crossover-tipping-point-they'd-flee-to-other-undergrounds-but-now-that-the-long-tail-makes-everything-effectively-popular-those-distinctions-don't-matter-anymore-so-it-really-is-an-economic-designation—"

"—but-then-how-do-you-explain-all-the-like-all-the-identi-fiable-stereotypes-right-like-what-are-skinny-jeans-but-the-millennial-beret—"

"—or-like-the-overgroomed-beard-a-perfect-emblem-of-masculine-ambivalence-emerging-from-a-progressive-sub-culture-rooted-in-regressive-nostalgia-and-pride-mingled-with-shame-not-to-mention-sincere-aestheticism-performed-through-ironic-mediums—"

"—who-love-good-coffee-but-complain-about-what-good-coffee-places-do-to-their-neighborhoods-and-who'll-collect-vinyl-from-the-nineties-but-sneer-at-the-bands-they-followed-three-years-ago-whose-breakout-success-they-themselves-enabled—"

"—hold-art-openings-in-vintage-clothes-stores-music-shows-in-car-washes-bars-in-converted-barbershops-in-an-again-ironic-expression-of-the-sincere-impulse-to-live-the-bohemian-lifestyle-while-evoking-the-authentic-vocational-self-sufficiency-of-the-parents-who-bankroll-their-freewheel-ing-endeavors—"

Linda was stunned by the ecstatic tsunami of irritation massing and cresting inside her as she listened to this tedious pukesome conversation—she glanced from idiot to idiot, as if observing a Ping-Pong match between players who missed the table every time. She drank her whiskey.

"—but-since-self-awareness-and-semiotic-savvy-is-pre-requisite-they-can-tweak-it-enough-to-conform-but-not-enough-to-be-pigeonholed-and-so-as-a-subculture-it's-un-precedentedly-sprawling-unbounded-by-geography-fashion-demographic-so-it-feels-more-like-an-all-pervading-endgame-than-any-countable-anthropological-system-and-like-I-know-like-it's-trite-even-to-point-it-out—"

"—or-even-to-point-out-that-you're-pointing-out-that-you're-pointing-it-out—"

"—still-what-I-mean-is-it's-a-heuristic-worldview-a-mass-postmodern-covenant-unallied-to-any-value-system-but-that-of-signification-itself—"

"—well-because-bohemianism-was-once-defined-by-the-insiderism-of-outsiders-and-the-tyranny-of-recherché-taste-but-like-Zygmunt-Bauman-says-there's-no-more-outside-to-be-inside-because-of-the-appropriation-dissemination-and-fragmentation-of-tastes-via-the-Internet-like-there's-no-more-culture-as-such-only-content-coursing-through-platforms-enthroning-everyone-atop-their-personal-microaristocracy-of-arbitrarily-differentiated-taste-and-yesteryear's-*comme-il-faut*-fascism-of-exclusion-is-passively-enforced-by-posting-flattering-images-of-you-performing-yourself-as-streetwear-model-or-art-critic-or-social-agitator-or-party-photographer-or-globetrotter-or-fabulous-trainwreck-inflicting-upon-everyone-pinhole-exposure-to-a-glamorous-lifestyle-residing-in-some-unreachably-distant-nexus-of-cool-which-was-a-sewer-tunnel-in-Bushwick-of-late-and-is-now-some-ineffable-IP-address-whose-glamour-is-only-the-shadow-of-the-medium-so-that-everyone-exists-in-an-outside-generated-by-the-inside-like-Baudrillard's-remainder—"

"—everyone-here-is-one-definitely—"

"—and-I'm-not-saying-it's-even-a-bad-thing-I-mean-look-at-us-like-oooh-we're-standing-here-drinking-forties-and-wearing-whatever-we're-wearing-and-bullshitting-as-if-we're-above-any-of-it-but-nobody-is-and-it's-not-like-we're-hurting-anybody-or-there's-any-such-thing-as-authenticity-even-if-you're-*not*-striving-for-it-so-ultimately-it's-just-a-sociological-category-and-an-arrangement-of-fashions-and-if-it's-this-or-temping-then-so-be-it."

They turned jitteringly to Linda. "What-do-you-think-Liza?" Linda looked around—what could she kill them with?

Those ironikitsch gold record wall clocks? Sheer contempt? Linda was torn by her almost horny desire to put them in their place, and her disgust for the antimatter vortex of taxonomy. The word that tainted every tongue that spoke it; the self-love that dared not speak its name. Deny you were one and you were one; call yourself one and you were a failed one; criticize one and it backfired instantly, since only the aspiring hip or resentfully unhip had a stake in disparaging hipness. It was a pejorative, but one that boring people overextended to malign all creative people. Why and where to draw distinctions for the transcultural culture of distinction? Who gave a fuck about the generation?

With a start, Linda realized the two guys were one guy standing next to a mirror. And where did they go? She looked around, flinching when she caught her own reflection.

To her relief, a fresh infusion of drunk people came clomping in from the stairwell, refugees from other parties, hefting bikes and twelve-packs. When the DJ went to the bathroom, Linda put on UGK and flicked up the master volume. She nudged through moving bodies into yet another living room, where the music was playing from recessed wall speakers. She sat on an ottoman and scooped out some coke with her white press-on pinkie nail, snorted behind a privacy curtain of hair. She hated the pretentious rituals of conspicuous concealment, everyone breaking their necks whenever two people walked toward a bathroom. Integrity meant doing your drugs in public and alone.

Having done them, though, it was nice to walk through bodies in a strobe of glamour, champing at the insides of your cheeks, eyes tracing the newly interesting rooms like a machine die. Pleasure might be a deceptive sophistry, but it was better than subscribing to some hoary ideal of seriousness, of subtlety at the expense of the obvious. Seriousness was articulation. Leave the body out of it.

Leave the body out—Linda realized she was dancing and nobody else was. She stopped and stood vanquished near a ficus. An underdressed girl in sunglasses was wending through the crowd with a large messenger bag. Linda would've thought she was a panhandler who'd wandered in if not for her bike helmet. The girl sidled up to a group of people, laughing whenever they laughed, then broke in and squashed their conversation flat. She tried again with a second group as the first laughed at her. When she passed nearby, Linda recognized the round butt and gnarled hair and felt a gong of surprise. "Oh my god," Linda called out, hooking the girl's sleeve. "Hey. Hey. Cory!"

Cory turned. "Oh, whoa."

They embraced over Cory's lumpy canvas bag. "'Sup hoodrat! What's with the indoor sunglasses," Linda panted.

Cory took her sunglasses off, and her face gave its eloquent account. Hammocks of violet flesh hanging under her eyes and a cheek zit requiring clinical drainage. "Work's fucking me up," she said.

"Come sit." Linda patted Cory's back through her dense cables of hair and eased her onto a couch. Linda felt a throat-squeeze of compassion for Cory's bustedness. This was not shabby chic—it was the beauty sleep denied. "Do a bump with me."

"I still don't do that shit."

"Whaaat? You smoke weed like err'day."

"Weed's not a—" Cory seemed to want to say more, but let out a leonine yawn that probably began as a scream.

A nearby subwoofer splattered out dubstep that made the loose folds on Cory's T-shirt blur on the downbeat. Linda had already keyed out a small hill of drug and offered it to Cory, the other keys jingling on the ring. "Do it."

Cory shook a baggie of white powder at Linda. "I'm on this already. Excedrin and baking soda. Jesus, I'm gonna pass out."

Linda took the bump and licked the key clean. "Girl, you look like you just learned about death. Go get some sleep. And *food*."

"I can't, I'm working. We're promoting at private parties now. My company. There's no cover here. I have to go to three more tonight. You know whose party this is?"

"No. Do you?"

"Some Internet rich guy."

Yes, it was a dickhead party. Linda's critical apparatus switched lenses from telephoto unease to wide-angle disgust: the framed Chris Ware panels, the wall-mounted collector's guitars and Godard poster. Everyone had very uncreased necks, which meant no prolonged inclining of the head, which meant no reading. (Linda's own neck looked like a finger, but she reassured herself that the creases were like tree rings marking her substance.) She hated that she was legitimizing it by being here.

Cory let out another yawn you could walk around in. "Ulgh. I have to go. Good seeing you."

"No, c'mon, stay."

"Sorry. Work."

Cory hugged Linda and pressed a glossy flyer into her hand, affixed with a small baggie of her fake coke. Linda considered leaving with Cory, since she'd be goddamned if she left with Eve and Jared, but Cory had already moved on. How had they fallen into such low profile? Success had seemed so foregone in college, when Cory was doing her hunger strikes and Linda was at least still writing. When they roomed together in college they'd finely balanced their negativities—Cory's distaste for coolness had shamed Linda out of several Adorno-quote tattoos she would've definitely regretted, and Linda's sarcasm had shamed Cory out of claiming that she ate only chickpeas with hot sauce to be frugal/healthy/vegetarian. Plus Cory had den-mother tendencies that had found their perfect subject—even that one time Linda passed out in Cory's bed and then wet it, Cory made her raspberry leaf tea and filled a knotted-up T-shirt with microwaved dry rice to rest on her forehead. Though their rapport wasn't based on caretaking so much as mutual admiration for qualities they didn't covet themselves, which made everything easy. Cory once said she had an intricate recurring fantasy about intervening in a sexual assault and then counseling the almost-victim through her trauma and reporting options, which Linda found hilarious and touching.

But now Cory had blundered into the hamster wheel of nonprofit, and Linda was here.

Linda was feeling the squirming beginnings of vomit when a mustached guy in a serape approached her, offering a long slender glass pipe. She took it from him and asked what it was. "Opium. You'll like it," he said.

She examined the slick brown lump in the bowl, lit it, and her lungs filled with a thick, dead-tasting greasiness, like boiling Vaseline. She took three more hits, letting the bitter smudge seethe from her teeth. "You said this is opium?"

Retrieving the pipe from Linda, the guy took a luxurious hit and said through a bush of smoke, "Actually it's heroin. Actually it's better than heroin. It's death. But some people get all faggy when they hear the H-word. It's all opiates."

Her hands and cheeks warmed, matched by a queasy remorse that she was accustomed to pushing through. The thing she was indignant about was sapping her indignation. The pipe guy was still talking, one of those guys who became their drug preferences. Interrupting him, Linda rose like a fever up from the couch and headed outside to clear out her lungs with a cigarette.

When she couldn't hear her own footsteps in the stairwell she realized how loud it had been inside; the sidewalk outside seemed muffled. She posted up by the stoop, near three girls with faces phosphoresced by their phones. Linda regretted breaking hers. Now she never knew the time.

She twisted the filter off an American Spirit, lit it, and crossed her eyes to stare at its gray-orange cherry. Cigarettes made ideal partners: they made you look good, let you be needy for five minutes before replacing them with another. Stimulation, orality, the breathplay of carbon monoxide. An unlit cigarette smelled like a raisin, a lit one like a cigarette, your fingers afterward like soy sauce. And yes, the romance of smoking was pure product placement, but it was still the sexiest way of hating yourself.

Her thing with Henrik had not been a cigarette but a campfire—blazing, oxygen-hungry. And she'd kicked dirt and pissed on him until he was out.

She went back in. Someone was switching the light off and on in time to the music. While she splashed gin into a cup, she noticed a guy slouching in a corner as if being punished for his lanky height. When they met eyes, he approached, and she began to plan his evisceration, until he passed under a black light and Linda registered something familiar in his shrewish face: dishonor, trouble, evil—

"Fuck, fuck, fuck."

Since she'd left him, Baptist had grown his hair to squire length, though still with those side-flopping bangs. He wore tortoiseshell glasses and a full auburn beard that was mangy over the cheeks, a brown leather jacket distressed like a golem. She might not have left him as quickly if he'd looked like this, able to make good on his testosterone.

Backing away, Linda cut the bathroom line and slipped in just as someone else left, locking the door. As she searched the tremendous bathroom for a window to dive through, Baptist entered through a second door from the master bedroom, and locked it as well. He clutched Linda's arm, another appetizing show of dominance Linda had assumed he wasn't capable of. They ignored the guy passed out in the bathtub. Baptist's pubescent voice echoed off the shiny black tile. "I just want to talk."

Linda threw off Baptist's grasp. "Nice glasses, fuckface. You look like a professor of douche studies."

"I've been trying to contact you. You're living with Eve and Jared now."

"The fuck you know Eve?"

"I know Jared. Eve works with my girlfriend. Everyone knows everyone."

"Does your girlfriend know you're stalking me?"

Even in the bathroom, the music was loud enough that Baptist had to lean in close to Linda. "I was tripping last fall, but I'm over it. My mom set me up in this apartment and helped me pay down my bills. I'm sober and I met a girl who loves me. I'm not stalking you, but I've been kind of obsessed with figuring out what happened with us. If you let me say something I promise I'll leave you alone forever."

Someone battered the bathroom door. Linda leaned against the sink. "Fine."

Baptist pushed his bangs back and they swayed forward again. He stuck out a counting pinkie. "First, you're insecure, like everyone. You're conflicted because you want to be liked, but want even more to be *resented*—to be stared at, to make people ashamed of their inferior wit and taste. The sincerest form of flattery. Feels good, right? You wouldn't even be letting me take you down like this if it weren't proof in itself that you got under my skin."

She reached over and curled Baptist's pinkie back into his fist. "Anxiously awaiting substance."

"You make yourself unapproachable. So you provoke, because if you're awful and people still put up with it, then you must be special, and you justify being shitty by pretending you're being even harder on yourself. Also, for someone who complains about 'fashions' and 'topicality' in books, can I point out that your hobbies, clothes, even the way you talk couldn't be more contemporary?"

Linda half smiled and belched, as if intentionally. She was hearing about 60 percent of what he was saying. More slapping at the door. "Cool. How much do I owe for the session?"

"Okay, last few things. I'm sure you know that all your posturing just covers up your thin résumé. Which makes you loathe yourself, even more so because you know the only people you're impressing are those whose admiration you despise, like me. You hate anyone who's not as smart as you aspire to be. Because you can manipulate them, or because they don't try hard enough to see through you. Even worse is that you both resent men and live for their attention, and your attention-getting makes other girls either despise or lose respect for you. Basically, you're lonely, and exploit desperate guys for validation, being sure to make them suffer so that you're not technically serving them. But ironically that makes you, like, metaneedy—you need their need. And finally you inflate this loneliness to existential proportions, convince yourself it's more than just self-manufactured twenty-something drama. But that's all it is: drama. Sorry I'm rushing this; I had more to say."

"Well, friendo," Linda said, hair-flipping over each shoulder, "I mean, thanks for the tête-à-twat. I wish I had half as much to say about you, but you're just another dipshit techie man-child who thinks women are Rubik's Cubes, and *just* realized that having money doesn't make him interesting or any less of a cunt."

"Thanks for proving my point. Whenever anyone gets real with you, you shrink them and squish them. You're good at it, because you can do donuts around most people intellectually. But then you're invincible and alone. Stuck thinking, 'Why isn't my life as great as me?' That, I do not envy."

Linda was struck by the cunning of Baptist's accidental checkmate: that she was wrong for being right, and her reflexive comeback—that she'd already heard everything he was telling her—forced her to admit *he* was right. "Sure, man," she said, pushing in her cuticles until she located the rhetorical fire exit. "So, what, like, I'm supposed to feel contrite and start crying? That's what you want? Fuck you."

Baptist shrugged and extended a hand that Linda left unspliced. "We're good. I'll mail your stuff to Eve. And chew some gum, you're stank as hell."

He exited into the bedroom, while Linda, not to be seen

leaving with him, left through the hallway, shoulder-checking past a gauntlet of hisses and snack-missiles from the long bathroom line. People were dancing in the living room, and every horizontal surface was covered in drinks. Linda picked up the nearest cup and drank from it, stopping when she saw a long red hair plastered to its inside, half-immersed. How shitty of Baptist to ambush her while she was fucked up. And how shitty of San Francisco for being too small to churn away consequence. There was no getting lost.

Hearing laughter, Linda turned to make sure it wasn't at her. Three guys sat around a glass coffee table, which held something that looked like a nude baby and, on second glance, was a nude baby. One of the guys was pouring vodka into its mouth. Linda dropped her drink and pushed bodies out of the way—*What the fuck!*—but on third glance the baby was a doll, the kind that wet itself. They were doing baby shots. She was going to murder them if they laughed, but they offered her the doll instead, and to save face she grabbed its floppy legs and drank down six ounces of rubber-smelling vodka. She dropped the doll and walked away, wondering if anything smart could ever be said about this.

As she dreamily removed her jacket and laid her head against the armrest of the couch that she was apparently sitting on, exhaustion snuggled up like an enormous grub in her head. Her consciousness bobbed between this room and its shadowy double in Hell. She closed her eyes, and an unwanted insight lit up before her: *PARTIES AREN'T FUN.* That you could have fun *at* a party only confused matters. Alcohol, drugs. Bad dancing to bad music with the wrong number of people. Crowded hallways. Photos. Groping on a bed of coats. Something spills or breaks, someone pukes. A fight. You might meet someone new and interesting, but broadly speaking people were less new and interesting every day.

Eve and Jared were at her side, wearing their coats, along with a pudgy bald stranger in a polo shirt. "Linda, we found a ride. Let's dip."

Linda stood and leaned on a wall, or a door, or a floor. "What for? You hired a sitter."

"The scene is sketch as fuck."

"This shit's not good for my recovery," Jared added.

"Aw, booboo doesn't drink! What the fuck did you expect at a party?"

"Well, we got up at seven, so we gotta go now or we'll be wiped in the morning."

"Oh, we'll be, be'll we? Fuck your conjugal we. And who's *this* shithead?" Linda ran up on the bald guy.

"He's driving us home. Don't get outta line."

"Ew, those shitty piercings. You're that guy who can't think up a good tattoo and just goes for maximum holes."

The bald guy turned to Eve. "She's coming with us?"

"No way I'm going with this fuggin . . . bald-ass Drakkar Noir fuggin faggot."

"Linda, this shit is *not cute*."

Linda slapped the guy's jaw, gave him a sturdy headbutt, then went grabbing at his ears. He pushed her off and sank into the dancing crowd. Eve rested her fingertips against her temples, and Jared called after the bald guy.

"Whatever. Go watch your movie. Boring cunts."

"Jared, let's go. Bitch, you're out of our apartment. Handle your shit."

Eve left, and Linda touched away a warm spot on her brow that, no matter how much she looked at it, was blood. Blood was so sincere. Must be why people made promises with it. Maybe it was sincerity itself—she should write that down. Where was her purse? Forget the pen, she'd write in blood. Write her epitaph. Epigraph. Prologue. Foreword. Backward. The sleeve of her leather jacket hailed from behind a couch cushion, and she yanked it out and put it on. She needed a ride but she was too faded to find an exploitable guy. The inside of her dress smelled like not quite yogurt. She wouldn't even make good prey.

Someone was yelling at her, pushing her forward. On her way to the door she seized the edge of a table and overturned it, sending plastic cups and beer cans spinning to the floor in pinwheels of foam. This was becoming her personal cliché: exile from a strange home, a hasty scramble down dark stairs, unnecessary things left behind. That was the last thing she would recall, later.

?. ????????

It was later. A thin white horizon grew, uncurtained from above, and was nothing but a ceiling. She couldn't move; with great effort she observed herself. Limbs muffed in gauze dangled from slings and cables in stiff angles of salute. When she tried to move her leg, the bone snarled in pain, feeling nailed to a plank of wood, and her vision wobbled with tears. Then she was all nose, and the tubes that ran up it gouged and gagged her. Her lungs slurped whenever she inhaled.

This was Linda drained of Lindahood, less a person than a sentient body, no realer than words on a document, struck from subject into object—that is, things that felt terrible felt like her. Possibly this new pain would be her great achievement, possessing all the qualities she'd wanted for her writing: a pioneering agony that both straddled genres (thriller, mystery, horror) and defied them, baroque and maximalist, enveloping her with its belabored detail and longeurs, high modernist in its stern insistence on a total universe, its difficulty.

As soon as she could speak she screamed. First that she'd been blinded, though it was just that her contact lens was knocked out. She punched the nurse call button for attacks of gas, dementing face itches, and her sordid bedpan concerns. She requested wet towels and pled for cigarettes until her nurse brought in the resident doctor, muttering about Linda's "acute supratentorial issues" as if she couldn't guess what that meant. The doctor read the damage, a list that would be difficult to memorize if not for the rote tutorials of pain: three cracked ribs, broken right wrist, clavicle, right fibula. Palms, feet, and knees icy with abrasions. "Also," he added, "you've got really high cholesterol."

He added that, considering her injuries, she really ought to be dead. He was right. She was tragically prehumous; since she was a reader, most people she cared about were dead or fictional. In Valéry, Phaedrus complained that he couldn't hear or see in the underworld, and Socrates replied, *Perhaps you are not sufficiently dead.* Always it was the freckle of vulgar life, bringing pain, seeming to persist no matter what, that denied her the immortality of death.

In her first conscious hours she enacted every convalescent cliché. Will I be all right? ("Everything's going to be fine.") Be honest, is it bad? ("It's not good. We'll have to insert a metal rod in your arm.") She even begged for a mirror. Both her top front teeth were punched out, a bottom incisor snapped down to an angled shard. Her tongue was speed-lined with road rash, and a trail of black stitches ran along it from tip to center. Her upper lip split at one peak. Touching her teeth together completed a vile circuit that sent currents of frost and flame through her skull. She stared at the holes. Only money would fill them. How much sex work would it take to pay it down— how many shudders, what pledge of remaining innocence? No, nobody would pay for that now. She'd need a job that didn't require a face. Office manager, paralegal. And she would have to keep her mouth shut.

An SFPD pig came visiting in his black serge and flat cap to collect a statement for the incident report, assuring her that she wasn't in any trouble, and she thought that was funny. What do you remember, he asked. Nothing. Nothing at all? I remember . . .

II. A Vehicle

The rain outside Baptist's apartment made the asphalt sear with vertical files of reflected neon. The night was curved like a lens. The street gave her two directions to home. She lunged into the slut-shaming chill of night, posture muscles limp but thighs steady under their swaying elastic freight. Near the corner she slipped on a shred of someone's discarded wig and went stumbling into a wall. Cars sped by, sucked up the ramp of asphalt, hissing black rainslick under their tires. Then the street sped by, and Linda bent at the knees to fix her purchase on the ground. She reached the corner but she couldn't read the signs. Now there were twice as many ways. She hitched one arm around a lamppost and dropped an orange scarf of vomit.

From here it was trick-camera and split-screen. Memory to be constructed into something less obviously stupid and trivial than it obviously was, filtered through consciousness, refined into language, rolled and toasted into literature. Someone had to choose the words. Every account was a frame around chaos, excluding this and highlighting that, thus fiction by omission, no matter how factual. No accident that modernism and cars arrived at the same time; inevitable that they should collide.

The only witness surges downhill on Dolores at two A.M., acceleration putting a tickle of freefall into his stomach and making worms of rain sprint across his windshield. Fleshy blur where his face should be. He pokes at the Seek button, blows cigarette smoke out the window, freeing it invisibly into the wind.

Theirs is a meeting of misdemeanors, jaywalker and speeder, two trajectories in the vastness of spacetime converging in a bursting asterisk. *Deus ex machina*—here was a last-minute metaphor all right, a narrative vehicle stinking of ye olde emergency conceit, the overpowering heaviness and all-transformingness out of nowhere and zoom, it's off with the plot. The way that all failed metaphors smashed together the irreconcilable; how they rammed aside the real to advance someone's cheap tidy idea of the world.

She who lives by the metaphor, etc.

At this speed Linda is no more than a startled flash, a single spooked frame registering nothing but its own displacement as her body takes over the car's hard motion. How far she flew, struck through. Going up. Turning over. She hits the curb with her chest and rolls to a stop between a mailbox and a trash can.

The record contains only loose sense-data for this interval of ink and void: the smell of close wet concrete, a trembling bubble of shame expanding from her mouth, hazy glowing edges where the rainbow of consciousness bands off into ultraviolet. Every blink reshakes the kaleidoscope. The sound of a city night returns, distant acouasms of traffic, and seeing the lee shore of waking she understands she's dying. No more shame. Her torn dress and jacket, the night, and the forked lightning strike of her blood across the sidewalk are fragments of the same blackness. A rotating fire draws close, licking, licking across the building fronts. Something lifts her up and back down, uncoiling things and tying them to her arm. She lightens and unexists. A weighty phantom on top of Linda tries to shout with her voice, but her mouth is full of her tongue.

What had she tried to say? If only she had the talent to remember.

III. Not Sufficiently Dead

. . . nothing.

After the officer left, her resident informed her that they hadn't been able to reach her mother. Which was fine, her mother couldn't afford to help. Anyone else she'd like to call? She didn't know any phone numbers offhand. "I need a computer," she rasped.

The male nurse held the loaner laptop in front of her as Linda pecked at it with her unslung arm and glared at it with her one lensed eye: **hey buddy ive been hit by a car. spazzed out in traction at sf general. don't be a stranger xx lt.** She bcc'd six recipients and dismissed the nurse, flipping off his departing back.

Hours crept by disguised as days. Whenever her breath

slowed into sleep she sprang awake with detonations of rich coughs, making the pulleys of her traction squeak. When they brought her semisolid meals, she sneered at the oatmeals and milk cartons, the soggy cutlets of no animal in particular. She chewed with crooked deliberation in her cheek. Linda thundered at her nurse to turn the television off and the radio on, finding the airwaves occupied by the moneychangers of Mainstream.

Time was losing its orderly candor, time was now officially weak—fitting that she should live out her bad writing. In her exhausted half-waking, Linda reviewed the canon of the car-struck: Camus, Sebald, Barthes, Italo Svevo, okay. Frank O'Hara and Randall Jarrell. Nathanael West, T-boned on his way to Fitzgerald's funeral, ha. Margaret Mitchell, Stephen King—so there was money in it yet.

Her thumb learned the rhythm of her glowing green morphine button, sending the drug discoursing through her bloodstream on the hour and making her head fill the moon, anchored only by the hyperdense dot of her aching body. Where was the nicotine button, the Bloody Mary button? Well, give her the morphine—*and* the fentanyl, the Mylar balloons, condolence cakes. If she was going to go broke for this, let them go for broke. The nasal tubes made her retch and drool, the IV made her piss, the bandages made her sweat, the suppositories made her shit, the breakthrough pain made her cry, and she wasn't getting paid for it. Having a male nurse sponge her down was humiliating. There had to be all-female hospitals somewhere, only run by, only treating, and if those . . .

She woke later to silence, to the shush of her bed and the ministrations of her pain. Will was reading his phone next to her. Hearing Linda inhale deeply, Will pocketed his phone and stood beside her at his concise five foot four, asked how she felt. She wheezed. He read the accident report aloud from his phone. It had happened three whole days earlier, suspect unknown, no witnesses.

"So, uh. What's it like being Jane Doe? Usually only corpses and amnesiacs get to know that." She didn't respond. "Well. At least the fucknuts who hit you probably read this article and is shitting hot water right now."

Trust in Will to draw solace in vengeance. She was grateful he wasn't patronizing her with tenderness. It was a little sad that the only person to visit her was someone she'd seen only once in the past two years. She'd never spent much time with Will, and who knew if she'd see him again after today. He was that guy she'd always liked yet never really befriended because they had nothing in common but Henrik, and he'd occasionally pull some inferiority complex bullshit when he was drunk and say things like, *Admit it, the only reason you'd ever talk to me is because you're dating my friend, ADMIT IT.* But he was here, and she doubted she would've visited him likewise. He'd come along since college: more self-aware, better clothes and hair. It was fun sharing the secret of having been dorky undergrad pariahs, though she felt fraudulent around him for that reason.

"I'm glad you're here," she said. "I hate hospitals. I wish they'd put me straight in the dirt."

Will was reading his phone again. "Do you have health insurance?"

"Are you being funny?"

"Then we should get you out of here soon as possible. They're probably raping you with the bill. It's so stupid to have drugged-up patients dealing with this bullshit."

Linda rolled her head on her pillow. Of its own accord her

hand tensed around the morphine button, and her arm bloomed and warmed. "As soon as my piss goes back to a normal color I'm leaving. Through a window if I have to."

Will gave a loud laugh, not because it was funny but because he hated the soft laughter that people offered the infirm. "You need me to bring you anything from your place? Where do you live?"

"Nowhere."

"I said where do you live?"

"I said *nowhere*."

"Are you being melodramatic or are you actually homeless or is it the morphine?"

Linda gauged the length of a full explanation at about two pages and did not elaborate. Instead she coughed.

"Okay. Interesting." Will grasped his chin and mouth. "Vanya's away. You could catsit for her. They're toilet-trained."

Linda turned her head to face Will, putting her nasal tubes painfully aslant. Constructing sentences felt like trying to remember in utero existence. "Maybe," she said.

"Good. All right, I'm going now. Call me if you need something."

"No phone."

"Jesus, okay. Well, I've been meaning to upgrade anyway, so take this one. Can you set it up with your phone carrier?" They looked at each other desperately. "Fine, I'll do that too. Now, who's your emergency contact?"

"My mom. But she doesn't know I'm here."

"Your dad?"

"In Rome. And an asshole."

"Then put me down. It'll help me get you out."

"Will, you don't have to."

"It's fine. Vanya's away, so I've got time. If I jerk off any more I'll crash the Internet."

"Okay." Linda yawned. Morphine brimmed her head like a full soapy bath. "You're being so nice."

Linda seemed only nominally aware that anybody was in the room with her at all. She babbled into her pillow, saying she was grateful, she loved him, she hurt so much. Will didn't know what to do until she said, "Something smells good."

"Oh. It's my lunch."

"What is it?"

"Pastrami and corned beef on rye. Sauerkraut, brown mustard, Thousand Island."

"I want it."

"Uh, it's my lunch."

"But I want it."

Will grunted and took half the sandwich from his bag. He unfolded its butcher paper and steered the more succulent corner into her mouth, and she bit with startling ardor, taking away a crescent of paper, bit again before swallowing her first crammed mouthful, drawing blood from his thumb, three more chomps, and it was gone. "Any booze?" Linda said. Bread lint and threads of sauerkraut stuck to the brown mustard at the corners of her mouth.

"That would kill you right now."

"Give it to me or I kill *you*."

Will reached inside his jacket to unscrew the cap, then stood with his back to the door as he tipped and tipped the bubbling leather flask to her mouth and said, "Glenlivet, eighteen-year." Actually it was twelve. Linda gulped it like apple juice, pushing the flask away with her tongue when it was empty. The last nip spread down her chin and darkly into her gown, and she swabbed her lips together. "Mm."

Will rescrewed the flask and wiped her chin. "Anything else?"

"You're going? Nooo."

"Yeah, you should rest."

"Please don't go. Please. At least hug me."

A weird writhing embarrassment, like an eel in his ribs, made Will blush. He maneuvered unskillfully around her traction to press his ear against hers for ten seconds, squeezing her shoulders rather than reaching for a full embrace, and he felt her warm good arm around him. She sighed as he drew back. Her eyes were red and brimming. "Listen, I'll be back tomorrow," he said.

"Wait. Before you go. Tell me how you get your arms so hairless."

"Diet and prayer. Are we good?"

"Yeah, um. Hang on. Can you tell me if I look okay?"

"Sure. You'll live."

"No, not okay as in healthy. I mean cute."

Will's forehead wrinkled; he felt a shy curl of empathy. Linda was wearing the customary blue gown and a low-lidded expression. The teased snowbank of her hair still held flecks of dirt. Lake-shapes of dried drool on the collar of her gown, tubes in her nose and arm, a big square bandage on her right cheek, scabbed lips, a puke pot at arm's reach. She seemed flattened and foreshortened, and without her front teeth she spoke with an arid draftiness. Some of her eyeliner and mascara was still on but faded, making her eyes beady and wide set. It felt uncanny to square this needy version of her with the intimidation he'd always associated with her, embodying as she did that unicorn species of hot girl who he'd been trained to assume looked down on him and thus deserved to be resented. It was hard to hold eye contact with her. Was that, in fact, the only reason he was here? Even though he had Vanya, that loserly imperative to get as near as possible to hot girls and stare at them and be useful to them and get their approval had never withered, like he'd hoped it would. Visiting Linda was probably charitable, though possibly he should've shunned her out of loyalty to Henrik.

Anyway: yes, he still would, he totally would. With that one leg elevated in traction, helpless . . . Jesus. Good thing he wasn't in the habit of taking his thoughts seriously. "You look fine," he said. "Except your teeth."

"Thank you." Yawned tears ran down both sides of her nose. "What time is it?" she asked.

"Two thirty."

"Stay," she said, and immediately fell asleep.

Will closed the door behind him, holding the knob twisted so it didn't click when it closed. In the hallway he contemplated all the good deeds he'd just been pressured into, and left with a qualm of guilt for feeling so pleased.

They meet late in a year of record lows. The fifteen-degree summer. Invasion abroad, recall at home, Schwarzenegger by a landslide. A SARS quarantine on campus. Mars draws near to Earth.

Henrik Fenn has just transferred to Stanford after a summer pumping gas at a New Haven Amoco, and on the way to the library he stops by the coffee cart and sees her. An elfy brunette in sunglasses and a teal hoodie. There's no line, but he wishes there were one, so he'd have more time. He decides against a smoothie, or anything else with an emasculating straw, orders coffee and a banana instead. She doesn't bother to set down her book to ring him up. In her bug-eye sunglasses he sees only two of himself.

He sits at a table to eat his solitary banana, recalling that his psychiatrist warned him against caffeine. The daylight hides her in the cart's shade, though he shouldn't be ogling anyway.

From deep behind her sunglasses, Linda Troland sees him too, and knows he's lurking precisely to be seen. Courtship as sit-in protest. At first she's just like, well hello, who's this stuttering pork tenderloin? Relaxed-fit jeans, dangling canvas belt, Brewers ball cap, Patagonia microfleece, carabiner keychain. Just like his coffee: a tall plain drip.

Out of boredom, however, she speculates. Remember, she's

seventeen: she listens to Nada Surf and Moby, wears a clear laminate retainer; at night her shins still pulse unaccountably with growing pains, and, having lost all faith and good standing in academia, she's determined to fuck up, off, with, and around until purged of all purity and inhibition.

She spends her shift drawing his butcher chart. During a lull, she walks over to his table, hands in hoodie pockets. "Yo, why are you staring at me?" she asks. "Do I fucking owe you money or something?"

He doesn't respond or look up to see her indulgent tilde of a smile, instead ignores her attentively, ears and scalp turning a meaty red through thin blond locks. If he were a lizard his tail would drop off. She softens her knife a little. "For real, though. Were you gonna say something?"

"I don't know."

"Coffee. Banana. What's not to know?"

"Nothing. That's why I didn't."

"But you wanted to talk to me."

He nods.

"Maybe spit some game? Little bit?"

Blank, oppressed silence.

"But you decided against it. Indulge my curiosity here."

He looks off to the nearby red fountain, shaped like a costume halo, the falling water blurred by a crosswind and sending students racing to shield their books and papers. Something big is downloading. At last he says, "I came up with a bunch of reasonable noble-sounding excuses. Like, girls are constantly getting approached by pushy guys who think they're owed attention, and I'd be no exception. It's sleazy to hit on someone who's trying to work, and hey, I'll talk to her if I see her some other time when I'm wearing deodorant and have something to say. My nervousness is a sure sign of unhealthy expectations. And it feels so transparently shallow to flirt with someone when you both know physical attraction is all that's driving it, reinforcing the idea that people are worth approaching insofar as they're good-looking. Plus the likelihood of a scarring rejection outweighs the tiny chance of a satisfying exchange. I know strangers talk all the time without pretext, or can supply their own pretext, but I suck at it. The real reason I didn't say anything to you is fear."

She waits for him to punctuate. This is fun. "So he talks."

"Sorry."

"So it's hard for you to flirt but easy to rip your guts open?"

"It is easier to fail on purpose. Though I wouldn't call it easy."

"Regardless, here we are. Try me."

He scratches behind his ear. "Okay, um, what do you study."

"Nope. If we're doing small talk, I'm out."

"Sorry."

"Oh, don't be sorry. Be interesting."

"Okay."

"Sorry and okay, he says. You're so nice. Don't you hate stuff? That's how I spend, like, two-thirds of my time. I eat popcorn and I judge. How can you not hate?"

"I do hate."

"Oh yeah?"

"A lot. Like, a Walmart of hate."

"Name one thing."

Motionless pondering for twenty seconds. "Misogyny."

"How brave. Why not just say war? Or airplane food?"

"I know, it makes me look pious and now I regret saying it. I guess I specifically mean male romantic entitlement, the thing that made it seem wrong to talk to you. And how it's formed this sort of ecosystem of creep archetypes that feel almost like Darwinian adaptations to feminism."

"Like what?"

"Well." Seeing him muster his words is like watching a hydroelectric power plant. "First you have the sociopathic bros who see life as a nonstop pussy safari and devise entire social conventions around exploiting female fears. The Apex Creep—alpha-male and pickup-artist types. Just relentlessly catcalling and macking. Polishing an exoskeleton of confidence. They're usually considered idiots but actually they're as rational as mosquitoes. They play the numbers. Emotions are just levers on bipedal sex kiosks. Existence is reduced to sham evolutionary behavioralism. They muffle their consciences by insisting that women play the same game—gold diggers or skanks who want to be dominated, and any who deny it are ugly fat dyke feminists.

"Then there's the Rage Creeps, those wounded pressure cookers. If out of sheer resentment they don't aspire to become Apex Creeps, then they'll define themselves to the contrary, which convinces them they're good guys. They think it's romantic to aggressively offer themselves up for exploitation, be kind attentive friends for however long they think it'll take for the girl to come around, but when this doesn't pay off in sex, it putrefies into stalkery rage, so they get to play both victim and tragic hero. I'm sure this isn't news to you so maybe we should talk about something else."

"No. Proceed," she says, lighting a cigarette.

"The Noble Creep. The high-minded ambitious dude whose band or social cause or novel is so important it dwarfs any woman's needs. If his girlfriend says he's negligent or domineering, she's being petty. Why's she gotta be like that? Can't she be supportive? Any philandering or abuse is justified, though if she tries to be equally aloof then sayonara. He might be self-aware enough to tell himself he's not sexist since he treats everyone equally like garbage, though the practical truth is that women have to put up with a lot more of it. On the other hand there are Needy Creeps with disabling dysfunctions, addicted, lovelorn, mentally ill or whatever, who consciously or not use their brokenness to make women responsible for fixing them, especially those who can be convinced it's a form of empowerment.

"Women can and should hit back. But some end up calling their harassers fags or virgins or saying they have small dicks, which is more effective than calling them creeps, but it validates creeps' cynical assumption that women are shallow bitches who only value masculinity.

"This stuff bothers me because I'm implicated. Even while I'm tempted to flatter myself for my self-awareness, this one aspect of misogyny haunts me only because it affects me. Which makes me one of those Enlightened Creeps who's read a few books and declares himself an ally, even delivers feminist sermons and beatdowns to the point where feminism becomes another arena for male competition. They'll say mock-humble stuff like 'I hope to empathize, but I'll never truly understand the struggle of women,' though they secretly think they deserve extra credit because, unlike women, they're being altruistic.

"All my self-flagellating right now is the worst kind of self-pity because it's actually bragging; look how sensitive and self-aware I am. Even pointing out how I'm bragging makes me look knowing and forthright. And pointing out that I'm pointing it out makes me look complex and quirkily neurotic. It's exhausting but I don't know what else I can do except acknowledge it.

"I'm sure there are men out there who do treat women fairly, but I assume some enabling x factor of privilege, like it only works because they're rich or good-looking, or worse, because they don't think about this stuff. Men can be feminists, but I don't know if straight guys can avoid being creeps, not here and now. The structural power advantage is always there, even if it's not leveraged. So usually I avoid women, confirming the guilty suspicions that feminist men are silly effete intellectuals who would be sexist if they were man enough, so that sexism becomes almost this sexually selected trait. It's also just defensive pessimism: 'I'm not shy, I respect women!' A vicious circle that keeps me insulated from and sensitized to emotional engagement, amounting to nothing except a feeling that I'm right. Which I'm not."

She shifts her sunglasses up. "Jesus."

"Sorry."

"If you think it's so hopeless, why are we talking?"

Another pause long enough to fix a martini in. "I don't know. So far all I've done is embarrass myself. Either you think that's funny, or you enjoy not having to impress me. But I'm lonely and invested enough to accept it now that it's begun."

"Enough, stop it."

"Sorry."

"Listen, I agree and I disagree. You're like me. If you didn't hate yourself a lot you wouldn't like yourself at all." She snuffs her cigarette. "I'm E," she says, not offering her hand.

"E, like the letter?"

"No. Like the drug."

It is a nickname she's just invented, an algebraic symbol

designating her new variable self. "C'mon, let's go do something. Let's go shoplift."

With startling composure he says, "Do you have tinfoil?"

It circumvents theft alarms, he says, and begins explaining how Faraday cages work. He takes visible solace in academic talk, as it can be nuanced and factual without having anything to do with him. Returning to the coffee cart, she spends the rest of her shift fortifying her bag, and afterward they walk to the Stanford Shopping Center. Playing the bored purse-holding spouse at Bloomingdale's, he lifts a sweater and exits nonchalantly, handing her the purse.

"It's like you just handed me free money for life," she says, petting the chenille.

"Just like my pops taught me," he says, knowing she'll think he's kidding. "I can take off the antitheft tags too. With a rubber band."

"Yes. Next time. You will show me."

Cool, she thinks. She pens her number on his wrist and takes her leave with a noncommittal nod. Petty larceny is weaponizing her intellect. Forming the vision of her desires: the auratic, anesthetic, deterrent power of prestige—though the young and green will content themselves with its basest form, cool. To dictate the terms of male attention and take whatever she wants.

For the next three weeks she is a crime wave, mopping basics at H&M, swiping skinny jeans and houndstooth circle scarves from Urban Outfitters, wearing tube dresses under her tube dresses out of Forever 21, thrift-lifting a D&G jacket and a Prada bag. Corset tops, rib crop tees, bobble lace halters, stretchy shiny bandeaux, strappy chunky wedge heels, the visible spectrum of Lycra leggings, skinny ties, and a fucking beret. Never again the athletic sock or the solitaire stud. Not one more banana clip. She will awestrike. Get ambitious about her hair. Read smoky eye tutorials. Wax.

Soon she's gazing upon a full wardrobe. All hers. She reconsiders Henrik. His gameness in the face of repeat humiliation. Someone she can bombard with new identities. Zero risk of catching feelings. It is her first time on the pedestal. She will see what sort of bust she makes.

CHAPTER 9
Everyone Else's Problem

Now I hate to tell such a plain truth, but I must—the bulk of San Francisco's liberality seems sometimes actuated by a love of applause.

—Mark Twain

2/2/08

It's so *me* of me to start a journal, especially knowing nobody will read it. In theory I hate navel-gazing, so not writing felt justified: the supreme negative poetics. So much for that. I've hit a bottom, & not even rock bottom—just plain dirt bottom.

Let the exposition be brief. In Jan I checked out of SF General w/ an impossible bill. Instead of taking Will's offer to stay at his place, I went back to Eve's—up until the accident I'd been turning in solid diaper changes, & they'd never pass up free babysitting. So I cabbed to their place unannounced, figuring my damaged steez would arouse her maternal pity. It did. "We know you'd been going thru a rough time," Eve said, courteously rationalizing my shittiness. Which is not the same as saying she likes me.

I've been here about a week looking after Mercy, who's tripled in size. The baby teeth she has coming in are the same ones I'm missing. She looks constantly amazed at being able to stand & grip the rail of her crib in her hooded lime-green onesie. I give her la-las in the morning, poochie-poos at night. Again I hold a green binky in her yap & wait for the latch. Again I accept diaper payloads, handle refrigerated bags of milk pumped out of my friend, & slather rash-paste across a thankless butt. The only time I hear my voice is when I'm talking to Mercy's life—oops, are we hungry? Did we drop our binky? Did we shit our diapies again? Fitting that I should narrate the subjectivity of someone who hasn't even constructed one.

If I'm going to let my ambition die shouldn't I at least be paid for it?

2007 Report Card—Silence: B / Cunning: D / Exile: A+

2/17/08

Jared is that guy who's talented but only paints shit like yetis on skateboards or pterodactyls eating astronauts. He's got the bloated face of the ex-junkie who doesn't sublimate his addiction into exercise. Back in Brooklyn he tried to be a party photographer & would lure girls to his apartment w/ drugs to sit for photos, twenty-somethings who cultivated a grueling look of underage skank: I was that girl.

Street art is his thing now. You can smell the rubber glue from the alley whenever the bathroom window's open & all he talks about are his "ideas" for where to get up— supermarket produce, mail, the plastic shield over photo-

booth cameras, so people's faces come out tagged. Tonight over dinner he tried showing me how to bite the nib of a glitter pen to make the letters drip but it exploded in his mouth & sprayed all over the tablecloth. Eve yelled, the baby cried, I yawned. Not that I'm one to disdain anybody's way of making his stupid mark.

I could go out to get away from the noise, but not with this grill. For purposes of laying low it helps that I'm approaching absolute ratchet. Scabs, bruises, & did I mention the acne rosacea is back? It is. Now that my hair toner's washed out it's this rank candy-corn yellow w/ shitty brown roots. Even some saddlebag softness where I hate to be soft. Day & night my gumholes make protest chants of pain. I can't bend my arm all the way—blots of stiff pain in my elbow, like the pins are stripping the bone. Last week the casts came off & my leg's got this puckered greenish tint, impervious to scrubbing & sunlight. I'm getting mouth lines. And I think a yeast situation is a-brewing. So begins life as a hag.

2/23/08

I thought living w/ Eve and Jared would be ho-hum— two parents who change from work clothes directly into sweatclothes to stare at a TV over the sounds of a screaming baby. But the shelter has gone skelter. Jared's trial period w/ sober partying has gone about as successfully as you might expect from someone who once shit in my couch (yes, __in__ it: he lifted the cushion). Yesterday Eve comes home & finds Jared passed out in an armchair w/ Mercy fallen on the floor. Me, I was applying to copyediting jobs in the next room—fuck me for entrusting Jared w/ his own daughter. So Eve investigates the premises—both those they live in & those they live under—quickly finding a grip of OxyContin in Jared's windbreaker.

2/28/08

Around midnight, when I'm putting Mercy down, Jared comes in w/ the stern look of someone who's been pacing for hours before a decision. His earring clashes conceptually w/ his pajamas. "So you couldn't sleep either," *he says, leaning on the doorframe, either for balance or for dramatic effect.*

I said yup, li'l jerk wouldn't go down w/out a fight. In that shushing voice.

"Can I hang?"

It's your house, I say, just don't wake her.

"I can tell you care about Mercy."

Yeah it's my job, I say, while a light goes red in the dash of my brain: I, you, care.

When he stumbles to the recliner I can tell he's throwed on pills—floaty, noddy, & I don't smell booze & he has to get drunk to shoot up. "It's really cool having you here, Linda," *he says in a voice weighing about half a gram.*

Thanks? I say.

"You take care of Mercy & it's not a big deal. Eve's been cutty like a motherfucker. The milk's got to be <u>this</u> warm, Mercy's got to sleep on <u>this</u> side and it's like, can I live? Just raise the fucking kid, hey?"

I say yup.

"To be totally honest," (I <u>do not</u> want total honesty) "I kinda think we should've dated instead."

I say the only thing I can: ew.

"In New York I thought it'd be lame to date someone w/ a fake ID. But now it's like, we click. You totally get it. Come on, you know it's true."

Here I'm trying to contain the fury—you know, that seething star-core of indignation that goes supergiant whenever some dickhead makes his sexual entitlements known. I saw this coming; he's been texting me while we're both in the apartment, always shit like "haha hey" and "whats up." I tell him he's a bit premature for a midlife crisis. He tries to say more but I cold shut him down. You should probably go to bed, I say. (Before I fucking put a knife in you.)

"We'll move to Omaha. Buy some land, make art, raise our own—"

Nope, nope, nope. Your side-chick-homestead ambitions are about to meet their death.

"No but you hear what I'm saying? I'm in love w/ you. Linda, I <u>love</u> you."

Actually, I considered it? I calculated logistics—how to bone w/out waking the baby, whether this Omaha farmhouse would have Wi-Fi—but virtue triumphs, I guess. I leap forward & pull his blissing ass off the recliner (I am the strongest bitch alive when I have to be) & I kick him out. Mercy makes those pre-sob hiccups, then starts howling, needle in the red. I'm up for another two hours. Boys are vile.

I feel it's best to keep the whole scummy affair mum from Mom. What's one little horny bucolic fantasy, ten-

dered in an opium-addled night rapture? Jared's idiocy is status quo. Babies need status quo.

3/2/08

God hell fucking dammit. Status quo? Never you fucking mind.

Today Mercy teeters flat-footed over to me, gripping couch cushions for balance. "Ummumma," she says.

Eve, who's eating dinner at the kitchen table, drops her silverware. "That was—"

I say, no, I don't think—

"She called you Mama."

Now I'm on the high wire. No way, I say, babies don't make that kind of mistake, they just don't.

"Linda. She was looking right at you."

I tell her Mama's an easy word—that's why it means what it means. Open your mouth twice while humming & that's it.

Eve takes Mercy from me (kind of unsafely!) & starts dandling her in perfect anguish. "This is so not what I need right now. Linda, it's OK, I'm not mad. You've helped a lot. But we need to talk about your plans."

"Umma, um. MUM-ma," Mercy enunciates from the dale of Eve's bosom, grabbing out to me w/ her face bunched. Eve joggles her double-time like she's trying to make up for lost parenting, & glares at me like, usurper.

At first I protest: doesn't it mean I'm doing a good job? But I'm also thinking: bitch, you may not have the life you asked for, but you have a life, & now you're booting the girl

w/ no work, money, friends, close family, or front teeth,
who's been raising <u>your</u> fucking baby.

So I tell Eve she's been so checked out that she hasn't
even noticed I've been fucking Jared, all this time he's been
turning me out like a dirty rubber glove, et cetera.

I don't blame her for slapping me: that's sort of what I
was going for.

She gave me the ol' ho-heave, and with cab fare as my
severance, I brought my duffel bag to Noe Valley to cash in
on Will's offer of sanctuary. Will was too tired to object, so
he pushed a key to the downstairs studio into my hands &
slammed the door in my face. He's a good guy.

3/29/08

This hag has not left Will's apartment in 3 weeks. It's
your basic hardwood-&-whitewash affair, screaming real-
tor from every sconce & track-light. Big round glass table,
daybed, lounge chair so overstuffed it leans you forward.
Huge flat-screen on the wall where portraits of ancestors
might have once hung. On the breakfast bar is a dusty can-
dleholder w/ linen-scented candles, still shrinkwrapped.
Dishwasher & laundry. Backyard terrace with potted
plants & patio furniture. A purgatory beyond my price
range. Will's girlfriend's wheelchair creaks the floorboards
upstairs. The sky outside a featureless white, like the fluorescent panels they hung my X-rays on.

TV isn't numbing me: that means trouble. Last week
I binge-watched <u>The Wire</u> & thought shit, about time TV
killed the social novel, that sad oxymoron. A social novel

needs a society, & society wants to be shown, not told. I hate to hork up the old gravamina about the death of literature, but I cannot take being outdone by entertainments I thought I was aiming higher than. Channel by premium channel, there goes period drama, self-help, chick-lit, fantasy, horror, cookbook, travelogue. The news beggars satire, and the verse line will never outrun the headline crawl— QUESTION DOCTOR'S SLEEP, NIPPLE MIX-UP ADVICE / GAYS WORSE THAN TERRORISTS LAWMAKER SAYS. *Then you go online & read the public affirmations of the First World. At last the mass can sing of the mass. What writing can survive? The inverse in verse, the antisocial novel?*

Fucking why even trip when all I'm doing is writing journal entries to myself about myself by myself for myself against myself <u>in spite of</u> *myself? I can admit certain things now: That I can't be alone. That ambition, transgression, and righteous vengeance weren't enough after all. And finally that my writing urge has nothing to do with talent or expression. It's not that I have a way with words; it's that I have no way without them.*

My birthday's next week. Retired dominatrix, tired bellatrix, failed belletrist, bailed fellatrist by 22. No existential justification no problem.

"BABY," VANYA CALLED out into Will's living room, where Will was reading eight blogs. "Come eat breakfast."

Since Vanya's apartment was being gut-renovated to accommodate filming, she and Will were living together for the first time. It was temporary, and she worked East Coast hours, but cohab was cohab.

She'd made garden omelets that sat on two round white dishes redly squiggled over with Sriracha sauce, and was photographing them. She and Will sat at the kitchen table in their usual tandem-work catercorner.

"I know you hate when I ask you, but I'd like you to take some tests," Vanya said. "To develop your onscreen persona."

Will sneered at his photogenic omelet, which somehow symbolized Vanya's firm, broad, unambiguous selfhood. Through years of personal optimization testing and strength-finding, she reckoned herself a Type A Left-Brain ESTP Post-Wave Feminist True-Cost Social Capitalist Progressive Independent Compatibilist Challenger Mahayana Buddhist Straight Mono Switch Femme; a Carrie, an Aries, and a Ravenclaw. Last year she'd had her DNA sequenced and found she was part Polish. In this galaxy of metrics Vanya had rigorously defined herself. *You're more than that,* Will wanted to say; but could he insist she was more complex than *she* said she was?

From her laptop Vanya administered the omnibus quiz— Myers-Briggs, enneagram, NEO PI-R, and Holland Code. "I've filled out the boilerplate. Okay. Religious beliefs?"

"None."

"Aren't your parents Buddhist?"

"Yeah, and *I'm* an atheist. The universe is a random-number generator."

"You're just saying that because it's trendy. Atheism is actually really extreme," Vanya said. "You literally believe there's no *possible* undiscovered thing that explains consciousness? You're *positive*?"

"Nobody's positive."

"That's agnostic then. Doubt means agnostic."

"At least put igtheist."

"There's no menu option for that. Agnostic it is. Okay—political affiliation?"

"None."

"Baby, you vote straight-ticket Democrat."

"I hate conservatives and I'm lazy."

"Basically a Democrat. Okay, now rate your agreement with these statements, scale of one to five. I am worthy of love?"

"I meaning you?"

"No, I meaning *you*."

"This test blows. Loved by who? Worthy meaning what?" Vanya searched Will's face as if for Spartacus. "Baby."

"Three."

"I rely on others for my emotional well-being?"

Will glared. Vanya clicked.

For the next half hour Will sliced smiles into his omelet as he self-reported his workspace tidiness, feelings about lions killing antelopes, drinking habits, relationship with his parents, attitudes on justifiable violence.

"Okay, it's loading," Vanya said. She popped her knuckles with an ice-crunching sound while a server in some Latvian barracks digested him. "I knew it. INTJ, obvi."

Will used his mobile VNC client to spy on Vanya's screen. Two columns were labeled **WILL** and **VANYA**. Amid the other data was a light blue box that said **COMPATIBILITY SCORE: 56**. His own column read **DEATH AGE: 52**, while Vanya's was **84**. Will pocketed his phone. "These are just horoscopes for people who went to college."

"You're actually right," Vanya said. "Horoscopes get you thinking."

Vanya went quiet as she worked toward inbox zero, leaving

Will to quietly process the everyday aggressions of the word *actually*.

Later, as Will was reading twenty blogs, someone knocked at the back stairwell; it was Linda, on a crutch. Will had told Vanya that Linda was staying downstairs, but they'd never met, and with apprehension Will observed this encounter between the two scariest girls he knew. Vanya, soft and sylph-like and porcelain, flashed a peace sign at skinny-sexy-hoarse Linda.

"Hate those stairs," Linda said. "Can I borrow your mixer?"

"So nice to meet you! Ooh, girl, I love your ink!" Vanya said. "I googled you before but you, like, don't exist online. You're so cute! You want to be famous?"

"Not for being cute."

Linda averted herself from Vanya's lapel camera. There was Vanya's type of hot girl, who loved cameras, and Linda's type, who didn't. "Don't worry, it's off," Vanya said. "I'm just practicing wearing it. Oh, listen, I'm so sorry about your accident. Any interest in doing a spot about recovering from an accident?"

"Vanya," Will said.

"What? I just think she'd be an amazing online personality. A spokesperson."

"For accidents?" Linda said.

"Will says you're into reading, yeah? We might need a Books editor. You could do video reviews."

Will was worried that Vanya was going to go into her spiel about how dead-tree was obsolete and how the five-paragraph essay would give way to the three-minute video clip and how books were paywalls, and Linda would combust.

"So I'd do, like, video blogs about William Blake?" Linda said. "Or something."

"Retweet links to hot new Melville apps."

"I know, you're being snarky, but yeah, you get it. If it traffics, we might even pay." Vanya handed her a slim business card, emblazoned with only her name, framed in a search box. "We're always looking for creatives to join ship. The teeth would have to be fixed, though."

"*Vanya*," Will said again.

"Baby, I'm sure she's planning on getting them fixed."

"Will, can we talk?" Linda said, beckoning.

Will followed Linda as she clopped down the back stairwell. He admired the ass sculpted in black leggings, the black bra through diaphanous ivory blouse. They reached the downstairs studio, where Linda had been staying, joined last night by Henrik. Peeping through the door window, Will expected to see flames and shattered glass, but Henrik was asleep on the couch in skintight borrowed sweatclothes.

"Your girlfriend's very realistic-looking," Linda said.

"What do you want?"

"Just to bum a smoke."

"I told you, no smoking indoors."

Will took his cigarettes from his shirt pocket anyway. Linda hadn't worn makeup since the accident, and with the oily gleam and orange-peel pores near her nose, she looked mortal. Her hair was just long enough to knot, and an oniony sprig of it popped vertically. Will looked through the door's window. "How's he doing?"

"I gave him all my Valium and Xanax. Homeboy does not want to be conscious."

"Are you getting along?"

"Misery loves misery," Linda said. "Now will you tell me who he is?"

Jesus, Linda was still pretending not to recognize Henrik. Last night, when she'd let him in half-nude and he'd locked himself in the bathroom, Will had been too drunk to deal with it, and had no idea what was happening, except that Henrik was in trouble.

Will asked Linda if she perhaps remembered being *engaged* to him, and she shook her head. Will asked if this mightn't be an idiotic ploy to avoid confrontation. Linda shrugged. Irritation rose from Will's chest into his head like bright sparks up a flue. "Cut the fucking shit!"

"Yo, look at my teeth. You're suggesting there's something convenient about all this?"

Will inspected her with silent, finalizing disgust. He lit his own cigarette, and soon they were in a curly white booth of smoke. "Not convenient. Opportunistic. You know that lady-tears will make Henrik accept anything you say. To be honest, it might not be good to have you around him."

Linda made a gesture indicating the expansion or explosion of her head. "I don't even *know* this jamoke! My situation isn't as bad as his?"

"Stop talking. Now, I need you to do a major tangible. Actually, I *command* you. I cracked his Walgreens password and filled his bipolar meds. Go pick them up and make him take them. Here's cash."

"Wait, he's *what*? Bipolar?" Linda's eyes biggened. She really could ham it up. "Is he, like, unstable?"

"Not compared to you." Will wished he had the integrity to disdain hot women effortlessly. "Either look after Henrik or leave. You've already been here six weeks."

"I can help," Linda said, tucking her lips, nodding.

"Go to the pharmacy now. And see if they have anything for lying sociopaths."

UNTIL RECENTLY, ROOPA had been annoying but harmless—*obnocuous,* Barr might say. But the common-cause camaraderie, the enemy-of-my-enemy amity, had vanished, and fights became regular. One evening Cory came home from work to find Roopa knitting naked in the common area, all her surfaces porpoise-sleek, with the word SLUT written across her chest in purple shimmer paint. It was an experiment, Roopa explained, in rehabilitating nudism as a "refutement" of body-shaming through embodied sex-positivity. "Plus it's reclaiming the word 'slut'?"

Roopa, of course, was refuting nothing with her perfect body. Mostly to spite her, Cory said, "New word definitions don't just erase older ones. The B-word, the C-word, the N-word, they're all still toxic."

"At least we're creating safe spaces to use them."

"Who *wants* to use them? I'd rather we just *didn't.*"

"I think maybe, as a white cultural elite, you should be careful about policing language?"

"Oh, *I* police language? That time I called 8-Ball 'him' and you scolded me because he identifies as questioning, even though I didn't know he was trans?"

"If you'd ever talked to zim *once,* you might've known. Marginalized people need to empower and define their identities against their oppressors."

"The real 'marginalized' people don't have access to these rarefied discourses of gender identity—which by the way come from the academic tradition you call bourgeois—"

"All the more reason to keep raising awareness. Cory, don't you identify as queer?"

"Yes," Cory said, becoming magma.

"And doesn't that—"

"I know! Okay! Fine! Yes! I know!"

Later that night, while Cory worked on her Rec & Park proposal in Iniquity's common area, Roopa was doing pelvic tilts, still nude, while talking about a screenplay she was working on. "It's a dark satire about Columbus's arrival. You know how he called Native Americans 'Indians'? Well, since the Norse came to America before him, my indigenous characters call the Spaniards 'Vikings.' Isn't that funny? It's called *BC: Before Chris.*"

Cory closed her eyes so she could roll them. "Columbus landed in the Bahamas. I'm pretty sure the Norse landed in Canada, centuries earlier. It's not like they'd remember, or call them Vikings."

Roopa shut her red notebook and made an affronted stutter. "Cory, you haven't even read it. It doesn't have to be a million percent historically airtight; it's art. It's satire."

"What are you satirizing? Spanish explorers?"

"Columbus was a murdering rapist slave-trader who made Hitler look like a toddler. Is there a *problem* with debunking his myth?"

Cory slid her pencil into her notebook's spiral binding, obliged to humor Roopa's humorlessness. She was shriller than any workaday activist, like one of those trumpet novices who could blow a high-C precisely because her chops weren't slack with practice. Why were idiots so tireless? Was stupidity a privilege? But Roopa wasn't exactly stupid, not even ill-intentioned—just unconditionally confident, which was sort of worse.

"It's *been* debunked," Cory said. "Everyone already *knows* it's bullshit and *they* still don't care. That's the real problem. You're just taking a sanctimonious potshot that wouldn't offend anyone but historians."

"I'm not sure what I did to earn your random hostility today," Roopa said, "but it is not cool having this negativity in the house. I know you're stressed and all, but what's the point of tearing down someone's work?"

Righteous irritation aerated Cory's bloodstream. What, Cory thought, did Roopa know about *work*?

"Roopa," Cory said, "what *the fuck* do you know about work?"

Roopa took her notebook and rose with a collected lack of haste, her face a freshly stretched canvas of restraint. "Namaste," she said, and left.

Cory was glad to get Roopa out of sight and mind. But Roopa made a big sonic footprint in Iniquity, especially at the hour of night when Cory craved the silence to hate herself. The hard vast emptiness of the warehouse acoustified the skiffles and bumps of Roopa's body against Henrik's. Stage-moaning followed by twenty minutes of pro wrestling. Roopa giggling like a smug piccolo. To her it was a sport, played in weekly exhibition matches, and she gloated over every boink and tee-hee, her scenic routes to climax, where it stood in this season's bracket.

"I'm so into Henrik," Roopa said the next morning, across the long communal dining table. She seemed to have forgotten their fight, which meant she'd won. "I wish you'd introduced us earlier. He was such an awkward turtle at first! But he, like, *legitimately* gets how to physically communicate. Last night he almost gave me a *nipple* orgasm. I told him afterward how amazing he was, and he was like, 'I guess I have to be good at something.' I love self-depreciating humor."

"Self-*deprecating*," Cory said, abandoning her breakfast and leaving Roopa alone with her almost-orgasmic nipples. The next morning, she moved her soap, pillow, blanket, and tooth-brush to the office. At this stage, she would not let the scale of her concerns be diminished by piddling twenty-something drama. Only sacrifice mattered now.

THE MONTHS RUNNING up to the launch of *WHEEL & DEAL with Vanya Andreeva* were the sort of busy that Vanya would approvingly describe as "slammed." From January onward, Will and Vanya went out every night, a social decathlon unpleas-antly similar to Will's bachelor yesterlife. They held meetups, camped in line for the MacBook Air, made appearances at DEMO, the Crunchies, SxSW, Maker Faire, Web 2.0 Expo. At afterparties in Mission apartments, he wiped the street grime off Vanya's wheels and piggybacked her up stairwells; when they entered, some white guy would invariably call out to Will, mistaking him for another Asian guy.

As the recession dwindled Will's freelance clientele, he went full-time at Sable. Officially his title was CTO, but his duties spanned the whole org chart. He made coffee runs, tested camera lighting umbrellas, vetted press releases, built the brand database for social intelligence monitoring, and filed Vanya's 2007 taxes (which, thankfully, had yet to include ven-ture capital income and business outlay). He advised the UI designers to blow up the headers and push static content into extra-long footers. He adapted Vanya's notes into blog posts:

"Five Easy Hairstyles You Can Do with One Hand"; "The 14 Worst Accessibility Design Fails"; "Watch This Deaf MC DOMINATE a Rap Battle (Wait for It!)."

Prep notes for the show landed in Will's inbox:

From: va@sablemedia.com
To: wn@sablemedia.com
Subject: Best Practices for Will
May 21, 2008 7:09 AM

Hi baby :) Here's some personalized ground rules for W&D on-air personalities moving forward. Email if you have questions, I'm too slammed for f2f atm.

BEST PRACTICES FOR WILL v1.0

- "Active" schedule is **6 AM to 10 PM**, so we'll probably want to get to bed around **11 PM** unless we're at an event. Take melatonin to help transition.

- We get **four 15 min. blackouts** a day while we roll ads. Use them whenever, but time bathroom breaks accordingly.

- **No swearing.** Hit the dump button immediately if you mess up. Practice alternatives (shoot, freak, jeez, etc.).

- **No smoking.** Like it or not, we're role models now, and it's bad for our lifestyle focus (and yr health) :)

- **Enunciate.** You mumble and talk too fast. And use strong active verbs.

- **SMILE!** Your default face is grim! I've also noticed **you pick at it** a lot—stoppit :)))))

- Copying this into a shared doc & will update.

<3 u baby xoxoxxoo

VANYA ANDREEVA
va@sablemedia.com
Sable Founder/CEO/HBIC. Maker. Serial Entrepreneuse. Idea Bot. Fashion Victim. Former Little Miss. Queen of the Internet. *Sable—What're *You* Looking At?*

Will replied and asked what he would do if he happened to need the bathroom more than four times a day (**Plan ahead**), what to do if he got sick (**Please don't**), and the gas issue (**If you really need to, separate your cheeks so it's quiet**). It was demeaning, but Vanya never erred on lifestyle—she'd been right about not wearing black with navy blue, and quitting video games, and cleaning his ears with Q-tips instead of compressed air.

Once the Series A funding went through, Vanya expensed thirty new dresses, a mani-pedi, porcelain veneers, and nightly business dinners. On her wheelchair's backrest she stenciled the word DIRECTOR. She groomed until she came to resemble her smiling photo on the About page, an attractiveness unto abstraction, like millions of photos of herself averaged out.

Style is strategy, she advised in another email. **I want to be a projection screen. Help others be themselves by embracing every aspect of myself. When they see me, they should think: I could be her, and she can be anything.**

For Will, she expensed a sousveillance rig, consisting of a TLDR-700p wearable livecasting webcam (built-in EV-DO and 802.11n support, 64 GB MicroSD), a pocketable Wi-Fi hotspot, and a dual-port USB battery extender. Vanya also earmarked $2,000 for a style refresh—twill and chambray shirts, three suits, rosewood-framed glasses, all purchased online, since department stores never carried his size. He'd always left his Facebook profile pic blank, but she uploaded one of him in jubilant midjump, which he'd originally taken to make fun of people who did that.

And he got a haircut. This was traumatic. Already Will's hair ran to about $800 annually for styling, mentholated conditioners, shape creams, and finishing ointments. His salon in Hayes Valley was all steel and theater silk; the receptionist fixed him a doppio as the bored stylist worked in a tea tree oil conditioner. He specified: no highlights or frost, no bangs, spikes, choppy edges. As she circled his head with considered snips, Will didn't add what he meant, which was not to make him look Asian. It wasn't that he didn't want to look Asian, just not like *other Asian men*. The otaku ponytail, the laissez-faire buzz cut, the bed of nails, the cue ball, the K-pop swoop, or the fugly center part, accompanying smooth or acned faces, hoodies and T-shirts, jeans with ornate stitch patterns. This syncretic aping of Western fashions was doubly agonizing, for in matters of race you couldn't join them so you had to beat them, those who aligned you with the stock: good at form, bad at feeling, tech-savvy, word-dumb, cunning drones, uncanny clones, kowtowing kamikazes, the overseas sweatshop that processed dishonor into convenience. But just give it time; eventually the stereotype overran everything, becoming as plural as individuality itself. Until you were not reduced, but particularized to a stereotype. Asian men—it wasn't that he saw himself in them, but that he resented having to pity them, and resented that to everyone else he *was* them, and they were him. And they were certainly something, but what? There were no occasions to think or give a billionth of a micron of a fuck of a shit about Asian men unless one was your dad. Ridiculing North Korea, dreading China, resenting Vietnam, fetishizing Japan; the rest a vast, humid resort full of greasy food, smog, death, monks, beaches, and affordable sex. So he was depatriated: Asian by occident. None of this Asian-American bullshit, the hyphen devised to hitch two cultures to an identity. A hyphen was just half an equal sign, a minus. We knew we'd stolen America from Native Americans, built it with black slaves, given the hard jobs to Latinos, and that Jews had an all-around rough time. Each possessed collective authenticities of oppression. But Asians? Fuck 'em. Not so easy to prove negative bias, indifference, suspicion, condescension, disrespect, against which one could only whine. If you were going to be alienated, you might at least feel the more exceptional for it. Yet the sense of Asian men was of conspicuous arbitrariness in a culture of the special. Whose social modes of being had been enshrined in national policy: internment and exclusion. Conforming yet abnormal. Another and an Other. Asian men lived in the infinite corner of their Chinese room, over there. Asian men wore glasses, or didn't; either way they looked more Asian. The Asian men you saw everywhere once, in subways, under bedsheets, from the sky. Millions lost in revolution and famine. Those who stood beside, behind the point, except when they murdered you. Asian men were good in a bad way, or bad in a bad way, or in a bad way. What was the point? You never knew, because Asian men never explained why they were Asian, and for some reason we needed them to. *Where* was the point—geographically, emotionally—when one was least Asian? What were Asian men if not Asian? Asian men couldn't possibly be human, and they were too clever to be animals; so what were they, so tireless so cheap so networked, so remote so threatening so uniform, so skilled so useful so ascendantly many? Not men, not beasts—but computers. And they, Asian men, were problems, with problems. And the problem's denial, the allegation that Asian men had created their own problems, had become Will's problem, though it would be everyone else's soon enough. Would it be a problem if there were no Asian men? Like Stalin said: no man, no problem . . . There'd be no Will. Would *that* be a problem? For Will? For what was everyone else's problem: Was it everyone else, or Asian men, or Will, or his problem?

Will tipped the girl thirty dollars to make up for his hysterical crying, and left the salon with an upscale variant of his original swoop: not generically Asian, not aspiringly white, legibly hetero, expressing nothing else but what it cost.

5/15/08

Oh what fresh hell. So, Henrik shows up last month. We're sharing the studio but he won't talk to me. Instead he lies around on the daybed, only getting up to go to the bathroom, where he doesn't even turn the light on.

Henrik, I say.

Nothing.

HENRIK, I say.

I give him an apple. He takes one bite & spends the next half hour watching the air tan its flesh. No response when I offer him the bed, no preference for TV on or off. How typical of me to envy him for this purity of feeling, his legit hunger art.

If he won't talk, I will: bullshit naturally. File under C for Coprolalia. But to lie, you need a quantity of truth to mortgage, and my truth's run low. How long do I keep up the reverse-Scheherazade charade? Maybe he's curious enough to hear me out, or even believes me. Maybe he's <u>humoring</u> me . . . god no, I can manage my own delusions, thanks. So either I'm deceiving-exploiting him or he's deceiving-mollifying me. Our whole college ~~relationship~~ entanglement, D.C. al fine.

What is the small nasty Lucifer in me that prefers labor-intensive irony to the unslant truth? Some belief that reality wants my autograph, or that the inclusion of falsehood forms a fuller picture than truth alone? Henrik once said I just liked saying no. Well, no: it's more complicated than that. I'm adversarial, I believe in dialectics. Agreement fixes nothing. (Nor does confession—it's like defusing a bomb by pointing at it and saying hey, check out my bomb.) When there's nobody to disagree w/ I can always controvert life. At least lies can be fair.

HENRIK'S EYES OPENED the way they did when you realized you didn't know where you were. Linda stood across the room brushing her half-blond hair, swollen with static and dented in the middle where she'd tied it earlier. A light trail of scars ran from cheek to chin.

A tremor plummeted down to the deep-chest spot where a swallow ended. The cut of sunlight from the drawn curtains had passed about a foot over his outstretched body since he'd fallen asleep. Linda's pills weighed in his blood; he felt his brain encased in some hard amber sap.

"Morning," Linda said. Henrik startled to see her sundered teeth, though he'd been startled by the same sight hours earlier. A rattling item arced across the room and struck Henrik's shoulder, a pill bottle the size of a soup can. "Will says take it," Linda said.

Next to him on the floor was a dish bearing a green apple and a slab of toast smeared with honey. He could tell it'd been sitting out for a while because the honey was foggy and granular and beads of air clung to the inside of the glass. Henrik wrenched open the pill bottle and drank down eight pills. His breath stank, so the water was sweet. Will was probably forcing Linda to play nice. Linda took the apple from him when he failed to remove its sticker.

"A few months ago I got hit by a car," Linda said, slicing the apple into ramps. "I suffered some kind of memory loss. Will says you and I were close, but I don't recognize you at all. Whenever I try, it's like trying to think of a color that doesn't exist. I'm not pretending this isn't implausible. Online they call it lacunar amnesia. You know how every memory is split up all over the brain, so you can retain emotional associations to things without remembering them? That explains why I feel like you're about to kill me, but I don't know why."

Henrik fixed his eyes on the water glass as if trilling a sonar wave into it.

"I also read this study on memory loss in divorcées and widows. How it's caused by their partners' physical absence, since they use one another as memory cues, like when they finish each other's sentences. So losing your partner is like losing part of your mind. It's probably pop science bullshit."

Red symmetries were forming at Linda's cheeks and neckline. Of course memories were stored in different places. His were all over, at Stanford, New Haven, Goshen, Reno, Twenty-nine Palms, and in a truck that might still be moving. And the one place he thought they might have been safe: Linda.

"Bullshit," Henrik said.

"Well," Linda said, placing the apple slices back on his plate. "It doesn't matter if you believe me. Here's my idea. I think it would help if you told me everything you know about me. I know you don't owe me anything. But we have free time. We're both here. The zipper is down. Let's talk."

"Let's not," Henrik said.

Linda copped a Viennese accent. "Subject responds to offer of open-ended discussion with sullen disregard. Presents signs of echolalia."

Henrik made that platter-lifting shrug with one hand. "Least it's not amnesia."

The way he elongated that last word, as if he were teaching it to her, made Linda's forehead itch. "If you want to believe I'm lying, go ahead. I can't prove anything."

Henrik put an apple slice into his mouth and chewed. She knew he was allergic.

CORY'S LABOR WAS acquiring a fateful poignance, as if she were assembling a large bomb she would later wear. If she was exhausted and missing her periods, if she ate only chickpea salad and drank only lemon seltzer, if sunglasses no longer fully concealed her raccoon eyes, if she had to rinse her hands in warm water every ten minutes, or hide her calf bruises under wool socks, or ice her inflamed toes and cheeks, or track the violet map lines on her calves, it only proved she was working as hard as she had to.

Her ledger became smudgy with pencil lead as she added vendors, and expense receipts stuffed her file cabinet by the baleful. She picked at the cat's cradle of logistics: to make room for vendors, she'd have to close traffic on Dolores, which pissed off the Mission Dolores Neighborhood Association. The ISCOTT panel said the earliest street closure was the last weekend of June, Pride Weekend, two weeks before Socialize's debt deadline. DPW wouldn't clean the park after the Dyke March on Saturday if Socialize was going to mess it up again on Sunday, so Cory agreed to handle cleanup. And hire 10B rent-a-cops for security and traffic, SFMTA PCOs, and paramedics, all in high demand. And make road signage.

She caved and bought a cell phone. Balking at the glassy unaccountability of smartphones, she bought the dumbest one she could find, a small red clamshell. Lo: she was texting and emailing, collapsing her time into button presses and screen checks. She responded to vendor queries, discovering that being prompt with email was like diving into a vat of leeches:

sry we dont provide tables or chairs. read the vendor guidelines :)

u r responsible 4 cleaning ur space, plz bring own receptacle it's in the guidelines :)

LISTEN IM SRY IF U PAID 4 10x10 LOT U CANT SET UP
15x15 TENT. I DONT C WHAT IS HARD ABOUT THIS! BASIC
PHYSICS :)

She paused often to fight low blood sugar, and in lengthen-
ing blinks she dreamed of an afterlife in which the turfy fire
blanket on her head was brushed out into a blade of satin and
she had a big scary wardrobe and hit Pilates every day until
she'd burned off the paradoxical melancholy of feeling worthless and underappreciated, of doing work that was frivolous
and insurmountable.

Since her weed hookup had moved out, she had no eight
P.M. bowl to relax with. She took long sitting showers and
slunk into bed with cold wet hair. She was finally starting to
comprehend money, its gold fangs and green fur. How it sig-
nified importance and bought kindness. How it enabled the
losers who considered poor people losers. Corporations argued
money was free speech because it talked—actually it was expensive speech, and it screamed. Time was money and work
was money; when Cory forced herself to brush her teeth while
nodding off, that was money; when she drank coffee until she
trembled and beer to calm down and threw up without even
meaning to, that was money. Soon she'd have enough money to
start making some *money*.

But her revenue projections were diminishing with hidden
shakedowns. She had to buy event insurance and a sound
permit, rent porta-potties and generators, and hire a CPA to
help with the 990. A Rec & Park bureaucrat told her commercial events on public space required "donations." A letter
from Handshake claimed that the Terms & Conditions of her
registration obliged her to credit Handshake in the marketing

material of any new business endeavors. And food problems, always food problems: not all of the carts and trucks had the $10K permits they needed, and because Dolores Park adjoined Mission High School, she needed an exemption from the anti-obesity ordinance banning food trucks near schools. Food trucks required health and fire inspection, and had to cook their meat in enclosed spaces with refrigeration, ventilation, and three-compartment sinks; carts were regulated differently. Maybe she'd hire shared facilities—but only after she'd verified business licenses, liability insurance, and food handling certifications. The paperwork made her hungry.

Then, street promo. Mission turnout looked likely, so she canvassed Van Ness, Divisadero, Embarcadero, Sunset, and Haight in the finger-stiffening spring mist. Cory was reminded that her rap had never been very effective—she'd never cleared the daily quota by much when she'd canvassed for Equality CA after college. (Their top earner had been a shameless tall hot boredom-proof Scandinavian with a fathomless bladder who positioned her messenger bag strap strategically between her boobs.) She felt guilty, as usual, for competing with the homeless for the scarce goodwill of pedestrians—no one would ever stop more than once.

"Recreate '08! Local DIY fair! June 29! Design, crafts, food, performances! Support your neighbors!" she chanted across miles of sidewalk, everywhere tasting the same exhaust and surrounding ocean in the air.

It is a long season of affectations; of self-definition by process of elimination. He teaches her the Tao of the freebie—music off Soulseek, movies off BitTorrent, booze from house parties, furniture from Craigslist, craggy lemons from the bushes on West Campus. He knows she's out to transgress, but she also has a puritanical streak that makes her wary of fun qua fun; everything must be a step toward metamorphosis. So he scores her a fake ID from a guy in Sunnyvale so they can get into bars in Mountain View, where he stealth recharges her whiskey glasses from his flask. On weekends they take the Caltrain up to the city and he buffers her against butt-friskers at Popscene and Frisco Disco, elbows her to the front of the crowd when the headliners come on at the Rickshaw Stop, his ears packed with toilet paper.

Two months of this and it's understood that they're in something. Are they happy? It doesn't feel that way; or maybe happiness withers under that sort of doubtful probing. It's more of a monotonous amnesia of chillness, with no events or progressions, and at any rate it is very chaste, only partly because she's underage. Not even a kiss until date seven, just to see how he'll respond to getting pushed into deep criminal territory.

He's no longer Force-choked with anxiety when he keeps her company while she's working, or when she visits him in his room. They can't stop talking, hours of recirculating bullshit. Why the left-hand horse on the Marlboro logo wears a crown, and whether whales menstruate. Fuck Bush, marry Rumsfeld, kill Cheney, become Rove. Occasionally midconversation she'll do some weird shit like slap him or sit on his lap and start pissing, both of them discreetly aware that his appeal will be measured in the shit he lets her get away with.

He's glad to indulge; it's incredible for the world to want something from him. He reckons that relationships are about maxing out intimacy ASAP, eliminating secrets. No, he doesn't tell her about the bipolar or the suicide attempt / transfer, but he's medicated now, and anyway, he'd rather get to know her. He googles her name, chows down her book recommendations, listens to her music. Charts her PMS to the day. He knows she prefers Cabernet, Pantene, Aleve, Trident, Xiu Xiu, and that whenever she can't find her hair clip it's always attached to her purse strap. He develops a ratlike intuition about her frequent puking—when, how much, whether migraine- or alcohol-induced, that look of concern on her face when it's coming.

Though, being institutionalized in solitude, he can't shake the conviction that all commitment is temporary and kindness has an agenda. For him the grapes will always be sour.

For her part, she enjoys that he's nakedly unsocialized and a little rednecky and so doesn't constantly nod and say uh-huh when you talk to him. He keeps doing things that make her snicker. One nice thing about books, he says, is you can't bore them. Balloons make him wince ("You just never know about them"), and whenever he lights his Zippo on the first try, striking the flint-wheel off his knee, he goes, "First try." His favorite band? Oasis! Even his most annoying tendencies—broad rationalization, narrow sciencizing—indulge her favorite pastime, disagreement.

Not enough to settle into anything, obviously. She's just coasting on inertia when he invites her to an annoying costume party at his house on Mayfield Avenue. She gulps down the free booze, feeling way overcute in her fringe dress and pin curls while a guy in a Pikachu costume hits on her by explaining chore divisions in co-op housing. Before dinner is even served, she tells Henrik to take her to his room. It's unclear whether she's flirting or steadying herself when she takes his arm to climb the stairs.

When they switch on his room lights, there's an Asian guy in headphones laughing at a photo of a bloody corpse on his computer. Linda clocks the bare walls, the bare hangers, the duffel bag in the wardrobe prolapsing with undershirts and sweatpants, decommissioned sneakers behind the door, a desk set with a field-stripped Zippo and no lamp, situated beneath a double-lofted bed that signals his low expectations.

Will N——————— says hey. Instead of waving, Linda just straightens her fingers with her thumb still hooked around her purse strap. "Linda," she says, forgetting that she's been going by E. "Pretty snug in here. You guys share a bed?"

"No," Henrik says.

"I was kidding."

"Oh. Me too."

"Wait, you really do sleep together?"

"Only when we're fucking," Will says.

Will receives Henrik's psychic telegram and leaves the room with his laptop.

"Do you want anything?" Henrik says. "Tea?"

Without replying, she scales the teetering bedframe, readjusting to sit sidesaddle on the mattress; he climbs after her, with vague concerns about bearing capacity, and sits uneasily beside her. She's still hunched in her jacket, heavy-eyed. She wriggles her toes and arches to loosen her heels and waits for sex to occur. And occur it does not. This makes her feel undesirable, then annoyed at her reflexive self-blaming, then indignant because what the fuck, this was supposed to be easy.

When he gets up, sensing that he's unwanted in his own bed, she yanks him back down by his shirt. He has no idea what to do, except the usual: make things explicit. "Do you want me to kiss you?"

"Oh god, are you seriously asking permission? You're killing me."

But then when he leans to kiss her, she shoulder-blocks him. The quintessentially Lindaic gambit of exploiting his inexperience to misdirect him from her own.

"I'm stumped," Henrik says.

"How many relationships have you been in?" she asks.

"None."

"How many girls have you slept with?"

"One."

"How many times? Protected?"

"Three. Condom."

"Let's see a picture," she says.

Incredibly, this strikes him as reasonable, and he doesn't question why she wants or needs to know. He fetches his laptop and pulls up an online photo of the redheaded Yalie pretending to drink from a keg tap. Linda laughs through a raspberry. "Tight, dude. You dated Princess Keg Stand?"

"'Date' isn't the word."

"Kind of questioning your standards here."

He knows she's joking, but also that she won't let up until he throws the redhead under the bus. "She's much cuter in person when I'm drunk." This makes her laugh, so he continues. "You're better-looking."

"Aww, that's so vague of you."

"I like your mouth."

"What? That's weird. You can have a nice smile or dimples or lips or teeth. But mouth? Ew."

"Should I compliment your eyes instead, or is that cliché?"

"Any dumb cunt can wear eyeliner. So did you just give up on my mouth or what?"

"Come on. I like the whole package."

"By which you mean my looks."

"I mean, you're so good-looking it's hard to appreciate only your mind."

". . ."

"That was totally a compliment."

"!!!"

"I'm sorry."

However clumsy, his artlessness ends up convincing her that he's incapable of deceit. She kisses him. He assumes that her stiff, poking tongue and the way she's gripping his head must be deliberate, she must be trying to correct something he's doing wrong. The sex is very much what his retractile, uncomfortable personality led her to expect: his hands are unimaginative tourists, bumbling around her most obvious landmarks before wandering in circles around her back and thighs. She works his pants down halfway and seizes the fourth dick of her life—*come on,* she thinks, *admire me, be into me, don't make me regret hooking up with someone lame, it's your goddamn move.* She gets his shirt off and microjudges his coronas of nipple hair, his dunes of flesh, the pit hair frosted with deodorant. Straddling him, she begins the chore of erecting him, grinding fast against the sway of the bed. She manages to roll the condom on, but then getting it in is like trying to swab an ear with an uninflated balloon. The way she's worrying the corner of her lip makes her look like she's jumping her first car battery. She still hasn't removed her jacket.

The drama is abrupted when the lofted bed collapses at one end with a thrilling snap of timber and they go skidding off the mattress. She won't stop laughing as he helps her up with his pants down and the condom still on. She pats him on the shoulder. "Next time, brosef."

At least it was funny, they both think.

Back at her dorm, she can't sleep. Insecurity proves as contagious as yawning, and she wonders why it didn't work—was it timidity, or did she fuck it up—and this queerness, this sensation of her internal organs somehow latching to his, and the urge to see him again right this minute: Has she become dependent on him, or dependent on fucking with him, or is it just relief that he's not the kind of creep she's used to, mingled with fear that she may only like creeps?

Still awake and still drunk at two A.M., she gets up and walks back to his house without understanding why until she gets there. From the curb she squints to see whether the light in his window is on, not knowing why she needs to know if it's on, why it matters, but it is, she does, and it does.

CHAPTER 10

. . . No One's Business

I know no speck so troublesome as self.
—George Eliot

Vanya had always given herself the chemical edge. Her medicine cabinet was filled with glossy brown bottles of unregulated nutraceuticals. There were naturopathic supplements with Tolkienesque names: valerian, tyrosine, eleuthero, melatonin; and there were the more Philip K. Dick synthetics: L-theanine, CDP-choline, 5-HTP, ALA, GABA. But when scheduled drugs started showing up in her purse—the Xanax, Ambien, Adipost, and Adderall—Will secretly counted them daily to make sure she wasn't abusing them. The cornflake crunch of her grinding teeth at night was keeping him awake, and he noted how she'd been speaking rapidly with unmoving eye contact, and drinking enough vitamin water to put a hippo into renal failure.

"Cancer," he said over dinner.

"Something's always giving us cancer," Vanya said. "And you smoke cigarettes, so don't cancer me."

"I'm concerned. It's a lot of pills."

She rolled the elastic from her wrist and secured her hair in that absentmindedly expert way. "It's not like I'm drowning my sorrows. Even if it shortens my life-span, I'd rather be focused and productive. Quality over quantity."

"Okay, but is it legitimate?"

Vanya released a glassblowing breath. "How can a mental state not be legitimate? Don't feed me any moralizing horse apples about 'earning' your emotions, because it's all just neurotransmitters swirling around. It's this reactionary Cartesian sentimentalism to see our brains as these special black boxes we're not allowed to hack. If it helps me access my full potential, I'll do it. My body, my choice."

"What if it alters your personality? Or your feelings for me?"

"Oh sheesh, that's insecure. And also just wrong. Caffeine and nicotine alter feelings too. We were both schnockered when we met. Does that make our relationship a lie?"

"No—"

"Because there's no philosophical difference. You're always who you are. Think about what 'artificial' means, all right? Your glasses are prosthetics. So's my wheelchair. Storing info in your phone, that's artificial cognition. We're all cyborgs. Progress is unnatural. There's nothing but the body. When bionic legs are chic and functional enough, I'll use them. Will you stop loving me then?"

"No, but—"

"And feelings are *totally* artificial. Love is literally a drug. When we touch, our brains release oxytocin and we bond. I wouldn't mind if you took Viagra."

"Um, what?"

"I'm saying hypothetically, if you needed it."

"I don't need it. I have you."

Yes, he had Vanya at maximum strength, and the long-term effects of relationship abuse—marriage and kids—were cal-

culated trade-offs. Will considered doing a Cory-style lament
about how Vanya's drugs were all bourgeois palliatives for capitalism. But that was too academic for his purpose now, which
was to make Vanya do what he wanted her to do, while making
her think she was doing what she wanted to do, by doing what
she wanted him to do.

"I saw this talk on prospect theory that's totally relevant
here," Vanya said. "If *not* taking Adderall *diminishes* your pro-
ductivity, isn't taking it a no-brainer?"

"No."

"You're being contrarian."

"Yes! I'm being contrarian!"

She waved him off as if he were an odor. "Okay, well, if I
get cancer, you win."

Soon after this, resigned to defeat and ready to make a home
of it, Will attended the Sable launch party, a yacht gala leaving from Pier 40 to sail around Alcatraz. He sat at his reserved
table, intercepting every Riesling-bearing caterer while he explained his last name to Vanya's parents, as Vanya emceed. In
attendance were Sable's investors and board, the president of
the American Disability Foundation, friends and Chi-O sisters, the young, the cool, and the maimed. There were talks by
Robert Scoble and Ray Kurzweil, and a surprise video greet-
ing from Stephen Hawking. Webcams captured the party from
eleven angles, livestreamed and projected onto the ceiling. A
fleet of full-accessibility party buses greeted them at the harbor
and shuttled them to live-band karaoke at the Marriott.

Beginning the next morning, they assumed the biorhythms
of the New Media elite. A seven A.M. East Coast videoconfer-
ence, an allergy-triggering tour of the Conservatory of Flow-
ers, lunch at Delfina while Vanya was interviewed by KQED,

a trip to the top of the Transamerica Pyramid. Will had never seen Vanya in full-on professional gothic; the camera rig on her purple wheelchair drew onlookers. Her acting skills, insofar as it was acting, highlighted her knack for relentless monologue: "Alrighty, so now we're taking the wheelchair lift to get on the Forty-Eight bus. I'm always blown away by the lift tech, even though the noise is one of the little head-turning nuisances people with mobility issues always deal with, just begging for a little innovation. But at least you get to know your lovely Muni drivers! See the dude who's folding up the accessibility chair for me? Gracias, señor! You're on the Internet!"

When Vanya spoke to Will at all, it was to frisk him for content. "What's on your mind, baby? What are you thinking?"

"Uh. Nothing."

"No? Nothing's going through your head?"

"Not when you *ask* me."

She sighed and stabbed her dump button. It was too late to worry that Vanya was putting on airs for the Internet's lidless compound eye, and anyhow, by the only metric that mattered—raw duration of company—they'd never fared better.

In bed that night, Vanya typed her inaugural blog post while video-chatting with viewers as Will wore a shoe on his head at their request:

> What it do, Sablers! DANG y'all were looking cute today in the Yay Area! You know how there's this temptation for people with mobility issues to hole up and say they're "introverts" with "social anxiety"? Well, as a wise uncle once said: CUT IT OUT. It is the actual worst!

Even with the stares and negative comments, being out in plain view is always worth it, because it makes us part of society instead of invisible minorities . . . check out <u>this list of 20 ways</u> introverts aren't actually loners, they just need time to "recharge."

All you wheelchair potatoes: extend your battery life! **Don't sit out, stand out!** Figuratively, duhhh :)

We hope you'll visit Sable to share, connect, win the Internets—then go play outdoors! (Our mobile app is dropping soon!)

S/O to all my Internoodles tryna break a glass ceiling!

V.A.N.Y.A. <3

They drew 32,000 uniques on launch day. Over the following weeks, inquiries came in: wannabe correspondents in Seattle and Sydney; top billing on TechCrunch in a roundup of young women in tech; a digital anthropology professor at Amherst who wanted to archive the footage.

But it was Vanya's TED Talk (@CCESS @BILITY: *Shattering the Able Ceiling with Web 2.0*) that gave them the breakthrough bump. Fame arrived subtly—their whole project made paparazzi redundant, but in bars Will thought he saw strangers pointing their phones at them. Vanya took it calmly, presuming nothing, until the afternoon when, waiting for the J-Church, a bearded redhead in a striped T-shirt pointed at Will and yelled *"Baby!"* Vanya giddily waved at him, and then twisted nearly fully in her wheelchair to smile at Will. "Baby, he means you! He means *you!*"

Was the world their bedroom, or was there no more bedroom? Vanya denied that privacy was a right or even an asset in the attention economy. She wanted sticky content everflowing. Sex had stopped, and he'd replaced cigarettes with his own Adderall prescription. His blackouts were becoming speed-orgies of vice and chore, doing squats with a toothbrush in his mouth and rinsing with bourbon; watching porn on the toilet dual-wielding his phone and dick (masturbating on Adderall always felt alien and intricate, like polishing a remote control, and the time constraint added a freakish urgency, like cleaning evidence off a murder weapon).

The Sable developers licensed a back end that analyzed their video feed and quantified its "interestingness." When Will's first try returned a 24.4/100, Vanya reminded him that it wasn't exactly mind-blowing for viewers to watch him doink around on his computer. The algorithm preferred movement, faces, contrast. Just go out more, Vanya said, even though she knew he hated going out. Some charitable hypocrisy had enabled her to overlook this essential truth about him. But this was the choice of life under glass: to be seen or not to be.

AFTER A MONTH of canvassing, Cory was so used to being ignored that she was disquieted when opportunities started coming in—the commercial sniffers and cool-seeking missiles. Buzz was finally radiating into significant ears. She got an email query from a guy named Roland Drodzst, who said he'd been following Socialize's work, and they arranged an interesting phone call, followed by an interesting meeting.

Entering the café, Roland surprised Cory by being black. He was six foot, spindle-legged like a stork, with a waxed mustache that swept down and out so violently it looked like he'd sneezed it out. They shook hands, and from a puck-shaped container he offered a tablet of miracle berry gum that weirded your taste buds. Cory worked it around her sensitive molars as Roland ordered a fruit plate.

"I'm surprised you've heard of Recreate," Cory said. "We've barely started promoting."

"Yeah, it's what I do. I got that life-event connect. I'm sort of a general marketing ronin. I do UX, brand consulting, event organizing, trendspotting, all that good shit. It's my job to identify influencers in emerging demos. One thing I do is scout for cool underground creatives and hook them up with sponsors. That way, companies don't have to throw Astroturf events, and their money supports projects with good causes. The company reps with the community, organizers like you get to throw legit events, the proceeds benefit the world, and I get paid. Wins all over the damn place."

"Where do I fit in?" Cory said, wishing his mustache was less interesting, and that his thighs were thicker than hers.

"I hear you're booking Dolores Park. It sounds like a good chewy project. Tell me your plans, and I'll see if I can help. Try that," Roland said, passing her the Tabasco bottle on the table.

Roland spoke with remarkable presence while using his phone. In his white linen coat and green knit cap and wood-framed glasses, he seemed to embody one of the emerging demos it was his job to serve. Suddenly paranoid that he might be some kind of corporate saboteur, Cory gave an abstracted account of her plans for Recreate while sampling dabs of Tabasco that tasted like donut glaze.

"Cool," Roland said. "Yeah, I've done outdoor festivals. It's crazy you're doing this by yourself."

"I'd rather *not* do it by myself. I feel like I'm digging a well with my forehead."

"Then let me help. PBR's Bay Area team is closing their books soon, so they're looking to spend. Could be a good fit."

"PBR, like, the beer?"

"Yeah, and other companies too."

Cory drizzled more sugary hot sauce on her tongue while Roland listed the clients he'd worked with (Levi's, Clif Bar, Greenpeace) and those he'd declined (Microsoft, American Apparel, Target) on the studied basis of their social agendas. He deflected Cory's concerns about corporate sponsorship by arguing that philanthrocapitalism was a crucial avenue for immediate good, operating at sufficient scale to tackle global issues short-term. If PBR was gonna make it rain on social projects, why not bleed the beast? "Bottom line, I want to be involved. I got this," Roland said, offering his credit card to the waiter, whom he somehow sensed approaching from behind. "What do you say?"

"I'm intrigued," Cory said, truthfully. His arguments struck at her recent doubts that her essentially commercial event was nothing more than yuppified pollyanna bourgeois activism, the simony of the offset. The important thing, the principle that Cory sheltered like a votive against a slanting breeze, was that she wouldn't profit no matter how successful she was. "It'd be good to collaborate. I'll definitely consider it," she continued, aware that she could put some flirty top spin on this, yet erring to professionalism. "Can I ask you something random?"

"Do it."

"Guys like you, you're always guys. Bronins. Why no female marketing ronins?"

"Sexism. Or they're working real jobs in PR, like my girl-friend," Roland said.

Cory released a never-ending sigh in her mind. She zinged Tabasco sauce into her mouth and gagged against the surprise burn, aspirating more sauce as she doubled over, coughing until lights appeared. The gum had worn off. Roland slid another puck across the table. "Take more. I oversaw imports for these guys."

"Thanks," Cory said, dabbing at star-filled tears. "I love it."

VANYA GAVE WILL full admin privileges once *WHEEL & DEAL*'s user forums opened, but if she was trying to impress him with the Sable community's cohesion, the moderating queue achieved exactly the opposite:

> mmmyeah id rape dat ass. sum1 betta shove a phat dick in her mouf so she stop talking doe
> Posted at 9:22 PM 5-5-2008 by anonymous | Reply

> DA FUQ IS THAT POOPOO PLATTER IN THE SHOW FOR, HE AINT EVEN CRIPPLE. LOL PROBAY RETARDED
> Posted at 8:10 PM 5-5-2008 by pikachoad | Reply

> the asien guy . . . I bet isher (faggot) friend,definately not is a Good actor tho..sounds like revenge of The nerds
> Posted at 7:39 PM 5-5-2008 by anonymous | Reply

> great post. very insightful. check out this link meet AMO-ROUS moist hotties in your neighborhood http://tinyurl.com/owf3o
> Posted at 7:27 PM 5-5-2008 by anonymous | Reply

NIGGERS 卍卍卍卍卍卍卍卍卍卍卍卍卍卍卍卍卍卍卍卍
卍卍卍卍卍卍卍卍卍卍卍卍卍卍卍卍卍卍卍卍卍卍卍卍卍
卍卍卍卍卍卍卍卍卍卍卍卍卍卍卍卍卍卍卍卍卍卍卍
卍卍卍卍卍卍卍卍卍卍卍卍卍... [read more]

Posted at 6:12 PM 5-5-2008 by WAFFLECOCK | Reply

> Queen of the Internet

UGH kys bitch pls

Posted at 5:59 PM 5-5-2008 by ki11j0y | Reply

Will was allowed to delete these, as they breached community standards. They didn't much bother him—all online comments were either gush or spew, nasty nickels clinking into his brain hemorrhage piggy bank. But a week later, something popped up in the queue:

> ok internutz get this. my gf said she went on a craigslist date with the asian guy once. he just awkwardly stared at her the whole time and at the end he tried to grab her tit. LOL FOREVER RONERY. he sent her like 100 butthurt PMs afterward when she didn't call him back, will deliver screencaps soon. oh and here's his old online dating profiles for great justice. anon I SUMMON YOU to dox this shitbird. ohhhhh the things we do for the lulz.
>
> Posted at 4:25 PM 5-11-2008 by alsoTHEGAME | Reply

Another post followed with a massive paste-dump of his emails. Yes, it was all there, every strained joke, casual typo, and horny innuendo. A cremora of rage exploded in his mind. Vanya refused to let him ban or delete the comment, fearing a Streisand effect. "He's not violating ToS," she told him. "Yes, it's embarrassing, but this'll ease up once we implement cross-site identity. You shouldn't have sent those emails in the first place." After drearily tracking the commenter's IP and contemplating retaliation, Will let it drop.

But soon Vanya started to feel the flames. During blackouts, she hosed Will down with misplaced indignation— against users calling her out for dressing sexy ("I'm *supposed* to look good! That's the *point!*"), being too white-bread ("Have they not noticed I'm dating *you*?"), being privileged ("I'm a self-made entrepreneur! So I like wine, so freaking what? Privilege, god! I'm a disabled woman!"). She was even touchier about the swoons and crests of her web analytics, which functioned as line graphs of her mood. She thrilled when traffic spiked from a Boing Boing link, considered it a net win when Valleywag called her an unctuous fameball, despaired as registration plateaued for a week, boosted time-on-site by wearing deeper necklines. The uneven user segments also irked her. "Some members aren't even really disabled, they're just *old*," Vanya said. "They post all those creepy gifs of babies and angels. One guy says he has ingrown teeth. That's not even real, is it? Then these *temporary* disabilities. I mean, obesity? Give me a freaking break!"

"Well, who did you expect to—"

"Power users! I don't just want uniques or impressions, eyeballs are cheap! I want young, cool, engaged, *legitimately* disabled influencers who'll bring in other active registered goddamn *users*!" She slapped her armrest and glowered at her glowering screen. "We only get one launch."

It was odd to see Vanya not yet winning. She even committed an outright blooper as they were heading down Church Street to brunch. Distracted while texting, she let her front wheel drop off the curb, and her phone, wheelchair, and body all flew at right angles from each other. Will rushed over and she pushed him away, pointing at her wheelchair and hissing, "*Dump the feed!*" Will hit their dump buttons and helped re-throne Vanya. "I *cannot* believe that happened," she said, fixing her headband and priming the dump button a few more times. Freckles of blood spotted the elbow of her white silk sleeve. Tears rinsed her contacts. "Everything has to be so goddamn hard, doesn't it. I know you're expecting me to mess up." Will chose to assume that she was addressing herself, and he again dumped them both out.

5/27/08

I'm the kind of idiot who'd have no identity without idiocy to condemn; overcontent with half-knowledge, deploring received knowledge so much she refuses knowledge wholesale. And I'm prone to pompous symbolic gestures. Like this project with Henrik.

"I'm not a storyteller," he says.

To which I say, fine, just describe it to me like it's a movie. What's insane is he agreed. I took some of Will's beers & we went out to the backyard terrace. We're at the patio table in the fangy shade of a fern, beer bottles puckering their labels with sweat, clouds standing so clear against the blue overhead they look sliced out & taped on. Notebook on my lap. He asks where to start. I say from the beginning, everything.

"Well. Start with a title card: Rome, 1985. You're being born. No wait, first there's a black-and-white montage—

your dad's a married English lit professor & he meets your mother, his student. They fall in love. There's courtship, then scandal, then you. Now we're in color. A plane or a boat leaves for America. Then another montage I guess. You're standing, walking, sitting in Catholic school. Raising your hand to answer a question or something. God this is ridiculous."

(When he said "Catholic school" it was like a hypnotist's trigger word: I saw my fiberboard desk, my pencil falling out of its groove whenever I opened the lid, all smelling like PB&J after we made sandwiches for the soup kitchen. Sister Stamm who tossed her ratty foam football at inattentive kids. Detention = JUG, for Judgment Under God. Joining handbell choir to be like the row of girls in black velvet dresses & elbow-length gloves—but they gave me the luggish two-handed G4 w/ the ugly plastic strap instead of the dainty lacquered handles, a rusty tongue that threw me off-tempo.)

Keep going, I say.

"We shift from warm soft focus to day-for-night. You're 12 & your father sits you down. Ominous cello music, sound of your mom crying in the next room. He confesses he's got a second family w/ some criminologist in Boston. You've denied that this whole episode gave you a daddy complex, but you don't get a say over that." (Tough to argue that w/ Henrik.) "Anyway. You and your mom move to Waterbury. Smash-cut to a mildewy basement apartment where you can hear the feet of mice etching around on the Styrofoam-panel ceilings."

(Mom really took her lumps then: first the divorce damning her Catholic soul, the novelty of breadwinning.

We can't live on an associate professor's child support, so Mom takes a cashier job at a stationery store & my supervision is halved.)

"Your new school sucks. I picture one of those supermax prison cafeterias, everything concrete and lined up in rows. On the one hand you're skipping grades, but you've got no friends, & when puberty hits it's blood in the water. Still wearing big oval glasses but also getting into mall fashion & trying on your mom's perfume at home."

(Out came the spaghetti straps, scissored-out collars, ripped tights, one-inch pins. New opportunities mistaken for freedom.)

"8th grade English class, split-screen: on one side, your teacher is adjusting something on the overhead projector, & on the other side, a boy one desk over sharks down your scoop-neck peasant shirt. He's got his dick out too—maybe that can be a picture-in-picture."

(Whatever violation I felt was baffled by the novelty of being noticed—I thought it meant I wasn't powerless. Not only had I forgotten I'd told this to Henrik; I'd forgotten the memory itself. So I <u>do</u> have amnesia, sort of.)

"During lunch, that same guy lures you to the boys' locker room, where his friend Jeremy is hiding—they whip their cocks out—"

(& when he pushes me to a kneel Jeremy fucking <u>alights</u> it on my shoulder. Mute humiliation is read as consent. My male anatomical knowledge was restricted to a bathroom scrawl of a cock that looked like a tommy gun, and somehow I thought boys had three balls. Even back then, I insisted on pretending to know what I was doing, so I look at his junk & say, Where's the third ball? Oh what a laff

riot, found ourselves a dizzy one here, fellas. David says, w/
his cock bobbling at me: Do it like a cow, bitch. Every day
I grieve for my million squandered retorts: I'm supposed to
suck your cock like I'm milking a cow? Aren't cows female?
Am I a cow or am I a bitch—which is it? You don't milk
cows with your mouth, you shithead.

Yet all I did was comply. I'd never even kissed anyone.
It's nauseatingly warm, I wonder how it's warmer than the
inside of my mouth when they're both body temperature, &
my soft palate flexes, I gag up a big dopey glorp, more laughing. The bell rings & I bolt, wondering how I'll <u>apologize</u> to
them later! Then word gets out that I <u>lured</u> them into the
locker room. So I become the school slut. That cornerstone
sexual inversion—male conquest vs. female shame—
reminds me of that X graph from Honors English with the
ascending line labeled MACBETH & the descending line
LADY MACBETH: unsexed woman is lethal, whereas the
more sexed, the more unmann'd in folly . . .)

"About a year later your mother gets involved with your
orthodontist—"

(Scotty—widower, 56, swollen knuckles, potbelly, old-
guy soul patch. I tried to let them have their volupté in
private but Scotty wrangled me into every mall outing &
community theater night, prohibited reading at the dinner
table. He was the Man who provided Structure. Which
made it hilarious when after five months of playing Ward
Cleaver he started "accidentally" walking in on me while I
was showering & eventually came into my room & tried to
convince me, in the same tone he used when putting spac-
ers between my molars, to let him take my virginity because
his "medical training" would make the experience safe &

comfortable. Mom brought her Catholic A-game when I told her about it, denying it outright. Two horny bad apples in a row? Impossible. She made me apologize to Scotty for bearing false witness. Scotty forgave me, and they kept on, tho remarriage was a Luke 16:18 no-no. He never outright forced himself on me, but he still got off on clothes-shaming me, making me scrub the shower and toilet, fondling my foot while he put silver nitrate on my toe wart.

I remember one health class where we submitted anonymous questions in a box; at the beginning of the next class the male teacher says, "I'm disappointed. Half these questions were about being molested. You guys need to take this more seriously." I read somewhere that sexual trauma can distort or suppress memory. Is there, then, an epidemic of female amnesia? Of perpetrators who deny, and victims who forget? No, I haven't forgotten.)

"—which is when you start dating Gavin what's-his-name." (Mosier.) "You really want me to go on?"

(This was the Reign of Gavin. I had no friends to warn me about him, & it never struck me that a held-back 19-y.o. senior who dated a skipped-ahead 13-y.o. freshman might not be in excellent standing with his peers. We took Algebra II together, & it was two weeks of peeks across the classroom before he came to my locker door. I remember staring at his flaky red nostrils while he went through his repertoire of put-downs and pickups. "Do you think I'm hot? Be brutally honest." I couldn't see the binary trap then: either he's hot or I'm brutal.

Finally here was the intimidator I wanted: a guy who convinced me I had to prove myself to him. Nothing outwardly impressive about him—spiked hair, puggy eyes, pepperoni acne, a chin like a Barbie doll's ass. He wore fingerless wool gloves & a ball-chain necklace w/ a knit jacket that signaled toughness only insofar as he was underdressed for winter. Sometimes he wore eyeliner & nail polish & a feather boa, not to genderfuck, just to disrupt things in a way that authorities couldn't prohibit, & when he got into the inevitable fistfights, he'd get beaten worse on purpose, knowing it'd help his case in the principal's office, though he was always careful to land a jab on his opponent's throat.

Sometimes I like to pretend Gavin taught me how to be deadly prey, but no, he only convinced me that perversity was sophistication, and submission was initiation; that we were the only ones smart & fucked up enough to understand that. The usual teen bricolage of contempt & template identity: parallel cuts on my thighs, IM convos about suicide & atheism, calling other people "normies," reading Burroughs, Bataille, Poppy Z. Brite. I think I knew I was faking it—or am I just retrojecting this awareness into myself? The plain fact that he drove a car & could buy cigarettes made it easy to forgive him when he threatened to cut off his pinkie finger if I didn't break curfew to make out with him. Or when he made me help feed his 7-foot boa constrictor, which slept in a tiny vivarium with its scored flab pressed against the glass, & I held it while he fed it frozen rats that he thawed in his microwave.

You could call this "abuse"—but I <u>hate</u> that word & how it predestinates every choice & feeling. Far more interesting is the ensuing lifetime of disabuse. The disillusionment you crave as innocence curdles to shame. His mom once called me to thank me for being a good influence on him.

He also kept a drawer full of smutty letters & cybersex printouts he solicited from other girls like me, & he made me read them aloud to him. Nothing sadder than an 8th-grader trying to front like a slut: "Hi cutie. Ummm guess what I'm doing? I'm fingering myself! Are u getting excited, if u know what I mean. I hope u r haha." He had me reply to them; so, w/ straight-capped Ts & sharp-angled Ws, I was his smut amanuensis, & he was the psychopomp rowing me into adulthood, claiming my firsts as his toll. First kiss, first handjob, first swallow. He pierced my ears and gave me that goddamn barcode stickpoke.

& my first drink, when he took me to the lake w/ Ryan & Odie during the early springtime when the nights are still winter. I felt translucent & secondary around them, & to loosen me up Gavin gave me a vodka w/ a sugar-free grapefruit mixer called Fruité. I said I was getting tipsy, figuring if I acted drunk then I'd be drunk—I exploded out of my clothes & sprinted to the lake, cannonballed into the big freezing plane of ink. When my lungs could move again I splashed around shouting I'M SO WASTED! while thinking <u>Jesus christ I am so sober</u>, I'm about to drown just to impress these jags. The next thing I remember is Gavin shaking me awake in his bed at six A.M. I couldn't even speak & I threw up twice. He'd drugged me. He dove in after me because he knew I'd drown. He tried convincing me I'd blacked out and I was just hungover. "Almost lost you, Jesus, gotta get you back home."

"Rape," from "rapere," to seize. Better than "abuse" but not much. I think the Latin is "stuprum," giving us both "stupid" & "stupor." There's the word. I wasn't there to witness it. But we both knew it.

My whole life became this tape loop, OK OK jeez fine whatever. The first time Gavin parked us in the middle of an empty meadow & said he wouldn't drive back until I'd gotten him off twice, I didn't say no, because I assumed he'd probably say no to my no & there was definitely no saying no to that. Consent made everything less complicated. I figured he'd been leading off third so long I might as well wave him home myself; he's already taken my virginity so what does it matter; better him than Scotty; & who was I to withhold something my boyfriend wanted. I'd even worked myself into that delusion where sex = maturity = agency, when really it's just capitulating to stupid men's wants.

This worked up until the night he hectored me into spit-lubed anal—I said no, it happened anyway, & I thought: yes, that counts. Afterward he smoked a cigarette, too stupid to understand the insanity of a postcoital smoke after raping someone.)

"You're failing classes. You realize that getting rid of Gavin will take more than aloofness. So you devise your perfect revenge: everyone punished, without even knowing it's punishment. You tell Gavin that Scotty raped you."

(*He gives me too much credit. There wasn't much planning, I just saw an opportunity to tell him something "fucked up," don't even remember the particular night. I draw out the silence to savor its excellent pregnancy, brush back my hair, & tell him Scotty raped me. I could've phrased it differently, but he got the point.*)

"What makes this so quintessentially Lindaic is that you told this to your <u>actual</u> rapist. I used to think it was pure perversity, but now I see the design: it gave him an opportunity to expiate his guilt, since confiding in him *implied that <u>he</u> didn't rape you, & now he could redeem himself without apology. You made him swear not to do anything, guaranteeing that he would.*

"Three nights later, a ski-masked goon swings a crowbar at Scotty's head in your driveway. While Scotty's down, the goon empties a pillowcase & out falls a huge coil onto Scotty's chest. A boa constrictor. Screaming & wrestling. Scotty gets a fractured skull.

"The giant pink bow on the whole thing is when you fink out Gavin w/ an anonymous police tip. Gavin implodes at the first ratcheting of handcuffs, confesses immediately, & w/ his one phone call he calls you. When he asks you to feed his snake, not knowing Animal Control's already put it down, you hang up. Scotty presses charges & leaves your mom. Ta-da! Two men down, guilt-free. Another skipped grade, perfect SAT scores, a year of college courses, & you're high-stepping off to Stanford."

The sun is already behind the tall backyard fence, so the fern's shadow's gone. The SF weather is doing what it always does at sunset, instantly plummeting sixty degrees. I forgot how much I'd exaggerated my own life to Henrik— the official record is oral apocrypha, a boring pomo narrative ending in me. But having someone disassemble your life & show you to yourself, what a luxury.

Final irony: wrote as fast as I could but couldn't get Henrik's verbatim verbatim. Only what I remember.

JUST WHEN CORY had forgotten about meeting with Roland, he emailed her an offer: if she'd allocate one of Recreate's vendor slots to PBR and include them on the event banners, they'd foot $3K of concessions and decorations, plus fifty cases of PBR, and Roland would provide support. That was all—no plugging or shilling, and Roland would handle the paperwork.

Cory agreed, and soon Roland was saving her life daily, as he took point on vendor booking, secured a license for public drinking in a cordoned zone, and tutored Cory in strategic planning and creative management. One Saturday afternoon they had a chalk session in his massive loft apartment on Capp Street, conducting SWOT analyses and Six Thinking Hats brainstorming. Identifying pain points in vendor registration. Calculating earnings subject to unrelated business income tax. Ensuring against inurement. He made Cory articulate her value proposition as he plinked pizzicato on a Les Paul. "What experience are you offering to the citizens of San Francisco?"

"Activism. San Francisco is progressive."

"Activism's not an experience," said Roland, chugging into a Johnny Marr riff. "Strap on the cheddar goggles. Your target audience is young and hip and likes parties. Remember, you're not competing with charities, you're competing with Pride Weekend."

"Ulgh. *Panem et circenses.*"

"Hey, it's your project. I'm just giving advice, not tryna front."

Cory squirmed under the mentorship of a hot guy who always knew what he was doing. Because admiration was a feeling easy to mistake for both inspiration and attraction, that evening she attempted what she'd lacked the energy to do for several months. Lying on the bedroll next to her desk at the office, she slid her hand between practical cotton and crinkly bush and swirled her fingerpads around as if trying to efface an ink spot. As usual she toggled between her fantasies, each delimited by plausibility: tourists cruising for loose Americans, experienced older dykes, homely celebrities.

Something felt stiff and not-right, a faint purling itch. She felt a cobbling of hard bumps leading as far inward as she would dare to explore, interspersed by slick ouchy patches. She kept afloat on denial for a few minutes until she turned on her bedside lamp to straddle and squint at her mirror. Continents of rashes throve across her whole situation. Her body was protesting itself, staging an immune-system intifada to tear down the system, seize the means of reproduction, agitate. An STI? Literally impossible. Cory indulged in online self-diagnosis: Had she engaged in sex with multiple partners? No. Intravenous drugs? No. Foreign travel? No . . . and she resented her answers. It would've been nice to *earn* an STI, but hers was an immaculate infection.

She spent a minute envisioning cervical cancers and condylomas, working out anagrams: A RECORD LESION, COARSE RED LOIN. There was no one she could call. Linda, maybe—Linda would make someone pay for this. But she was probably out partying, freebasing between three-ways. Cory often felt like Linda's Dorian Gray portrait, absorbing her ugly excesses.

Giving up, she dialed her phone. Barr answered. His deep voice, grainier than usual, rattled the phone's plastic diaphragm. Cory had the uncanny sense that the phone *was* her dad. "Cordy. It's late."

"I know, I'm sorry. Is Mom around? It's sort of urgent."

"Your mother is away on business."

"Again?"

"Not again. Still."

Cory's mom was a talk-circuit epidemiologist who tended to minimize feminist issues like the pay gap because she made three-quarters of a buttload, never attributing successes to the civil liberties that enabled them. She went on long medical missions—tsunami relief in Indonesia, AIDS education in sub-Saharan Africa. It was good work. In truth, her mother should've remained childless. "Your voice sounds weird, Dad."

"I hope you didn't wake me up for no reason," Barr said.

Cory covered her eyes to avoid seeing the words leaving her mouth. "I've got a female rash."

"I see. Allergies? Prickly heat? Have you been wearing breathable panties?"

"Ew, yes."

"Describe it to me."

A shudder of awkwardness tripped down her sternum like a xylophone mallet. "It's like, clusters of red bumps. *Not* an STI."

"Cranberry juice might— "

"Wrong tract."

"I see. See, I wish you'd taken my health insurance coverage. For now try Vagisil—the cream, not the foam." *How did he know about the cream and the foam?* "When I'm at Dr. Heiselman's tomorrow I'll ask for Valtrex samples."

"Dad, it's *not* an STI." Why was she fighting him? Clearly this was for his sake. "I mean, like, sure, send it if you want."

"Good. Did you follow up on my email?"

"Yeah, I went to Handshake. Helpful, I guess."

"Will you be home for the seder? Deedee's coming."

"I really can't. Things are crazy here." Cory figured she could absorb some blame. "I guess they're always crazy, though."

"*De te fabula narratur,*" Barr intoned.

When she hung up, all was silent except for the trickling circulations of the radiator. She itched and felt afraid, but it didn't matter. What difference did the existence of one frightened heart make on the scale of calamity? The optimistic forecasts gave us fifty years until the seas rose, then drought, mass displacement, resource wars. It was perverse: You wanted scientific consensus to be wrong about the ice core data, the carbon bomb in the permafrost, the declining albedo. You prayed that the delusional idiots were right. But the only comfort was that they'd suffer too.

Cory went to the office kitchenette and used a belt and a green company T-shirt to lash a sack of ice to her crotch in an improvised breechcloth. She brought Pascal's almond butter from the office fridge into the bathroom and sat on the rim of the bathtub with the light off, paddling scoops of almond butter onto her tongue. She chewed until it liquefied and spat it into the toilet in a gummy blob, flushing at every fifth spit.

Returning to her bedsheet on the floor, she rolled her blanket into the width of a person and threw her limbs around it until it warmed to her own body and breath, which never failed to feel like she was embracing something she loved.

For the rest of junior year the four of them are airtight, eating all their dinners together and avoiding campus parties in favor of grilling on the rooftop porch at Will and Henrik's co-op. Will is briefly suspended for assault; he switches rooms with Linda upon his return, and everything is normal. Every day it's studying and drinking Sierra Nevada and doing whatever drugs are on hand. They stage a moonlight raid of the cactus garden with hacksaws to steal three stalks of San Pedro and brew them into a viscous bitter olive-drab tea, which they drink in Henrik and Linda's room, then watch the windows drip off the walls. For senior year they will land two adjoining rooms in the queer-friendly co-op.

To celebrate Linda's nineteenth birthday, Henrik finds a riverside cabin to housesit after spring break, and the four of them drive up to Guerneville in Will's Camry. With an open beer between her bare knees, Linda lights cigarettes two at a time and feeds one to Henrik while he drives, the filter tacky with lip gloss. At a Korean convenience store they take pictures of the sign on the broken refrigerator that says NOT COOL. Cory plays a Joanna Newsom album and Linda calls it Eine Kleine Vagina. Over the roar of highway air they play road games. "I got one. The Sun Also Rises in My Butt."

"Their Eyes Were Watching God in My Butt."

"Shakespeare's comedies. The Taming of the Shrew in My Butt."

"All's Well That Ends Well."

"As You Like It."

"How about movies—A Few Good Men . . ."

The car pulls into a long dirt driveway. While everyone else drags backpacks and coolers into the cabin, Linda claims the master bedroom by sprinting in and stripping off her clothes everywhere, inspecting the rooms; she walks out to the deck in her underwear to find Henrik in a primal Midwestern tableau, stacking a pyramid of charcoal in a grill beside a rack of Coors Light, his curly hair squashed out from under his ball cap. Will trips Henrik when he walks by and Henrik shoves him off his chair, then pulls him back up, both laughing. Cory rolls her eyes: dude energy off-puts her. She takes a deep chest hit off of her pipe and proposes a hike, but Will hates fresh air and Linda has cramps, so Cory and Henrik drive off to the Armstrong Redwoods.

They hike a ruddy walking trail through the chirping forest, whose pillared trees vault straight to heaven. Hiking with Henrik is like walking an obedient dog: silent and inquisitive, occasionally pausing to sniff a plant or inspect a fat banana slug flexing across the path. He lets it crawl over his finger. Cory realizes she's never been alone with Henrik for more than a few minutes, and that everything she knows about him comes through Linda. The trail is abrupted by a puddle so large and still that Cory wants to rest for a bit rather than disturb it.

"It was nice of you to plan this trip," she says, propped on a log mangy with slime-green moss. Henrik nods in acknowledgment. "You do so much stuff for Linda," she adds, implying some distant insult.

"It's my girlfriend's birthday. I'd be an asshole if I didn't."

"Well, she can be tricky. Especially when people do nice things for her."

"I figured she'd like getting off campus. She always complains how she never got to travel or do nature stuff growing up."

"Oh, you know what I mean. It's not so easy to get gratitude out of her. She's not super forgiving. Sorry, I don't know why I'm being such a B-word," Cory says.

Henrik stands in a patch of sunlight nearby. "I know what you mean. She hides most of her warm feelings in this impenetrable performed aggression, partly to indulge this idea of herself as transgressive, partly out of the tendency to repay poor treatment, partly for attention, and partly because she suspects she won't be taken seriously no matter what she does. Since I'm the nearest I wind up taking the biggest hits. I can't strictly say I even trust her. But it's moot because I'm aware of all that and still love her. If that makes me a doormat I guess I don't care. That must sound all kinds of screwed up, and probably you'll say something about me having to respect myself and be my own person in order to function in a relationship, but self-esteem is secondary to me. I'll do anything for her. My only goal is to make her happy; that's it."

This, and Henrik's secretive smile, makes Cory fluttery and a little sick of herself. She should be grossed out by his total self-abasement, but she's only envious; she too would settle for being the doormat. Why is she trying to solicit damning opinions from him? To bait him into revealing something that she can report back to Linda, or to form a bond with him that excludes Linda? Despicable either way. She gets up from the fence and starts off straight through the puddle, getting cold mud in her sandals. "That's really nice, Henrik."

Around then, Will is browsing the VHS collection in the cabin's darkened living room with Linda curled like a prawn on the couch behind him. He recites kitschy taglines. "Five Kids. One Sea Lion. No Rules," he says. "It's called *Slappy and the Stinkers*. Oh god, and here's a copy of *Mac and Me*. Wait— what if the guy who owns these is being ironic too?"

Linda moans. Her cramps feel surgical. "I hope my uterus is still under warranty."

"Did the Tylenol kick in yet?"

"No, but the Xanax and Percocet did."

"Ever wonder what it's like to be sober?"

"Ever wonder what it's like to get laid?"

Will makes a strange whinny intended as laughter. Linda sits up. "No way."

"What?" he sulks.

"You're a virgin? Dude."

"Whatever. Like it's not obvious."

"But you've kissed someone before, right? On the mouth?"

Will turns away and changes through a few phases of matter. "You should take thirty more of those pills."

"Gosh. Can I give you some advice?"

"You're seventeen."

"Eighteen today! Seriously, this is some vital inner-sanctum girl info. Come here and I'll whisper it to you. I need to tell your brain directly."

"Oh wonderful, advice." He goes and takes a knee beside her where she's lying. "I've gotten every piece of girl advice there is to give. You can't tell me shit."

"No, this is a secret. Nobody knows it but me, and I'm telling it to you," she says. Her breath, slightly foul, moistens his ear. "Are you listening?"

"Yes."

"It's okay to touch girls. All you gotta do is convince us to want you to."

"No shit. That's your secret?"

"Out of desire, curiosity, pity, boredom, it all works. If all you want is to touch."

"You make it sound easy."

"It is easy. I would say too easy."

She turns his head by the chin and moves in to collide with a kiss that he tries to feint, only she presses on to lunge off the couch until he's on his back. She clutches his shirt in both fists and all he registers is force, his glasses mashing against his eyelids. It's not pleasurable and feels nothing like the crook of his elbow. When she lets him go, she slaps his cheeks bracingly, *pap-pap-pap*.

"You're such an asshole," he says. "That's not even an original move."

"What, you don't like secrets? Come on, I didn't even use tongue."

Will gets up and goes into the bathroom so she can't see him pout. His face in the mirror looks the same. "Henrik will not be thrilled about this," he calls out.

"Go ahead and tell him. He'll think it's funny."

"It's not."

"Bro, quit tripping! I just did you a favor. You made out with a barely legal teen. Now you're blessed."

Sometime later the screen door squeaks open, and Cory and Henrik enter carrying grocery bags. "You guys have fun?" Cory says.

"Both of us very much!" Linda says, across the room from Will, who folds his arms.

The day is still bright and Linda's cramps have yielded, so she puts on her black bikini, Henrik mats down his chest hair with sunscreen, and they both drop molly and take turns inflating the muddy blue raft they find under the porch, its valve smelling like a new shower curtain. The two of them float down Russian River on their mingled breath, straddling a picnic basket. Hot sunlight hits them through damp water-cooled air. Henrik drags his arm in the dimpled brown water, the raft turning as it glides. A jumping smallmouth bass tail-whips a spiral of water beads into the air. They discover a slow leak when their butts start sinking into the raft. Henrik can't swim, so they get out and cling to the raft and tread water. When it's fully deflated they kick themselves over to the shore, taking their picnic basket and abandoning the raft to the current.

Dripping, shaky, they limp over the searing gravelly bank that dries their footprints instantly and spread out their picnic. The sun keeps dimming to a sharp white pupil behind shredded clouds. Linda feels dementedly carefree, gorging on bread and smoked gouda, summer sausage and Peroni. "Look"—she wedges the empty bottle up into herself almost to the label. Briefly she's reminded of impressing Gavin by jumping into the lake, but no, this is empowering, she's establishing the terms of what's permissible. To dare herself better, get him to follow.

They return to the cabin just after sunset stinking of each other. Linda turns on the outdoor hot tub without bothering to skim out the slimy leaves and acorns that have fallen through the vinyl cover. They climb in before the tub warms, the cool water scalding the sunburns on her back and arms. Once the tub is going, she sees Henrik staring at her with an oblique smile, and she lets him, slumping down to let the scummy froth tickle her chin. She wonders if she's gone too far in letting him please her this much, whether she has any obligation to turn down favors; but let him enjoy himself, she thinks.

When they enter the cabin wrapped in soaking towels, Cory and Will are playing Scrabble next to the spattering fireplace. Henrik and Linda change and make out in the bedroom before rejoining the others. "Will ate all the guacamole," Cory says.

"I offered you some," Will says. "You're the one who got me stoned. Hang on." He plays the letters IMSO_Y and laughs until he coughs. "See? I'm sorry."

They keep playing, with Linda advising Cory over her shoulder, and Henrik pecks around Will's iPod looking for Beach Boys songs to play through the TV speakers. A barn owl makes predatory screams outside the open window. Beer yields to wine.

"Hey, guys?" Henrik says, standing up. "I want to say something."

The attention crystallizes. They are all curious to hear what an occasional speech from Henrik will sound like, and he thought he would come up with something, but he decides it would be grandiose and goes straight to the crux. No need for a ring, he just gets down on his knees—plural. "I want to get married," he says to Linda.

The air in the cabin condenses with heat. Will, arms crossed since the afternoon, crosses them tighter and squints. Cory covers her mouth, and her eyes zip between Henrik and Linda. The pause is longer than anyone would like, while Linda chews her lip and considers. A bit sudden, she thinks, but right on schedule. She knows he's had these ambitions, in his sad devoted way reminding her that he only wanted to be with her as long as she wanted and not a second longer. Clearly there was no way she'd lock it down, but she doesn't want to harsh an otherwise perfect weekend. There's no malice, really, only denial and cleverness that froth together into one word: "Okay!" As in: okay, you want me to marry you, good luck with that. Even as he pins her arms to her sides in an overeager hug, even while she's crying, she knows he thinks she means *Yes*, when she actually knows she means *Not really*. Or so she thinks.

While Henrik pours prosecco, Will and Cory golf-clap and trade glances, having versions of the same guilty thought: that this is not only disastrously ill-fated, but a vandalism of the group spirit, making them third and fourth wheels, or more properly, the two wheels on a tandem bike that Henrik and Linda are riding. They toast to the engagement, and they drink to drink. Four bottles are slain and a fifth is spilled before Will calls Henrik out for a smoke.

They go onto the deck under total night. Will decides, at the strike of his lighter wheel, not to bother telling Henrik about getting kissed by Linda, because he'd just rationalize it as horseplay, and not even Will thinks it meant anything to her. Beyond this, Will realizes no advice will work because Henrik would just claim privileged knowledge of Linda, and Will would become the guy who tried to get between them; even if Henrik did take it, Will would become the guy who ruined his chance at happiness. "Some stunt in there," Will says.

"Sorry. I didn't want to make a big show of it."

"Have you been planning this long?" Will scratches his cheek with his cigarette hand. "Seems hasty."

Henrik nods several times. "I haven't talked about it with her but I have thought about it a lot. It could end badly, but I'm not sure that's a reason not to do it. In my head nothing's changed."

Will feels himself engorging with disbelief. It bugs him that supporting Henrik means letting him ruin his life in a relationship that will almost certainly exclude Will. With a hard pull on his cigarette he almost inhales the filter, and the half-second spin of nicotine heartens him. "Dude, Linda is playing you, I gotta say it. She's smart and hot and all, and I think she really does like you, but this is all a big amusement to her. She's going to grind you up like a cider apple, okay? You might have trouble getting angry but I fucking don't."

Being very him, Henrik does not increase his energy to match Will's, instead tilts his head and reflects. "You don't have to be more concerned for me than I am."

"Just have a modicum of fucking dignity is all I'm saying."

"I have enough."

"You're for real about this?" Cory asks Linda, who's doing weird fake ballet moves all around the living room.

"Sure am," Linda says. "Who am I to back down from a dare?"

"I don't think you get how serious Henrik is about you."

"I'm serious too."

"Then I don't think you get what serious is."

"Girl. Either I break his heart by saying no, or I give him a shot and we change our minds later and none of us have to regret not trying. Simple choice."

"Yeah, everything's pretty simple when you set up a fake-ass dichotomy."

"Don't get mad. It's my birthday," Linda says.

"I'm just saying. You're so young. You hit voting age literally today."

"You're condescending to me because of my age, Miss Twenty-Year-Old? I'm not hearing that shit. I've dated more boys than you, I know what I'm doing."

"That right there? Is how your inferiority complex makes

you overreact in spite of yourself. Reassure yourself that you're still edgy enough to self-destruct. That's what I'm warning you against. Also fuck you too."

"Whatevs."

"Right. Whatevs."

Doom settles in the next morning when they wake up, poisoned by fun. In the chilly stench of ash and opened cans and sticky floors they drop trash into trash bags and slosh water out from the coolers. Nobody wants to look at anyone else. Linda's loud vomiting in the bathroom prompts no inquiry.

Nausea keeps trickling through her on the ride back to campus. She'd convinced herself she was being clever in accepting Henrik's proposal, but now she knows she felt it, that exquisite twinkly rapture, the sensation of her internal organs somehow latching to his. After all her effort to make nothing out of something, she'd meant *Yes,* and her tears had been as real as they were wet. It's not fair, she thinks. How did he trick her into tricking herself? She's dealt with so many needy pricks, now this one wants to plant a flag on her? Hell no. This was supposed to be about agency and choice and she's taken the first fucking bid. She isn't graduating with a fucking MRS. Out there is the world. More is coming to her. But first she must conceive an end.

CHAPTER 11
DIY

Pride will spit in pride's face.
—Thomas Fuller

Turnout for yesterday's Dyke March was huge, and in the pre-dawn hours before Recreate '08, Cory was scrambling around Dolores Park with trash bags to chase down muffin wrappers, beer cans, soggy pink streamers, plastic tiaras, paper bags translucent with grease, and inside-out latex gloves, all tumbling around in a circular breeze, her neck pleading uncle at each stoop. After two hours she lay back on a dewy hill to rest. Dark-bellied clouds menaced the sun; the forecast had been waffling between partly cloudy and occasional showers. She blew upward, as if to swizzle them away with her feeble dowel of air. The sky peered down, gradual and unmoved. With a flabby exhale she fell asleep.

She woke under a sky the color of baby clothes. She was rapt with a soreness whose ambitions surpassed the body, springing up her back in a fountain of sparks and multiplying into her shoulders. A torus of stiffness constricted her ribs, and the forgotten locations of her obliques were illuminated in red flashes of ache. She pulled herself up and made uneven sandalprints through the mud and male-pattern grass toward the Muni tracks, where her piss both looked and felt like old-school Listerine.

The weather was chill but bright enough to go jacketless. Paralyzed with dreaminess, Cory stood at the park's north terrace and glanced across the bay. Pink clouds hulked over the alpenglow like raked sand. The park's pastured districts were empty of their defining memberships: the Fruit Shelf, the Dogpatch, Hipster Hill and Fiesta Flats and the shelters of palms. A trail wound to the pavilion on the flank, abutting the bumpy sandlot and the filthy bathrooms. On warm days the breeze smellshifted as it changed direction: sunscreen, charcoal, weed, sod. A sandy playground rested low in the center, tennis and basketball courts up north.

It was full morning by the time she donned her staff lanyard and went down the hill to measure out vendor lots with checkered speed-tape. She greeted the Barr None van her father had sent to help move the booth supplies from the office. John, Pascal, and Martina arrived at nine A.M., each given staff lanyards and dispatched to their Socialize Action Tables, outfitted with flyers, petitions, and suggested donation tills. While Cory inflated a hundred balloons, the first vendors arrived: the vintage tennis apparel shop Beforehand, the LGBTQIA-BBQ, and the Election Year Eatery (LOCAL NO. CAL. LO-CAL/NO-CAL CUISINE: STEM CELERYSEARCH - $2.99 / IRAQ OF RIBS [V] - $7.99 / ABORSCHTION - $4.99 / UNIVERSAL HEALTH CARROT CAKE - $3.99).

Setting up was like installing thousands of tiny lightbulbs on a moving carousel. She'd grouped all the food carts in one plaza, but the vegan bakers complained about being near the walking-taco trailer—tough shit! Nothing unvegan about smelling meat! A jeweler asked if she could pay half and have others take over halfway—hell no! The programs were printed! The SF Mime Troupe, hired to replace Luis's drag queens, had arrived to perform a commedia dell'arte, which, following their stipulations, Cory had not previewed.

Claiming a rack of PBR as her pay, Linda limped in carrying a crate of soul LPs with an iPod balanced atop, the sleeves of her faded black sweatshirt pushed up, wearing white sunglasses and cowboy boots, teal leggings, door-knocker earrings. The scabs on her cheek had healed into a shiny pink archipelago. Cory pointed Linda to the DJ table where the PA was set up.

Roland arrived at eleven A.M. dragging what looked like two body bags. These were the banners, and when he lashed them up, they hung twenty feet across, one between two poles over the eastern steps, the other in a break of the tree line by the tennis courts:

"Yo, where's our logo?" Cory said. "We spent three hundred bucks on logo design. Why is our text so tiny?"

"Your part is smaller because you gave me more text," Roland said. "And I emailed you for the hi-res logo two days ago."

"Okay, and why does it say Levi's and Red Bull?"

Roland pointed. In one lot, a blond woman in a red bikini and sneakers was unloading a large duffel from a van with a tremendous Red Bull can erupting from its roof, the other end of the duffel being carried out by an identically dressed woman who was also blond or may as well have been. Cory grasped Roland's flannel. "Who's they? I mean, who're they?"

"I thought we resolved this."

"We agreed on *one slot for PBR*."

"I assumed if other sponsors were interested, we'd offer the same deal."

"You assumed wrong!" *She'd* assumed wrong assuming he'd assume right. The banner stretched and sagged with gusts of late spring. "Sorry. I appreciate your work. It's just not ideal."

"Shit never is. Everything's still on." Roland reached down to squeeze her shoulder. "That crowd. Focus on the customer."

Cory shook his hand and returned to field vendors and acts. She hadn't kept track of time, and didn't realize the event had started until people were dribbling in—passengers disembarked from the J-Church carrying sunbrellas and coolers. Stroller-pushers pondered the safest route into the park from the steep northwest. The portly ganja treats guy patrolled with his walking staff and knapsack. A stout Latino in plaid flannel pushed an ice cream cart. Obama campaigners went afield in their boxy blue T-shirts. At the park's west, a bucket was being lowered from a second-floor window with a sign reading HOMEMADE COOKIES $3. Cory did not feel the heart-spreading warmth of achievement she was supposed to feel. She'd probably feel it after she'd slept.

6/5/08

Hey Linda. Maybe this is an invasion of privacy but I figure this is the simplest way to work things out. And frankly I don't have anything else to write on. I know if we talk we're gonna twist each other up into balloon animals just like before. So I'm handing you the home-field advantage. I haven't had much luck with writing, hell my last journal got me committed. But this way there's no shouting or interruptions. I'll say my whole piece and then you can laugh at my bad writing, win-win.

No point getting defensive I guess. "Procatalepsis is for pussies," like you used to say. But to really quote you properly I'd need more quotation marks, "'like this,'" since that's how you talk, in scare quotes. That way you're never wrong, just verbatim. Man, its obvious now! Scare quotes mean you're scared.

So first of all of course I don't "'believe'" you about your memory loss. I don't even believe you'd believe I'd believe you. No, I know from a goddamn stretcher and I've read my DSM-IV. "'Lacunar amnesia'"? More likely its pseudologia fantastica, pathological lying . . . file under M for Mythomania. Not fact or fiction but factition, the intentional fabrication of subjective complaints with no external incentive. By proxy. Its linked to high verbal skills and a rough childhood. Or if it is "'lacunar amnesia,'" then its probably a symptom of Korsakoff's, whose other symptoms include anhedonia, apathy, lack of insight, and making shit up. Caused by drug and alcohol abuse . . . stop me if this sounds familiar.

I know its tempting to diagnose your unhappiness. To

turn your life into a pathological seismograph. The real puzzler is why you'd lie to your <u>own diary</u>. A dry run before you lay it on me? Doctoring your future memories? This whole "'reverse-Scheherazade charade'" is obviously a trap to get me to engage with you. But the trap itself is bait in a larger trap: to make the whole process as interesting as possible. That's so completely your M.O. Writing a whole made-up story about me right in front of me, then planting it in the trash for me to fish out. You think "'nobody will read it'"? <u>Fucking yeah right</u>. You knew I would and secretly you think <u>everyone</u> will and everything you do will be held up to criticism.

At first I thought this was all some role-play puppet therapy where <u>I'm</u> the puppet. You shove your arm up me and put pretentious words in my mouth like "'"quintessentially Lindaic"'" even though that phrase and strategy <u>and</u> pointing them out are all quintessentially Lindaic. (Even more quintessentially Lindaic is doing the exact thing that you say you're not doing <u>by saying you're not doing it</u>!) You and the Henrik-puppet bond over a rough history, you have mature little epiphanies about writing and trauma and loneliness, and boom-shakalaka, forgiveness.

But now I'm starting to think you believe writing something makes it literally real. Its not "'Lucifer'" in you, its Maxwell's demon, converting ordinary chaos into unnatural order. The amnesia lie leads to another lie about me telling your life story. Rape, violence, tit-for-tat, and you're the righteous victim who gets revenge . . . by lying.

Jeez louise just describing it makes me sound crazy. I imagine that was the intention. Let me try and sort out the possibilities here.

Case 1: You were never raped and you made everything up. Maybe you'd invent a story like this to pull my heartstrings. But it's extremely unlikely, and to be extra clear I'm not in any way doubting you were raped. There's no way I'm pulling the pin on that shit. One-in-six, I know. For the same reason I'll wager you never lied to Gavin about being raped. But I think you would lie about having lied.

Case 2: You were raped and everything you wrote about it is true. Unlikely, since you confessed to your "'reverse-Scheherazade charade.'" But for argument's sake let's say its all true except when you say its not. Why pretend something's true just to undermine it by presenting it falsely? And why launder it through a fictional version of me? If you wanted my sympathy you could've told me what happened. Its probably worse than anything you did to me, plus you could avoid any appearance of fabricating the rape, which I know you hate when women get accused of.

Case 3: You were raped but lied about how it happened. Probably. But how? Maybe you were raped by the middle school boys but not Gavin. Or vice versa. Or Scotty did, and you made up the Gavin story to justify using him to retaliate. Maybe you were assaulted in some other way entirely and you're working through it with a more digestible shadow account. Or by fictionalizing what happened, you can insulate yourself from your frustration about not being believed? I can only speculate.

Now I bet you're nodding and saying: yeah, pal, this is what writers do, transform reality into art. But "'confes-

sion fixes nothing,'" right? Plus who cares if its art? Actually you want to get caught lying and then have everyone play along anyway. Lie out in the open. Have every motive point to you. Having, wanting, or losing you, its all the same. Even getting hit by a car ups the ante. Even this lecture goes straight into the bank, you love a postmortem. Putting concepts before people, assaying every experience for usable material and all material for its breaking point, its almost scientific. Except scientists have ethical standards for human experiments.

Its all so warped and narcissistic. But what do I know? Maybe this is what every "'~~relationship~~'" is like. Yeah-yeah, I hate that word too. Too broad to define, too easy to disqualify. I bet you crossed it out because its cheesy, but also for the same reason you call sex "'fucking'" or "'boning'" or "'porking'" like teenage boys do. You'd commit suicide before you "made love." It makes sense: we actually never made love and never were in love, we were just porking. And now we've got beef.

Not wanting sex to be sex, writing about not writing, getting engaged without following through . . . actions without consequence. Now you're denying reality wholesale, and denying you're denying it.

You always used to shut me down by saying "'it's more complicated than that.'" Sure. But you're the one complicating it. There's such a thing as a simple proposition, True/False. Yes/No. For example. Was there an abortion or not? It doesn't matter now. Go ahead and lie, but you better sell it to me. I want it in writing.

—Henrik

THE GRASSY HILLS at Dolores Park were not congenial to Vanya's wheelchair, so she'd gone downtown to cover the Pride Parade, dispatching Will to cover Cory's event by himself. He was drunk and every cab was taken, so he waited for the 48-inbound Muni bus amid costumed Pridegoers and a flock of children on a weekend field trip. The bus came late, a zero-emission model tethered to an overhead cable, with an electric motor warbling like harmonized theremins. Will waited for it to kneel and allow the elderly to board, and he slapped the fare box that retched his limp dollar back at him. More bodies crushed in and the seated passengers drew in their legs and moved shopping bags to laps. The bus kicked forward and everyone heeled into each other.

Will stood at eye level with chins and armpits, his wrists tingling from straphanging. The collar of his gray oxford crinkled in the heat. Through the window whitened with scuffs, he saw people strolling in pink T-shirts, VOTE FOR LOVE / UNITED BY PRIDE. The bus slewed left and the children screamed in delight; a skinny elbow shanked him in the side. Will busied his eyes with the shipping labels stuck to the windows, tagged with territorial ideograms and dingy with pick-and-peel— nothing was uglier than a half-removed sticker, with its furry white scar.

After three stops the children herded off and Will slipped into a seat, immediately feeling his nuisance antenna twitch at a conversation directly behind him. He faked staring out the window to catch the speaker's reflection—an Australian teenager with a green bandanna, addressing the teenage Asian girl sitting next to him. "Your sort are more laid back about it all," he said. "More feminine too. You lived in the States long? Are you from here originally? Come on, give us an answer."

"No," the girl said.

"Where you from, then?"

"Seattle."

"And where's your family from?"

"Seattle."

"Right. Going to the park? I've got whiskey. It's Pride Weekend, everybody's drinking. I bet you blush when you drink. Hey. Smile for me."

Fighting to control the temperature of his ears, Will turned in his seat with words already splattering out. "Hey kid, can you pipe down?"

The kid glared. "Fuck off."

Will pivoted as much as his spine would allow. "Listen, dick. She's not interested. Do you think she's some little shivering lotus petal who's just too turned on to respond? And yeah it *is* my business, because I have to sit here, listening to you being an annoying *fuck*."

The bus slowed and the electric engine went mute. The kid sat in amused ease, rubbing a frizzy muttonchop. His arm veins cast shadows. "Mate, you fuckin' mind—"

"What do they even call rednecks in Australia?"

"—before you get your head smacked, right—"

"Settle down," the driver called over the loudspeaker.

"—you dumbshit." The caffeinated cinders in Will's stomach made it difficult to steady his volume. He made a petitioning scan of the other passengers, who glowered at their phones or out the windows. The moment hung like a spun coin that would not collapse on its final wobbles.

"You're embarrassing yourself, right," the kid said. "Shouting like a fucking monkey."

"Oh, *there* it is, you racist little shit."

"What the fuck you mean, racist? You wanna go me, you cunt?"

Will addressed the Asian girl. "He's bothering you, right?"

She gazed down the aisle, gripping her bag to her hip. She had a plain face, high-foreheaded and maybe fifteen, dressed for some kind of sport, though she wasn't carrying equipment. Maybe she was a runner. "Don't get intimidated," Will said, "just speak up."

"I don't know," the girl said, oppressed.

"You're *kidding*." Brambly heat from Will's ears pumped out to his scalp. He was weightless with rage. "So you're okay with random Asian fetishists harassing you?"

"He's an Asian fetishist just because he's hitting on me?" the girl replied, and now that Will was seeing her face-front, it was possible she was hapa. Though that counted.

"Yeah," Will said. "It may not be obvious to you because you're young, but yeah."

"Leave me alone," the girl said, absurdly. "I didn't ask you to rescue me. You're both creeps."

"Right, there's your answer," said the kid to Will. "Fuck off now."

Will queried his thesaurus for Australian slurs—dingo, boomerang, vegemite. Great Barrier Reef. "Shut up. She's just feeling awkward."

"Oh, you daft midget. Go play with your little Chinese cock."

"You *racis*—"

The instant Will grasped the kid's shirt collar he felt his head snapped back, his glasses whipped off, many arresting strengths pushing him down in the aisle. Will thrashed his legs and, instead of the expected beatdown, he heard the kid give a short surprised laugh and with shocking agility he yanked and freed Will's belt, jeans, and boxer shorts down to his ankles. The driver was shouting and another teenager went *Ohhhh!* Will shook off the arms and pulled his jeans back on, walked to the stairs in front of the rear door, realizing his stop was five stops ago. The bell-cord Klaxon sounded a doubled middle A. He remembered his lapel camera and held down the dump button. His glasses had fallen off, but he wasn't going to frisk around for them.

He waited in the witless staircase, feeling the bus's camera blaring its security at him. At the stop he yelled, *Back door,* and the bus released him with a pneumatic hiss. Will stepped into the blurry afternoon, where he was not known.

BY TWO P.M. Cory's aluminum water bottle was empty and her bladder was full. The insides of her cheeks were taking on the grainy texture of mackerel. She'd been shooing off the street vendors she caught laying out blankets at the periphery of the park to sell battered DVDs and belts; likewise the bonneted woman selling pastries, whose enormous breasts hung bare from unbuttoned hatches in her dress. A homeless man was harassing the Good Vibrations vendors. On their performance stage, the mime troupe had gone entirely nude and were hamming up the negotiation of their arrest with the 10B officers.

Cory tried to accept that opportunists signaled success. With more limbs, she might have managed it, more Cories, though the last thing she wanted more of was herself.

The time felt right for an announcement. She stood on the hill by the marketplace with her megaphone, signaling Linda to cut the music. "How's everybody doing?" Cory called out. A few people whistled or hooted. "My name's Cory! Thank you guys *so much* for coming out and supporting local artists and merchants! Our profits go to Katrina reconstruction, AIDS research, and . . . all that good stuff! If this is a success, we can make it a regular—" Cory lowered the megaphone with a crackle, swallowed to resharpen her voice, then raised it too quickly, smashing the receiver on her teeth. "Ow! A regular thing. Uh, I was gonna say something . . . oh! Make sure you see the booths up by the J-Church stop, okay? Lots of cool stuff there, don't miss it. T-shirts . . ."

The crowd picked up again. She'd missed her window. *I did this for you,* she should have said, *and if you're not enjoying yourselves, it's because you don't know how hard this was.*

Pascal was hurrying up the hill to where Cory was standing, rolling her ankle on a hidden pothole and tumbling down, shouting across the remaining distance: "There's a problem!" She pointed southeast.

"What is it?"

At Eighteenth and Dolores, some three dozen people had gathered. Cory cantered down the hill, juking around off-leash dogs and toppled garbage cans, across the barricade of gray porta-potties, the curvy inflatable couches by the Red Bull Blogger Tent, the booth babes at the Levi's Letterpress Kiosk and the PBR Cheap-It-Real Merch Station, and dodged under the drinking cordon to reach the edge of the crowd. She turned her staff badge to face outward, then searched for a leader in the enviably diverse multitude, which included white girls in zebra-striped bikinis and pink boas, working-class Latinos, middle-aged couples with toddlers, drag queens, Valencia hipsters in plaid shirts and black glasses. A large adult tricycle blared "Fat

Bottomed Girls" from a mounted speaker. A portable grill and trampoline were in use, and people held fluorescent signs, implacable placards in stencil and marker and printout:

¡¡¡¡¡BASTA!!!!!
CORPORATE WHORES

KEEP YR <u>PRIVATES</u>
OUTTA MY <u>PUBLIC</u> AREA

RENTERS & OWNERS
4
PEACE & <u>QUIET</u>

Nearby, a short woman with curly bobby-pinned hair held a sign that said KEEP DOLORES LOCAL. Cory tried explaining that Recreate was *all about* community, and Socialize itself was a local nonprofit, that the corporate sponsorship was minimal. The woman had valid, civilized rebuttals about preserving the park's noncommercialism, but she declined Cory's offer to discuss it later in a public forum ("This *is* a public forum, and we're trying to keep it that way").

They attracted other protestors, who redirected their chants at Cory. In the front line, wearing an extravagant smirk, was Luis. He carried a rhinestone bullhorn, and his gold-painted face was glossy like a statuette except where the paint flecked on his stubble. Cory tried to take him aside, but the protestors encircled them.

"You put this together to fuck me over!" Cory said.

"Oh, hon, I hardly did anything," Luis said. "Everyone was fighting this from the start. It figures that you never saw the blog. The NIMBYs were already lobbying for fewer Dolores Park events, and you scheduled the event on Pride Weekend. And then you got corporate sponsorship—for a DIY event! It is to laugh! By the way, your giant beer banner is facing Mission High School, which is illegal?"

"This was approved fair and square."

"Whatever. We both know approval's all about who's willing to pay for permits and sit through boring meetings. That's so you. Lame enough to ask for permission to gather on public space, establishment enough to take it over." From this close up Cory could see the taut speedbag of his uvula. "All I did was send some emails pointing out that these groups had common cause. They ran with it. I only came to watch." Luis took in a broad chestful of air, as if it were a luxury he could enjoy only on this particular afternoon.

"You are"—Cory squeezed at imaginary cotton balls—"so unbelievably—"

Luis held his palm out and blew a plume of brilliant dust into Cory's face. She spat and saw glitter on her hand. Someone squished a wet finger into her ear, and she pushed it off as she stumbled away from laughter and photo-snapping. She couldn't risk having the rent-a-cops disperse them; that would make them look good. Transferring glitter between her face and hands as she swatted it off, she saw Roopa at the edge of the crowd, dancing by the boombox. "Why are you here?" Cory said, approaching her.

"8-Ball invited me," Roopa said. Her pink pleather crop top gleamed under a fence-net shirt, and her leopard-print tights were sheer with fadedness. Her face was painted in angles of silver and black like a dazzle ship; across her stomach, in coruscating gold letters at the point of her dagger tattoo, was the word CUNT. "I had no idea this was *your* thing. Are you really taking corporate money?"

"They're only providing concessions. Look, are you here to protest?"

"You should hear them out," Roopa said, still somewhat dancing. "They're really well organized."

"It's not organized at *all*, there's just lots of them. What're they even accomplishing? It's already happening."

"They're making themselves heard through direct action. You gotta admire them for being here when they could be out partying at Pride."

"They *are* out partying. This is a party to them! You need to clear out. Take everyone with you," Cory said, giving side-eye to Luis.

"Sorry. Have to show solidarity."

"Okay, Roopa?" Cory said, shaping the resolve behind her words as she heard herself speak them. "If you don't leave now, I am kicking you out of the house."

Roopa craned her head at various angles, as if to see around Cory's bluff. "You're serious."

Cory stuck her gaze down at the word CUNT. "I'm done with you. All the passive-aggressive posturing. Everything you call community and inclusion is just this motley blanket fort of privileged dickheads. You would never include anyone you disagreed with. Even when we back the same causes, you're so smug and reductive you make me *not want* to back them. It's Pharisee idiots like you who make progressive movements commit suicide every fucking time."

She hoped that Roopa would have exploded into a heap of bloody feathers at these words, but Roopa replied, "Everyone in Iniquity knows that *you're* the negative one. Selfish, bossy, straight-up rude. Even now you're ranting like a fascist. Why work for the people if you don't like *people*? Because you use self-sacrifice to justify being nasty. That's your truth."

"You and your friends," Cory said. "You're all out of the house."

Roopa tossed her hair. "You can't kick us out."

"Except I can, because *my* name's on the lease!"

"The landlord likes us, and he's dating my new roommate. You haven't even been *sleeping* there. I can tell you right now that the consensus meeting will not go your way."

Cory experienced a profound absence—the sense of not standing on the sidewalk, and not turning away from Roopa, and not feeling the snivel fluking in her chest. She turned again and lifted her megaphone to her chapped lips. Her voice was felty and muffled. "Guys, thanks for coming out, I love seeing the community getting engaged! But we need to clear the sidewalk! I'm sorry!"

"We have megaphones too, sweetie!" Luis's voice crackled through his bullhorn, and he gave it a loud staticky smooch, drawing laughs. "This is a fake grassroots event! Look at that fucking banner! She's a corporate shill! Are we going to leave?"

"NO!" the crowd responded. Signs hoisted and twirled. Someone said, *Get it girl*.

"What do we want?"

The sidewalk faithful were divided on this, shouting in illegible unison.

"Everyone!" Cory said, unable to hear herself even through the megaphone. "We all want the same thing! Stronger social programs! No more war! Marriage and wealth equality! Local f—"

Cory's vowels turned to air. She swallowed a painful teaspoon of spittle and tried again, only straining out a rasp through her puffy larynx. She looked around for Pascal and instead saw Linda jogging over, shifting her white sunglasses up. "Glittery," she said, pointing at Cory's face. "Everything okay?"

Shaking her head hard, Cory clasped her throat and mouthed, *Can't talk*. With her arms she made bulldozing gestures toward the protesters.

"Want me to make them leave?" Linda said.

Cory nodded. Linda declined Cory's megaphone and walked back to where she'd come from. A minute later came what sounded like a shattering chain of transformer explosions. Cory hurried toward the noise, thinking that Linda had finally done it, her hipness had finally radicalized into terrorism. The blare thundered from the PA. Linda was at her DJ table, munching her cuticle as Cory pointed at the speakers and made a throat-slashing gesture. People near the table cringed and covered their ears.

"You wanted crowd dispersal!" Linda shouted. "I'm playing Autechre!"

So far Recreate was succeeding—they'd drawn a big crowd, vendors were vending, people seemed entertained. It no longer required her. She couldn't lose money now. But she didn't want to win it. Here, for the majority losers and the lost, she silently declared an unwinnable war against success.

She walked to the top of the park, powering her phone off and untangling her lanyard from her reefknots of hair, passing two nude handcuffed mimes being escorted to a squad car. The shadows of palm trees lengthened toward the distant highrises, away from the amphitheater of sinking daylight. After an hour, the pack of protestors vanished without seeming to move, like smoke after a windless report of cannons. Sleep pulled her down, and when she woke the park was empty of everything but trash.

6/9/08

Henrik,

JESUS CHRIST. *Whatever you meant to do, you've turned my whiny little penetralium into a goddamn text. And not just any text: an epistolary. "Home-field advantage"? No, you've turned the form against me. It demands such goofy suspensions of disbelief — people sitting around, accidentally composing full novels in correspondence by inkwell and oil lamp, with scenes and dialogue and total recall. Fiction is already a rube's game; the epistolary doesn't even try. You swallow the lie up front. So maybe the epistolary's perfect for us two, sitting in a room together for literally months without speaking. I need more belief than I deserve.*

I can't handle people reading my stupid writing. I feel like I've just found a hidden camera in my toilet. Still, I'm glad you're reaching out, even to mortify me—don't pretend that's not part of the deal. The moment I saw you on the doorstep, looking like a vengeful wraith with your white boxers and fucked-up hair, I knew: so art thou to revenge.

Why do I lie? Trust me, I'd love to be taken at face value, stifle that academic impulse to disregard everything but subtext. But there's no communication without performance without artifice. Sincerity is a fief of the subconscious, one you only stumble over by parapraxis. Here, with my elaborate botched lie, you're getting more honesty than

I could ever consciously give you. All failures are honest, including failures of honesty.

I always knew narrative was oppressive—narrowing things down to one or even a thousand perspectives is still an abridgment of infinity. I have real pity for fictional characters, the clueless dupes of dramatic irony—especially the female creations of male novelists, the Lolitas, Caddies, Bovaries ontologically fucked with, their every foible delectably plated. Hester Prynne didn't have to get preggers, Miss Mowcher didn't have to have cankles, Winnie Verloc didn't have to die—except to serve their narratives, of which they're denied basic awareness. Vessels for the writer's outlook, for the reader's vicarious experience. For them there's no nature or fortune: just guile. Forced to be interesting, plausible, coherent, deep, through the corrupt brokerage of a narrator. The better the novel, the more enchanting the characters, the more their mysteries are spread-eagled, the greater glory to their creator.

You call it denial, resentment, narcissism. I call it Catholicism. No, I don't think "'writing something makes it real'"—I think reality is text-based. Not poststructurally— postscripturally. We lapsed Catholics have long had our reality debunked as fiction, but we're still in the habit of worrying that Providence is hashing us out. Another reason to pity fictional characters: their Providence is a <u>person</u>, whose subjects are his objects. No matter how a character acts out—gets vengeance, gets closure, breaks it down, sees it through—it all serves narrative progress.

Postmodernism was supposed to plug the leak. And it did: like a backed-up septic tank. The revenge of text on author. Tempting; but I can't let go of the Self and become some layer cake of context. Not after all the shit this Self has gone through. Whose teeth are missing? Mine.

Doesn't this all sound suspiciously like the double bind of female embodiment—that having an observable body renders you nothing but; but concealing/erasing it demotes its status as a real thing? Either way agency is forfeit. I have better things to be than my body but I'd still like to <u>have</u> one.

So I've picked Door #3: militant solipsism. Any imperative for the female educated American literary PYT—I'll pass. I'll play no part, no merit awarded by pity, no weakness forgiven by trauma. Predictability is suicide. Death before determination! Murder before membership! Execution before explanation! More than anything I refuse to make my past <u>mean</u> anything, to have the imposed cliché of mistreatment-by-shitty-dudes matter in any way. I eat my way around the universal. If style is fate and character is destiny, I'll reject both. I want impossible self-authorship: to be sui generis, valuable in myself and flawed by my own hand. I'll become the archangel of wry suffering, producing only ephemera, marginalia, juvenilia—a print so fine it doesn't exist. Being unwritten, unread, hiding out in an apartment, in subtext, unnatural, unnurtured, refusing to be emplotted like a good little subject, that's my whole deal now. One by one the positive ethics go out the window: first optimism, then eudaemonism, contentment, redemption, acceptance, coherence, finally existence.

Now, to the charge of narcissism? Nolo contendere. All love is projection. Stuffing your experiences and hopes into whatever objet petit a, then embracing it. And don't forget, dude, we've discussed how self-loathing is narcissis-

tic too: dwelling over your shortcomings, insisting on your own worthlessness over everyone else's objections. Hating is, after all, caring. So narcissism is fine by me.

What I really fear is being an echoist. A helpless nymph who loses her voice for loving it too much, loses her body for loving a narcissist. Nothing but a dumb attention-hungry repetition of other people's words. The cliché made flesh, then robbed of it. Wherever will collapses under fate it makes an echo. Is Ahab Ahab. I can't go on I'll go on. The horror the horror. Tomorrow and tomorrow and tomorrow.

Sorry for the comp lit paper. Here's my point. For months I've been looking for somewhere to stay, then somewhere to go. Obeying the mandates of desire and transcendence, I've avoided the past, kept plowing ahead like the worst kind of reader, impatient for an ending. But I haven't even begun.

NOT ONLY HAD Will's webcam picked up the Muni debacle and fed it live to the Sable homepage, but the highlight algorithm, smelling a hit, had automatically posted the incident, becoming the site's most watched video in less than three days. Another passenger who'd recognized Will had recorded the fight on his phone and uploaded it to YouTube (**Chinese Guy MELTDOWN on Bus during Live Webcast [dick slip at 2:31]**). The videos circulated among the commentariat—speedily reposted, memed and macroed, and recut to an autotuned parody montage (**CALIFORNIA CRAZIANS ***ORIGINAL VERSION*****), a shameshow of fobby runts throwing tantrums in broken English. Will conceded it was pretty funny and well edited.

The clips cleared eighty thousand views in a week—a piddling figure on the grand scale of virality, but far above Sable's average traffic, and Will was certain that it skewed heavily local, so he'd be recognized if he went out in public, which he would certainly not. And the signal of his cock, transmuted into a data-bearing transmission, however degraded, would waft out into deep space for some advanced civilization to laugh at.

To be so hideously remixed! Crushed down to a clip! So it went that the medium best suited to disposable content eternalized all. Will's paisley-shaped cheek bruise in no way matched his humiliation, and Vanya was hopping. Her head an ominous lab flask boiling with some acid tincture she'd pour into his ear. Will pointed out that viewers liked drama, traffic had never been higher, and time-on-site, returning visitors, and click-throughs were all up. Vanya hit him with an organ-harvesting grimace—she was *not* looking to make a quick buck off a trashy reality show. She wanted to change the world by expressing herself, and therefore needed to prove to investors and sponsors that livecasting content was reliably on-message.

Vanya agonized over whether to take down the video and thereby draw attention to it, or to allow it to linger atop the homepage's Most Watched list. She called an all-hands video-conference to talk damage control, barring Will, though he eavesdropped over VNC. At three A.M. she took the website down for "scheduled maintenance" and made a short post on the Sable blog, hammering at her space bar as if it delivered electric shocks to Will: **Aloha Sablers! By now you've probably seen the video everyone's talking about, an embarrassing little "outtake"** . . . She pointed out that Will's **chronic sleep disorders, a disability with which he continues to struggle,** had made him **irritable and disoriented, but there's obviously no excuse for physical confrontation,** so Will would spend a few weeks **regrouping,** and Vanya hoped that the community would continue to support them **as we keep living our crazy random lives**.

"You said I have a sleep disorder?" Will said, standing at Vanya's door, disbelieving his phone.

"If I didn't say *something,* people might've gotten this crazy idea that you *pointlessly attack kids*."

"That 'kid' had forty pounds on me."

"You were being psychotic!"

Will straightened up, then reverted to a median slump. "So I have to take random shitstains calling me racial slurs?"

"He wasn't doing *anything* until you got up in his business. And even then, when you're wearing a *camera,* you do not *hit people*. He could sue Sable. You could land in jail! Think they have Wi-Fi there? Baby, this is going to sound mean," Vanya said, "but the show does not depend on you. You're a cohost, not an equal partner."

"You'd *regret* it if I left."

"If that's a threat, it's hilarious. I'm as clean as cling wrap. If you go rogue, and I'm only saying that because that's what it sounds like you're threatening, you'll only hurt yourself—god, you are just this ha*bit*ual naysayer who can't stand it when I succeed because you've gotten nowhere on your own!"

"Watch it."

"Right now the thing that's not working is you. Nothing depends on you, do you get that? I wouldn't even need to *replace* you."

Will felt his breath stoppered by an anger like a swelling second heart, and left Vanya's apartment, frustrated that he couldn't slam her automatic door, pissed that she was right: the worst thing about her was him. He thought about how he could damage Vanya just enough to demonstrate his worth. She said she was clean, but dirt was doable. It was only the revealed, exhaustible mystery of the body; the impression, not the fact, of a broken censor.

At home he drained a quarter bottle of Balvenie and hot-keyed to his porn folder, opening the most recent project file. It was grainy and underlit, but with some careful touch-ups, you could see it: his homemade Vanya porn. From this template it was easy to generate more. He watched them on loop, his virtual Vanyas with faceless men. At five A.M. he sent Vanya a blank email with a thirty-second clip attached. Then he passed out or something.

The next afternoon he woke with his blood feeling solid. The possibility that Vanya might smash through his front door seemed real enough to confine him to his room, composing and deleting futile apologies.

But Vanya proved just as eager to move forward, not because she was sorry but because it was unproductive. She texted: **bb come over tonite we'll discuss yr future on the show.** It sounded climactic.

She wasn't wearing her camera when she greeted him at the door. She led Will to the living room, where there were two full wineglasses. She hoisted herself gymnastically from her chair onto her couch and readied her laptop. Something was amassing in her bearing. She was about to pitch.

"Baby, I hate fighting. I know the show's been putting us under some strain, and neither of us meant what we said or did, so let's not even talk about it."

"Fine," Will said, sitting and finishing his wine.

"I've been thinking about the root of the tension, and I have a plan. I want to hear your thoughts, but you have to hear me out fully. It'll sound extreme."

"I'm hard to shock."

"Okay. I want you to consider a procedure"—here Will was thinking castration, or lobotomy—"a really simple one to modify the epicanthic fold on your eyelids and create a supratarsal fold right—"

Will stood up. "Eyelid surgery? You're *shitting* me."

Vanya's glare struck him like the beam of a flashlight. "You said you'd listen. Sit down." Will sat farther away, and Vanya continued, "It's a one-hour outpatient procedure that'll put a subtle crease in each eyelid."

"Oh yeah? If it's so 'subtle,' why bother?"

"Because, listen. This incident has convinced me that you need to start taking steps to confront your persecution complex. First you get suspended—"

Vanya was referring to that time in college when he'd been heading to Cory's dorm from Sweet Hall, and was passing Kappa Alpha when a drunk shirtless white guy ran over and picked him up, flipped him head-over-heels as easily as if he'd been filled with feathers, and placed him back down on his feet to the applause of his brothers. Will left and returned wielding a ginkgo branch he'd taken from a landscaping heap, found the guy sitting in a butterfly lawn chair, and swung twice, bloodying the guy's ear before being tackled (professionally, by a Cardinal fullback), his face pushed so hard into the lawn he couldn't close his mouth, until campus security arrived. After a disciplinary hearing, where Will unsuccessfully argued that he'd been the victim of a hate crime, they were both suspended.

"—and now this."

"So the solution is to make me less Asian!"

"Perfect segue to my next point, where I convince you that there's no such thing as 'less Asian.' Do you know where this surgery is most popular? South Korea. With *Asian* Asians."

"So? That's cultural imperialism."

Now Vanya's glare struck him like the handle of a flashlight. "*Don't* condescend to me. I was going to address this later but might as well do it now." Vanya checked her notes. "What does 'looking Asian' mean, exactly? Supposedly it's a set of morphological features: dark straight hair, brown eyes, gracile build, flatter facial bones and brow ridges, and epicanthic folds."

"God help me. Where'd you google this from?"

"But none of those traits are exclusive to East Asians, and not every East Asian has all or any of these features. So for instance"—Vanya turned her laptop toward Will to show him a photo of a scraggly white guy—"here's the native Ainu in Hokkaido. They have blue eyes and red hair, but they don't look European. An eyelid fold doesn't make you less Asian— that's like saying straight hair makes you less black. No trait is a necessary or sufficient racial qualifier. It's a multivariate social construct."

"Yeah, no shit," Will said. "So if I'm no more or less Asian without it, then once again: Why bother?"

Vanya hid her nose in a steeple of fingertips before speaking again. "Here's the issue. You walk around thinking that whenever people see your face, they pile on every awful Asian stereotype. You think, oh no, they're thinking ching-chong, math, kung fu. But that paranoia is just another prejudice that makes you resent total strangers. People overreact to your overreaction, and it spirals from there." Vanya tapped Will's wrist, her way of refreshing his attention. "It's your problem, not anyone else's. This isn't about changing your identity, but managing how *you think* other people perceive you—your projected *self*-image. Nothing'll really change except your outlook." Vanya sneezed and then recovered disconcertingly quickly: "I'm aware I have a different comfort level with cosmetic surgery. I've had procedures."

Will sucked his tongue. She might know he knew, and be maneuvering to entrap him.

"Nose, lips, boobs, boob fix, browbone, Lasik. Does that make me 'fake'? Do I look okay?"

"Very okay."

"I never brought it up because it doesn't *matter*. I don't do it to please men. I do it because, for better or worse, I feel more like myself this way. Everything I am is deliberate. The real issue here isn't race, it's fashion, which is about expression and self-determination. Identities don't happen to you, you create them. You wear what expresses you."

"Unless you're a minority. Then you wear what other people put on you."

"Do *you* dress quote-unquote Asian? No: you've adopted Western fashions. Imperialism, cultural exchange, whatever—it beats isolation. North Korea is effed-up because it's isolated. South Korea has the highest rate of plastic surgery in the world, and it's flourishing."

"Korea's also hypernationalist and racist and homophobic and patriarchal, if you really want to fuck around with meaningless correlations."

"Now my second point is about your mother, who doesn't have an epicanthic fold. So you wouldn't even be distancing yourself from your family or your genetic haplogroup."

"Vocab?"

"Your gene pool," Vanya said. "Tracing you to your geographic roots. Southeast Asians are usually in group C, D, or F."

"All the bad grades."

"You're being absurd."

"It's, like, quasi eugenic. Like how sperm donors have to be at least five eight; I hate that shit." While Will spoke, he could see Vanya chambering her next argument, wearily leaning on her armrest and flicking at her trackpad. "The demand for short men's semen is so low that most sperm banks won't bother storing it. And Asians are shorter on average, so guess what happens? As for Asian plastic surgery, the Chinese have this really cool height-enhancing surgery where they snap your shinbones and insert—"

"Point number three is that you've already *had* your body modified—braces, nasal polyps, circumcision."

Will chopped an X into the air. "Ridiculous. The first two were medical. And I didn't *renounce* my foreskin."

"The motive makes no difference. Okay, now I'll hear you out. Let me open my notes. Okay. What's your attachment to the shape of your eyelids?" Vanya sat alert, index fingers at J and F, a blinking cursor in her eyes.

"I don't have any. But, I mean—" Will sighed to signal his exhaustion, though this appealed to a type of pity Vanya lacked. "I shouldn't have to compromise anything."

"Because it's so terrible to be liked! You always talk about how lonely you used to be before we met, always getting overlooked, abandoned. Might this somehow relate to your allergy to compromise?"

"I can compromise with you. Not with fucked-up social expectations."

Vanya typed a bit. "Then compromise for me. I'll give you

a three-day decision period. I've recorded our conversation, so I'll link you to the audio file and my notes if you want to review them. Okay?"

It was not okay.

Will left Vanya's apartment and plunged down a fathomless clickhole, linking Vanya to a battery of eye surgery videos: steel shims levered under eyeballs, incised eyelids tweezed off in tatters, laser-smoke billowing up from dark pink gore. **It's surgery what do u expect,** Vanya replied. Will linked her to horror stories of accidental cauterization causing permanent weepiness, and excess fat removal creating ugly hollows, infections, scars. Vanya replied that with enough research, anything would kill you. Then Will argued it'd be too expensive. **We'll expense it,** Vanya replied. **And cost shouldn't be a factor when it comes to self-actualization. Admit it, your problem isn't with the money or the operation. It's about your fear of change.**

He wasn't afraid of change, but of being wrong; afraid that the operation would indeed solve his problems, proving that his world-filling rule chart of perceived outrages and dignified withholdings, the emotional calculus that had given him his only secure basis of self-esteem, was after all invalid; that he'd made himself a lifelong victim only of habit. But the only way to prove that it didn't matter was to do it.

At the end of the decision period, Will texted her:

set up the appointment + let's stop talking about it

excellent thank u baby
also i was thinking
maybe get eyebags done too?
if ur going in 4 a procedure anyway :)

wtf is an eyebag

bulges under eyes
also lasik?
not a big deal ;) just spitballin

fine

k what day works best

yesterday

ur absolutely 100% ok with all this? just making sure

i rly dont care tbh

no
i'm asking to make sure u *do* care

uh okay
i dont not care

Vanya didn't respond, but a minute later Will saw she'd tweeted: **The opposite of caring is not not caring. #mantra**

The next day, Will drove to the oculoplastic surgeon's office in Marin for his consultation. He nodded along as the old Turkish surgeon walked him through the dual transconjunctival blepharoplasty and the epicanthoplasty—a full incision for the upper lids, lasers to fix the lowers and eyebags in one shot. The surgeon snapped Will's photo and loaded it into a cosmetic-surgery simulation app; the result came up on a cuttingly hi-def thirty-two-inch monitor. Two swan-backed arcs overscored Will's eyes. In the gestalt of his face it *was* subtle, even obscured by his glasses; what troubled him more, at this resolution, were his eyebrows (bushy, thin), mouth (wrinkled his chin when closed), pores (potholes), and nose (a stingerless stingray). This was indeed who he was.

He filled out medical history and insurance forms, setting the appointment in impossibly short order. In six days Will was nude under a blue hospital gown at Saint Francis Memorial, with a Latina nurse taking his vitals. Her breaths struck his cheek while she drew rings around his eyes with a felt-tip marker to direct the blades and lasers. He registered the difference between eye contact and someone looking at your eyeball. The surgeon helped Will up onto the table in the ER and covered his face with the anesthetic mask, having him count backward until he was dazzled into repose by the honeycomb stare of the surgical lamp that left nothing dark.

A few months before the end, Linda gets the university email reminding her to register for graduation and order her cap and gown. She takes it as a final notice. If she hadn't stagnated in this relationship, she could've written a book, made better friends, maybe learned how to DJ . . . at least become reassured of her path to seriousness. Instead all she's done is get a middling GPA and acquire a wardrobe she's already sick of.

Admittedly she could just tell Henrik to give her some space and he'd give it to her. But if it's not mutual—or better yet, his idea—it's *no bueno*. She shouldn't have to bear the guilt of dumping him; such guilt would imply that her feelings for him were real. What does she owe that she hasn't already paid? He's the one who's dragging things on past their expiration, taking her hostage with his abandonment issues. And with all her posturing and restyling, all his confessed projection and idealization, is he dating her at all? No, only the idea of her.

Plus he's been weird. It's bad timing; too many of the wrong drugs, not enough of the right ones, and lack of sleep to boot (he never does get comfortable sharing a bed). He stops eating and his body seems to cook down in sweat. His thoughts come from elsewhere, fast. One night at three A.M. he comes from the bathroom and wakes her to insist he's heard a voice in the shower drain screaming for help; she writes it off as sleepwalking. She doesn't take his tripped-tongue monologuing as a sign of incipient anything, nor his new interest in sex—she figures he's just getting his fill now that he senses her drifting.

I'll just disappear, she thinks, *peace the fuck out.* She sleeps in the library and the lounges of other dorms. But he never could do subtext or irony; the more she ignores him, the longer and oftener his emails get. Cory tells her that Henrik's been sitting shiva in his room and she had to talk him out of filing a Missing Persons report. Will texts Linda saying she's being a real fucking hatchet wound. So she avoids them too—may as well cut all the balloon strings.

She stealths back to their room during one of his lectures to get her laptop, but he's there, and something's up. He is untame. His eyes have trouble closing. "I don't get it," he says.

"I don't get what you're not getting."

"Why you're avoiding me."

"You really don't want to hear it," she says, meaning: please don't make me say it.

"Actually I do."

Instigate, she thinks, coax something real out of him. But it's like trying to juice a golf ball. "You've got no life of your own and it puts the burden on me to be interesting for the both of us. It's dragging me into mediocrity."

"Okay, I apologize for that."

"Of course you do."

"I don't know what else to say."

"Oh, stop. Please stop fucking boring me with your sheepish apology voice. It makes me want to rip my body off. The whole knee-jerk reflexive steez is pathetic. I don't care if you're sorry. It doesn't *do* anything. Apologizing is way easier than being a person, isn't it? How long do I have to wait until you form your own opinions? Or come up with something to do besides watch movies and grill and go to bars? Like, you haven't even given me an orgasm. Don't you fucking say you'll try to change because then you're just obeying me again. And I'm four years younger. I mean, Jesus."

Here the echo begins. She knows exactly what he's thinking: *I knew it; I called this, and I deserve this.* His null hypothesis—that he has nothing to do with anybody else, is fundamentally unable to bring joy to anybody else or have joy reflected back onto him—has been confirmed.

"It's an impasse," he says. A tower imploding inside him. "You think I'm oblivious to what you want, but you still want me to intuit your feelings, even though you deliberately mislead me about them, possibly to test my intuition, which you use to gauge the depth of my understanding and caring for you. You pretend that doesn't mean anything to you. If it doesn't, then you should just break up with me."

Midfight she will not admit she's been faking anything. Escalate, she thinks. Screaming is easy. Provoke, retreat, and repeat. Shoving out dramatic soundscapes as enormously as possible, even though now it feels pro forma. "No, the issue is you're an insecure fucking loser who's constantly trying to get his own niceness validated by being overbearingly apologetic to the point that I have to feel like a total asshole if I don't forgive you and tell you everything's all right. You're the one who's projecting on me."

She tells him he's so insecure he's postmodern. He says she's being emotionally litigious. She says things might have worked if he'd been less eager to please. He says he won't let her get away with the past tense. Once it's clear words are getting them nowhere, she splashes a glass of water across his waist and leg, then slides open a window and drops his laptop out. He knows her method: picking an absurd fight, then using his wrong-footed reaction as proof that he hates her, when it's clearly the provocation itself he hates.

"You know, I fucked another guy—" Utterly, she lies. "You forgive me for that?"

That should be that. He turns away; *great, he wants me to yank the thorn from his paw,* she thinks, until he reaches up to the ceiling fan and snaps a blade off. He wings it at the mirror on their door and it cracks in a spider-legged burst. "There. Violence. Drama. Isn't that interesting?" he says. "You can have the room, I don't need it." He leaves, slamming the door: shardfall.

Wow, she thinks, that sort of worked. Inwardly she thanks Mr. Hyde for the leverage. It is the middle of the day, so nobody's around to hear, and too bad, this kind of insolence thrives on witnesses. She stops by the bathroom to puke— not unusual for her, though she must smother down an ugly epiphany that putting their relationship in jeopardy is making her affection quicken, like how a propeller seems to spin faster just after the motor cuts. Cheap orchestrated conflict is still titillating. The kind of excitement that might've reignited the relationship if she weren't so determined to extinguish it.

Having submitted the lie, the deed itself is simple rectification. Not adultery; *adult* isn't the word. Closer to its root, advoutry, committed first in the heart. To conceive the end is to reach it, and much mischief followeth thereof.

At a Chi Theta Chi party she drinks by herself until some fancy haircut approaches to sniff and mount, a philosophy grad who's writing a monograph on Merleau-Ponty. He smells tangy and muscular, and the fact that he's Persian counts for something. Yeah, all right. They repair to his room for some low-stakes cardio. She's vexed to find that she's too timid to ask him to use a condom; his bush is an outrageous loofah and he sort of cuffs her neck to pretend-choke her. He tilts her to his advantage and pummels her with upthrusts until she feels like a paddleball. When she moans he tells her to stop. But whatever, it doesn't matter—at least he doesn't propose to her. This is it. Sex should be fun, it should be fucking, not some gloomy I-and-thou shit.

When she sneaks out in the morning, puffy-eyed, her mouth tastes like a crypt and a heel is missing. On her barefoot odyssey home, she wonders if it's reasonable to regret sex that you sought, initiated, consented to, and heartily enjoyed, and whether this regret stems from using sex as a means to an end, to *the* end . . . nah, that's just Jesus talking. She enjoys the lightness of her whoredom. She is a balloon, a bubble: floating, festive, roundly full of nothing.

The next time Henrik approaches the coffee cart, she's ready to turn up the house lights. But he says he's checked out *The Ethical Slut* and *Love Without Limits,* and dilates at painful length on "negotiating boundaries" and "communication games" and "primary partnership." Oh, this is impossible. Boundless niceness is impossible. At last he has proven himself an Overbearing Creep, the currency of his attention rendered worthless by inflation. Who the fuck wants unconditional love? She abandons the cart. Literally sprints.

They've come to this quivering fulcrum of resentment and contempt and all it needs is a push, one tiny plot point—but, staying true to her aesthetics, she opts for decadent overkill. A time-honored, irrevocable gesture, with a genre and everything: a tidy inversion of the melodrama where the rapacious harlot contrives a pregnancy to snare a nobleman into wedlock. The sociopathic girl prodigy will contrive an abortion. It is important that it's a fait accompli, something to enrage him inalterably and send her beyond the pale of being loved, a goal she's been moving toward for a long time without quite knowing it was her goal. In hindsight it's also very Catholic of her to immaculately conceive someone just to sacrifice him for absolution.

Of course every objection must be anticipated. If he insists it's some other guy's, since they used condoms and the pill, she'll tell him she hadn't started fucking around until a month ago, so it had to have been his. She comes up with an exact time and date, even picks out the clinic and mocks up a false invoice. Her finger is braced on a big red button labeled MY RIGHT TO CHOOSE. Tying up the final loophole, she tells herself that if he believes her, it only proves he doesn't get her.

A week from graduation, she arranges a meeting in a semi-public corner of the coffeehouse. With her expression brave, her ponytail correctly dire, she serves her enormous overworked lie in a tremolo of repentance and defiance. "Last week," she says.

"Credit card," she explains.

"Twilight," she specifies.

"I'm fine," she reassures.

Try me, she thinks.

But she is *not* prepared for acceptance. No demands for proof. Does not balk at raising a kid, even someone else's. The fact that he's sad it can't happen makes her sad it didn't. He gives her only her own lie to live with. He turns away. After two years of talk he's gone back to silence. She wishes he'd say something, give her something to shred, but she doesn't try to make him.

Everything has run against her understanding: ridiculous to sublime, farce to tragedy. A lurch from the tar pit of irony into the honey trap of sincerity. The joke has become an exception. At the time, mastering the terms of her narrative was more important than succumbing to a love she had no control over, love in spite of her best hopes. But love is exceptional. Only when there's some unfair bargain accepted or perversity tolerated, some cherished scruple suspended under emergency conditions, does love ever qualify. Not passion, duty, or amiability; certainly nothing like what you think you deserve. And boy does it tie your hands.

Love is a form of spite—for her, at least. The wretch who needs something sterner and sturdier than hope. All the clichés come clear: You fall in love because it's a trap. The line between love and hate is thin because spite governs both. It comes when you're not looking for it because no sane person seeks it in the morass of shit where it dwells. Purely a fabrication maintained by each's desire to believe, each's willingness to give in. And when the need for delusion outweighs the desire for truth, it gets real.

Leaving the coffeehouse, she has the impression of crossing some vast bitch Rubicon. The matter remains between the two of them, concluded.

Until he comes back to her, under circumstances that feel like fate, are technically coincidence, but add up to something intermediate. Plot? Providence? An ordered network of consequences? What's wrong with calling it a poor kind of love?

Sincerely—
Editta Linda Troland

CHAPTER 12
The Plan to Quit

Hatred is a partisan, but love is even more so.
—Goethe

I. Afterimage

A tense visor of discomfort constricted Will's head; it felt like two eggs, freshly boiled and shelled, were crammed in his eye sockets, held in by two gauze pads and five front-wet layers of bandage. The rainy sound of typing was nearby, and as he moved to feel his bandages, it stopped. "Baby, don't touch it. Drink some water," Vanya said.

"What time," Will gurgled.

"It's eleven in the evening. How do you feel?"

"Ducky."

Linda's high, hoarse voice: "Does he want more pills?"

"He's already had two. He'll be fine."

"Let him sleep," said Henrik.

Thanking Henrik telepathically, Will slept and woke again. "What time."

"Nine in the morning. How you feel, buddy?" said Linda.

Will was too exhausted to gag on the smells of ointment and his own breath. It was hard to feel awake when you couldn't open your eyes. He wanted to dash his bandages off and blink furiously, and his stomach turned a horrid suplex when he imagined the sound it would make.

"Where's Vanya?" Will asked. He heard a gravelly scuffling; an ice pack lowered onto his face. He cooled his cheeks with the sharp corners and planes of the cubes through cotton, and with squints he urged the cold to leach up to his eyes.

"She's doing her show. She asked if I could take a shift. I haven't heard from her and she's not picking up her phone."

"Email is better for her," Will said.

"Here's some aspirin. I'm out of Vicodin."

Will chased two tablets with apple juice from a straw and chilled his face. It felt like a curtain rod was pushing through his temples, soon accompanied by come-and-go twinges of vascular microtear, like maggots chewing slow zigzags around his eye sockets, which he mistook for the itch of recovery. The doctors would later surmise that the aspirin had aggravated his intraorbital bleeding, worsening with each clogged sneeze and noseblow triggered by the spring pollen, each pang of reactive hyperemia opening the door a little wider to the pseudomonal panophthalmitis that would barrel over his immune system.

Linda lit his cigarettes and cashed the butts into a beer bottle. As the itch crawled deeper and became entwined with pain, he had Linda dial the oculoplastic office, where a scheduling nurse told him that the surgeon was out of town for the weekend. So Will was in slow agony until Monday, grating the skin around his bandages with the sides of his fingers.

Tuesday came, and Will and Linda took an eighty-dollar cab ride to the oculoplastic surgeon's office, with Linda steering him by the elbow. Will joggled his legs on the padded exam table, envisioning the spree of blinking and scratching he would enjoy when the bandages were off. The layers became stickier and wetter as each was unwound. "Hast seen the white Will?" Linda sang as the last was peeled off.

Something wasn't right. He saw as if through greased goggles; the hand mirror showed only a blur of fruity reds and purples. The surgeon flicked the light switch and shone a penlight into Will's eyes that Will could sense more than see. He instructed Will not to touch his face, excused himself, and made a phone call in the next room.

An ambulance drove them to an office at Marin General, where another doctor examined him, left, and returned to deliver a diagnosis with a straight-sounding face. Orbital cellulitis had broken out in both eyes; the inflammation was strangling the optic nerves, and his vitreous humors were turbid with pus. They put him on oral antibiotics and held him for monitoring.

"When is this coming off," Will said, while they mummified his face in fresh gauze.

"There's no timetable," the surgeon said. "We'll monitor how you respond to the antibiotics and wait for the Gram stain. But the infection is advancing rapidly, and in the worst case, enucleation could be necessary."

"What's that?"

"Removing the eyes."

Linda gripped Will's shoulder. "Both of them?"

"If the infection spreads, it could go back through the optic foramen and into the brain. Even without enucleation, some vision loss is possible. It's a last resort, but—"

By eight the vendors had left. The performing stage was empty. All warmth had faded with the sun and the crowd. The grass was cicatriced and shiny from the day's trample. Pascal and Martina were returning the kegs and helium tanks. Cory was repeating her errand of twelve hours earlier—before her now was the exact volume of garbage cans she'd underestimated by, the scattered blue Solo cups, balled-up burrito foils, waffle cone sleeves, fairy trails of glitter, moon-colored condoms, four cell phones, a crack stem with a blackened bulb. She goaded herself on by lying to herself: only five more minutes, five more, five more. The only one helping her was a homeless man, with his shopping cart full of tight clear bags of empties. Tight clear bag of empty: that, in the least Zen way possible, was how she felt. She was glad she could at least provide someone a livelihood with her refuse.

After sundown, Cory dizzily rested on a playground swing with her pulse throbbing in every toe before pedaling home on her still-seatless bike—not to her office, but to Iniquity, in a fatigue that hardened around her brain like cooling glass. She let her bike fall to the ground as she stepped indoors and yanked the banister up to her room. She fell on her pillow and wrestled off her clothes. The bed felt unoccupied even as she lay in it. A balloon was inflating in her chest, struggling but unable to pop. All she wanted was sleep, something only she could give herself and at last denied herself. Instead a deep shiver budded between her lungs, and a sickle-moon of migraine cleft her skull, smearing her vision. She pulled her hair into her mouth; when her fingers snagged, she pulled harder and moaned in formless schwas, hoping to discharge the pain as sound.

She woke the next morning to find her pillow pithed from its case. She was sore in her thickest muscles and her scalp itched. Turned to see a mass of hair on the bed, like a bird's nest that someone had given a good kick. Reached up to feel much of it missing. Some of the uprooted clumps were still tangled to the hair on her head. She fled to the bathroom with her heart clapping at her throat, and twenty minutes later she left naked and bald, with her deadlocks coiled inside the wastebasket looking like a head had fallen there from the guillotine. She levitated to the kitchen and mindlessly washed a mug, turning it around under a shaft of cold water that stiffened her hands, then wandered to the fridge and opened it, looking for nothing, letting the frosted air move down the front of her bare chest, stomach, legs.

Behind her, clogs clapped on the concrete floor; it was Roopa, topless and startled, maybe because she was surprised to see Cory at home, bareheaded and smiling madly—

"Hey, Roopa, good to see you! So, I've been thinking about stuff, and I realized you're right. You've been a hundred percent completely right all along. I'm really sorry for all the trouble I've given you! I'll be moving out soon, but don't worry, I'll come up with the rest of the month's rent. Sorry again!"

—though Cory liked to think, as she left the kitchen, that Roopa was dumbstruck by the scourge of Cory's perfected ugliness, given nothing to oppose.

DURING HIS HOSPITAL stay after the operation, Will told the nurses to refuse visits from Vanya. In the name of sparing himself more explanation, he didn't call his parents, but he kept his phone on his lap, and when it rang he skated his fingers across its featureless surface until it picked up. (He'd have to buy a new phone—no, an *old* phone.) If it was Vanya he hung up; if it was Linda he put in a dinner order.

It took him five minutes to get bored of touching stuff in his room, and a day to become bored of sleep. He spent the rest of his time inventorying his unhappiness. Not seeing, no longer having. The sterile, silent, painless way it was achieved. All his life he had light and then he woke up and didn't. He clutched at his sternum when he felt its bolts tighten, and his nubbly blanket stiffened the more he wiped his face with it. He understood that he'd mistakenly prized loneliness above other miseries, when it was just a species in the genus of neurosis, family of suffering, class of comprehension, phylum of thought, kingdom of consciousness, domain of being—being being the basic option of life.

Blindness was not some fantastic peephole to the eternal, just plain darkness that felt closer to him than his own face, with the occasional fleeting sunburst or serpent undulating across numb space. He could envision Vanya's bangs, the doorknob on his parents' house, his driver's license photo, and generic ideals—clock, breast, moon. What the mind beheld directly. But he couldn't see anything he'd never seen before.

After six days he was discharged into Linda's care wearing a double eye patch. As they entered his house, Linda's guiding hand gave Will's a startled squeeze. "Vanya's here," Linda whispered. She led Will to his recliner and excused herself downstairs.

"I'm going to help you through this," Vanya said. Her voice was bled of its principal timbre of optimism. She must have gotten in with the hidden key in the back stairwell, which had no stairlift. She must have dragged herself up. "Who knows more about overcoming disability than me? I'm plugged into every vision impairment resource there is. You can still work for the company, obviously. You can inspire people with your story—a recently vision-impaired man re-learns the ropes."

"No."

"No what?"

"No show. No relearning."

"That's silly. You've invested so much in your tech training," Vanya said. "Once you transition with some occupational therapy and get familiar with voice-command and screen-reading software, you'll be able to work like before."

"I hate work."

"And bionic eyes will be robust in a few years—you could end up with *superhuman* vision, who knows. But first we're going to sue the sardines out of this quack. He should have been available the instant you reported discomfort."

"I'm not suing anybody."

Vanya slapped her lap. "What are you going to do, then?"

"Nothing," Will said.

"Baby, if I'd done nothing but sit around and feel sorry for myself after my accident, what kind of person would I be today?"

Will tilted his head up. "I don't know! Paralyzed?"

"It's normal that you're responding out of pain right now," Vanya said. "But to rise above this, you need to have things to look forward to. You can't give up. If you believe you'll fail, you're right."

"Well, at least I'm right."

"Okay, I'm getting to the point. I found the ring in your jacket." Vanya put Will's hand around her finger; she was wearing it. "I know you wanted to propose. I'm here. Ask me."

"What? Fuck no."

After many silences, Vanya said, "Elaborate."

"Has there ever been any actual love? Like, really? No. Just a bunch of organizing."

"Baby," Vanya said, "I totally understand why you're lashing out. Things are bad. But if you keep saying things you don't mean, you'll regret it."

"I already regret everything. I can take more."

"So that's your plan. Self-pity. How will you support yourself?"

"With my money."

"So you're just going to waste your talents? Do nothing?"

"No, I'm doing something: I'm quitting. And you were fine with that when it was convenient."

"All right, baby," Vanya said in grave tones. "I'm giving you *one* chance to admit you're being ridiculous."

He slid the ring off her finger and flicked it away. It landed soundlessly wherever. "Yeah, well."

Vanya drew back, lowered herself to the floor, and he heard her crawling away one hand after another, her body swishing behind her. The stairwell door clumsily opened, and after a moment, when Will was tempted to hear a hiccup of true hurt, it closed.

Will sat there, quitting for as long as that would take.

II. Lares and Penates

With Recreate finished, Cory found that she could be highly productive when she wasn't working. She canceled her cell phone plan. Enough hair had grown back to restyle into a pixie cut. At the free clinic she learned that she was malnourished, anemic, hyponatremic, and had minor but literal cases of scurvy, telogen effluvium, and iodine deficiency, which her doctor had never seen before in America; he administered an electrolyte solution and a multivitamin. Later that afternoon her women's center OB/GYN diagnosed her with vulvovaginal lichen planus, likely stress-induced, not sexually transmitted.

On her way back home she stopped at Whole Foods to buy a rotisserie chicken, which she ate with her hands straight from the carton while walking, brown grease gliding down to her elbows. She was sucking the last gray tatters from its thigh when she arrived home and checked her email for the first time in a month. One came in from Roland: he wrote that PBR was psyched with the turnout and wanted to continue the partnership. They'd put Socialize on a six-month $100,000 retainer, and if the buzz was good, they'd talk promotions and contract renewal. It wasn't an acquisition or anything, Roland said; the company might have to change its tax status, but it would still be Socialize, Cory would still be in charge, and Roland would be around for logistical heavy lifting—*Think on it and get at me*.

If she took the offer, she could finally promote John, Martina, and Pascal to full-time as promised. The work would be steady, no more hustling.

While she decided, Cory was determined not to remain in Iniquity long enough to be voted out. She would find a sublet. She invited Linda to help her pack and move boxes into a Barr None truck. Linda arrived with her new bleached hair wind-fluffed, and ripples blown into her green cape coat. She sat in front of the closet sorting through Cory's clothes, comfortably prim with her bad leg outstretched by a glass of Charles Shaw Shiraz, while Cory winnowed her piles of neglected mail.

The phone rang. It was Socialize's CPA, who said there were questions about the nature of her sponsors as declared in her 990 and their relevance to the company's mission. Socialize's exemption status was in danger.

"Looks like I fucked up again," Cory said, hanging up. "With the sponsorship thing. Apparently I might be a white-collar criminal." Linda tilted her head, and Cory held her breath to steady herself. "Be honest," she resumed. "Since you've known me. Was I always ridiculous? Do I always—*always* set myself up to fail? I mean, is this why people hate me? Am I one of those clueless, earnest, humorless—"

Probably to feign casualness, Linda continued folding a tank top. "Sometimes, yeah. That line of questioning is one example."

"I try to do the right things. Then I do them wrong. And then they end up having been the wrong things all along."

"Doing the wrong thing is supposed to feel good."

"But I don't. I *never* feel good. And then you see all these shitty people everywhere getting what you want, which tricks you into thinking you deserve it. But it's not like anyone gets anything *because* they deserve it."

Cory meant to reel in some of this messy whining, but she opened her mouth to a staircase of dry sobs. Linda did not offer a hug, no, too cool for that; instead she'd gotten up to pace around, in her typical way of disengaging at the wrong moment. She was making odd balletic motions—poses, static postures.

"I used to just hate my mind and body. Now it's worse. Now I believe in the soul and I hate it most of all. I mean the conscious part of me. Maybe I've tricked myself into thinking it's part of the social contract, you know: I do useful work, and you fix my soul. That self-love is moot if you're selfless. But it's an ego trip after all, like everyone said, and when I'm standing on the corner bothering strangers I'm just begging for attention."

This was what she ought to have shouted at the Recreate

protest. If it didn't matter what she said, she could've at least said what she meant. Meanwhile Linda whisked the belt from her waist.

"Whatever, this probably sounds eye-rolling and weepy to you. I hate that too. I resent my friends."

Linda went liquidly into point and then bent in a shaky plié, and with one hand she undid her blouse, revealing the white bra and pale scalloped torso underneath, both reflecting lamplight. Cory's puzzlement slowed her crying. "I'm including you, Linda. You never helped me."

"I was in the hospital," Linda said, easy as that, shucking off her shoes and flashing wine teeth.

"I know, I know, and I wasn't there for you either, so I can't complain. I guess since all I *do* is complain, I can hardly blame you for keeping a distance." Linda seemed to be thinking about something in the other room. Leaning aside, she skimmed her blouse off the shoulder and down the arm, draping the cloth like a matador. Cory turned away. "I hate my soul, I annoy my friends. So all I have is my awareness, and it's all twisted up with self-pity and dread. There's no going back on awareness."

"You're wrong," Linda said.

"I definitely *feel* wrong."

Cory lowered her head, but before the shiver in her chest had time to open her lips, she felt a swift shrinking of personal space, and a hand on the back of her neck—Linda was kissing her, ridiculously going for it, her tongue giving chase. Was she serious? Cory toppled back into the instability she'd been heading for, letting her tears wet Linda's face. They made a unison stumble to the futon. Cory tried blocking Linda's hand from reaching between her legs, but Linda kept scrambling it down, crossing the mat of hair until it reached soft concealed skin that flinched. Some of Cory's clothes were struggled off, others half removed. There was nothing gentle about it: Linda's skirmishing fingers were a little offside, doing quick circles and come-hithers, and when things just had to get better, Cory steered her to the soundless chime at the center. Time went along, escorted by bliss. Cramps of lust squeezed up through Cory's stomach in a widening cone, ribboned down into chattering feet. It was happening; she arched and strained like a longbow; it happened, it was over.

She shrank to a more familiar scale of shame. She wanted to say it was nice, though it wasn't nice, it was pity. But not the worst way to be condescended to. Cory waited through a stupid shy smile that came and went before she turned to face Linda, who lay prone. "Why did that just happen?" Cory said.

"Dunno! I must've seen it on TV or something."

"Seriously, though."

"Because I fuck." Linda hadn't removed her bra, and was rashing where its straps and cups had chafed. "One does like to fancy oneself a writer, but where raw talent is granted, one is essentially a fucker."

"That's insanely self-objectifying."

"Whatever," Linda said, and then rolled onto her back; her stomach bore a pale engraving of the sheet's rucked creases. "Hey, have you talked to Will lately?"

"Not really. He gave me some computer help a while ago. Why?"

Linda rubbed her nose, and Cory felt a nibble of regret to see Linda's skin disappear back behind the fastenings of her white blouse. "Put on some tea. It's bad news, but it might make you feel better."

SOME TIME AFTER Vanya left, Will heard the stairwell door open again. Socked feet approached him. "I wasn't eavesdropping," Linda said. "Thin walls. You okay?"

"I'm such an idiot."

"But an independent idiot."

"What is it about hot girls?" Will covered his bandaged face. "It's like mind control. I get bored of everything; how did I never get bored looking at her? As long as she was hot I could tell myself anything. It felt nice having that kind of drive. But it leaves you so fucking raw. I mean, I was really planning to marry her." He bit his lips. "Do you think I hate women?"

"I don't suppose it's as simple as that," Linda said. He waited for a better answer. "I think it's nice you're asking," she added.

"Fine. And I know I'm a shitheel for thinking you could give me a pass. Then let me ask you this. Did you ever think Vanya and I would actually work?"

"This thing just had to play out, trust me. That said, um, she does post a lot of dumb shit online. Maybe it's better you didn't settle."

"Yeah, I settled. I settled for a smart, rich, successful, beautiful nymphomaniac. I deserve better." He turned in her direction. "I always wanted exactly what you and Henrik had. And I fucking got it, all of it."

"Let's change the subject," Linda said, and moved to sit on the ottoman in front of him. "So now what?"

"Now you leave."

"Will, come on."

"Don't suck up. You just landed a sweet caretaking gig, good for you. Now go away."

"You think I'm here to mooch? It might kill you to hear this, but people *like* you. I do," Linda said, with shyness wobbling her voice at the rare moment of wanting to get a compliment right. The leather couch cushion inhaled as she got up to pace. "You're the only one who visited me in the hospital. You let me and Henrik stay here. You're generous."

"It's not generosity when you're rich," Will said. "See, watch. Henrik, you there?"

A pause. "Yeah, man."

He took his keys from his pocket and threw them somewhere. "Want my car? It's got, like, a thousand miles on it. Sell it, drive it into the sea, I don't give a fuck."

"Okay."

"And there's a ring somewhere around here, take that too. I paid twenty G's for that. See? I'm fucking loaded. Now leave."

"Will, you shouldn't be alone," Linda said. "You hungry? I'll make you a milkshake."

The laugh that began in Will's throat dropped into his chest, and he shook his head while he cried. The terrible news of the present kept coming in, how right life always was. He reached to cover his face but withdrew before he touched it.

Linda pressed a tissue into Will's hand. "Okay. I really don't know what to do. Henrik? Got anything?"

A pause as Henrik muttered in his head. "When Euler lost his eye, he said, 'Now I will have less distraction.'"

"Henrik!"

"What? I don't know! Sorry."

The nap of Linda's sweater kept grazing Will's neck as she made ironing strokes across his back. "Will, what do you want?"

Will had no answer. He'd probably need a seeing-eye dog. Somehow he'd have to feed it and clean its shit. It would sleep at his feet, mush its damp snout into his palm, conduct him through the world of solids. Some kind of Labrador, with its jiggling pink tongue and plain pedigree. He would never know what it looked like, but it's not like dogs minded. He would get a dog and have it until it died.

"I need air on my face," Will said.

"Does that thing come off?"

"It's not supposed to, but it does. You're gonna want to look away because—"

"I know. No eyes."

With slow crackles, Will peeled up his sodden mask halfway and gave the inflamed rims of his hollows a tender scratch, aware he was every last bit a terror.

"It's not that bad," Linda said. "Don't touch it, though."

"Get my laptop. Help me shop for eyes."

"Right on. State of the art. Laser beams and GPS."

"Just normal glass ones."

"Brown still a good color?"

"Yes, and before I forget, there are some things I need you to delete."

CORY CALLED BARR, having free time and no excuse not to. She dialed the number while smacking on a cube of chilled sugar cane she'd stolen from Roopa, spitting the pulp into her palm when the line picked up. "Barr Rosen," he said. His voice still sounded grainy.

"Cordelia Rosen," Cory grunted back. "Just calling to tell you I'm finally getting around to returning your van. And yes I'll fill the tank."

"Very good."

"So yeah, I think I might be scaling back my company involvement. I could probably come home to visit soon. But I should warn you, I sort of got rid of my hair."

A pause followed that felt disapproving. "I suppose," Barr said, "I should warn you likewise."

"Likewise of what?"

Barr seemed to wait for her to guess. "I wish I had better news, but the news is thyroid cancer. Fairly advanced. Or *un*-fairly, I should say."

Cory felt shoved while remaining in place, like the grasping reflex that woke you from a falling dream, as if she would seize the bygone minute in which Barr was indefinitely well. "You're what?"

"It was tricky finding a proper moment to tell you. Uncle Adam outlived his prognosis by seven years. I'm excellently covered. Surgery and radioiodine treatments are through, and adjuvant chemo wraps up in a while. I'm told I won't be able to enter an airport for several months without setting off Geiger counters. Isn't that interesting?"

"Does Deedee know?"

"Your sister visited for the seder. The evidence is tough to conceal."

"Seder? So, three months? *She* knew for *three fucking months*?"

"I told her not to worry you. You've been busy."

Cory brought out her special-occasion cry, the good silver and bone china. She hugged herself to contain the bucking force of her sobs, and didn't wait to stop crying to say, "Did you think you were being *noble* by not telling me?"

"Well, I was discouraged from having visitors while taking nuclear medicine. And I'm telling you now. I was respecting the independence you've always strongly defended."

Barr was right. And she'd always depended on Barr's wrong-ness to index her rightness. A memory came over her—him driving her to private school, listening to *OK Computer* on her Discman and tracing an anarchy symbol into the mist of the passenger's-side window, Barr powering the window down and up to smear it away. Anarchy, an ideal suited to obscure dis-order. The symbols had come first, then the anger, then the books. But now Barr was right.

"I'll admit. I'm surprised to have felt a measure of shame. Shamed by sickness. But my care is managed, and in the worst case neither you nor Deedee will lack. In fact, you stand to inherit."

"That's awful to say. That's so awful."

"I'm sorry. Ha. Illness is a gross entitlement to self-pity. I'm only saying that I know things will work out. Still, we need a plan. Let me offer you a job as my assistant. Twelve hundred dollars a month, plus my health benefits. Until you're twenty-six, anyway."

"Dad, no."

"It is an offer of employment in a down economy."

"Why not hire a nurse?"

"Because I wouldn't. I might be dying but I hate being con-sidered sick." Barr coughed, then cleared his throat in ascending tones, as if to disavow any significance to the cough by sending it off musically. "My energy is gone, and my head's a mess of chemo brain. I'm not gathering the mourners. I just think you're the person for the job. You understand my preferences."

"No more loans," Cory said.

"A wage, not a loan. But as you're keen on squaring your debts, I'm prepared to withhold some of your salary. Or you can consider it an advance on your inheritance."

"Oh my god, Dad, that's not funny."

Barr laughed. "Illness gives me that monstrous entitlement. The decision is yours. I won't force you to leave your work, nor have I asked your mother to."

"Why isn't Mom at home with you?"

"Away on business."

"Still?"

"Not still. Again." So he'd been in that huge three-story house alone. Barr did not sound bitter. He seemed to scrutinize the notion as he would a mosquito on his finger. "Your mother and I have grown more independent. But separation would make us no freer. Work took over." Barr ahemed. "It's been tough, being idle. But in the meantime I've enjoyed the Recreate '08 coverage."

"Recreate? What coverage?"

"The *SF Bay Guardian, SF Weekly,* and the *Examiner,* the closest thing to news outlets in our benighted region. I have all the clips. Some are negative, but criticism is good. Means it's a real accomplishment. I should have known you'd succeed. The egg on my face is frying."

"Stop, stop." Cory cried again until her stabs of hiccups lengthened back to breathing. "No more gags. Just don't. It's just something we do instead of argue politics."

"We did argue. It was never necessary."

"It's *always* necessary. Everything really is political. Like, you want me to take care of you," Cory said, rubbing her eyes, "but I'm not qualified. Even with the salary and everything, it'd be welfare. Caring, the big libertarian loophole."

"What I've offered as support, you've scorned as privilege. And you've tried to dismiss it even when what you value most, your liberal education, comes straight out of it. Well, I don't think I have to tell you that you can't get rid of your privilege. From what I can tell, you've tried to earn it by extending it. If that's what you want to do, that's fine."

"You're shoehorning me into your ideology again," Cory said, feeling beyond worthless for scolding her dying father but hoping he would see that she was not mollified by pity.

"Our ideologies are maybe not so different. Take your advanced socialist states," Barr said, winding up into a comfy oration. "France, Sweden, Greece, Singapore. National health care, arts funding, vacation time, what could go wrong? With all that comfort the Enlightenment scaffolding feels obsolete, so they kick it away—close off, become nationalist and conformist, turn against foreigners and minorities. We both hate tyrannical majorities, we hate panacea and utopia, we like dissent."

She disagreed, which meant she agreed. As he spoke she heard his stubble grate against the receiver. She pictured him in the mutt-colored easy chair in his study with his slippers pointing toward the bookcase at Ovid, Sophocles, Heraclitus. She'd never thought Barr *thought*. "You're abusing Plato."

"Ideally parents would make things safe but not easy. A tricky balance. If you're worried about redeeming your privilege, you have to work at being happy. Conscience you've taken care of. Now you must be healthy and strong and effective. Having everything you've got, then being sick and miserable, that would be the real waste."

"I'll come home. But I'm not taking any money."

"Cordy, never mind the job. You've been away a long time. We'll just have a rest."

As soon as the phone dropped in its cradle, Cory eased down to her sore knees and elbows and, lacking knowledge of the particulars and in no tradition, petitioned to whatever had time for her. It was quiet and easy. She was sure it accomplished nothing and meant nothing. But if she could believe in anything it was her own doubt.

Picking herself up, she wrote Roland a courteous three-line email thanking him for the opportunity, though she couldn't accept it at the time for personal reasons, but she hoped that they'd have more opportunities to collaborate when the timing worked better on future projects. Then she deleted it and sent another one: **NO.** She sent another email to her employees, pronouncing Socialize dead. They had enough cash to make the last payroll and severance. If anyone wanted the directorship, she'd be glad to talk transition. Nobody replied. The concern was gone.

AN EMAIL CAME in from Eve, sent at 6:20 A.M., which seemed dire until Linda remembered that's just when parents woke up. Eve needed a favor, and asked to come over; Linda gave her Will's address.

Opting not to explain who Henrik was, Linda stepped out around noon to meet Eve under the backyard patio's awning in a downpour that made the sidewalks fizz. Eve carried a large pastel go-bag and a foldaway crib, with Mercy flopped over her right shoulder, clutching Eve's drenched coat collar.

Eve was not a crier, more of a deep frowner—every part of her face was downturned as she brought Linda up to speed. Eve had locked Jared out after he came home late last night in full-fathom relapse. He kicked at the door, and when the cops came they found him passed out in the stairwell and tossed him in the drunk tank. Eve wouldn't press charges and wasn't worried he'd get violent. But she didn't want Mercy around;

worst case, he could run off with her, or Family and Children's Services could get involved. "And my parents already hate Jared," Eve said. "I just need someone to watch her while we make shit right. A week, max."

Linda nodded, relieved she could take the woman's side here. "Sure."

"I wouldn't ask if I weren't desperate," Eve said. "Offense sort of intended."

"None taken. You know, with Jared, I didn't actually—"

"Oh, Jared's a straight-up bitch. He'd never."

"I feel bad, though."

"Girl, don't. One of us should be happy. I wish we could both be you."

Eve turned away, and so did Linda, though she still overheard Eve muttering something to Mercy. *You're a part of me.* Or *You're apart of me, par for me, pardon me.*

Returning with brimming eyes, Eve pecked Linda's cheek. "I'll drop off the rest of her shit after work. Yours too. Baptist sent it along."

"Nice of him," Linda said.

Eve handed off her child and went back out into the hard weather.

FROM THE COUCH, Henrik glanced up from his book to see Linda bump through the studio entrance carrying an armload. Her hair dripped with the rain falling outside in thousands of cellophane crinkles. The storm clouds were green drab and inside, one table lamp was on. The thing in Linda's arms had arms, and Henrik gawked at them, counting dates in his head to make sure it wasn't his, even though it was plainly impossible—he would put nothing past Linda, not even having his black baby. Forgetting that he couldn't speak, he spoke. "What is that?"

"It's a little baby. Mercy, say hi!" Linda waved Mercy's arm at Henrik.

"What are you doing with it?"

"Only thing you *can* do. Keeping it alive."

Linda set the crib down and unfolded it, pinching her finger in the hinge. A crib was a cage. Wombs, cribs, rooms, tombs. She laid the bedding in, and the baby on top of it.

"Don't worry, it's easy," Linda said. She bunged the pacifier into the baby's mouth and it was like she'd switched it off. "Diaper, bottle, binky, burp, sleep, hold. That's all she needs."

Cars, clothes, skins, skulls. In physiology textbooks you saw red muscles, vascular cables of red and blue, off-white bones. But light didn't reach that far into you. All day you were mostly night. You began there, in someone else's darkness.

"I thought you hated babies," Henrik said. "You used to say they're atavisms."

"That does sound like me. But I came around. They're never condescending. You know they need you. And they're never wrong. Don't argue with a baby; you'll lose." The baby was belly-up, sucking her pacifier like it was full of sleep. "It's weird that she won't remember this. Her week with us. Though Lacan would say—"

"Let's not with the L-word."

"—that when she cries and we feed or change her diapers we're reinforcing her connection between need and demand and sucking her into our symbolic discourse." Linda tumbled onto the couch beside Henrik and zapped the TV on. "It helps her sleep."

They sat in benign existence, watching frantic chefs prepare meals against a timer, until the commercial break. "All right, can we talk?" Linda said. "As much as I love a good brood war, we can get through this quicker by talking."

Henrik turned his TV glaze toward her. Without front teeth and with her wet hair she looked desperate and hurt. "Since negatives come easiest to me," Linda said, "I'll say what I don't want. I don't want to promise you I'll change so you'll 'take me back.' Any shrink would tell you to set healthy boundaries and cut me off, but I don't want that either. And I don't want to be just friends, or friends with benefits, or least of all your ex."

"Doesn't leave much."

"You're right. *If* we go by what actually happened. We don't have to—wait, hear me out. We had a pretty good relationship built on lies. I don't see why we can't do it again."

"Because relationships are based on intimacy and intimacy is based on trust and trust is based on honesty."

"You think every functioning couple knows themselves and expresses what they want and hears what the other is saying perfectly? That we're not pumping everyone else full of prejudices and fantasies with no connection to reality? The only thing holding relationships together is intention. It's not a matter of fact or reason. We get to say what happened because we're the only ones who care. My problem isn't that I lie but that I used the wrong lies. Selfish and romantic ones."

"Sheesh."

"Listen, couples omit and revise their histories all the time. Telling their parents they met at a barbecue instead of on a fetish website. Or saying some fleeting episode of infidelity didn't count. Faked orgasms, coworker crushes. Or, better example, you not telling me about your bipolar while we were dating."

Henrik did not dispute this.

"Usually they're lies of convenience. But sometimes the poetic truth of a cover story suits their understanding better than what actually happened. Like how when we hear Robert Johnson sold his soul to the devil, it doesn't feel true but it feels right. This always gets framed as pathetic or delusional but at least reality never gets the best of you."

"Difference is I'm not asking you to lie to me."

"You could watch me try," Linda said, turning the TV off. "Will you?"

Henrik inhaled and exhaled. The medication wore down his protest.

"Say we move to Sacramento after college," Linda says. "I don't want to live there but it's the only place we both got decent job offers so we can stay together. And after two years and a slipped condom we end up with a situation."

"You never wanted a baby," Henrik said. "You said that to raise a kid was to get PTSD after catering to some helpless idiot for eighteen years in the hope that he wouldn't eventually blame you for his miserable life on some blog."

"Naturally my stance changes once it happens. What the hell, we're married and insured. And we get the amnio and everything's fine. So I quit drinking and smoking, we take gross photos of my belly each month until the kid pops out. Of course I resent the mundanity, that my biggest problem is basically: How can I write and be myself when I'm always tired from working to pay student loans and pumping breast milk?

"Then I trip in the shower and knock my front teeth out, and we get into a big fight about spending money on something cosmetic. Slowly we realize our relationship in college had a lot to do with circumstance and lack of experience, that we were all so intensely codependent that we had to exceed friendship. So I move back to SF because that's where our friends are, and you move here because that's where our baby is. While we're looking for a new place and making new plans, we figure it's cheapest to both stay with Will.

"That's it. It's not an exciting story. But it got us here."

"It sounds like you just want to be let off the hook."

"There shouldn't be a hook is what I'm saying," Linda said.

"What do I get out of it?"

Linda thought about this one. "Me," she concluded.

"Why would I want to let you do this all over again? Give you all the power?"

"Usually the power belongs to the one who wants the relationship less. That would be you."

Linda noticed Henrik tracking her hand with suspicion. She offered a dainty cat-paw for him to examine. On her middle finger was Will's engagement ring. Its sapphire was deep, clear, and extremely real, and the band, a gray-and-gold braid speckled with diamonds, shone with its price. "You said you didn't want me to forgive or forget," Henrik said. "How is this not forgetting?"

"It's not. It's a choice between options, one factual and the other truthful."

"Double think."

"The sign of a first-rate mind! But I knew you'd have this hang-up about facts, so I made this." She reached under the cushion of the daybed and took out a notebook, handed it to him. Opening it, he found some ninety pages of tight script full of cross-outs, carets, footnotes. *They meet late in a year of record lows.*

"Hang on to it," she said. "But don't show anyone. It's pretty embarrassing."

He put the book aside. "So, we're dating again. All of a sudden you're hot for commitment."

"Let's not call it anything. I just want to talk again."

"My feelings for you always have been unambiguously romantic. Keeping it vague lets you pull me back into the kind of relationship I don't want."

"Oh, really? You don't want someone to look after you right now? That's a second-rate kind of affection. Listen, you can send me packing whenever you want. This time it'll be your choice."

The sleeping baby gave the room a faint stink. He heard the water spattering outside with the distant shipwreck sound of thunder. The choice, he felt, was between it and this treacherous girl, who was trying so hard to seem like she cared for him, as if that in itself was enough, and possibly it was. Then again he could never tell if he was really thinking what he thought rather than what he was trying not to think.

"If you're making a vague offer then I'm giving you a vague acceptance."

"I accept your acceptance."

"So now what?" Henrik said. "Just continue? This doesn't last without money."

She looked down at her damp clothes. Her skin was uncreased and lightly furred, all tattoos colorless in the dim light. She rested an ear on Henrik's shoulder and flicked a lock of damp blond-tipped hair across her chin. Behind her back, she switched the ring to another finger. She could look after Will and Henrik until she got antsy and broke, gave in and pursued one of those higher degrees you didn't earn so much as contract like a wasting disease: advanced, terminal. She'd have to take tests again, assemble little packets of talent to submit to strangers who would reject her, or admit her on promise. But that was all hypothetical and she would still need money. Words had been good for something, not everything: the question was whether they were enough. "Don't worry about that. If I go broke I can sell the ring."

"No sense being impractical. It'll appreciate."

III. The Unemployment

On the last day at Socialize, Martina asked if Cory wanted to liquidate the office furniture. Cory looked out over the desks, chairs, scuff mats, cord caddies, modular bins, desk phones, computers, printers, cables—all that work. She scratched an itchless bump on her arm and yawned. "Just grab whatever you want and take off. I'll handle the rest."

They struck the office in an afternoon. Cory claimed Taren's record player, and from his desk she saved a packet of ballpoint pens gold-embossed with the Socialize logo. Martina and Pascal ro-sham-boed over the conference table and divided the office supplies. Cory helped load the copier into a Barr None van with John, and trashed the Gandhi quote and the wall calendar, whose anxious lists of errands leading up to Recreate now looked so angry. She took apart the modular storage and yanked the phone lines from the wall with a twang, half expecting blood to well from the outlets. She worked the door keys off her key ring and set them by the front door in little silver sardine rows for the landlord.

Holding a shoebox full of tools, Cory felt nothing but pleasant light-headedness and cool air on her scalp as she watched the Barr None van crackle away down the alley. The slick patches of pavement from last night's rain flashed with sunlight.

She went inside and made a phone call, then cleaned through the rest of the daylight along to Leonard Cohen and Joan Baez records. After sundown there was a twist at the front doorknob and two loud knocks. Linda entered first, leading Will by the hand, and Will held the door for Henrik, who carried a rack of Tecate and a liter of Maker's Mark. Will was guided to a desk chair.

"How you feel, Will?" Cory asked.

He adjusted his sunglasses. Cory looked at Linda. "Will isn't talking," Linda said. "He says he's sick of expressing himself. He says no matter what he says people only hear what they see. But he's going to get sick of the third person soon, isn't he?" She pinched his cheeks until he swatted her arms away.

Henrik rolled beer cans to Linda and Cory, and Linda cracked hers in one hand, dripping spittley foam. "Toast."

"To what? My company shutting down?"

"To your event. To having some time off. To me. Who cares?"

As Linda raised her can, Cory's eyes widened at the ring on Linda's hand. Well, that made sense. Linda reset the record and handed a loaded pipe to Cory, who examined it like it was a bullet casing she'd found in a sandwich. "Christ, it's been forever." She sucked in a magnificent hit that went to her temples instead of her lungs. Holding it, tasting and smelling the moments the weed transformed from green to orange to white, she watched Henrik pace around before taking a seat against the wall. And Will really was just sitting there. She couldn't even remember what they would do together. Seeing them in her gutted workplace sent a current of mingled nostalgia streaming from her nostrils. They were lounging in the concreteness of her failure.

"What are you doing for money?" Cory asked Linda, having little else to say.

"Nothing. But Henrik and I came up with a plan," Linda said. "Easy money."

"How?"

"ART."

Across the room Henrik shook his head and laughed.

"Shut up, I've done the research," Linda said. "Whatever else I am, I'm white, twenty-two, educated, and I clean up nice."

Linda told her about ART. It had made big advances in the past few decades. Nobody could agree on a precise definition, and its long-term effects hadn't been studied, but ART had low rates of morbidity and mortality. It could trigger early menopause and make her fat, she'd have to quit drinking, and her tattoos might hurt her market value, but ART paid: twelve to twenty grand. "Enough to cover my bills and keep off the student loan creeps for a minute."

"Huh," Cory said, though by this point, knocking the ash out of her spent bowl onto the floor, she was distracted by remembering how much she loved weed. She felt herself get walleyed, expand and disrobe into a headless fume, all her identities pleasingly reshuffled like a clever anagram of herself. No more hardlining, no tireless cause-and-effect along the same weary grooves of dread. She went to sit by Henrik. The large smooth warm stone in her chest felt like forgiving him for something. "So you and Linda worked it out," she said. "I'm glad you're back on."

"Um, not back on, exactly. We're just staying together at Will's."

"Good. That's good. Together is good." She gulped her beer. She kept forgetting and remembering that there was no work tomorrow, each time triggering bursts of panic and relief. "Can I ask you something?" she said.

"Yeah."

"Why Roopa? *How* Roopa?"

Henrik glanced over at Linda, just out of hearing range. "I don't know if I should say."

"I really really want you to say."

Henrik sucked in and said on a sigh, "I responded to her ad online."

"Like, a dating ad?"

"A one-hour date."

"You don't mean—"

"Uh, yeah."

Some inner tectonics made Cory's lips warp and buckle until they let out berserk laughter. She slid down the wall, and now lay on the floor, squirming in mirth like an itchy dog.

"There's more to it than that," Henrik said. "We didn't—"

"Nope, I don't want to hear it," Cory said between heaves. "What you said is perfect."

When she caught her breath the heat of her heart was on the skin on her face. She mouthed a few syllables, to establish that she could: *luh, guh, buh*. She dragged her hands down her cheeks. "Linda. What. The hell. Was in that weed?"

"I really don't know," Linda said, attempting a headstand. Her dress fell down over her head so she was all bare belly and legs. "Definitely something!"

"So if you've moved out of Iniquity," Henrik said to Cory, "where are you staying tonight?"

"Here," Cory said.

"Um, you can probably stay with us. Will?"

Will shrugged.

"No, I'm staying here," Cory said.

"Oh shit, are we sleeping over?" Linda said. "We'll need more food and drugs. Someone give me their phone."

Nobody had one. Linda proposed a supply run; Henrik was the only one with a license, and they made Will come along. "Cory, *vamanos*."

"I have to finish moving and cleaning."

"Tomorrow!"

Cory's mouth started to talk. "I can't because I'm driving home in the morning to move back home with my dad and it'll probably cost too much for me to ever move back. So I won't be around anymore." Everyone looked at her like she'd said something very wrong, and she decided to go with that. "I feel so great that we're here and so bad we weren't here, you know? It's so stupid how that works. I fucking hated you guys so much for having nicer lives and I spent so much time obsessing over how unfair it was, but why should it matter, you know? It's just not a real thing, because the world will not be around much longer, I'm very sorry to say. God, I actually love you guys. I love you."

It became apparent that the music had stopped a while ago. She wondered if she'd made it stop and laughed and wiped her eyes. Will nodded, feigning comprehension; Henrik and Linda sight-checked each other. Linda's mouth kept opening, her rosacea aflame. The air grew rich with delay. Cory laughed. "It's fine, it's fine," she said, "take your time. No, don't even say anything, I know how it is. You can't say I'm wrong, though."

Linda went over and kissed Cory's cheek. "Back in a bit," she said.

They left. Actually there wasn't much to do besides sweep

and bring out the last chairs and cleaning supplies—plastic crates, mop buckets, a dolly. She filled some crates and took them outside, thinking she might catch up. She looked for where she'd stacked the other office remains in an unobtrusive heap that afternoon, at the alley's inlet. But they were gone, everything was claimed: file cabinets archiving nothing, pencil caddies, desk phones bound up in their cords, obsolete computer towers. All that was left was the whiteboard, face up, where she'd written in permanent marker over the faded green, red, and blue of erased plans:

FREE
HELP
YOURSELVES

Acknowledgments

The latest of continual thanks for the support of my writing groups and the writing of my support groups: Daniel Levin Becker, Mauro Cardenas, Max Doty, Jen duBois, Anthony Ha, Alice Sola Kim, Reese Kwon, Greg Larson, Karan Mahajan, Anna North, Vauhini Vara, Esmé Wang, Annie Wyman, and Jenny Zhang. And no less, the fearfully symmetric MFA cohort: E. J. Fischer, Evan James, Carmen Machado, Ben Mauk, Mark Mayer, Rebecca Rukeyser, and Bennett Sims.

An unrepayable student loan debt is owed to Adam Johnson, Elizabeth Tallent, Sam Chang, Michelle Huneven, Wells Tower, and Marilynne Robinson. Endless praise for the administrations of Deb West, Jan Zenisek, and Connie Brothers; the Jentel Artist Residency Program; the MacDowell Colony; and the Copernicus Society of America for the Michener-Copernicus Fellowship. And I sure won't leave out my agent Ellen Levine, my editor Margaux Weisman, and my copyeditor Laura Cherkas, all of whom I've exhausted at various points in the process just by being myself.

But my first thanks are to my mother, father, and sister, beloved enablers.

Lydia White

About the Author

Tony Tulathimutte has written for *VICE, AGNI, The Three-penny Review,* Salon, *The New Yorker* online, and other publications. A graduate of the Iowa Writers' Workshop and Stanford University, he has received an O. Henry Award, MacDowell Colony and Truman Capote Fellowships, and the Michener-Copernicus Society of America Award. He lives in New York.